Advance Praise for *HYSTERICAL*

"Completely absorbing and entirely believable, *HYSTERICAL* is both a lovely work and a treasure. This is the book we all wish Anna Freud had had the courage to write."

—**Jeffrey Moussaieff Masson**,
author of *The Assault on Truth: Freud's Suppression of the Seduction Theory* and former Projects Director of The Freud Archives

"...[A] wonderfully insightful fictional glimpse into the Freud family dynamic and, most notably, its impact on Sigmund's theories about lesbianism. How did Freud père receive the announcement that the daughter to whom he was closest—his right-hand girl and protégé—loved women? How did he deal with her long domestic partnership with another woman? Coffey's presentation of what may have happened between Sigmund and Anna is nuanced, intelligent, and wonderfully persuasive."

—**Lillian Faderman**,
author of *Naked in the Promised Land: A Memoir*

"...[A]bsolutely fascinating and interesting. Reading it brought up a lot of tears because of the memories it evoked about the people and the time. I was so happy to have Freud's relationship with his daughter revealed."

—**Sophie Templer**,
95-year-old daughter of controversial Freudian psychoanalyst Otto Gross

"Rebecca Coffey's imagination knows no bounds. She makes you believe this is exactly the way it all happened. *HYSTERICAL* is sad, funny, painful, strange, outrageous, and disturbing. If we can't have Anna's diaries, this is the next best thing."

—**Ellen Bass**,

author of *The Courage to Heal*

"Moving, irreverent, often very funny, and a remarkable tour de force, *HYSTERICAL* lets us eavesdrop at the keyhole of the Freud family. And, oh, what we learn!"

—**Leonard Foglia**,

Broadway director of *Thurgood, Wait Until Dark*, and *Master Class*

Hysterical

Hysterical

Anna Freud's Story

Rebecca Coffey

SWP
SHE WRITES PRESS

Published 2014
Printed in the United States of America
ISBN: 978-1-938314-42-1
Library of Congress Control Number: 2013933277

For information, address:
She Writes Press
1563 Solano Ave #546
Berkeley, CA 94707

For Kay and Joe Coffey

Contents

Author's Note

A yenta brought along an assistant to a conference about a bride. This assistant's job was to agree with every claim the yenta made on the potential bride's behalf.

"The lady in question is cultivated and elegant," said the yenta.

"Very elegant," said the assistant.

"She is an able counter, and can outwit tricky merchants," said the yenta.

"Very smart woman," said the assistant.

"And such a kind heart!" said the yenta, "Wouldn't hurt a fly."

"Kind as kind can be," came the echo.

"She is handsome in her own way. Magnetically attractive."

"Very attractive," repeated the assistant.

"However," the yenta began to admit at long last, "she does have one very small problem. There is a slight hump on her back."

"And what a hump!" said the assistant.

It's an old Jewish joke. Sigmund Freud, the founder of psychoanalysis, loved Jewish humor, as did his intellectual heir, his youngest daughter Anna.

For all I know, Sigmund and Anna enjoyed this joke in particular. Or at least I like to imagine them enjoying it. For although Anna came to be an enormously influential and even revered child psychoanalyst in her own right, she never stopped parroting the ideas of her father.

And those ideas had "humps"—bulging, grotesque ones that she never pointed out. Two of those humps weren't only troubling on a theoretical level. They endangered Anna herself, and to her very core, thwarting the growth of her spirit and personality in much the same way that a strong pair of root clippers keeps a bonsai tree weirdly small.

But let me make this clear from the outset: Anna Freud grew free of the small container built for her by her father. That's the story of this novel. She may have been his best defender. She may have been even his "pet" of sorts. Arguably she was deformed by the singular struggles of her coming of age. But over the course of her long life, her independent contributions as a child psychoanalyst became many and impressive, and they were especially remarkable for what they reflected about both her common sense and her humanity. Read quotations from Sigmund alongside quotations from Anna. His will seem academic and self-consciously literary. Hers will make evident that she was a hugely original thinker motivated by deep kindness and a determination to rescue whomever she could from whatever was killing them or clamping them down

As I've said, there were two ugly humps. The first was Sigmund's set of ideas about female morality. Sigmund believed that women are inherently devious. According to him, it is only through committed consort with a man that a woman can gain moral and emotional fortitude. Lesbians don't enjoy intimacy with men. And so, in Sigmund's world, the very act of making love with another female sets a woman on a path towards breakdown.

Published excerpts from Anna's diaries and correspondence suggest that she began having intensely romantic feelings for women by her early twenties. Undeniably, by the time she was thirty she had begun a monogamous relationship with Dorothy Burlingham, heir to the Tiffany fortune. Neither woman ever publicly acknowledged the relationship as sexual. But it did continue, merrily, committedly, and concertedly, for more than five decades.

Anna's biographers have largely ignored this central relationship in her life. Sigmund's biographers have, too. Why? Most of the biographers have themselves been Freudian psychoanalysts. At the risk of sounding like I'm trying to analyze the pros, let me suggest that the biographers may have been ego-invested in upholding Sigmund's reputation as a theorist—and even as a family man.

The "family man" aspect of this long-ignored secret may be the real key to understanding the child she was and the woman she connived to become. Not only did Sigmund consider lesbianism a gateway to mental illness, he taught that it is always the fault of the father. In other words, Freudian theory holds that if Anna were a lesbian, Sigmund was the selfish father who ruined her emotional health and any chance at a "normal" adulthood.

The second "hump" in the theories that Anna so patiently parroted is that Sigmund consistently warned his students and colleagues that psychoanalysis is inherently an erotic relationship that one should never, ever engage in with a family member. Regardless, during two separate periods of her young adulthood, he analyzed Anna, most probably six nights a week. What they primarily discussed were her masturbation fantasies.

The analysis was an open secret among the Freud family and its circle of friends and colleagues. (So, for that matter, were Anna's fantasies.) Still, as with her preference for partnering monogamously with women, most psychoanalytic biographers have refused to comment on this analytic relationship. It was an unaligned biographer—political scientist Paul Roazen—who disclosed the analysis. He did so in 1969. Not until 1994 did a psychoanalytic biographer mention it. Even so, in *Anna Freud: A Biography* Elisabeth Young-Bruehl assigned not so much as a hint of impropriety to the arrangement. Historian Peter Gay did, however. Not being a psychoanalyst and therefore having no need to buttress or endorse Sigmund, in his 1998 book *Freud: A Life for Our Time* Gay called Anna's analysis "most irregular," and labeled Sigmund's decision to analyze Anna "a calculated flouting of the rules he had lain down with such force and precision."

Please. Imagine growing up homosexual in a household where your world-renowned psychologist father has pronounced lesbianism to be a moral and emotional death sentence for a young girl.

Imagine then being drawn by your father into an erotic power play. Imagine that he psychoanalyzes you for a total of about one thousand clinical hours.

When doing so, keep in mind that your father has also defined the birth of civilization as the moment that mankind realized that incest is *verboten*. This means that even if the verbal foreplay of your psychoanalysis makes you occasionally feel (way too) heterosexual, nothing that is aroused is going to be consummated.

What might have happened to your sexuality and sense of self during those years of analysis?

What might have happened to your love for your father?

What might have happened to your sibling relationships and to your relationship with your mother? By the time that lengthy analysis had ended, where might you stand emotionally in relation to your family, given that you were the only family member with whom your father ever expressed an inclination to transgress?

How would you feel about what had become of your youth and your possibilities? How would you feel about your life choices?

"Hysterical" is a word that has been defined in rather a lot of ways over the years. Possessed by erotic desire (Sigmund's understanding of the word), laughing helplessly at the irony of it all (Borscht belt comedians' understanding), feeling distraught and more than a tad berserk (modern psychiatrists'). Any way you look at it, the word may describe how Anna felt. And again, at the risk of sounding like I'm analyzing a pro, I suggest that "hysterical" in all of its shades can explain why Anna became a committed emotional rescuer—especially of children.

HYSTERICAL

The life of Anna Freud (1895-1982) spanned two centuries, three continents, and both world wars. Her public life in Vienna and London was, by any standards, extraordinary. Owing to her father's prominence, she encountered in her home some of Europe and America's leading intellectuals and artists. A tumultuous whirl of ideas and activities undoubtedly shaped her.

Anna was the last born of Sigmund Freud's six children, and the only one of the siblings to follow in her father's professional footsteps. As her father aged, she became his collaborator, his closest companion, and his nurse. As he became increasingly frail, the two of them even shared a bed. Upon his death, her active devotion to him did not lessen. On the contrary, she proudly defended his ideas about women and, indeed, hysteria from detractors and competitors. And as she accomplished all that she did, she loved women. With one historically notable woman in particular, she partnered permanently and co-mothered children.

I wanted to know how Anna Freud accomplished all of this given the theoretical prison her father had constructed around her. This novel is the product of that curiosity. In writing it I have relied heavily on facts and materials from the historical record and on commentary from Anna's and Sigmund's supporters and detractors. (The bibliography in back lists my sources.) But I have also relied on invention. I have created dialogue, scenes, and situations based on both fact and imagination. I have followed implications to their logical and sometimes outrageous conclusions, and I've made small adjustments to chronology in order to better relate a complex story within a sound dramatic framework. I have invented no characters, although I have sometimes given personalities to characters about whose actual singularities I am unsure. I am particularly indebted to Michael Burlingham's *The Last Tiffany: A Biography of Dorothy Tiffany Burlingham.* From his facts I was able to spin stories about the woman and children whom Anna loved so well.

The photos in this book are from the Freud Museum in London.

Many of the jokes are classic Jewish jokes that Anna would surely have known, given her father's fascination with wit and with Jewish humor in particular. Others are merely ones I've heard or read over the years. In all cases I've tried to identify their provenance and have come up with nothing helpful. If I've stepped on toes by using them without attribution, I apologize for the failure of my best efforts to identify and acknowledge their creators.

Although typographically it is laid as a joke, the fish anecdote in Chapter 36 is a folk a legend—or so I believe. At any rate, it is not original with me.

By and large, my aim in writing has been to create a compelling tale guided by research but not limited by what is not available or known. Truly, much about Anna remains a mystery. Perhaps it always will. Information about her is held at bay by The Sigmund Freud Archives, an independent organization founded by a small cadre of psychoanalysts who had strong personal loyalties to Sigmund. The Freud Archives holds the copyright to Anna's diaries and papers, and decides who can and who cannot read them. Much of the written record Anna left of her life remains sealed.

—Rebecca Coffey

Prologue

October 10, 1982, 7:00 am

Sitting alone in a just-tidied kitchen, Paula Fichtl was glad for her second cup of coffee. Being English coffee, it was not good, but it would do. After all, mediocre coffee had sufficed for all of the years that she and the Freuds and Burlinghams had lived in London.

Better than her second cup of coffee was the fact that the Freud Museum was closed for the week out of respect for Miss Freud's passing. The absence of museum visitors meant that Paula did not have to accept murmured condolences from people who meant nothing to her and whose names she couldn't remember.

When the museum was open there was no avoiding such people, for the museum was part of the home in which she and Miss Freud lived. Paula was Miss Freud's maid. The fact that Miss Freud had died and the museum was temporarily closed did present Paula with a problem, however. That nice young researcher with the Bermuda shorts would not be available to lift the boxes of books she was trying to organize. Paula had no intention, at her age, of lifting books herself. And surely he would have offered. And just as surely, it would have been a treat to watch him bend over and hoist.

Oh, nonsense! Paula knew that such thoughts were not wrong. Even in the very old sexual feelings are normal and healthy. In the Freud household they had been part of everyday conversation, always, and of everyday jokes.

"A man goes to a psychoanalyst," Miss Freud had said only a few weeks ago to the nice young researcher now occupying Paula's thoughts. "The doctor says 'You're crazy.' The man says 'I want a second opinion.' 'Okay, you're ugly, too.'"

Wait. That one wasn't even sexy. Come to think of it, it wasn't very funny either. Evidently Miss Freud had been gently testing the nice young man's appetites for humor and all the rest of it.

And he had shown real hunger, though for what she and Miss Freud had not been immediately sure. Hearing "ugly" had made him howl with laughter and then begin snorting air like pigs sleeping on a Sunday. That sound made Miss Freud and Paula open their own mouths wide and howl along with him. They'd opened so wide that they'd shown off the dental work on their back teeth. Of that Paula was certain, because when the researcher saw it he'd howled and snorted even more loudly.

Nothing wrong with that, either.

"How many Freudian analysts does it take to change a light bulb?" the nice young researcher had quickly volunteered.

"How many?" Miss Freud had asked.

Before he spoke again, he started up with more of that pigs on a Sunday business. But then he stopped. "No, no. I'm sorry," he said, wiping his nose. "Give me a minute to think of something else."

"As you were saying…" Miss Freud had insisted. She could be stern when she needed to be. You could almost imagine her tapping her foot against the floor and frowning through half glasses (which she didn't wear). "Tell me what has come to your mind, young man," she prompted cheerily. "Always do so, as soon as it comes to your mind."

The answer, as it turned out, was two.

"One analyst changes the light bulb while the other holds the breasts, I mean ladder."

Topped! Miss Freud had been topped! His joke was funnier—and sexy, which Miss Freud hadn't even dared. Miss Freud had immediately shown her dental work again, and so had Paula. And then they learned that the nice young researcher had three fillings of his own on his back teeth.

Ah, well. Without someone to do her heavy lifting, today's accomplishments would be limited. Paula rinsed her coffee cup, dried it, and put it in the cupboard. She walked upstairs, carefully holding the handrail as she did so. Once at the top, she opened the door to Miss Freud's bedroom.

A rush of melancholy met her. She stood for a long while with her hand on the doorknob; her eyes were reluctant to leave the sight of her mistress's bedclothes, which were still wrinkled, and which still emitted Miss Freud's baby powder smell. The outline of her small body could still be seen in the white sheets. Her large pile of knitting lay on the bedclothes right about where her knees would have been.

Paula was relieved to see that, when she had died, Miss Freud's pillows had still been nicely plumped. Paula had always kept them just so. But she was aghast to notice that she had never removed yesterday afternoon's coffee tray from Miss Freud's room. Of course, the coffee had gone cold, and the cream had curdled. Such a waste.

"There's no fool like an old fool," she scolded herself.

Paula lifted the tea tray from the nightstand and placed it carefully on the hall table. Then she opened a window to let a little autumn into the bedroom. All of London was glorious that morning.

The single most miserable part of the day's work would be dealing with the bedclothes. Just by changing the sheets, Paula would eradicate the last traces of Miss Freud's living form. Washing and tidying, however, must be done. Indeed, the bed must be made up again prettily, freshly—exuberantly even.

Paula believed in exuberance. It was where she had always placed her faith, much in the way that other people place faith in God. In some of the crises she had survived with the Freuds—wars, hunger, Nazis, deaths, impossible children, possible ones, separations, suicides threatened and real—she'd had little time to grasp what was happening as it happened. Thank goodness understanding wasn't her job. The

Herr Professor'd had the brains for understanding. So had Miss Freud. But they hadn't had exuberance. That had been Paula's responsibility; tidying up requires it.

"All right," thought Paula. "Bedclothes last. Dusting first."

She looked forward to it. Dusting Miss Freud's bedroom she would once again hold objects she'd tended for years. On the top of the mahogany bookcase were Herr Professor's pocket watch and the neatly arranged display of colored ribbons that Miss Freud had treasured for as long as Paula had known her. One shelf down were the penny bank that doubled as a toy guillotine and the cigars that the guillotine beheaded. There was a frog skeleton that Miss Freud affectionately called "Prince." There was a rat skeleton she called "Ernest." There was a statuette of Venus with a broken spear. It was a genuine antiquity, probably Greek, Miss Freud had told Paula. The most recent item in the collection was a many-paged memoir that Miss Freud had written during her infirmity.

The memoir was only her most recent project. Miss Freud had been writing one thing or another for almost as long as Paula had known her. She had authored so many articles about children that it had taken eight big, hardcover books to hold them. Not until writing her memoir, however, had Miss Freud laughed while she wrote. Certainly she had never before cried.

Picking up the manuscript, Paula noticed on the cover page two titles. *The Unauthorized Freud, by The Unauthorized Freud* was crossed out. In its place, *Hysterical* was written with a desperately weak hand. Brandishing her duster like a sword, Paula drew it across, around, and underneath the manuscript before hurling the entire stack of papers into the trash.

Keeping order—physically and otherwise—was her purpose on Earth. And what good had being hysterical ever done anyone?

Paula cleaned picture frames and *tchotchkes*. She accosted wood with linseed oil. She shook sad thoughts free from her own brain. And she charged exuberantly on.

Part 1

The Origins of Hysteria

(1895-1902)

Sophie (rear, left), Mathilde, Martin, Anna, Oliver, and Ernst Freud, 1889.

Chapter 1

If you had seen my Papa in my young years, you would have noticed the light burning in his eyes. The nights are long in Vienna midwinter. And when I was born, back in the time of royals and castles, even in broad daylight coal dust darkened the sky. Thankfully, light beamed out of Papa's eyes morning and night on his tromps around the Ringstrasse. On his smoking-and-thinking walks he illuminated a path for everyone.

Funny, aren't they? The exaggerations in children's memories?

But I'll wager that each one of my siblings remember Papa's eyes that way and recall being obliged to troop behind him twice a day. Before breakfast and again just before supper we ran like mad to keep up, all six of us plus Nanny and a governess. Bundled in layers of wool, we dodged carts and made "unnecessary noise."

Summers in the mountains were best, though, for there we could relax. Our family hikes were leisurely, quiet, mesmerizing—just strolls, really. Papa and his brood in the mountains in the bramble. There were endless days of mushroom hunting, with Papa calling, "Come out! Come out! It's safe to come out!" and then, having enticed fungi, trapping them in his hat, much to our wild delight.

"One of life's real pleasures," Papa would proudly announce, "is rooting out wild things."

If you had visited us then, if you had seen Papa in his tall socks and warm-weather pants, you wouldn't have suspected. His Alpine attire held no clues to his habits and fancies. You wouldn't have known about his sunburned face going even redder at night while he talked to Mama. You would not have imagined Papa and the dog yelping together in the summer garden in the early morning dew.

Winters. Six children, Mama, Papa, my Tante Minna, one nanny, and one governess. Papa's patients. One bathroom. Papa always said that stuttering and lisping are upwards psychological displacements of conflicts about excrementory functions. We all lisped. Even Papa lisped sometimes.

My sister Sophie was Papa's favorite child; she was older than me by two years. She was far prettier, she hated me, and already she knew how to wrap a man around her little finger. My sister Mathilde, eight years my senior, was obedient and kind, and for these qualities Papa was grateful. I especially liked her kindness. But she often sang aloud to herself; she couldn't help it, even though extraneous sounds annoyed Papa. My three boisterous brothers were all loud, too, which set Papa on edge.

And so I developed a singular talent that afforded me my own special relationship with my father. I alone among our gaggle could promise to be quiet and then do it.

When I was five or so, Papa rented an apartment downstairs from our family's quarters. He used it as a professional suite. He couldn't really afford the apartment. He'd trained as a neurologist, but only rarely accepted neurology patients. And not all of his psychology patients paid him for his attention. In fact, he paid some of *them* to allow him to ask questions and learn. But poor Mama just needed him to bring home some bacon. In an unforgettable alto tone she would weep loudly about the added rent. And of course Papa's face would turn red.

Papa wanted deference. But he didn't want to shove away his entire family. So while I was still too young for school, he routinely invited me to accompany him downstairs to his suite of professional rooms.

While he met with patients in his consulting room, I played on the Persian rugs of his waiting room. Sometimes, between patients' visits, he read to me from books of fairy tales.

They're not subtle stuff, those fairy tales that have traveled for a thousand years through India, the Mideast, and Western Europe. They're not for the squeamish. Giants eat little boys' livers. Parents chuck children into the woods to fend off witches all by themselves.

Good always triumphs in fairy tales, of course. But whenever Papa returned to his consulting room, I wondered about the times when good might not triumph in time. It never seemed to when Sophie tormented me. It hadn't seemed to for the pure-at-heart children in *Jack and the Beanstalk* whose livers were eaten by the giant *before* Jack arrived.

The waiting room had no toys. Aside from my doll, I had nothing with which to entertain myself when I waited for Papa. Usually, right after Papa entered the consulting room with a patient, I stuck out my tongue at his consulting room door. Once, while proudly appreciating my tongue's length and flagrant pinkness, I noticed that my vision had changed. It had lost focus of everything except for the tongue itself. Of course, I'd just crossed my eyes. Still, I held them in their tongue-seeking position while I moved my head about. The effect was dizzying.

I didn't really dare walk that way. But I did stumble upon the discovery that, when my eyes were crossed, within Papa's ornately woven Persian rugs I could see more than the abstract designs that everyone else saw. I could see people. The clumps of wool and silk in one rug, for example, resembled women. If I jiggled my head while keeping my eyes crossed, those women danced. The spiky yellow and brown forms in a second rug became manticores racing about. A third rug's lumps resembled vegetables and fresh fruit eerily floating through the air.

My single boldest action while alone in Papa's waiting room was when I looked one day at my tongue while standing on my head in the middle of a large, circular rug. From that perspective I saw a tower and houses made of stone. I even saw village people. The rug itself was surrounded by a deep blue border, and so the village itself was surrounded by a sea to which tiny, woolen dots of children ran to swim.

Wouldn't you know, Papa walked in with a patient while I was enjoying the view. Evidently my cheeks were purple with blood flow and my eyes were, well, funny looking.

"If you fall, your face will stay like that," Papa warned, commenting not at all on the fact that my undergarments were on display.

And so I called my own halt to the tongue game. But I still enjoyed the rugs now that I knew they were neighborhoods.

I also took up a chalk-and-slate activity that today's psychologists might call "counter-phobic." For example, if Sophie had bossed me around earlier that day, I drew pictures of her bound and gagged. I often drew pictures in which I was bigger than she—bigger than Mathilde, even. With my crude sketches I changed everything I didn't like, even some of the fairy tales Papa read. In my versions, beanstalks didn't grow into the clouds; Cinderella's mother did not die; and Cinderella had no sisters.

Fascinated by what I created, between appointments Papa helped me turn my graphic tales into stories with words.

The drawings I made of *The Frog Prince* are long lost. Only the words I dictated have survived.

The Frog Prince

Once upon a time there was a princess who, when sitting on the edge of a lake, dropped a precious ball that her papa had given her. A frog retrieved it for her, thinking he might get a kiss in return.

"But I don't want to kiss a frog," the princess complained to her papa once she had the ball back.

With no problem at all, her papa understood and explained the problem to the frog.

The king walked with the princess as she led the frog to a wide creek, where she pointed him downstream towards the river.

The princess and her papa waved gaily as the frog lifted up his little butt and hopped in.

The frog swam away disappointed, for he had hoped that the princess would be his love. Still, he was pretty sure he could find the river.

"Bye, bye!" the princess whispered. She looked beautiful with her curly, blonde hair and her new princess shoes.

"Bye, bye!" the frog whispered back, without complaining. What a prince he was!

The frog went on to live happily ever after, and so did the princess and her papa.

Here's a good joke.

Mrs. Cohen," the psychoanalyst says. "I'm sorry to be the one to have to tell you this. Your son has a terrible Oedipus complex."

"Oedipus, schmoedipus," says Mrs. Cohen. "Just as long as he loves his mother."

Papa loved that joke. It's been a long time coming, but these days, so do I.

Chapter 2

As I write it is the autumn of 1982. I was born in 1895—though I think of my life as having started in 1881 when Mama and Papa met. Mama was a twenty-year-old traditional girl from an orthodox family. Papa was a twenty-five-year-old secular Jew who had just finished neurology training. Mama and her sister dined one evening at Papa's family's house.

On very first sight, something about Mama's flat, grey-green eyes, her thin face, and her thick, dark hair parted unimaginatively in the middle and pulled back tightly behind prominent ears made Papa fall in love. Or perhaps it was her passive manner. When he caught her eye with a meaningful look, she smiled.

The next time that Papa came to dinner, he gave Mama a rose. She allowed him to touch her hand under the table.

On Mama's third visit, Papa promised to love her forever. Her heart was the only prize he ever wanted, he told her. And that was true until he got it. Then he also wanted the Nobel Prize in Medicine and Physiology.

Unfortunately, when Grandmother Bernays realized that the nice young man who had given her Martha a rose was an apostate, she removed Mama from Vienna to Germany proper, where for almost four years she attempted to change Mama's mind about her romantic prospects.

Meanwhile, Papa tried to make a start at the sort of career with which he could impress Grandmother. He found employment as a researcher in a cerebral anatomy laboratory, and there he conducted experiments on the effect of cocaine on rats. Papa was the first person ever to discover that cocaine anesthetized rats' mucous membranes.

He also wondered whether it might anesthetize eyeballs, thus making cataract surgery possible. But before he could find out, he took a trip to visit Mama in Germany. While he was gone, his friend Karl Kohler performed exactly the sort of surgery Papa had imagined. Ironically, perhaps, he performed it on Papa's father. Kohler's operation was successful, and for it, he was nominated for the Nobel Prize in Medicine and Physiology.

In his later years, Papa referred to that as "The Eyeballs of My Father Fiasco." Still, during his research at the laboratory of cerebral anatomy, Papa did make one other important discovery: Cocaine anesthetized his own mucous membranes just as well as it did the membranes of rats. That, and it did wonders for his loneliness. He published his findings and began to make a small reputation.

Papa used cocaine throughout the years of his separation from Mama. During that time he sent her at least one hyperbolic letter a day. Nine hundred of them have survived.

"Woe to you, my little Queen, when I come! I will kiss you quite red. And if you are forward you shall see who is the stronger, a gentle little girl who doesn't eat enough or a big wild man who has cocaine in his body."

In 1885, with Mama still waiting faithfully for Papa in Germany, Papa moved from Vienna to study in Paris with the greatest neuropathologist of his day. Docteur Jean-Martin Charcot's workplace was the *Hôpital Salpêtrière,* a medical poorhouse for women. Studying with Docteur Charcot is when Papa's training in neurology began to blossom into a fascination with psychology.

At the time, all of Europe was in the grips of an epidemic of hysteria. The victims were almost exclusively females. No one knew hysteria's cause, but doctors had strong ideas about how to treat it. When symptoms included twitching, fainting, masturbation, hearing voices, talking in tongues, or paralysis, women were examined by neurologists. Some were given pelvic massages resulting in orgasm. Some were treated with opiates.

When neither cure worked, and especially when hysteria's symptoms included homosexual desire, patients were sent to surgeons for ovariectomies or clitorodectomies.

Docteur Charcot's patients got no treatment at all. With their symptoms unhampered, the good Docteur attempted to discern hysteria's cause. He found that, under hypnosis, most hysterical women recounted deeply traumatic experiences.

Upon his return to Vienna, Papa opened a small neurology practice and welcomed into his practice quite a few hysterical patients. He did not administer massages or opiates. Most patients were happy to let Papa plumb their psyches for evidence of trauma. Papa became quite the conversationalist.

In 1886 Papa and Mama finally married.

In 1887 Mathilde was born.

In 1889 Martin was born.

In 1891 Oliver was born.

In 1892 Ernst was born.

In 1893 Sophie was born.

And in 1895 my father suffered three great failures.

The first of Papa's failures was that he allowed his friend Doktor Wilhelm Fliess, an eminent nose and throat specialist, to convince him that hysteria begins in the nose. Papa referred to Doktor Fliess one of his own masturbating patients and encouraged Doktor Fliess to operate on her nasal passages.

Doktor Fliess successfully removed the suspect portions of Fraülein Emma Eckstein's nose. But then, when sewing up, he inadvertently left rather a lot of gauze inside the wound. Fraülein Eckstein hemorrhaged, and although Papa initially assumed that the flood of blood was an expression of unvoiced sexual longing, he did eventually recognize the need to call in a "patching up" surgeon who had to remove a significant portion of her nasal flesh. The nose couldn't be reconstructed. Fraülein Eckstein lay in pain for months. She had been beautiful but never would be again.

To Papa's dismay she continued to masturbate.

Papa's second great failure of 1895 was a medical book that he and a colleague published about hysteria. Drawing on the work of Docteur Charcot, *Studies in Hysteria* suggested that hysteria is not always a neurologic condition necessitating surgery, sedatives, or massage, but sometimes an emotional one requiring attention, sympathy, and talking.

Studies in Hysteria sold fewer than thirty copies.

Just to give Papa's professional failures of 1895 some historical perspective, that was also the year that French Captain Alfred Dreyfus was convicted of treason and publicly humiliated. Rudolph Hess, who one day would become Adolph Hitler's Deputy Führer, was born. Louis Pasteur died. Oscar Wilde was tried and convicted as a sodomite.

By now you may have guessed that I was Papa's third great failure of 1895.

Upon my birth, Papa wrote to his friend Doktor Fliess: "If it had been a son I should have sent you the news by telegram. But as it is a little girl … you get the news later."

Poor Papa. He did have one success that year. He stumbled upon what he considered to be the meaning of dreams. That discovery was the key to his hallmark creation, psychoanalysis. From 1895 onward, Papa lived in a rapture focused primarily on his brainchild.

I am the twin sister, if you will, of psychoanalysis. I had always to share my father's love with psychoanalysis, and to struggle against it for his attention. I even became a psychoanalyst. I have been one now for six decades.

HYSTERICAL

Occasionally, I have been a hysterical one.

No doubt, that's a comment that begs explaining.

After I was born, Papa waded even more deeply into the topic of hysteria. Intent on tickling the imaginations of esteemed colleagues, he authored three papers that painted the clinical picture of hysteria in bolder strokes than anyone had imagined. Docteur Charcot had shown that hysteria is linked to trauma. Papa and his colleague had written that it *can* be caused by trauma. Writing solo, Papa claimed that it is *always* caused that way—and that the trauma is *always* sexual and is *almost always* perpetrated by fathers on young children.

At the time, about a quarter of Papa's colleagues' daughters had succumbed to the hysteria epidemic. Papa had inadvertently raised questions, therefore, about the comportment of Viennese physicians. Not surprisingly, after his papers were published Papa felt the cold fog of professional disdain settle around him.

And so in 1897, Papa embarked on a career-saving about-face. He formally rescinded the idea that memories of paternal childhood rape were founded in actual rapes. Then he began work on another idea.

Theatrically, anyway, *Three Essays on the Theory of Sexuality* was stupendous; it explained away Papa's troublesome statements, and in doing so, intrigued nearly everyone. Hysterical females, *Three Essays* announced, are far more disturbed than even Papa had guessed. They have not been raped, not even the ones who clearly remember being raped. Rather, every one of those girls and women *wishes* she had been raped. Furthermore, all females wish for that, not just hysterical ones. It's normal; it's healthy. Those who become hysterical are the ones who refuse to acknowledge this fundamental desire. Women's failure to embrace their innate need to be sexually brutalized is the source of all of hysteria's mysterious symptoms.

This is an important idea and one likely to be lost in the shuffle as I tell my life's tale. So let me be clear. Papa suggested that some girls and women wish so intensely to be raped that they masturbate or have sex with each other, which makes them hysterical, and along the way, causes them to confabulate rapes. Other girls and women are so horrified at the strength of their desire to be raped that they refuse to feel sexual longing altogether, and that makes them hysterical. Presumably, healthy girls and women just go ahead and get themselves raped.

It worked. With Papa's new pronouncement he won respect as a controversial but careful psychologist.

Klaineh ganavim hengt men; groisseh shenkt men. Petty thieves get hanged; big thieves get pardoned, as my Grandmothers Freud and Bernays might have said.

Still, I loved Papa, preposterously so. Like my mother, I am loyal by nature, also preposterously so. I dutifully struggled to conquer my own hysterical tendencies, and I've analyzed many children afflicted with the same symptoms against which I once fought. To this day I defend Papa's kingdom, which crumbles.

I even tell Papa's jokes.

Herr Schwartz, the tailor, is on his deathbed.
"Are you there, my darling wife?"
"Yes, my dear husband."
"Are you there, my beloved son?"
"Yes, Papa."
"And are you there, my dear cashier?"
"Yes, Herr Schwartz."
"Then who the hell is minding the store?"

I am, Papa. Your daughter. And that's a good joke.

Chapter 3

Danger for proper women! Danger for little girls! Danger, danger! Keep out!

In 1900 when I was five, Papa and I began chanting the "Danger for proper women!" warning playfully. It was almost a ritual. We chanted it every morning as we held hands and walked together out of our family's kitchen at nine o'clock. We went down to his suite of professional rooms, and I stayed there until it was time for me to run morning errands with Nanny.

We pretended that I was Papa's guard. As I sat on the Persian rugs and imagined the life within them, I was to enforce a No Freud Females rule about the consulting room.

Even I couldn't go in there.

Of course, women in general were allowed in Papa's consulting room. Indeed, the majority of Papa's patients were women.

"No Mama, no Tante Minna, no Mathilde, no Sophie, no Anna!" That was the second part of the chant.

Except for Tante Minna, the females in my family weren't actually interested in Papa's work, so the rule was not difficult to enforce. Mama detested the very idea of the consulting room. I had heard her call psychoanalysis "pornography" and Papa's consulting room a "den of iniquity."

To be honest, I was afraid of the consulting room. Still, nothing could have been more appealing to me than the idea of peeking just briefly through the Danger Door and into that most precarious of places.

"What is a den of iniquity?" I asked Papa one day.

Papa said that it is a place where people feel free to behave more colorfully than they might otherwise.

"Then what's iniquity?" I asked. "Colors?"

"Colorful conduct," Papa explained.

"What's colorful conduct?" I wanted to know.

"Ask your mother," Papa replied.

Now, so many years later, the faces of most of Papa's patients escape me. I do clearly remember an exceptionally tiny dowager. She was always fashionably dressed, though I could often see hints of her underpinnings peeking out from corners of her clothes. She had entirely too many brooches affixed to her dress, and gemmed hairpins seemed to protrude from every strand of hair. She looked as though she had been run through an electroplating machine and then swept up in stardust.

I also remember a young woman. I even remember her name. Fraülein Ida Bauer presented herself at Papa's Danger Door first thing each morning, six days a week for a while. I am sure that I remember her more than most others because she was a *feinshmeker*—a "fashion plate"—who behaved colorfully, at least with me, outside the den of iniquity.

Actually, fashion was only half of what was memorable about this patient. She was friendly and clownish. She insisted that I call her "Ida" and forego the "Fraülein" and "Bauer" parts of her name. It made me uncomfortable to do so, but whenever I said the magic word "Ida" plainly, she would reward me with a schmaltzy wink. Not only were her winks excellent, they were contagious. I would wink back and, lickety-split, the two of us would start lobbing them back and forth while she knocked on Papa's consulting room door. The only thing that could bring a pause to our winking was her buffoonery. As she waited for Papa to answer her knock she would mime for me headaches, stomachaches, and great comic explosions of intestinal gas that the wonderful Doktor would, of course, address. When we heard Papa's footsteps approach the door she would mime Papa's walk, with his hips tucked almost too far under his torso and his back hunched just a bit. But when Papa opened the door he always found a demure, composed Ida, whom he greeted with a professional smile and a nod and handshake.

As Ida entered the consulting room, Papa cast a surprised scowl at me for staring bug-eyed at a lady the way I stared bug-eyed at Ida.

"Do you see Ida wink and hear her pass intestinal gas, too?" I asked Papa one night after supper.

Papa slowly put down the newspaper he was reading. He didn't bother to correct me for saying "Ida." He tapped the ash from his cigar and seemed to stifle a sneeze. He allowed that, no, she had never winked or passed intestinal gas in the den of iniquity.

"Never?"

"Never."

It turned out that Ida had not been doing or saying much of anything with Papa in all of the weeks they had met. Learning that Ida had personality that she expressed with me but not with him is probably why Papa invited me to join them in the den.

To understand what I am about to say, you probably need to know that I was especially small. (I still am.) Papa took advantage and feigned to Ida that I was just barely four years old ("Won't understand a thing...") and that I was sometimes allowed to sit on his lap during sessions. He said that he was experimenting with theories about an atavistic form of parenting that would allow children to climb at will, monkey-like, onto laps for security.

This was the golden age of archaeology. Dinosaur hunting had firmly captured the popular imagination. Only a few decades before, Charles Darwin had spouted astonishing theories about evolution. Partly in hopes of capturing public notice and partly because his own imagination had been stirred by the work of evolutionists, Papa had recently taken to speculating about the prehistoric roots of certain modern behaviors.

But of course I should not have been allowed in that day. I have to laugh at the idea of a benefit to a young child of constant lap access to adults who are talking about delicate matters. Anyway, so it was that Papa contrived for me to be there. He did assure Ida that I had a singular talent for a child so young. If I promised to stay quiet I could.

When Ida raised her eyebrows questioningly at me, I promised that I could, indeed, do exactly as Papa had said.

I followed Papa and Ida into the den of iniquity.

Ida walked ahead of Papa. He waited for me to enter and then firmly shut the Danger Door behind me.

I stood aquiver by the door as Ida sashayed confidently towards a couch. Papa walked behind her.

Prior to lying on the couch, Ida handed her hat to Papa. He smiled winningly, admiring the hat, making an occasion of it. Then he extended his hand and helped her lie down gracefully. She crossed her feet at the ankles and folded her hands peacefully on her chest. Papa covered her feet and the lower extremities of her legs with a small, tufted white rug that he kept folded at the foot of the couch.

They have done this before, I thought as I watched the practiced symphony of their movements. *She may not pass gas with him. She may not wink. But they have something special that they do, and this is how they do it, every time.*

Papa sat in his chair and motioned for me to join him. I rather lurched across the many kilometers of floor separating me from Papa. I could feel Papa's and Ida's eyes on me. I looked about for someplace to rest my own gaze and found myself communing with a gargoyle on one of Papa's bookshelves.

I settled into Papa's lap, squirreling into a position that, if I craned my neck just so, allowed me to see both Ida's and Papa's faces while not blocking the gargoyle's view of what was about to transpire.

Papa looked for a few moments at the tufted rug covering Ida's feet and then looked away from her and towards his humidor. Although later in Papa's life he chain-smoked through all of his appointments, back in those days he never smoked in the presence of a lady. I could tell when he looked at the humidor that he longed to.

I remember that Papa often needed to clear his throat as Ida talked.

And talk she did. Papa said later it was the first time that she had spoken freely.

Ida told of truly dreadful circumstances. Her syphilitic father was engaged in an affair with a very young married woman, a Frau Kleinstoffer, with whom Ida herself regularly shared a bed.

Ida's mother was so repulsed by her husband's infection that she vigorously, endlessly, monotonously scrubbed herself, her house, and Ida.

Herr Kleinstoffer, the cuckolded husband, had taken to dropping by Ida's home with increasing frequency. For some reason, neither of Ida's parents ever seemed to be present when Herr Kleinstoffer stopped by. Invariably, Herr Kleinstoffer took the opportunity of the adults' absence to grope Ida. She always resisted firmly. Even so, Herr Kleinstoffer's visits and gropes continued. He had even attempted to rape Ida, and although she fought him off and reported the attempted rape to her father, Herr Kleinstoffer went unpunished. He was still a welcome guest in the Bauer home.

Ida told Papa that she suspected that the visits continued because her own father had "promised" her to Herr Kleinstoffer in trade for unimpeded access to Frau Kleinstoffer, and that her mother had agreed, however reluctantly, to the arrangement.

As Ida talked, I sat on Papa's lap and felt his legs shift slightly under me. Then he shifted them again, as though to get rid of something.

Am I too heavy? I thought. *Does he want me to get off now?*

I somehow knew that my presence on Papa's lap had become improper. I started to clamber ashamedly down. Papa stopped me just as quickly as I started.

He cleared his throat and lifted me for a moment before resettling me on his lap. After a few seconds of uncomfortable silence, he rather disjointedly asked Ida whether, perhaps, she suffered from occasional gas pains.

She seemed amused at his perspicacity. She admitted that, yes, she did. Then, smiling at me and avoiding his eyes altogether, she relaxed and talked more—about her shortness of breath, her inability to eat without vomiting, and her curious habit of rushing past any older man in animated conversation with any younger woman.

"Is this hysteria?" Ida wanted to know.

I had no answer to offer her. I looked to the gargoyle, but he had no insights, either.

Papa didn't offer his. But he did ask a question. He asked Ida whether she truly was repulsed by the sensation of her attacker's uninvited penis pressing against her thigh or whether she instead found the sensation appealing.

"Behind every strong fear is an intense, infantile wish," he explained.

Ida seemed taken aback. Perhaps she had been counting on the Papa of her attentive little friend to see her symptoms as she did—as manifestations of the trauma of Herr Kleinstoffer's assaults.

Unfortunately, Papa had already jettisoned his "hysteria is caused by sexual trauma" idea and was in the midst of formulating his "a little sexual trauma is what women want" idea. By Papa's new line of thinking, Ida's digestive, breathing, and intestinal problems exposed a lustful, engorged inner self in need of enlightened reclamation.

At that point Papa lifted me entirely off his lap. Setting me on the floor and tapping me lightly on the bottom as though to hurry me along, he suggested that I run off and play, which was just fine with me.

And that is all that I directly know about the psychoanalysis of Ida Bauer.

Papa used to tell a joke:

Frau Schlaussburg, an old, old woman who has always been barren, goes to see a doctor. She finally has female complaints, as they say. The doctor asks her to remove her clothes. The doctor helps her lie down on the table. The doctor examines her.

After a long while of silence between patient and doctor, Frau Schlaussburg says, "Herr Doktor, might I ask you a question?"

"Certainly," says the doctor.

"Herr Doktor, your mother knows that from work like this you make a living?"

After I left Ida in Papa's consulting room it was to the Persian rugs that I retired. I heard no untoward sounds coming through the Danger Door. However, in the many years since then, I have read and re-read all of Papa's writings. His records of the remainder of the sessions with Ida do seem lurid. The records also say that, just a few weeks after my visit past the Danger Door, Ida abruptly discontinued analysis. Papa, she said, was pursuing a line of reasoning that she found tiring.

I imagined Ida sitting up on the couch for the last time, and with due deliberation and *savoir-faire*, removing the tufted rug from her feet and legs.

I imagined Papa politely walking her to the door of his consulting room, distracted from the impact of what Ida had just announced by his habit of basting in his imagination the meat of that session's discoveries. "Today we have tunneled very deeply," was what he might have said to Ida; it is how he later closed many sessions with me.

I imagined him lisping a goodbye, assuming that she, like most of his patients, would be back. And she was, but it was several years later and only for one visit.

I didn't actually see any of their parting moments, because I was on the safe side of the Danger Door when Ida called Papa's treatment tiring. She did look weary when she emerged from the den of iniquity.

I called "Ida!" out to her as she gathered her umbrella and coat. In response, she afforded me one last wink. When she left, she was very careful to close the door.

It must have been the click of the closing door that shook Papa out of his post-session reverie. Moments after that door shut, Papa emerged from his consulting room looking like rapture lost—face red and eyes aflame.

Danger. Danger. How is it that we can be so thoroughly taken with someone? How is it that we are so transformed and confident while love lasts and so sniveling and ugly when love leaves?

I was alone with Papa as he struggled mightily with an urge that I did not understand but knew to threaten our family to its very core. I was so afraid. I thought of the Frog Prince, who in the end did not have love but did have courage and dignity. He raised his little rump and hopped into the water all by himself. He swam off, sodden map in hand, down the creek to the river and down the river to the sea, and what the salty sea eventually did to his green skin no one but him ever knew. But, you know? Maybe the river and the sea were better off for his lonely visit. Maybe the Frog Prince was better off, too.

In his case notes, Papa claimed to have cured Ida Bauer. Still, as often as I've read those notes, I don't know how he did. All I can reasonably say is that on the day Ida left Papa's care, Papa cried.

And from work like this Papa made us a living.

Chapter 4

It can be difficult for children to see mighty feelings in the face of someone they love.

It is also difficult when mighty emotions that once showed disappear.

Now, about Mama.

During the years of my youth, Mama's troubles with Papa increased. As they did, her passivity became extreme. Facial evidence of feelings disappeared almost entirely. No doubt this is why for me Mama became difficult to remember: Seeing nothing when I looked at her, I rarely formed whole memories.

Though I do have one from early in the spring of my fifth year:

I was walking. I was in the hills of Bavaria alone, although I should have been with Ernst, Oliver, and Martin. We were on a family vacation—just a visit, really, to the home in which we hoped to spend our August. I remember that the sky was loud. That is impossible, of course, but then the logic of memories is always constrained by perceptual abilities. My five-year-old mind perceived the sky as loud. It was so loud that it seemed to scare the neighbor's dog, with which I was walking.

It must have been the creeks that were loud. It must have been the melting snow that made the creeks rush so. As the dog and I approached a particularly loud section of creek, the sound became enormous. It was like a steam locomotive coming into a station. The dog shied away from the footbridge, wondering where on earth it could run for protection.

That spring, Mama wore a coat that I will always remember as making her look like her arms drooled. It must have been a coat of Papa's, for it was completely without fashion and the sleeves were too long. In pictures from that time Mama is usually half out of the frame. In some she looks at Papa as though looking for something lost. In those pictures, while Mama looks at Papa, I look away from Mama—and mostly towards the sky. It is possible that in those pictures I am not looking at the sky but only looking up and out of the frame, perhaps at my brothers. My eyes were often on the boys. I thought that their days were far more interesting than those of girls. Boys had fun. Boys had adventures.

I was excited about adventures. On the day that I walked alone in the woods, my brothers and I had prepared to set off on a big one. I helped them pack a mid-day meal. Then they told me to sit with the picnic basket way out in a clearing in the yard and wait for them as they gathered maps and hiking equipment. I did. From the clearing I looked back at the house we had rented, and I thought that it looked like a house in a fairy tale. It was modest—all we could afford at the time. But to me it seemed huge. I thought we were all so lucky to secure that house. So lucky and so special. I spotted my bedroom window. I felt all aglow at the prospect of a hike.

And then, gradually, I began to feel lonely, for many minutes had passed. I began to suspect that my brothers had gone on without me and had fooled me into guarding the meal in the yard so that they could make an escape. That was not what had happened, not exactly. They had not fooled me. They had not made their escape.

They had gotten distracted. And having forgotten their hike, they forgot their Anna. That is how it came to pass that I, a five-year-old, set off on my own adventure, bringing a picnic basket packed for four and a small, easily scared dog.

I walked sadly at first. I was weeping just a bit as I sneaked my hand into the basket and grabbed mouthfuls of fresh bread. The dog and I walked down the hill, past some felled, dry trees, past some young shrubs with red buds, past some not-quite-yet-awakened berry bushes, and into the beginning of woods. I was very, very careful to drop behind me a trail of pebbles as I went. Pebbles, not bread. I had learned from the story of *Hansel and Gretl* about the folly of bread trails, and I had taken notice.

Soon enough I was sobbing openly, imagining that I had been cast out of our home. I also imagined that in the forest I would meet animals that might understand me as no one but the neighbor's dog ever had. As the shadows lengthened I searched for a gingerbread house where the dog and I might be warmed, if there was a witch who wanted company.

The entire set of my outdoors survival skills was adapted from the Brothers Grimm. Still, I was surprisingly confident. Well aware that witches couldn't be trusted, I had a strategy. If I got hungry in front of a witch's fire, I wouldn't eat anything she offered. I would rely on the basket I had brought with me.

I also knew for some reason (I think it was Oliver, the most brainy of the boys, who had told me) that when you are lost in the woods you must never walk up hill to get a better view. "Children do that," Oliver once explained, "and children die alone and cold at the top." I must always walk down hill, for down the hill would be water and valleys, towns and roads. So it was with decision and intelligence that I led the dog farther and farther into the woods and headed down, I supposed, towards water and valleys, towns and roads.

I do not know how long it took for them to miss me. I know that the dog and I had not reached a town, though we did make it to the stream. I was very unsure of where we were and how to get back where we belonged. The weather was turning cold. I now hated my brothers for being the older boys I could never be. I hated Papa for having had boys and Mama for having had girls. I also worried about the boys, believing them actually too kind to have left me in the clearing, *ergo* they must be lost.

The wind agitated the trees. I thought I heard a wolf chewing dry bones and sighing with disgust.

The dog wandered away.

At which point I became distraught about Papa and Mama and Tante Minna, who would undoubtedly search for the boys and get themselves lost and possibly eaten, all the while not realizing that I was already on a rescue mission and had food that could save everyone.

I suppose that they first missed me when we all would have met at table for our mid-day meal, and I was not there. I heard later that Mama fainted straight off when she realized that I had been left on the lawn and hadn't been retrieved.

From far away, I heard voices shouting. Apparently, upon realizing I was lost and alone, Papa and the boys had raced crazily up hills and trees to get a better view and to look for me cold and dead.

Meanwhile, Mama awoke from her long faint alone in the vacation house. Pausing not even to straighten her skirts, she hastened to the edge of the woods and entered them precisely where I had entered them. From that point on, she was guided by my trail of stones.

A kilometer or two downhill is not a great distance for a frantic mother. But by the time that she got to me, a strong wind was shaking the forest.

"What have we here?" she called out with hysterical relief when she found me by the stream, gazing into its water. She began hollering loudly for Papa and weeping at the same time. She wiped my own tear-streaked face clean with a handkerchief and then wiped hers. She wrapped me in her sweater. She took me by the hand and hiked with me up the hill through the woods, swinging her free arm broadly as we made fast progress. And all the while that we walked, she sobbed—and all the while that she sobbed, she yelled for Papa. When I asked, she told me that Papa, Oliver, Martin, and Ernst would all be fine when we got back, and so Tante Minna, Mathilde, and Sophie would be. All would be as fine as we two were who were hiking so merrily right then. She said that, no, I should not worry and that, yes, we would all very definitely and quite soon begin to live happily ever after.

"Just you wait and see, dear child. Just you wait and see."

Part 2

Rooting Out the Wild Things

1902-1908

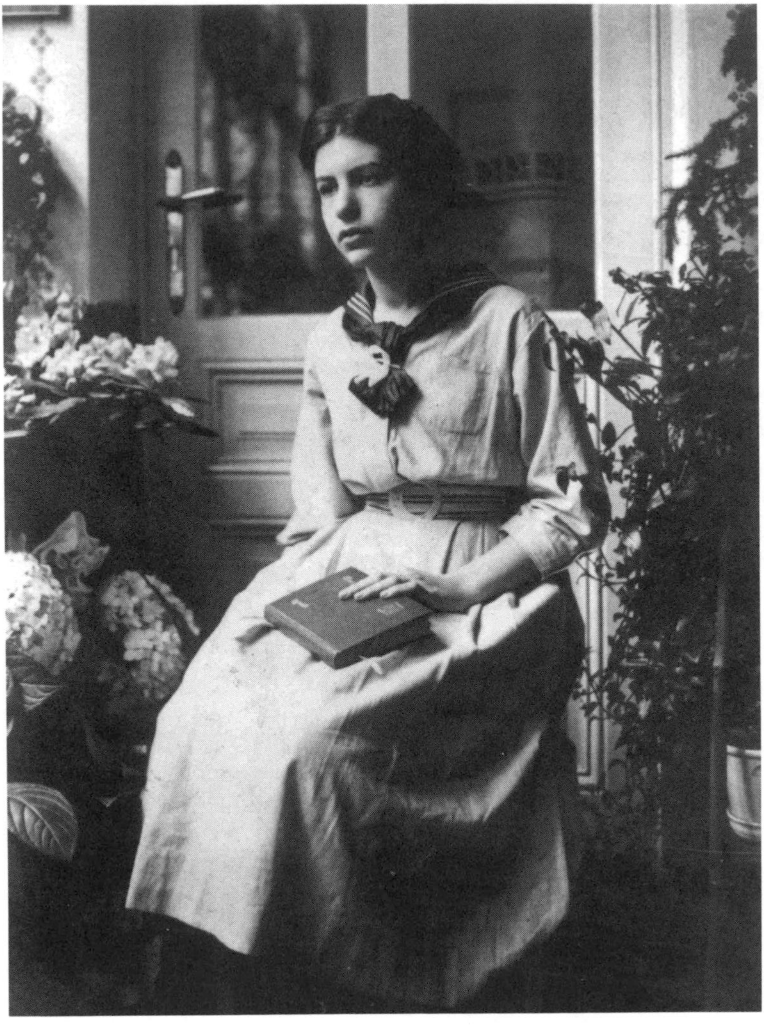

Anna

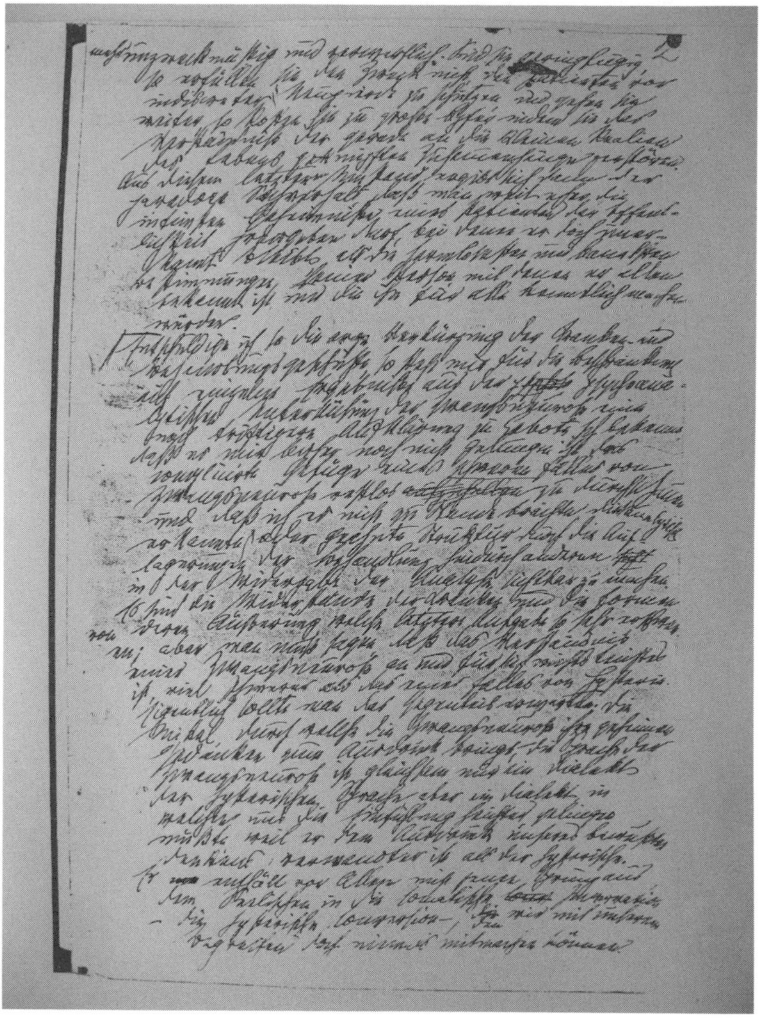

Excerpt from Sigmund Freud's notes on the Rat Man Case.

Chapter 5

In my sixth year, Papa's fame and fortune quotient began to improve at a steady pace. And by my seventh year, our family's spending habits had changed. We knew plenitude. Mama and Tante Minna no longer had to consider every krone. We had sweets and fresh vegetables with our supper almost every night.

In 1902 we splurged on an extra-long family vacation in Bavaria. We rented a nicer house, one on a lake. It came with a small rowboat.

My smart brother Oliver had learned from an astronomy book how to navigate by the stars. One cloudless night he took my siblings and me out in the rowboat. As Tante Minna and Papa watched us float away from shore, Tantie called out to Oliver, "You take special care of Anna. She can't swim."

"I know, Tantie. I will," Oliver assured her.

The three boys took turns rowing. Eventually, Sophie demanded a turn. Almost immediately, she dropped the oars into the lake. Then the wind blew us in the wrong direction. Oli watched the stars and narrated the course we were taking. I was scared, but I knew that Oli had kept his bearings. When clouds moved in and obscured the stars, however, even Oliver got nervous.

The night became so black that we couldn't see each other on the boat.

Sophie was the first to cry. Then Mathilde. Of course, the boys and I remained dry-eyed.

After enough of that, Oli announced that he had a sound scientific plan, and that it was high time to put it into action. It had to do with the mechanics of waves.

"I am going to jump in the water and make a big splash, right in the path in which we're moving. The displaced water will create a vacuum that will cause other water to rush in. The rushing water will push against the boat, momentarily shoving us back towards where we came. I will grab hold of the bow, kick with all my might, and use the new momentum to spin the boat around so that it is pointed in the right direction. Then I will kick some more, maybe all night, back towards shore. I will get cold. I may get eaten by a big fish. But I promised to protect Anna, and that's what I'm going to do. Martin and Ernst, can I count on your help?"

There was a long silence.

Fortunately, before Oliver could even remove his shoes, the wind shifted. The boat spun 180 degrees around, and we began to blow back precisely the way we had come. With the wind, the sky cleared. Sophie and Mathilde stopped crying.

Back on shore, Papa and Tante Minna were frantic about all of the changes happening in the weather. They had returned to the sand right where they'd stood when we'd sailed away. When they saw us approaching and heard Oli orating our navigational path, they raced out into hip-deep water to haul us in more quickly.

Tante Minna smothered Oli with kisses, and Papa pounded him on the back, congratulating him for being such a good navigator. I suppose that another child might have felt proud but, just looking at Oli, I could see his shame for ever having trusted Sophie with the oars.

Sophie complained about having been bossed around and inconvenienced. Martin and Ernst bragged that they had been about to help. I complained about Sophie's complaining.

Papa and Tante Minna didn't hear a word of it. Their concern had turned to relief. I saw that night in their giddiness an admirable urge to rescue and hold on to those they loved. It was writ large and pure. Oli's face held the same noble impulse, only etched more soberly. I watched him in the starlight as he secured the boat and sat for a moment looking into the shimmering sky.

I must say that I wonder to this day about the changes that boat ride wrought on my psyche. For shortly after, I developed a nightly fantasy about watching a nameless, faceless man dispassionately beat a nameless, faceless boy who meekly accepted the beating. Probably it was a revenge fantasy through which I was resolving feelings about Oliver having risked my life. Probably there was something in that fantasy about psychical impotence (mine) as well as actual impotence (Oli's in the face of Sophie's ineptitude). Possibly there was something in it about Papa's preference for tranquility.

At any rate, it didn't feel like only a morality tale when I had the fantasy, for it was a sexual fantasy. Every time the boy got beaten I touched myself intimately. I did this at night after I was sure that Sophie and Mathilde, with whom I shared a bedroom, were asleep.

Also in 1902, Papa and a small group of colleagues began the Wednesday Psychological Society. The group met in Papa's increasingly well-appointed waiting room to discuss aspects of psychology as they related to Papa's patients. All members were men; they were mostly doctors, but really all that was necessary to qualify for membership was an inordinate interest in either sex or dreams. All were Viennese Jews.

That same year, Papa received the title of Extraordinary Professor of the University of Vienna. "Extraordinary" in this sense was not synonymous with "amazing." It meant "unusual." Extraordinary Professors did not actually have jobs at the university. Ordinary Professors did, though E.P.s were allowed to lecture in the lecture halls as long as they could collect an audience and sweep up behind the audience afterwards.

Jews couldn't be Ordinary Professors.

Still, because of this honor, Papa was entitled to be called "Herr

Professor" rather than the lesser honorific "Herr Doktor." This galvanized him. In late 1902 he worked as if in a frenzy, meeting with patients all day and then either writing, talking, or teaching until late every evening. He paused only for meals and smoking-and-thinking walks. Curiously, he published very little.

By 1903 Papa needed a rest. He and Tante Minna traveled together to Bolzano, which is in the Dolomites. Bolzano is famous for walking paths that snake around medieval castles and plazas and then out of the city and into the hills. Although the Dolomites are part of the eastern Alps, the vegetation of Bolzano is Mediterranean. Palm trees, magnolias, cedars, agaves, and laurels line its paths. Papa and Tante Minna chased each other along the paths each day up the hills to the nearby vineyards, where they sampled glasses of the renowned St. Magdalena wine and had lazy meals of rabbit and soft cheeses.

Mama declined to join Papa and Tante Minna. Maybe she knew that all the scampering was beyond her ability.

A wife is like an umbrella, Papa used to say. *Sooner or later you take a cab.*

In 1904 our entire family made the acquaintance of a psychiatrist living in Munich. Like Papa, Doktor Otto Gross reveled in new and almost savage ideas. Indeed, he was famous for promoting bisexual promiscuity as the only healthy form of sexuality, and nudism as the ultimate self-expression. Soon after he and Papa had begun corresponding, he presented himself at Papa's office door for an unannounced hello, after which he came to our apartment for supper.

Cook was used to such surprises and was easily able to add another china setting to the table. She improvised an appetizer of onions, sherry-sautéed mushrooms, and goat cheese stuffed into a loaf of hearty bread. As we children thronged around the treat, Tante Minna poured wine for the adults.

Mathilde was a modest young woman of about sixteen, and already had her social skills perfected. Sipping water delicately from a crystal glass while her younger siblings elbowed their ways towards food, she asked Doktor Gross whether his train ride from Munich had been pleasant. And, of course, she called him, "Doktor Gross" when she did so.

"Otto," he replied. "Please, call me Otto."

Mathilde was unable to take the next sip of her water.

Unlike her, I wasn't shocked when I heard him say "Otto." Just four years before, Fraülein Ida Bauer had insisted that I call her by her first name, and I'd been able to do it. But for everyone else who'd heard Doktor Gross's request, it was as though he had set off a stink bomb in the room.

Not even Mama or Tante Minna could easily call Doktor Gross by his first name.

No one needed to explain this to him. He could see by the silence he had caused that an explanation was in order. And so he annotated:

Philosophically, he was an egalitarian. If Mathilde or any one of us were to use the honorific "Doktor" in addressing him it would impose on their relationship an unhealthy power imbalance.

"Call me Otto, children," he smiled magnanimously.

Mama looked pointedly towards heaven. She left the room with Cook, who also directed her eyes upward. Papa and Tante Minna stood side-by-side as Doktor Gross asked each of us siblings individually to call him "Otto." He started with Mathilde and worked his way down the line, by age.

Mathilde gave him her regrets.

Already embarrassed, perhaps by the matching sailor-style outfits Tante Minna had insisted they wear that evening, not one of my brothers would try for him.

Sophie, too, refused altogether.

When he got to me, he crouched down to talk to me. (Even though I was eight or nine at the time, I probably had the height of a five-year-old.) When he crouched, he put one clenched fist on the floor to balance himself. I was reminded of an ape I'd once seen in Vienna's zoo.

"Just, please, call me Otto," he said to me.

I was able to say "Otto" loudly and clearly on my first attempt. The girls screamed and laughed when I did; even Mama and Cook howled out from the kitchen.

"Again!" he prompted.

But I just plain couldn't call him Otto a second time, not if it was going to provoke such a reaction.

When the hilarity died down, Martin pointed out that we might all be able to stop saying "Doktor Gross" if we could, for example, call him "Doktor Otto."

Doktor Gross refused. "Doktor" was itself the biggest part of the problem.

Ernst asked the next question. Was there anything at all longer than an unadulterated "Otto" that we could say?

At which juncture, Doktor Gross playfully suggested that we could call him "Otto" by calling him "Call Me Otto."

"That would be four whole syllables," he pointed out.

And so the name stuck, like braid to a lampshade.

Chapter 6

In 1906, Papa celebrated his fiftieth birthday. A little more than half a year later I turned twelve, whereupon I also reached menarche. It happened in the middle of the night. I told Mama in the morning.

At first menstruation, the Jewish tradition is for the mother to slap the bleeding girl across the face. When I told Mama, I steeled myself for the hit. But although she had been orthodox until she married Papa, it never came.

She said we would create a new ritual. Then she enveloped me in a big hug and let me sob about all of the lonely washing I'd had to do all night long. Mama even cried with me, in loud, alto tones that echoed off her bedroom's high ceiling and would have made any ancient Rebecca or Rachael proud.

Tante Minna had a very nice idea for a ritual. First kissing me soundly on each cheek and saying a firm "Goodbye to Little Anna," she put a blindfold on me and spun me around three times. When she removed the blindfold she welcomed me into my new life. Then she handed me Dolly, the porcelain-faced, glass-eyed doll with which I had played on Papa's Persian rugs and slept each night of my childhood.

"Never forget, Anna, that you are still our little girl."

Tante Minna's gift to me of my own Dolly provoked more alto tones from Mama.

When Mama at last toddled off to bed, Tante Minna sat down in an old bentwood rocker that she had brought with her when she moved into our family's apartment shortly after my birth. With a large tangle of Mama's yarn in her lap, she teased apart the strands and bade me pull a chair near hers. Then she dodged into the kitchen and came back with a platter of jelly cookies and two glasses of grape juice. The two of us chatted into the evening, she correcting Mama's yarn so that it wound again into a nice, neat ball, and me holding onto Dolly while trying to appear grown up.

Tante Minna made me laugh with stories of her first menstruation, and she told me about Mama's, too. We spent hours together, and it was very late—the eight-day mantel clock had just chimed eleven—before I began to realize that, on her periodic visits to the kitchen, Tante Minna wasn't refreshing my grape drink and hers from the same bottle. As she got tipsy, she giggled to me of sexual urges.

"You'll feel on edge," she warned at first, tamely enough. Then, "He'll whisper words to you that you've never imagined. Even the restlessness of willows in brooks will seem unusually significant."

Then somehow we were leaping about onto topics like hands on bellies and heads between legs. She pulled my chair even closer as she whispered to me about her young love Iggy Schonberg, of her premarital pregnancy with him, of the tear in her womb and the loss of both her child and her ability to bear children, and of Iggy's eventual, sad death from tuberculosis.

I wasn't at all disturbed by Tante Minna's revelation of a premarital pregnancy. After all, Papa's work was sexuality; we all thought of it as normal. Indeed, I was grateful for Tante Minna's time and attention, and I admired her honesty. We had never shared secrets before or laughed and cried together easily. I mourned with Tantie when she spoke of her grief for her spoiled womb and for her Iggy, who had looked straight into her eyes with frank desire.

As I took the last, lonely cookie from the china platter, I thought to myself, *Well, I want an Iggy, too!*

Mind you, I wasn't sure what I thought of some of the particulars of lovemaking that Tante Minna had disclosed. Still, some of what she had said called to me just as surely as such knowledge had called to ripening women for generations on end. Undeniably, I wanted someone to look at me with piercing eyes and a heart full of plain, pulsing lust. I wanted to hear a knock, knock on my impenetrable chamber door and to present myself shyly but beautifully to behold. And oh! Great gods of my ancestors! From that evening on, at least for a few weeks, the whole world was precipitously and wonderfully damp with universal longing, longing that I welcomed into my newly fertile self.

I became more fidgety than usual. Willows waving restlessly in brooks seemed preternaturally significant.

I must find myself an Iggy, I said to myself lazily one night when I climbed into my four-poster. *Someone who will hunt me, get me, fill me, and then die young.*

So life was good for us all by 1908. Papa had his growing fame and a practice full of paying patients. The household hummed along busily, and my siblings did what middle-class Jewish adolescents did in those days; they went to school and tried their very best to achieve high marks.

I did the same, but I also had my sexual fantasy to enjoy. As I had since age six, I continued to touch myself intimately nearly every night while thinking about a man beating a boy. I now consistently imagined the boy as self-confident and having light, curly hair like mine was back then. I must have enjoyed masturbating more than ever, for I had started to make a bit of noise.

Or so I assume, for one morning Sophie imitated my moans at breakfast as Cook poured the coffee.

Mama told Sophie to be quiet at once, and she refused to pass her the sugar when Sophie asked.

Papa, though, looked disappointed, although he didn't admonish me. Theoretically, according to Papa, idle masturbation was perfectly fine for a boy. Indeed, he'd been treating a six-year-old boy who liked to touch himself. To the boy's father, Papa had defended the child's right to masturbate, and had pointed to the father's own sexual shame as the probable source of Little Hans's increasing social and horse phobias.

But according to Papa, a girl should never touch herself.

Still, that morning at breakfast, Papa did not scold me. Perhaps he was being realistic about the kind of rules and developmental schedules he could reasonably enforce. If so, he was right to recognize the limitations of his authority. As inclined as I was to take direction from Papa, it wouldn't have been easy for me to stop masturbating. For on the night that I'd made the noise that Sophie had heard, my beating fantasies had acquired a new dimension that I found irresistible.

Now there was a specific and serious misdeed—a mistake actually—that provoked the man to beat the curly-haired blond boy. Furthermore, the character of the boy was now that of a country lad. Not quite a shepherd and not quite a farmer, he had one responsibility only. He had to care for the willows waving significantly in brooks belonging to the beater, who now had a name: The Powerful Man.

And most expressively, the country lad had a name, too. It was Anna Freud.

I was the trans-gendered star of my own fantasy.

No longer confined to the role of observer, I got to be the one who was roundly beaten. It was I who was gorgeous and who had made the mistake. Out of sheer lack of attention to important details, I suppose, I had somehow fouled the brook. I had enraged the Powerful Man. I had made a grave error, and in a way over which I had no control.

The Powerful Man's soldiers drag me through a frenzied crowd. I become faint from the stench of hundreds of over-excited bodies. I am forced to stand in the hot sun on a high platform. I am sneered at. The clothes on the lower half of my body have fallen away. I am deeply embarrassed. But somewhere within myself I am also proud—wildly proud that I am good or at least good enough, proud of the mistake I have unwittingly yet honestly made. I plead. I explain to the crowd and soldiers. I bargain. I do it all with great dignity. All of my vowels are well-pronounced and my voice rings with earnestness and virtue.

But then there is a new and ugly tension in the air. I hear a thumping and a clanking.

"What could that sound be?" I wonder.

Then I see the first hint of the terror to come. The iron hand of discipline and order claws its way up the ladder to the platform—followed, of course, by the arm and the rest of its body. It is the Powerful Man. He has found me. He looks as though he wants to tear angrily at what remain of my clothes. He finds me with his piercing eyes and a heart full of plain, pulsing desire.

Fear. I have urgent and maddening and nameless feelings. Thick. I am nearly overwhelmed by the hissing and catcalls from the crowd and by the sound of brook willows calling desperately for my help.

Then my own hand moves quickly under my nightgown. I dissipate all of the tension that threatens me. And when I explode in heart and body, the boy is beaten. I am beaten by the iron-fisted Powerful Man.

Each night after I masturbated I went to sleep, and in the morning I woke up female.

Chapter 7

It was around the time that the fantasy took that evolutionary step that my visits to Papa's waiting room became more frequent. I no longer sat staring into the Persian rugs. Instead, I lost myself reading stacks upon stacks of Papa's psychiatric journals.

I read them all, and when I was through with them I continued to rummage, hungrily, through piles of Papa's unbound notes. Papa never warned me away from my reading. From it I learned about a variety of sexual behaviors, beginning with fantasy-assisted masturbation but proceeding on through adultery, necrophilia, pedophilia, bondage, and animal lust. I read so much so often that I became inured to the material's shock effect, deciding eventually that perversions (which is what Papa termed atypical sexual behaviors) were no more shocking than any other life choice a person might make.

From reading Papa's notes, I also learned about a patient he called Rat Man, a young lawyer who made his living settling estates. He was known for comforting office visits in which, with the deceased's relatives, he sorted through messy affairs, grouped and bundled papers with specially colored ribbons, and tucked them away into notched cedar drawers for safe-keeping and eventual presentation in court by a more brassy lawyer.

Mild mannered to a fault, Rat Man had strong sexual cravings that visited him not only in bed when he could tidily handle them, but also at times that were inopportune—like when he was consoling a widow or even dining with his own mother. The images accompanying the urges were, for the most part, reminiscences of a certain postal maid. The images were overwhelming and disorienting to him. And so, whenever he felt desire in a situation in which desire would not do, he conjured up an idea that a jar with a live rat was being strapped to his naked behind. The rat would use its teeth to tunnel through his anus. Rat Man's erection would usually dissipate. But so, at times, would his composure.

Over the past year, I had seen Rat Man many times while he sat in Papa's waiting room. He preferred to sit in a straight-backed chair in the corner, and I could tell it was because of the lamp on the cherry table next to it. The lamp's base and post were the trunk and limbs of a naked woman. Initially, I thought he was attracted to the woman's form. Later I realized that it was the lamp's embroidered shade that gave him comfort. He positioned it to obscure his face.

Whenever I saw Rat Man on the waiting room side of the Danger Door, I smiled reservedly, and he nodded in return. I never dreamed of engaging him as intimately as Ida Bauer and I had engaged each other.

Papa now occasionally allowed me to attend meetings of his Wednesday Psychological Society, which met in Papa's waiting room. I was allowed to attend only as a helper, and only on especially crowded nights. I was to welcome guests, hang coats, pour cognac, empty ashtrays, and open the windows a tiny bit when the room became stuffy. I was not to ask questions and I was never, ever to gossip about or in any way make light of what I saw.

I loved my rare nights with the Society; they held for me the same erotic draw that my beating fantasies held. In my fantasies I got dragged through fruity, farty smells and publicly stripped of dignity and defenses. Every Wednesday night that I spent in my father's waiting room I sat in the vicinity of overdressed, highly cologned, chain-smoking fat men. So much for aromatics. And, on the occasions when Papa or one of his friends actually presented a patient *in situ*, I watched humiliation happen.

HYSTERICAL

When Papa announced one night at supper that on the following Wednesday he would discuss the topic of sexual compulsions, he bragged that Rat Man himself would be attending. He expected, he said, an enormous gathering. He also said that he would need my help.

A Doktor Carl Gustav Jung was to attend the night of Rat Man's presentation. He was a young man—nearly thirty years younger than Papa—and yet was already second in command of the Burghölzli in Zurich. At the time it was Europe's most prestigious mental hospital. In correspondence prior to their first meeting, Doktor Jung had expressed his admiration for Papa's theories and had hinted at allegiance. That meant a lot to Papa both personally and professionally. And on the one time that they had met, they had talked theory, nonstop, for thirteen hours.

On the Wednesday evening of Rat Man's presentation, both Doktor Jung and Call Me Otto arrived late in the afternoon by carriage. They came separately from the train station.

I took their coats; Tante Minna gave them each a small glass of port and asked about their respective train rides. While they talked, Martin, Oliver, and Ernst bustled in and out of our apartment, grabbing every available chair and carrying them into Papa's professional suite. This was in anticipation of the huge number of attendees that we expected would arrive shortly before eight o'clock.

Alas, during supper, blankets of snow began to fall from the sky. The city came to a halt and a hush. The sound of carriages effervesced, as did the sounds of feet on cobblestone and of pedestrians' conversation. The hearty smile on Papa's face faded. No one could conceivably make it through the snow to sit in any of those waiting chairs, or so he and the rest of us thought.

At supper's end, the boys brought the extra chairs back to their stations in our apartment. Seeing the disappointment on my face, Papa said that, given the distances that Doktors Jung and Gross had traveled, his presentation would proceed. Furthermore, I could still attend. And so at eight o'clock Doktor Gross, Doktor Jung, Tante Minna, and I headed together down to Papa's professional quarters. Papa had already excused himself in order to prepare his patient for his appearance before the small gathering.

As we attendees waited for Papa and Rat Man to enter the waiting room I heard a knock on the hallway door. When I answered, in came a chillingly beautiful young woman bedecked in pearls and the silver fur of baby seals. There was a general pause of communal surprise at her loveliness, and I thought I noticed that clouds of snow had willingly followed her all the way in from the street to hover about her dotingly. Her hair was lustrous and fluffy, reaching everywhere yet somehow also staying within appropriate, upswept bounds. Her limbs were so delicate and her expression so consistently astonished that she looked almost as young as I. I have since calculated that she was a little older than Mathilde. She was twenty-three.

Her name was Fraülein Sabina Spielrein, and when she gave her card to me she was careful to say that she had just come all the way from Zurich. She asked if this was the professional suite of the great Herr Professor Sigmund Freud, and if so, whether the eminent Herr Doktor Carl Jung was available to greet her.

Tante Minna took Fraülein Spielrein's coat, for I forgot to ask for it. Doktor Jung was indeed available to greet her; he did so with glee. Proudly, almost deleriously, he introduced her to us all.

From the outset, Call Me Otto's behavior around Fraülein Spielrein was disturbed. I had seen him fluster other people before, but I had never seen him flustered. Now he was like a besotted schoolboy, recklessly vying for attention from the prettiest girl on the playground. I remember him singing a few lines of an off-color ditty that contained the word "Sabina." When kissing her hand in greeting, he smooched it. Then, during the minutes in which we all waited for Rat Man and Papa to emerge from the consulting room and join us, Call Me Otto leaned an ear against the Danger Door as though he were eavesdropping.

While doing so he smiled weirdly at Fraülein Spielrein, motioning for her to join him.

Doktor Jung frowned at all of Call Me Otto's shenanigans, but when he saw him eavesdrop and invite Fraülein Spielrein to eavesdrop with him, he wrapped one huge arm around her shoulders protectively. For her part, Fraülein Spielrein leaned cozily into the comfort of Doktor Jung's Teutonic chest.

Despite his jocular manner, Call Me Otto was entirely serious about eavesdropping. Yes, part of what he was doing was just show. But Papa and Rat Man really were in the consulting room on the other side of the door. And Call Me Otto really was listening in on their conversation. Little bits of what he heard elicited chuckles from him, more so as minutes passed.

Just to make sure I could hear nothing of what Rat Man and Papa said, I sat on a library ladder at the far side of the waiting room. I could not hear conversation, but I could hear Rat Man's cough. It rang out sharply from behind the closed door. Once, twice, thrice.

Behind every fear is an intense, infantile wish, I thought with each concussion, remembering what Papa had said to Ida Bauer so long before.

Chapter 8

At eight o'clock, the Danger Door creaked open.

I suppose it's because I had always seen Rat Man seated that I'd never noticed how tall and thin he was. He was attenuated to the point of seeming twig-like. His face was so clean-shaven that it looked to have been polished, and his sand-colored hair was neatly combed. That evening, when he walked through the Danger Door, he hovered close to Papa. The effect of his spare, spindly figure next to Papa's more burgher one made me fancy that Rat Man could get blown about were Papa to move too quickly.

No one spoke a word for a minute or so. The silence built dramatic tension. When Papa announced to us, "I give you Herr Lanzer," we responded by applauding with relief.

Herr Lanzer, of course, was Rat Man's real name. Despite our gesture of welcome, Herr Lanzer looked self-conscious. And I am ashamed to admit that, despite his evident discomfort, I gawked at him freely. We all did, hoping that Herr Lanzer's rat fantasy would soon become manifest before our very eyes.

I had always been the sort of child whose empathy with those around me tended to become physical. And so I soon found myself imitating Herr Lanzer's fretful sighs. I could also feel my shoulders creeping up towards my ears, just as his were doing. A gaggle of his coughs and nervous giggles collected near my own pharynx.

Quite consciously I chose a way to steady myself: I would review in my own mind Herr Lanzer's case notes, which I had re-read that very afternoon.

In addition to ill-timed sexual impulses and ideas about a rat, Herr Lanzer had what he called "omnipotent thoughts." He feared that if he thought ill of someone, that someone would die. On a less catastrophic scale, if he thought insufficiently well of someone, that someone would suffer a misfortune.

I was unable to concentrate very well on my review. For it had become evident to me that Papa himself was uncharacteristically tense that evening. Indeed, Papa was so on edge that, rather unprofessionally, he had left his presentation notes in the consulting room. He realized this only after announcing, "I give you Herr Lanzer."

Apologizing, he returned to the consulting room, pulling the Danger Door shut behind him.

Technically, Herr Lanzer no longer had an attending physician present. Neither did he have a larger, proximate form to give his airy figure ballast and a bit of cover.

Perhaps some misplaced sense of medical responsibility was what motivated Doktor Jung to approach Herr Lanzer. Wearing what he must have thought was a caring visage, Doktor Jung laid a gentle hand on one of Herr Lanzer's thin upper arms. He offered him a white-cushioned chair, and then he sat down in that chair's twin, which was immediately to Herr Lanzer's right.

Doktor Jung said, "God," as he looked Herr Lanzer in the eye.

Herr Lanzer seemed to comprehend readily that Doktor Jung had begun administering a word association exercise. It was what most psychologists those days did at the outset of any examination, and it was actually quite ingenious. Invented by Doktor Jung's superior at the Burghölzli, it was a structured way for psychologist and patient together to use seemingly unconnected bits of language to point them towards hidden matters at hand. Papa, evidently, had been using the exercise in his sessions with Herr Lanzer, for Herr Lanzer knew how to respond to Doktor Jung's prompts.

"Certainty," Herr Lanzer answered in response to "God."

"Love," said Doktor Jung.

"Lovely," said Herr Lanzer.

"Anger," said Doktor Jung.

"Hazard," Herr Lanzer blinked.

"Sex," said Doktor Jung.

Boy with blond curls, I found myself thinking. One of the giggles cowering near my pharynx almost escaped.

There came no immediate response to "sex" from Herr Lanzer, though he did sigh, almost as though he were exhausted.

"Sex," Doktor Jung repeated.

Herr Lanzer sighed again.

"Call me Otto," said Call Me Otto.

Call Me Otto placed himself in a plush armchair to Herr Lanzer's left and offered him a comforting smile.

"Sex," Doktor Jung said to Herr Lanzer again.

To no one in particular, Herr Lanzer explained, "Right now I want to be alone. I want to be in my bed."

Boy with blond curls, I thought again, illicitly, excitedly.

Call Me Otto leaned forward in his chair and took one of Herr Lanzer's hands as though to relax him. Winking, he said soothingly, "Ah, well. But it is snowing outside. It is icy and probably dangerous even for walking. I don't think you can leave to be alone in your bed quite yet." When he finished talking he did not let go of Herr Lanzer's hand.

"I need to be alone," Herr Lanzer replied.

"Do you ever have unwanted thoughts, Herr Lanzer?" Doktor Jung interrupted, clinically.

"Is there any other kind?" Otto asked Doktor Jung, as though to hush him. Meanwhile, he gently moved his thumb across the back of Herr Lanzer's hand.

Before Doktor Jung could answer, the Danger Door banged open and Papa re-emerged, in a hurry to make up for lost time. Upon seeing the *tableau* of Call Me Otto, Doktor Jung, and Herr Lanzer, however, Papa stopped, almost as an actor does when he makes an entrance too early and realizes he is about to "step on" a fellow's lines.

"Herr Lanzer," Call Me Otto said. "I just asked Doktor Jung whether there is any other kind of thought than an unwanted thought. Do you have an opinion on the matter?"

Herr Lanzer did not offer one.

"Remember that the only rule of conduct in psychoanalysis is to speak freely whatever is on your mind as soon as it comes to mind," Papa whispered to Herr Lanzer gently.

All eyes save for those of Herr Lanzer turned to Papa.

Herr Lanzer's eyes were on his own hand, the one that Call Me Otto still held firmly and caressed with his thumb. "But the man who asked me the question about thoughts is not analyzing me, Herr Professor," Herr Lanzer said.

"Then perhaps you and I should begin our analytic session," Papa suggested.

"I've already begun," said Doktor Jung. And then he said, "Sex" again to Herr Lanzer.

I wanted so badly for Herr Lanzer to take his hand from Call Me Otto's grasp so that he could concentrate on Doktor Jung's word association exercise. But when at last he did take back his hand, rather than turn his focus to Doktor Jung, Herr Lanzer said to no one in particular: "But…whatever are you thinking?" As he did, he waved the hand a bit in the air.

"Sex," said Doktor Jung for the fourth time to Herr Lanzer.

Just as he had before, Herr Lanzer waved his hand ineffectually in the air and said, "But…whatever are you thinking?"

Papa wrote something down on the notes he was carrying. The note-taking practically set me to dancing on my library ladder, for it reminded me that Papa, in his uncompiled case notes, had actually mentioned the very sort of hand-waving I was witnessing. Papa had written that, whenever Herr Lanzer was besieged at inappropriate times by intensely erotic urges, immediately prior to engaging the rat fantasy he waved one hand in the air and said to no one in particular, "But...whatever are you thinking?"

Someone in the room was currently arousing in Herr Lanzer an erotic urge. I thought through the list of suspects.

Immediately I dismissed Tante Minna. She was dressed in something flowery and flouncy and was plaintively munching on a beef sausage from a platter that Cook had made for the evening's guests. Yes, she had enjoyed a vigorous past, but now she was jowly, and neither the outfit nor the pose became her.

Certainly it was not I.

Of course it would be Fraülein Spielrein. Watching the evening's proceedings, her face was the image of beatific eagerness. Her loveliness could not have helped but arouse Herr Lanzer.

"But...whatever are you thinking?"

He asked it again of no one in particular, and this time he hadn't even been prompted by the word "sex" from Doktor Jung. Again, he waved his hand in the air, as he had before. This time, though, Call Me Otto caught the hand mid-air, almost as though it were a bird that he wanted to dissuade from yet another senseless flight. He placed the hand between his two knees and squeezed his knees together lightly, with just enough force to keep the bird from taking off.

"I beg your pardon?" Call Me Otto asked Herr Lanzer tenderly. "But whatever am I thinking?"

"BUT WHATEVER ARE YOU THINKING?!" Herr Lanzer screeched at Otto, and both Otto and I startled at the impact of the vocalization.

Recovering, Call Me Otto looked mildly amused.

Papa, too, was grinning when he volunteered, "Herr Lanzer, why don't you tell us what you think instead?"

Then Doktor Jung said, "Behind every intense fear lies an intense wish, Herr Lanzer. Surely Professor Freud has spoken to you about this. Tell us what you think. Tell us what you wish."

"Tell me your wildest desires, Herr Lanzer," Call Me Otto suggested. "Whisper them to me frantically."

As I've mentioned, during the hysteria epidemic that swept Europe in the late 1800s and early 1900s, it was predominantly girls and women who became hysterical. However, some boys and men did, too. Herr Lanzer, evidently, was the sort of man who could.

He did not bark, twitch, talk in tongues, or masturbate. He just looked unspeakably frightened, and then he swooned.

Papa moved assuredly to Herr Lanzer's side. Gently rousing him, he ushered him from the chair in which he sat to the waiting room's loveseat. Papa's firm hand on his shoulder seemed to steady Herr Lanzer emotionally. Tante Minna gave him a tasseled pillow for his head and a woven wool blanket. He lay down as best he could.

"My dear Herr Lanzer," Papa said, "you must excuse me for momentarily abandoning you. I hope you will also excuse the eagerness with which my friends have cared for you. I assure you that you find yourself in sympathetic company."

I believed that Papa's apologetic tone was sincere, for his grin had disappeared.

"Allow me to introduce everyone," he continued. "With you here tonight are two of my esteemed colleagues. They are Doktor Carl Jung, originally from Basel and now working in Zurich, and Doktor Otto Gross, originally from Graz and now working in Munich. Both are distinguished psychiatrists."

Herr Lanzer greeted them, and then Papa introduced Fraülein Spielrein ("Doktor Jung's friend and neurotic") and Tante Minna ("my wife's sister and, really, a second mother to all six of my children"). Then he introduced me.

"Over at the library ladder is my youngest daughter, Anna, whom you may recognize. She is a frequent visitor to my waiting room. I encourage you to appreciate that Anna, especially, wishes you the very best, Herr Lanzer."

Boy with blond curls. Boy with blond curls. Boy with blond curls. I curtseyed stiffly in greeting while everyone stared at me in horror and the women gasped.

Admittedly, I may have manufactured the memory of the staring and the gasps. I believe I had begun a quick slide towards the kind of instability I had just witnessed in Herr Lanzer. I did not ask aloud, as Herr Lanzer had, "Whatever are you thinking?" I did not wave my hand in a fluttering manner. But the entire waiting room did seem to froth away, leaving me in a perceptual void without the family and acquaintances who actually surrounded me. In their place I found a battalion of foul-mouthed soldiers in heavy boots. One reached out and grabbed my arm.

> *I am dragged by freakish soldiers through a gasping, frenzied crowd of overfed Austrians. They are neighbors, colleagues of my father, even relatives of my mother, and yet they revile me. I am forced to stand in the withering sun on a high platform. My skin burns in the heat. I begin to stink, just like the crowd. I watch in horror as the clothes on the lower half of my body fall away. When they do, the previously unexposed skin—the belly, the buttocks, the upper thighs—grows hot in the sun. All of me burns and I am in pain. I am also embarrassed, deeply so. But somewhere within myself I am also wildly proud—proud that I am good or at least good enough, proud of some mistake that I cannot quite name and that I have unwittingly yet honestly made.*
>
> *I have urgent and maddening feelings. Terror. I am terrified. Thick. The air is thick. I am thick. I have a thick feeling in my throat, in my stomach, in my pubis.*

"Anna? Anna?" Tante Minna had to whisper my name twice before I heard her. "Do sit down, dear, before you fall down."

I had left my perch on Papa's library ladder. Indeed, I had begun moving steadily towards the center of the waiting room, looking, I suppose, ill and oddly plucky.

Tante Minna had grabbed my arm. (I believe that hers was the touch I confused with a soldier's.) She had tried to tug me back to where I had been sitting. When the fantasy faded away, her hand was still on my arm and she was giving me an exasperated look.

No one except she had noticed this little drama.

The contagion of emotional instability is actually a well-documented phenomenon. Mass hysterical outbreaks were recorded in Japan in 1705, 1771, 1830, and 1867. In the western world, within the limited social science literature on the subject, there exists no disagreement about person-to-person contagion as a phenomenon, though there does remain a basic, unresolved question of what to call it. Some suggest that it is a sort of panic response, and this explanation makes sense enough to me. But call it what you will, I think it's safe to say that, when Herr Lanzer lost his emotional mooring, my own idiosyncrasies began to bubble.

Papa continued with the business of the Wednesday Psychological Society, and I missed some of the sense of what transpired next. I do remember that Herr Lanzer said again, "But…whatever are you thinking?" and then explained to Papa that he was ill and would like to be excused from participating further. I also believe that, when Papa asked for specifics about the illness, somehow Herr Lanzer agreed to continue with the presentation. Also somehow (and I wish I had noticed how, but I hadn't) Call Me Otto lost his tie and collar. A few remarkably long chest hairs pushed eagerly up out of the top of his starched white shirt.

Papa could see that Herr Lanzer was noticing the enthusiasm of Call Me Otto's chest hairs. He asked Otto to put his collar back on.

Bringing his hand to his forehead in exaggerated self-deprecation, Call Me Otto said, "Of course, Sigmund. My apologies if I have been rude." He reached for his collar and wrapped it around his neck. Then he began to fasten it in place, a set of motions that caused his hand inadvertently to ruffle the hairs that were peeking impatiently out.

This is the point at which my memories snap back into focus.

In the few seconds during which Call Me Otto's hands made his own chest hairs dance, Herr Lanzer started making strange noises like, "Nnnnn" and "Ggggggg." Curled into the loveseat, Herr Lanzer drew his knees up to his chest. Eventually, "Nnnnn" and "Ggggggg" gave way to loud, repetitive shouts of, "NO! NO! NO! GO AWAY!"

I began breathing heavily.

Call Me Otto seemed confounded by Herr Lanzer, although he clearly wanted to help him. Of whom did Herr Lanzer need to be rid? Doktor Jung? Papa? Frau Bernays? Fraülein Spielrein? Every time Call Me Otto asked for clarification, Herr Lanzer became more wretched. He seemed to flare up around the edges, much as a newspaper does when it combusts under a magnifying glass. I remember the crease in Herr Lanzer's pants near his buttocks stretching flat as, lying on his back, he banged his knees repeatedly against his chest and shouted "NO! NO! NO!"

When Herr Lanzer covered his groin with his hands, I realized that his rat fantasy had, alas, failed to obliterate desire.

Omnipotent thoughts were sure to kick in soon.

I remembered that, routinely, Herr Lanzer believed that thoughts and feelings of his that were not supremely cheerful could cause a small misfortune. What, then, would he anticipate resulting from thoughts and feelings that were entirely unbridled?

Herr Lanzer began to apologize to Call Me Otto.

"Nnnnng. Gggggg. But I hadn't meant any harm at all," he said. "And such a nice man you were. Nnnnnng."

"Am. I still am a very nice man," Otto assured him.

At which point Herr Lanzer's apologies turned into loud, penitent moans.

Papa lay a hand on Herr Lanzer and held it there for what must have been an entire month. Herr Lanzer's moaning eased. Then Papa said that he would like to ask Herr Lanzer a few questions; he hoped that Herr Lanzer could follow the custom of psychoanalytic sessions and answer by speaking whatever came to mind with absolutely no censorship and as soon as it came into his awareness.

"Do you feel like you're game for this sort of thing?" Papa asked.

I didn't hear Herr Lanzer's response. What I did hear, at first dimly but then with increasing volume, were "huzzah"s and "garrumph"s and "yeeeecccch"s and the like. The noises were soft but strident, animalistic. They weren't coming from Herr Lanzer, who still lay with his knees to his chest. It took me almost half a minute, perhaps, to realize that they weren't coming from anyone present that night at the Wednesday Psychological Society.

They were catcalls. A crowd's crude spirit had begun once again to fill the room:

> *I am on the wooden platform in the bright sun, but this time I am not alone.*
>
> *Herr Lanzer and I stand together. We smell the fruity, farty crowd that hates us. Herr Lanzer has been stripped of his dignity. He is naked below the waist; I am about to be similarly assaulted. I know this because I can hear the thumping and clanking of the Powerful Man. His iron hand is clawing up the ladder to the platform. At any moment the rest of his body will arrive. He will think medieval thoughts about me and tear at my clothes. Or so I fear. Or so I wish.*

I felt warmth on my right elbow. Looking down, I noticed Tante Minna's hand. I remember Papa saying many things, none of which I could comprehend. As my head cleared I heard him say, "The Herr Lanzer you see before you tonight is almost cured."

Oh, how I wanted for Herr Lanzer's sake for Papa to be right!

"Just one moment, Sigmund," I heard Call Me Otto say as I leaned stiffly into my library ladder, put my hand on my chest to quiet my heart, and hoped that no one but Tante Minna had noticed that I'd begun wandering again. "If I might be so bold: What could it be about Herr Lanzer that is almost cured? If he is anywhere near 'cured,' we haven't seen any evidence of it. On the contrary, we've seen extraordinary disorder and discomposure. Will you wave your hand magically in a moment or two, perhaps, and sweep fairy dust into his brain?"

Papa didn't say anything, but he did laugh at the very idea. So did Call Me Otto.

So, even, did Herr Lanzer. And so did I.

"Well," said Otto, seeing Herr Lanzer laugh. "Maybe our friend is a little closer to 'cured' than I thought. But surely you can humor and enlighten me. Of what will Herr Lanzer be cured, precisely? Surely not of fantasies about a rat, nor of omnipotent thoughts. Those seem far too ingrained to be quickly eradicated."

"There will be no need for me to address the fantasies of a rat. Neither will I address Herr Lanzer's omnipotent thoughts. I will address instead his wish, and once that has been dealt with, all of the contingent distress will vanish."

Papa continued: "The behaviors you just saw are elaborate defenses that Herr Lanzer has constructed to protect him from the force of wishes that are hidden from him and that he has self-defensively converted into fears." Papa said that as though it were self-evident.

"Wishes for the postal maid, you mean, Sigmund. Yes?"

"Not quite, Otto. Not quite. Of the postal maid Herr Lanzer has no real fear. Neither, actually, does he have desire. I'm not even sure that the postal maid ever existed. Indeed, I suspect that the postal maid in all of her glory is but a screen memory—a chimerical recollection that masks something that Herr Lanzer did a long time ago that was too terrifying for him to fully experience. Not having been adequately experienced, the action is therefore beyond complete remembering. Wishes of which he knows nothing arising from an action he has long forgotten are what torment Herr Lanzer."

"Terribly interesting idea, Sigmund," said Otto. "Are you ready to tell us what those wishes of Herr Lanzer's are?"

"To have sex with a man, of course. Herr Lanzer is a homosexual."

"I am?" said Herr Lanzer.

"I am?" I asked.

"Yes, you are," Papa said to Herr Lanzer.

"And how do you know that?" we responded.

Papa explained: "Far more significant than your outcry this evening in response to the sight of Otto's un-collared shirt has been your response to me—not so much tonight, but in analysis during regular hours. For a long while, Herr Lanzer, it's been clear that you want to have sex with me."

"I *do*?"

"Of course you do. All of my patients do. And I want to have sex with them. That's just part and parcel of what I call transference and countertransference—transference being the desire of the patient or 'analysand' for the analyst, and countertransference being the reciprocal desire of the analyst for the patient. Such feelings are inevitable in analysis."

Here I thought I saw Doktor Jung smile knowingly.

Papa continued: "They arise from all sorts of causes—imagined, remembered, and proximate. They are nothing of which to be ashamed for they are extraordinarily helpful to the analytic process—but only as long as the analyst calls them to the conscious attention of the analysand and uses them as fodder for a discussion about the analysand's past. Calling those feelings to your attention is what, right now, I am doing for you."

"Well, if erotic feelings in analysis are so common, why do you suggest that I am homosexual?" Herr Lanzer asked. "Are all of your male analysands homosexual? Are you?"

"Of course not. I know the unusual strength of your desire for me because I feel desire for you more strongly than I feel it for other male analysands. One of the techniques of analysis is that the analyst must learn to watch the countertransference for what it reflects about the transference. Which is to say that, in analysis, my feelings for you say nothing about me but speak instead to your feelings. I have felt strong desire for you, Rat Man, which can only mean that you are a homosexual."

Herr Lanzer looked skeptical. "So this is the wish of which I know nothing, Herr Professor?"

"This is the wish of which you know nothing."

"But what of the action?" Call Me Otto demanded. "Didn't you just say, Sigmund, that wishes of which the analysand knows nothing arise from an action long forgotten?"

"Indeed I did, Otto."

Papa explained to Call Me Otto that Herr Lanzer's homosexuality began when, as a three- or four-year-old, his father violently castigated him for masturbating after a sexually inappropriate encounter with his nanny in which, upon the nanny's invitation, little Herr Lanzer had crawled up her skirts and patted her "pretty parts."

As Papa explained to Herr Lanzer: "I suspect that your father caught you masturbating and beat you mercilessly. After that sexual escapade and beating, neither of which you remember, your erotic longing for the nanny no longer felt safe for you to hold. Mid-beating, mostly likely, you projected that longing onto your father. From that calamitous moment on, your father—and all men, but especially your father and, by extension, me—were 'holders' of your eros. Now that you know that even deeper within your original self your erotic longings are the same fierce, heterosexual beasts with which we all struggle, you needn't repress them. Retrieve your longings. Take them back from men, for you may now engage with women to your heart's content."

"But I already do," Herr Lanzer assured Papa. "To my heart's content."

"And now you will engage comfortably with men, as well," Otto volunteered happily, "rather than tying yourself up in emotional knots being afraid of that."

"No," said Papa. "Wrong, Otto. Not at all, Herr Lanzer. That wouldn't be civilized. Your task as a cured analysand will be to encrust onto any tarrying homosexual longings all of the harnesses worn by the rest of us—or at least by most of the rest of us. We are not, I repeat *not*, a homosexual society." Papa looked Herr Lanzer firmly in the eye.

"Well, all right then," said Herr Lanzer, conclusively.

"Wonderfully done!" cried Call Me Otto. "Sigmund, you've impressed me! Now, tell me, for I seem to be thickheaded tonight. I understand that Herr Lanzer will apparently no longer be ruled by the homosexual impulses of which he was decidedly unaware. But on what evidence must you insist that he is cured?"

"'On what evidence *must* I insist?'" Papa pounced. "Don't you mean to say, 'On what evidence *do* I insist?' With your unthinking use of the imperative, Otto, I believe that your slip is showing. I say that he is cured permanently and irrevocably because we have discovered the hidden context. It is the murderous rage that he felt for his father when his father beat him. It is also the resulting climactic moment in which Herr Lanzer thrust upon his father all of his sexual desire. Discovering the hidden context always effects cure."

"But how do you know? How can you say that 'discovering the hidden context always effects cure?' Where are your scientific data for such a claim?" Call Me Otto was a delighted revolutionary in the midst of freewheeling debate.

"In my consulting room," said Papa.

"But I eavesdrop on you in your consulting room, and I have never heard such evidence!" Call Me Otto announced.

"In my consulting room at night," Papa explained. "Each night I conduct a formal self-analysis. I have for years. Believe me, Otto, discovering the hidden context always effects cure."

"Sigmund! This is delightful! And what of you? Tell me quickly. Tell me everything. I am a-quiver with anticipation!"

This was not Otto speaking. It was Doktor Jung. Married to a rich, kind and competent Frau Jung and embroiled with his beautiful neurotic, Fraülein Spielrein, Doktor Jung had also, just that evening at supper, confided to us all that he had a "religious crush" on Papa, "something wonderfully naughty."

"Tell me about you! Tell me all about you!" Doktor Jung demanded.

"In my consulting room, Carl. In three minutes," said Papa in his sternest, head-of-the-family voice. And then, casting a powerful glance around the room and resting his eyes on Fraülein Spielrein, he added, "Alone."

Somehow Tante Minna had already left the room without my noticing. So it was only to Call Me Otto, Fraülein Spielrein, Herr Lanzer, and me that Papa said, "You will have to excuse us. But before I go, I would like to leave you with a little joke. It will soothe your psyches as well as be instructive in helping you understand how difficult it is for us to fathom our sexualities.

"One day The Lord came unto Adam," Papa began, and I heard the people around me begin to laugh nervously in anticipation. "The Lord said unto Adam, 'I've got some good news and some bad news.'

"Adam said, 'Lord, Lord, give me the good news first.'"

"The Lord said, 'I've got two new organs for you. One is called a brain. It will allow you to create the wheel and fire, live longer than you might otherwise, and have intelligent conversations with Eve. The other organ is called a penis. It will give you both great physical pleasure and will give Eve many babies. Eve will be very happy about your penis.'"

"Adam was ecstatic. 'Lord, these are great gifts you have given unto me! What could possibly be bad news after such glad tidings?'"

"The Lord looked upon Adam and said unto him with sorrow, 'You will never be able to use these two gifts at the same time.'"

Papa gathered his papers while Doktor Jung and Fraülein Spielrein kissed in parting. Then Doktor Jung rushed off to "gather one or two of my thoughts," as he said. Papa opened the Danger Door, walked directly into the consulting room, and closed the door firmly behind him.

Chapter 9

We had three minutes before Doktor Jung was due to join Papa in the consulting room. Call Me Otto was already leaning his ear against the door.

Danger. Danger. Danger for proper women. Danger for little girls. Danger, danger, keep out.

Those had been Papa's warnings. I was not to transgress the boundary of the consulting room door.

Regardless, I joined Call Me Otto.

At first, Herr Lanzer reacted to the sight of Otto's and my preparedness for eavesdropping with what can best be described as wonderment. I actually worried that he might swoon. He didn't. He took three tall, flat-bottomed crystal glasses from a *secretaire*. Herr Lanzer handed one glass each to Fraülein Spielrein and Call Me Otto, and kept one for himself. He then showed Fraülein Spielrein and Call Me Otto how to use the glasses.

"Prop one ear against the bottom of the glass while putting the glass's mouth flush against the door," he explained, miming.

Then, with a practiced set of movements that betrayed he had done this many times, Herr Lanzer removed a long-fluted conch shell from the top shelf of one of Papa's bookcases. Saying, "For Fraülein Freud who, I've learned, wishes me well," he handed the shell to me. He showed me that, with its long, curved chamber, I could easily pass sounds from the door to my ear, all the while peeking through the door's keyhole.

"Do you feel cured?" Call Me Otto whispered to Herr Lanzer with frank admiration while we waited in position at the door for there to be something to hear.

"I am a little unsure, Doktor Gross," Herr Lanzer whispered in return.

"Would you like me to leave you alone?" Otto whispered.

"No," said Herr Lanzer. He smiled confidently. "I am no longer feeling uncomfortable."

"Do you finally feel heterosexual?" Fraülein Spielrein joined in. In German, the word is *heterosexuell*. German was Fraülein Spielrein's third language, Russian and French being her first and second. As a consequence, perhaps, of language confusion, she had a habit of juxtaposing "w"s with "v"s and also (significantly for *heterosexuell*) "r"s with "l"s.

Perhaps the impossibility of responding to such a poorly intoned question caused Herr Lanzer to say nothing.

"Well, Herr Lanzer, we can certainly have coffee together or even something stronger later, once it stops snowing," Call Me Otto offered in a friendly manner. "But I'll bet it can take Doktor Jung a lot more than three short minutes to 'gather one or two of his thoughts.' If we have time before Carl and Sigmund start, and if you're feeling heterosexual, perhaps we four could fornicate. We have one good loveseat here, for which we could draw straws, and I believe the Persian rugs would be comfortable. Would you like to invite Fraülein Spielrein to join you? Or would you prefer Anna?"

I was long past any flush of sexual excitement that I had felt during the meeting of the Wednesday Psychological Society. I was not, however, devoid of feeling. For some reason, as soon as Papa and Doktor Jung had left the room, I had started to feel sad. Then I had gotten excited by the eavesdropping plans. Now I was—I didn't know. Afraid?

"But, come to think of it, would you mind doing Anna?" Otto continued casually. "I couldn't touch her. Sigmund would be furious. You do Anna, and I'll do Fraülein Spielrein."

I moved not a muscle. Herr Lanzer seemed frozen, too, though more in embarrassment than revulsion or fear. He coughed and looked away.

Fraülein Spielrein looked away, too, agitatedly. I could see that she hoped to find her lovely baby seal coat and make an exit.

"All right, then, I'll start," Otto said with a shrug. "But we'll have to do this quickly." He put down his eavesdropping glass and closed his eyes, making some hurried, quiet mumblings. They sounded, actually, like prayers or a mental casting of the *I Ching*. When he opened his eyes, he directed his attention at Fraülein Spielrein, who was by then sprinting rabidly about the room, opening and closing doors and cabinets to find the coat closet.

But then Call Me Otto hesitated. He pulled his attention away from Fraülein Spielrein and directed it instead at me.

He took off his collar and tie. His chest hairs waved hello.

I felt my breasts begin to tingle.

"To hell with Sigmund, Anna," he said. And then, more gently than he'd ever said these words before, he said, "Please. Just call me Otto."

And do you know what? Right away I thought about how Call Me Otto's eyes were nice. I had never noticed that before about him. They were blue. When I first mentioned Call Me Otto, did I mention the blue? They were blue like the Mediterranean Sea that kisses the home of my ancestors. I thought for a moment that I heard brook willows sing.

"Otto," I almost said, and I almost said it aloud.

Instead, of course, I screamed and dove for the floor. I put my head under a rug as though looking for mushrooms there.

"Otto," I had almost said, and for reasons that I couldn't explain, I feared that everyone I loved was thereby doomed.

"Doktor Gross, be sensible," I heard Herr Lanzer say. "Fraülein Freud, please do let me help you up." And then, "I was so pleased earlier this evening to see you with the others, Fraülein Freud. Your presence in the waiting room heartened me as it always has." As I brought myself clumsily to my feet and brushed stray bits of my hair back into place on my head, Herr Lanzer gave me a small, comforting pinch on the upper arm.

I had seen Herr Lanzer so many times before in Papa's waiting room. But then he had always been too ashamed to look at or speak to me. Now, though, he looked unreservedly into my eyes. Two miniscule tears of embarrassment were filling them. Despite them, I could see that his skinny face was nicely masculine. He took my hand in proper greeting and, once he had shown me how to take a few deep, calming breaths, he clicked his heels in a military way.

"I hope that you will accept my greeting."

"I will, Herr Lanzer," I smiled. "I will."

What a kind man! So engaging! And so unlike Papa. No sign of inspiration whatsoever. No bluster. And he didn't have much of a chin, but that was all right. He was what my Grandmothers Freud and Bernays would have called a *mensch*: worthy of respect and intending no harm.

Wonder and joy! I thought to myself. (Yes, young girls really used to think in language like that.)

Fraülein Spielrein began to titter with the surprise of the moment. Even her throat noises were lovely.

What is it about feet? For some reason, when she began to laugh, I became self-conscious, and my self-loathing focused on my feet. Certainly they were appropriately shod and normally sized. But they seemed so much clumsier than the well-appointed feet of Fraülein Spielrein. Focusing on the two serviceable clumps that protruded from the bottom of my skirt, I felt envy for everything about Fraülein Spielrein, and the feeling increased every time she giggled. Her hair was perfectly coiffed. Her hands and nails were just right. Her dress fit her like a glove in all of the places that fashion and mores allowed it to. In fact, speaking as a Freudian psychoanalyst more than seven decades later, I can safely say that, as the moments passed, the envy that I had for that sweet young woman became emergent, erect, and impressively sized.

I didn't know what to do with my pulsating discontent. It scared me—as did my new, strong responses to both of the men in the room.

Otto grunted something wonderfully animalistic. Herr Lanzer looked at me imploringly, as though asking me to accept the burden of his ongoing concern.

The psychoanalyst in me now knows that my first instance of homosexual desire was born in precisely the way that Papa said it had been born in Herr Lanzer. Not knowing how to cope with the heterosexual lust that he held so strongly, Herr Lanzer had hurled his desire for his nanny onto his father, whom he considered a safer target. Not knowing how to cope with the lust that I had so precipitously come to feel for both Call Me Otto and Herr Lanzer, I transferred my desire onto Fraülein Spielrein.

It was a *fait accompli* even before I knew what was happening. All I did was look at Fraülein Spielrein once more—she was still giggling—and I came alive from head to toe. I was filled, for the first time in my life, with a yen that I had in no way anticipated.

I did not spontaneously combust, as Herr Lanzer nearly had that evening in relation to Call Me Otto. Still, I must have looked taken aback.

Fraülein Spielrein stopped making happy, girlish noises. She regarded me with concern.

I contemplated giving her a winning smile in return but I thought the task impossible. I had laughable feet. I had unmanageable hair. Any smile that I might at that moment have conjured would have looked like a grimace.

Though I must have sneered in spite of myself, for apparently Call Me Otto saw it, and when he did he knew that something was newly awry for me. He backed a few steps away and his face registered concern.

Fraülein Spielrein seemed to think that I was ill. She took my hand, probably to help me feel better. It did make me feel, but "better" was not the specific feeling that her gesture effected.

Herr Lanzer was the one who knew what was happening within me. He smiled gently, first at Fraülein Spielrein and then at me; it was in the manner of a lawyer who knows how to gather messy problems into tidy bundles, bind them with specially colored ribbons, and then tuck them away into cedar drawers. He said, "Look at me, Fraülein Freud. I feel better. You will feel better, too, after a while. I'm beginning to think that you and I have a lot in common."

"What could it be that we have in common, Herr Lanzer?" I asked. I had to ask, just to be polite, but I hoped he would not answer my question, at least not aloud.

"She doesn't fear rats," Fraülein Spielrein quickly offered. "She didn't crawl up her nanny's skirts. She doesn't seem to be legally inclined."

"Well," Herr Lanzer said, charmed by Fraülein Spielrein's quick support of me, "let's just say that it has been a very interesting hour for both Fraülein Freud and me."

"It has?" I asked, my two tears erupting into many, though I knew not why.

All of his vowels were well-pronounced and his voice rang with earnestness and virtue.

"Yes, it has," he said.

For the life of me, my memory has it that sandy-haired Herr Lanzer was suddenly golden blond and that he convinced all of us to join hands with him, and as a human chain of resistance to madness and despair, together face a smelly crowd shrieking catcalls from the corners of my father's waiting room. Herr Lanzer spoke proudly and righteously to the crowd, declaiming as my co-conspirator in crime on the platform in the sun.

"Let it be known by all in the entirety of the world that Anna Freud is good despite what mistakes in her innocence and forthrightness she makes. She is blameless. We four all are. She is our friend and we are hers and there is nothing,

> *absolutely nothing, that any of you can do to stop us from loving her."*

But really we four were alone. It was by then very late in the evening. We did not hold hands, certainly not. It would have been an unthinkable intimacy for casual acquaintances in those days.

Herr Lanzer, Fraülein Spielrein, and Call Me Otto did, however, surround me. Cocooned by them, I wept.

As I did, Herr Lanzer spoke. Meekly he said, "It's been an interesting evening for me, Anna, but perhaps a more interesting one for you. Go ahead and have a good cry. Your time has finally come."

Chapter 10

My time had come?

I thought I heard my aunt's voice through the consulting room door.

I stopped crying. Call Me Otto, Fraülein Spielrein, and Herr Lanzer tipped the bases of their crystal drinking glasses to their ears and placed the glasses' mouths flush against the Danger Door.

I steadied my position in front of the keyhole and took up my conch shell.

When I peeked into the consulting room I saw that it was lit by moonlight as well as by a single Chinese lamp and the rosy glow of a fire in the broad, green-tiled coal stove that sat in the corner. Since my one visit as a five-year-old, the room had acquired many strange *tchotchkes* and Persian rugs. There were rugs on the floor, on the couch, and even one on a wall. Lit in this indirect and ghostly way, it resembled what I'd always imagined for the interior of Ali Baba's tent.

Through the keyhole I also saw Tante Minna quickly leave the very room that I had never known her to be allowed to enter. She exited by the seldom-used back door.

Papa was settled in his chair and fumbling to light a cigar.

Doktor Jung stood in front of Papa. His dancing shadow, cast by the fire in the stove, engulfed Papa.

Without speaking or even looking up at Doktor Jung, Papa impatiently waved him towards the couch. In shadow his moving arm made him look like a mage, casting out demons.

Doktor Jung did not respond, and so Papa waved him towards the couch again.

Doktor Jung neither budged nor talked. He was an immovable, stubborn spirit in an inspired chamber.

"Sigmund," he finally ventured in his resounding, Swiss tones. "But whatever are you thinking? I have not come here to be analyzed. I have come to hear you tell of your self-analysis."

"What did you say, Carl?" Papa asked through a thick puff of cigar smoke.

"I said that I have come to hear you tell of your self-analysis."

"No. No." Papa feigned impatience. He tapped his cigar into a cubic, blue-tiled ashtray that I recognized as the very one that he had once mischievously told Sophie and me was Pandora's Box. "I mean before. A moment before. What did you say?"

"I said, 'Whatever are you thinking.'"

"Not exactly. To be more precise, you said, '*But* whatever are you thinking.' Did you not?"

"I very well may have."

"'But whatever are you thinking!' Those are precisely the words that Herr Lanzer uses to ward off his fears about homosexuality. I invite you once again, Herr Doktor Jung, to lie down. We have much to discuss. We will begin with the rule that whatever comes to mind during the analysis must be spoken immediately, no matter how trivial or personally embarrassing it may sound."

The immovable spirit didn't actually move, but he did shift his weight impatiently on his feet.

"Sigmund," he complained, "you exasperate me. I was not impersonating Herr Lanzer. I was protesting that I had entered your consulting room at your invitation to discuss your self-analysis. Are you trying to turn the tables on me?"

"I hear surprise and anger in your voice, Herr Doktor. Continue." Papa added another ash to Pandora's Box.

"If you hear surprise and anger it is because I am surprised, and yes, even getting angry. Do you not recall inviting me in here?"

"Tell me, do I hear betrayal in your voice?"

"Oh, yes. You are probably beginning to hear betrayal," and here Doktor Jung tossed his head in irritation.

"Do I hear outrage?" Papa asked.

"Yes, you now probably hear outrage, as well."

"Tell me more, Doktor Jung," Papa said, and then another burning ash went into the Box.

"I will say nothing until offered a chair on which to sit in an upright position as your friend and colleague." Doktor Jung sounded plenty annoyed. He pulled himself up to his full height. It was impressive.

"You are my colleague, but I am no longer certain that you are my friend, Herr Doktor," Papa said. "You have brought into my professional rooms a young, almost unformed woman. You have transferred and countertransferred with her here. You have puckered her, and by doing so you have insulted my sister-in-law and my wife and daughters. Believe what you want and do what you want in your own quarters, Doktor Jung, but not in mine. Herr Doktor, here we respect marriage."

"But...whatever are you saying?" A burst of shocked laughter leapt from Doktor Jung's mouth.

"No, no, Doktor Jung. You have gotten your lines mixed up. You say, 'But whatever are you *thinking*?' when you feel those hysterically murderous impulses towards me that you undoubtedly now feel, being as you are my intellectual son but not my intellectual equal and certainly not the intellectual father because that is who I get to be. You want to murder me just as Herr Lanzer wanted to murder his father. But instead of taking the manly steps to do the deed rightly you have besmirched my honor with talk in front of my family of your 'religious crush' on me and with your ill-mannered eroticism with that unfortunate girl."

A minute, perhaps, passed before Doktor Jung tried to speak.

During that time he reached up and turned on the gas of the archaic chandelier lamp that hung high over Papa's head. If Doktor Jung wanted to dispel shadows, he succeeded. For at once the room seemed cheerful.

When Doktor Jung ventured a response to Papa's accusations, he was able to do so with what seemed like a fresh start. He walked to the couch and sat on its edge. He fingered the golden threads of the Persian rug that covered it. And he thoughtfully traced the ever-redundant, circular forms on the rug that hung on the wall behind the couch.

"Sigmund, I must say, you have upset me. There is a matter that I believe we must now address, for it is getting in the way. You accuse me of impropriety, and I admit that it is possible that I have not paid as much attention to the niceties of polite behavior as I should have when in your home and professional suite."

Here the two men nodded at each other in civil agreement.

"But, truly," Doktor Jung continued, "it is I who can be angry with you. And, now that I think of it, I am angry. I am upset much in the way that any son would be at the discovery of his father's imperfections."

"Whatever are you saying?" asked Papa, lifting one hand up to shield his eyes from the chandelier's unwelcome glare.

"I have spoken with Minna, Sigmund. She has told me that you are lovers. Your wife's sister! That is incest by the law of your faith, is it not?"

"Oh, that. You mean the little 'nose blowing' Minna does for me with her hand and her handkerchief. It's nothing." And then, "Would you mind at least dimming the two right-most flames, Carl? They're what bother me the most."

Doktor Jung adjusted the light, at which point Papa said, "Oh, my! Carl! My old friend the rhinologist was almost right! But sexuality is not rooted in the nose! With me it's rooted in the nose blower!" Then Papa started laughing, loudly.

"Sigmund, my God, get a hold of yourself!" Doktor Jung practically hissed. I could tell he was offended by what Papa had just said.

"Forgive me, Carl," Papa finally was able to offer after a few last chuckles. "Forgive me, for Minna certainly would. Let me assure you that my dealings with Minna are accommodations that she and I consensually and compassionately make to the poor state of Martha's health. Minna, especially, has only the smooth functioning of the family in mind."

"Smooth functioning of the family," Doktor Jung repeated, cynically.

"By all means," Papa assured him. "What Minna and I do is not incest. Yes, by rabbinical law it may be considered that. But we are not rabbis, so that law hardly matters here. Of course, it is possible that you speak of incest in the Wagnerian sense, the one that is so highly in favor at our city's Opera House. If so, my friend, by saying 'incest' you have hinted at the untarnished hope, youth, and innocence of twins separated at birth. Hope, youth, and innocence are not words that describe Minna, and they don't describe me, either. Look at me, Carl. I've already outlived my life expectancy, and Minna has almost outlived hers. Please, try to think of our arrangement as a quick relief of pressure that clears my brain and relaxes my back. And I do sit for so many hours in this chair."

"Then by all means, kind Doktor, lie for a moment on this couch!"

To my surprise and with a wry smile Papa left his rather plain chair for the lushly outfitted couch, and Doktor Jung left the couch for the chair.

"Looks like I'll have to paint that ceiling," Papa grumbled as he lay back and wondered about where to most delicately place his feet.

"Hmmm. Tell me, Professor Freud," said Doktor Jung, grabbing a cigar from the humidor near Pandora's Box. "These strong counter-transferential feelings that you say you have had towards Herr Lanzer: Do you think it is possible that he is emblematic for you of someone in your early childhood?"

"Carl, can you hand me the tufted foot rug, please? And will you turn that chandelier off entirely? It's hurting my eyes."

Doktor Jung returned the room to its original Ali Baba illumination.

"How do people tolerate lying back in this defenseless position?" Papa then asked, of no one in particular.

Taking the rug that Doktor Jung offered, he did some angry fumbling, some reaching, and some rearranging of his feet.

"Carl, by Minna's lack of discretion you know me at this moment more intimately than I would like. Ah, wait. I've got it there. Blast it, Carl, no I don't. The rug won't come up as far as my waist! How is a man to feel comfortably covered? Wait a moment. Expose the feet, cover the crotch. Now I've got it."

"Let me be frank, Carl," Papa said once he had arranged the rug to his satisfaction. "Let me confess that you see before you a man who is far less civilized than he would have you believe. I have not committed what I consider incest, but by my actions and by the acknowledgment of those actions to you I may have brought dishonor on my dear wife and sister-in-law. That is Confession Number One. Confession Number Two is that I have demeaned my sister-in-law in my attempt to retain your esteem. Minna is more than a mere functionary. She and I mean a great deal to each other."

"Sigmund, I am honored that you trust me enough to confide in me so deeply."

"Yes, Carl. But I am not finished saying what's on my mind as soon as it's come to mind. Confession Three: I believe that, this evening, in my fervor to impress you and Otto with my methods, I may have betrayed Herr Lanzer's secrets more liberally than he would have liked. I feel badly about having done that."

"Go on," Doktor Jung risked saying.

"And most distressingly to me, Carl, is that something that I said during my presentation of Herr Lanzer's case seems to have upset Anna."

"I saw no such upset."

"But I am her father and I did. I feel sad about causing it."

"I see," said Doktor Jung. "Would you like to tell me more about your feelings?"

"You say, 'I see,' Carl, and that implies, 'I know.' But *do* you know?

Do you really know on a fundamental level what it is to injure someone you love, even unintentionally, in the heat of a moment?"

"Go on."

Then Papa seemed to shiver a little as he lay, seemingly lost in thought.

"Oh, but this is so obvious," Papa at last remarked with disgust.

And then he sat up and made a certain gesture. Do you know the gesture some men make when the oblique becomes obvious—if not to all, at least to them? A carpenter makes it when measuring for a new door. He sees that, in addition to deciding where the door will go and which way it will open, he must cut the wood so that the bump that is the floor saddle won't hinder the door's movements. A tailor makes it when conquering unforgiving cloth. No doubt an astronomer once made it when noticing that stars shift position relative to other celestial objects. It is the gesture of the average and of the great. Darwin probably made this gesture when riding turtles on Galapagos. Dickens, Napoleon, and Gandhi probably all had their versions, a tugging of the mouth and nose that turns men fleetingly into gargoyles at the very moment that their intellects shine.

Papa did it right then, right when he said "obvious."

Then he removed the foot rug from his feet. He folded it neatly. And he asked Doktor Jung, "Are you familiar with the Homeric concept of *ate?*"

"I don't believe that I am."

"*Ate* means 'a consuming and compassionless need.' You don't know it? Are you sure not? Well. I do know it—and perhaps it is because I have it. *Ate!* Little, bookish me! I was, on occasion, compassionless tonight, especially with reference to Herr Lanzer's secrets, don't you think? I believe that the explanation for the thoughtlessness of my behavior is that tonight I was beset by *ate.*"

Whereupon Papa lay down again, pleased as punch.

"I struggle with my failings, truly I do, Carl," Papa continued. "I sit with Minna in this room each night as the fire dies in the stove, and I gaze into the shadows as much as I do into the firelight." Here he raised himself on his elbows, and the pace of his thoughts seemed to quicken. "*Ate* in the shadows. I can almost see it now, Carl. Right there, in the fire where it's dark! Can you imagine it? I can. It is dangerous and yet wonderful. An irregular black nothingness surrounded by brilliant hot spots, it makes my creativity burst and flicker. It no doubt powers my sexuality, too. But it also sometimes unkindly powers my tongue and my humor and even my anger. I am erratic. *Ate* makes me despair. So while my *ate* is a gift, it is also a challenging force I must learn to harness."

Papa lay and watched the fire and shadows some more. He covered himself again as best he could with the foot rug. I can only imagine, though, that with the direct overhead light extinguished and the Ali Baba mood infusing the room once again, that when he watched the fire some of the foibles that Pandora had long ago hidden in her Box escaped up and out into the room on a wisp of burning ash. For soon enough, a malaise seemed to descend on Papa. Indeed, he eventually began to shiver pronouncedly. When Papa's teeth began to chatter, Doktor Jung rose from his chair to cover him with his own suit coat.

"I'll get Minna," he said kindly and capably. "It seems, Sigmund, that you may have caught a chill. A man of your age should probably not…."

Papa roared out with a vocal force I'd never known he had. It was clear that Doktor Jung hadn't known about it either. "DO NOT TALK TO ME ABOUT 'MEN OF MY AGE!'" He roared. "NOOOOOOO! I've not caught a fever. NAYYYYYYY! I'm as hearty as… as…."

"As?" Doktor Jung asked, his suit coat now retrieved from Papa's body and clutched in his two hands.

"I am *too* hearty! I have *too* much *ate*! Can't you see? AAAGGGHHHHHH!" Here Papa's shivers really picked up steam. "My goodness, Carl. What I've caught is fear! I am scared of my own gusto-O-O-O-O!" After Papa hollered that word, he rolled himself into a fetal position and lay there, saying nothing.

Sitting on the very lip of the couch on which Papa lay, and using a textbook bedside manner, Doktor Jung questioned him again.

"Of what are you afraid, Sigmund? If it's *ate*, I think I can safely assure you that it sounds like just a Greek name for sexual hunger. Remember, you've already called sexual hunger 'libido?' And as you yourself have said, we all have libido, and we all must harness it. It sounds to me like you're just a normal man, Sigmund."

Here I thought I heard Papa growl. Slowly, he unfurled himself.

"*Ate* is not just another name for libido, you idiot. Not at all! And I may not be a normal man! Not at all! Haven't you been listening here, Carl?"

"Tell me more," Doktor Jung said.

"Tell you? Why in heaven's name would I need to *tell* you? Just read it! Everything that I could possibly say about me is already written. Here. And here. And over there, too," Papa gesticulated wildly about the room as though to indicate the many bound volumes of his published works as well as various loose-leaf manuscripts bearing his gothic script. His shivering was still running full throttle.

"It is psychoanalysis itself, damn it! Don't you see, Carl?"

Here Papa's physiological responses began to slow down. It seemed as if readying himself to give a long explanation was calming him.

"I'm beginning to see that, all along, I have been my own laboratory animal. The twists and turns that my theories have taken I now understand as the twists and turns of my own sick mind. No, no. Don't reassure me that I am fundamentally normal. I will not listen to your lame talk. After my disaster with Ida Bauer, I became famous for my writings about transference and countertransference. I hadn't thought about it until now, but it's possible that I wrote only about my own tendency to let my sexual desires wander where they shouldn't—not about *all* analysts' and analysands' tendencies, only my own."

"Do you mean that your erotic feelings for Herr Lanzer could, despite what you said earlier to him, be the result of your own lust, not his?"

The idea genuinely seemed to intrigue Papa.

"Goodness. It seems obvious now that you say it. Thank you, Carl, for illuminating me."

"You're welcome," said Doktor Jung.

But after a minute or two of contemplative silence, Papa started to shiver again.

"Sigmund," said Doktor Jung gently. "I see that you are no longer taking comfort from my insight."

"Comfort is not my concern!" Papa bellowed. "Carl, the safety of my friends and family is at stake! Do I speak and write about transferential lust because I am preposterously lustful? Do I write about libido because I am consumed by an amoral one? Frankly, Carl, I wonder. And I don't know the answer." At which point Papa began to rub irritably at his eyes while pulling at his face in a way that seemed reminiscent of neither the average man nor the great.

"Am I worse than most? Am I worse than most?" Papa moaned. "I really do not know."

"We have much to talk about," was Doktor Jung's optimistic response.

"Yes, well," Papa soon said. One exaggerated smile and deep sigh later, he continued. "Twelve years ago I was famous for my theory of hysteria and rape. I said that all hysteria was caused by childhood rapes. Over the next several years I changed that theory. I said that hysteria results from the *wish* to be raped. As of tonight I know that my rape theory *could*, like my libido theory, be about me."

"Your theory about childhood rapes or your theory about the desire for rape?"

"The first." Papa was now taking a turn at absent-mindedly tracing the patterns on the Persian rug that hung behind the couch. "Tonight I am newly re-concerned with the first."

"You are saying that your theory about hysteria stemming from childhood rape was, unbeknownst to you, actually about you?"

"Yes. About me."

"Let's be careful here, Sigmund. Rape is not a concept with which to trifle. Are you perhaps saying that you wrote about childhood rapes because you were raped as a child?"

"My gosh, I hadn't even thought about that possibility." Papa seemed taken aback—so much so that he also seemed amused.

"Forgive me, Sigmund. I've been stupid. I'm not following you."

"What an amazing idea! Tantalizing, yes! But, no. Probably not."

"But wait! You just said that the twists and turns of your theories might only reflect your personal history. If this is true, there is a strong possibility that you were raped as a child but have yet to remember it."

"Nonsense, Carl. Rape is something that happens to little girls, not to little boys."

"Certainly not. I, for one, was raped as a boy, actually as a young man. You must not let your prejudices about gender, size, and might get in the way of an understanding of power, violation, and violence."

"You were raped as a young man, Carl?"

"Yes. I was. Were you, Sigmund?"

"I hardly think so."

"Well then, what in God's name are we talking about?"

"I believe that we're wondering whether my theory about childhood rapes stems from my personal experience."

"But not as a rape victim."

"No. Not at all. If you must know, as a rapist."

"If I am to help you, Sigmund, I need you to stop this nonsense. Speak to me in terms of truth, Sigmund."

"To the best of my ability, I am."

Here Doktor Jung rose out of Papa's chair. Indeed, once again he pulled himself to his full height and cast a shadow across Papa.

"Not true!" he shouted. "Omission! You lie by omission and you control by omission! You conceal! You have the truth of your history and I need it. Give it to me. Give me the truth in the technical sense of the word and keep poesy and archaeology and criminology and literary analogy to yourself!"

Doktor Jung had begun to argue in a pitch that might best be described as unmasculine.

Papa tugged at his mouth and nose one last time and looked momentarily like a very wise man. He stared querulously into the front end of Doktor Jung's last sentence.

"Truth? In the technical sense? Can't you see, Carl? I'm afraid there's no such thing."

For all of the stentorian soul-searching that happened in Papa's consulting room, what was probably the more potent drama had played out in whispered voices on the waiting room side of the Danger Door.

My time, indeed, had come.

Three tall, flat-bottomed crystal glasses and one very recently smashed conch shell had been the drama's props. I had been its protagonist, Papa's overheard words the antagonist, and Call Me Otto, Fraülein Spielrein, and Herr Lanzer the Greek chorus, if you will. Their voices and faces had expressed moment by moment the bewilderment, agitation, horror, false hope, rage, and, ultimately, cheerlessness through which I had cycled. In the stillness of the drama's aftermath, a completely leerless Otto touched my head and stroked my hair. Fraülein Spielrein knelt next to me, weeping. Herr Lanzer waved his hand in a bird-like manner as he mumbled, "But...whatever are you thinking? Whatever are you thinking?"

Tante Minna entered the room at one point and tried to meet my eye. I deflected her attempt.

Anyone watching me in the waiting room, rather than Papa and Doktor Jung in the consulting room, would have seen the luminosity of a pubescent girl's spark diminish centigrade by centigrade. They would have witnessed childhood extinguished. They would have seen womanhood remain unborn.

At age thirteen, I had learned more about my father, my aunt, and life than I cared to know.

I climbed wearily into my four-poster later that night. I needed my customary solace. Still, I tucked my hands at my nightgown's seams as far as possible from the nightgown's hem, for masturbating would have required me to call up images of a Powerful Man about whose role in my life I had new ambivalence.

With no way to relieve my anxiety and dismay, I lay in bed and agonized, first about me and then about Herr Lanzer, who had been so kind.

What an awful evening it must have been for him, to sit as a freakish exhibit before a group of people whose own creepy peculiarities were not considered fair topic for discussion! I wished there were some way for me to tell him about the everyday oddities rampant in my own family.

For example, I could have told Herr Lanzer about Sophie. "When I was born she asked when I would die," I imagined myself confiding. "She sneaked bricks into my crib and onto my head so I would not grow."

I could have told him about my brother Oliver. Since the night when he was in charge and Sophie got us stranded mid-lake, he had taken to sketching plans for machines that could help people survive unexpected emergencies of any sort. Oliver had drawn plans for an underwater breathing system, a flying submarine, a time-traveling trolley, and a cutting machine with surprise, sickle-like knives on each side. "Slice, slice, slice!" he had taken to shouting.

I could tell Herr Lanzer that everyone in our family threw a pinch of salt over his or her left shoulder at the start of each meal.

I could have told him that Papa was afraid of certain hotel room numbers as well as telephones in general.

I could have told him that, nightly, Mama slept like she was dead, and that, daily, she read Tolstoy and wept.

I could have told him of a memory from my childhood. It is of my mother. She is sitting at the dining table, alone. Oblivious to the sound of our laughter, she is slowly drinking the soup from each of nine bowls. I see her through the window as I button up my coat. Papa, Tante Minna, and we children had decided to take our dinner *al fresco*. We forgot to tell her, that's all.

Those were the kinds of things that I wanted to say to Herr Lanzer the very next time that I saw him. I couldn't, though. To tell Herr Lanzer family secrets would be an impossible betrayal. Still, I was so tempted to help… so tempted to help.

I lay in bed with my hands at my nightgown's hems and struggled mightily to keep them from creeping underneath the cloth.

The muscles of the blond boy's chest were round and nice as he stood with his hands tied at his side and a look of beautiful innocence on his face. It was not really that the handsome young boy with a big chest and golden curls was suppressing a smile. It was more that a smile always lived there and that sometimes feelings like fear for his life had to visit for a little while on top of the smile.

He could have been a kind-hearted working boy. Maybe he was a careful and thoughtful shepherd, or a farmer in charge of willows and brooks.

Or maybe he was Prometheus, and what he had done was give mankind fire and blind hope when mankind had only war and disease and romantic haste and stranded rowboats and no reason really to carry on. Maybe the boy with blond curls was daring and fanciful, and like his brother whom he admired, knew how to rescue people and how to tunnel out of any bad fix that tried to bind him. Maybe the Powerful Man knew that and so secretly feared the boy as he secretly feared tunnels.

The Powerful Man raged at the boy for even thinking about sharing family secrets with Herr Lanzer. The Powerful Man snickered. He was angrier than he had ever been. The Powerful Man did nasty things in Latin to the boy's round chest muscles and strong, strong thighs. The boy's lip quivered, but the smile that lived there always bounced the quivering off. No one noticed that part, though, so he was not punished for possession of fearless lips.

Some people tried not to watch. Some people cried. Some people passed gas. Other people wished that they could be more like the Powerful Man, and they hoped that the boy with blond curls would make a mistake again someday. If he ever did and he was alone when he did it, they planned on doing even nastier things to him than the Powerful Man was about to do. Yes, they did. And then the Powerful Man....

A flood of feelings. Fear. Beauty. Thick. Smiles. Heaven. Fingertips.

After the night of Herr Lanzer's case presentation at the Wednesday Psychological Society, I drew an abrupt halt to my casual visits to Papa's waiting room. Papa brought directly to me whatever literature he thought might be appropriate for me, and I accepted his judgment about what I should read.

I did not again attend meetings of the Wednesday Psychological Society until I was much older. Which is to say that I had neither cause nor opportunity to encounter Herr Lanzer. I heard later than he died in the trenches during World War I.

Part 3

Behind Every Fear

(1909-1918)

Sigmund and Martha's silver wedding anniversary.
Oliver (left), Ernst, Anna, Sigmund, Martha, Mathilde, Minna (Bernays), Martin, and Sophie Freud.

Chapter 11

The year that I turned fourteen, Papa's work involved an elaboration of one of the jumble of ideas with which he had toyed in Herr Lanzer's analysis. That idea was that Herr Lanzer wanted to kill his father. Papa and Tante Minna took long thinking walks during which Papa sorted through all of the possibilities of such an urge. The result was Papa's theory of the Oedipus complex, based on the Greek myth of a young man raised by adoptive parents. According to Papa, the fact that Oedipus had killed King Laius, his biological father, and married Queen Jacosta, his biological mother, explained any son's murderous rage towards his progenitor.

That year—it was 1909—Mama lay passively in her bed for most of her waking hours, day after day. Her life as the family invalid troubled me, partly because it seemed so wasteful and sad but partly, I suppose, because in some way or another her approach to family life seemed just about right—for her and, perhaps, for me. There were many times when I wanted to lie down, take a rest, sleep endlessly, be indisposed. I worried about Mama and about myself. I exhaled lassitude like an atmosphere.

My siblings were hardier than I. Surely they knew that Mama was psychologically ill. Surely they knew that Papa's attentions lay with Tante Minna (pun intended). Surely they noticed that I had forgotten how to amuse myself. Still, they occupied themselves with being youthful and tending to the business of desire.

During summer in those days in Bavaria, the desire of many young men was focused on efforts to peek in the wormholes that they secretly worked into bathhouses and women's dressing rooms. Martin did that. Oli didn't bother to, but even Ernst, who was shy and anxious in general, did. My sisters greatly enjoyed the games of cat and mouse that the peeking created. In Bavaria during the summer of 1909, Mathilde and Sophie whispered to their friends whenever Martin and Ernst were about, excitedly ushering the girls into the lake's bathhouse just in time for them to display their undergarments' well-pressed seams.

That summer, while our siblings and their friends peeked and pranked, Oliver tended to Mama. He woke her in the mornings. He brought her meals. He read to her. He gave her an enlivening chocolate medicine three times a day. He joked with her. He even occasionally made her laugh. And whenever she seemed to be feeling even the slightest bit lighthearted, Oli took the opportunity to tell Mama forthrightly and to her face that he could remember a time long ago, "before Anna," when she had been lively, willing to walk briskly and have fun. He said that he deserved an occasionally vertical mother and would someday have one again, with her cooperation. They would approach things experimentally.

Mornings, Oli would set up shop on the small, rustic desk in the bedroom that Mama and Papa used that summer. First, he assembled gyroscopes to inspire Mama to regain her emotional and physical balance. She loved watching the gyroscopes spin, but she refused to get out of bed all the same. So Oli resorted to compasses, stuffing them under her pillows and tucking them in her bedclothes, all with the hope that, while she slept and lounged, she would osmotically acquire a sense of direction and purpose. Oli gave Mama books of architecture and art, hoping to infuse her with aspiration. He gave her tracts about women's suffrage, hoping to give her a will.

Oli also sang to Mama to calm her during the long afternoon thunderstorms that are typical of Bavarian summers.

Perhaps it was the thunderstorms. Perhaps one time there was an abundance of electricity in the room when Oli was standing close to Mama, plumping her pillows. Perhaps lightning leaked under the window sash during a particularly harsh crash, and what with all of the metallic objects that Oli had placed strategically about, created a cataclysmically charged atmosphere. Regardless, it is probably true what Papa said years later about Oli's sexual development: When Oli dribbled chocolate elixir onto a spoon for Mama three times a day and then watched her lap it with her tongue and suck it into her gums, he received at least as much carnal education as his brothers got from girls their own age.

There is an old Yiddish adage, "*Vee der Kedusheh is gresser, iz der Tumeh gresser*," or, "Where the holiness is greater, the impurity is greater." Grandmother Bernays used to say it and she would have said it about Mama and Oli, if she had been with us. Oli's intentions towards Mama were pure—devotional even. He only wanted to help. And he did help her, immeasurably, but in doing so he got swept away by forces that he didn't understand.

Here is the story of that:

After weeks of trial and nothing but error, Oliver stumbled on an approach to Mama's sadness that consistently lightened it, at least a little, and he pursued it. What he did was sing to her from her favorite book of the Hebrew Bible. It was *Song of Songs*.

Papa had recently banished from our home all use of Hebrew and practice of Judaism. He had even banned Yiddish. Anti-Semitism was increasing in professional literature and circles, and Papa thought it important to establish himself and his family as high Austrian, not low ghetto.

Alas, Mama had been raised with an Orthodox faith, and Oli correctly guessed that being forbidden to drink at all from the well of spirituality was adding to her distress. That, I am sure, is why he first tried, during a thunderstorm, to clandestinely chant a Hebraic verse or two from the *Song of Songs*, which he found in Mama's old Bible. Mama was so scared of the noise and light, and Oli wanted to calm her.

Surely there was no great risk in a little vocalizing. Besides, it was Papa who had forbidden Hebrew, and Papa and Tante Minna didn't seem to be about. Oli's warbling calmed Mama, clearly and right away. Not only did it calm her, as any kind of intoning or recitation might have, but the Biblical song produced a smile and a few notes from her. I am sure that is why, that evening, while Papa and Tante Minna were on a late thinking walk, Oli sang again to Mama. Indeed, he crooned to her, and by the end of the evening she was so enlivened that he promised to sing to her the whole *Song of Songs* bit by bit, every chance he could.

That would take quite a while, for the *Song of Songs* is the endless, dreamy cry of romantic longing attributed to King Solomon himself.

I have carried you off to Jerusalem.
You are fragrant still
Like aloes and myrrh.
Your vulva is a rounded crater.

And like that.

None of us had formal training in Hebrew. But it didn't take Oliver long to find a German Bible. There was one in the den of the house we were renting. At first he gave irregular little concerts to Mama alone in the late afternoons. Eventually, though, Oli realized that Wednesday nights were an ideal time, for Papa could be counted on to be at his meetings of the Wednesday Psychological Society, which, when we were in Bavaria, he hosted in the parlor. (Analysands and colleagues alike tended to accompany Papa on vacation and rent houses nearby.) Oli timed his concerts always to commence at bedtime, which was when Mama usually felt most forlorn.

My brother was a good singer. Each Wednesday night I crept with my other brothers and my sisters to just outside the door of Mama's room. We knew not to enter further until Oli had given Mama her nighttime elixir. Once the ritual of dribbling, sucking, and swallowing was done and the bottle had been capped and returned to the bedside table, we knew that we could move at least a few inches inside the room and sit quietly on the floor. With remarkable mutual consideration, Martin, Mathilde, Ernst, Sophie, and I formed two rows. Sophie allowed me in the front with her and Mathilde. Martin and Ernst, who were taller, kindly knelt in the back. Mathilde took out her hankie and wept whenever Oli got to parts of the song that I was still too uninformed to understand. Ernst understood those parts, though, and he finally complained to Oli that he should enunciate better.

Oli promised to. Indeed, the very next Wednesday, Oliver stood, took a bow, looked directly at us all, and burst into clear and beautifully enunciated song.

My, how we enjoyed Oliver's cantillating! We crept off to our beds much later that night, our hearts sated with a full meal of joy. Oliver followed us as far as Mama's doorway, where he stood, singing as much out into the hall and for our further pleasure as into Mama's bedroom and for hers.

Eyes closed, I lay under my bedclothes. Oli's voice continued to resound, and I heard in it all of Mosaic experience, lately denied us Freuds and now sounding as though it were somehow being heaved forth by an entire tabernacle choir. I rested my tired head—and I was weary in those days, as I've said. Diminished expectations had lately become for me a personal style. Still, I dared hope that, with continuing Wednesday night concerts, Oli could carry Mama and me out of our torpor.

Soon enough Martin, Mathilde, Ernst, Sophie, and I did away entirely with sitting politely on the floor. Instead, this became our Wednesday night ritual: We would brush our teeth. Then everyone but Oliver would call out a cheery, "Goodnight, all!" and hop under his or her covers. We would leave open our bedroom doors. Lying in our separate beds, we could see reflected in the hallway a glow of burning candles, for after urging Mama to make herself comfortable, Oli would fill her room with light. He would wrap himself in her shawls, making himself look like a cross between a rabbi and a shaman. Then he'd stand in her doorway and serenade about thighbones like jewels and pomegranates heavy on dew-dropped vines. He excelled so magnificently at articulating everyone's overheated longings that he seemed sometimes to lose his mooring. Intoning endlessly, and more inspired each minute, he caroled louder and louder until, carried away by a song, he showed signs of heaving emotion.

Or so Mama explained. We were in our own bedrooms and couldn't see. Mama called out to us one evening late as she saw what was surely a far-flung tear stain grow low on the shawl in which Oli was wrapped.

"Oh, see! Oh, see! Come see the miraculous little liquid drop that Oli has produced!"

"What? What? What is it? Ooohhh, Oliver, what is it?" my sisters and I, nearly grown but still completely innocent, gasped in amazement when we saw the stain.

Papa and Tante Minna stumbled through the bedroom door as we huddled around Oliver. They had rushed out of the Wednesday Psychological Society meeting to collect some papers. Seeing for the first time his own summer bedroom filled with joy and smiles and twinkling lights and one small stain, Papa growled to Oli, "A gentleman should not do such things, not even unconsciously."

Every family is entitled to one nervous breakdown. Sweet, inspired Oli was ours. Oedipus *Mensch.*

Chapter 12

Q: What's Jewish senility?
A: It's when you forget everything but the guilt.

Of the few weeks of summer that remained after Oliver's songfests ended I remember little, except for the antics of a chicken-eating dog that we seemed to have rented along with our vacation house. I walked the neighboring hills behind it as it wandered. I watched while it stalked and killed innocent fowl. It delicately ate their meat and bones and left their skin and feathers looking like the picture of peaceful repose.

Those same weeks I watched Oli sit in the parlor sadly, though I doubt that the word "sadly" is up to the task of describing Oli back then. "Coldly" fails, too, though he seemed devoid of feeling and warmth.

Tante Minna kept a fire blazing in the parlor and wrapped him in blankets.

Papa worked alone in a small room that had been a maid's quarters when the old house was first built. There he polished his ideas about the Oedipus complex while Martin, Mathilde, Ernst, Sophie, and I expressed no open concern for Oliver, had no real conversations, and had no fun. Mathilde and Sophie quarreled, which was just like Sophie but certainly not like Mathilde to do. Ernst seemed more anxious than ever, and Martin became affectedly libertine. We were all five trapped,

I now see, in a world of nausea and guilt. Guilt today, guilt tomorrow. No explaining our good fortune, no accounting for Oli's bad. No exit.

One time late that summer, the chicken farmer next door set a trap to catch our rented dog. I saw him set it up. I saw the dog approach it. And although, over the previous few weeks, the dog had become my primary companion and I had grown to care for it a good deal, I could not bring myself to stop the dog from being ensnared.

Never mind. The trap was gentle enough, a net made of long cords. The dog struggled for only a few moments before it gnawed through the main line. I followed it back into our yard. The dog was still wound in cord, and by then had a trail of angry hens clucking behind it. Papa tenderly bent down to release the dog while the hens hurled invective. One after another, Papa untangled those cords until the dog's neck, tail, and limbs were free of them. It trembled and whimpered as Papa worked, but it also looked at Papa with great trust. Sometimes, though, out of fear but never fury, it refused to bend a leg or an elbow. Papa was patience personified, and in just a few minutes' time the dog was released and running.

It ran to the farmer's chicken house and soon left another feathered carcass at the side of the road.

"Poor pup," Oli observed that night when the dog shat unexpectedly in the parlor, squirting yellow stain on the wall. "He wants so badly to be good. But something inside him just wants to kill chickens."

It was ten years before Oli was taken into analysis by one of Papa's disciples. (The name of this particular analyst I've forgotten.) I suppose that Papa had his colleague loosen the cords that bound Oli. I suppose that, despite Oli's fear and whimpering, he bent the occasional elbow and knee, allowing the man to free him so that he could run again.

But certainly for the remainder of my childhood, Oli did not run. Gone were his fantasies of empowerment and escape. Gone were the *Song of Songs* and the elixir on a spoon, the heaving emotion, and the aspirations to Mama's love burning as brightly as Mama's bedroom ablaze with candles. Gone were the gyroscopes and compasses, the flying submarines, machete machines, and time-traveling trolleys. After Oli cured Mama of her sadness, he stopped wondering about such things. He let go of wonder entirely.

We still asked our brilliant brother for explanations of the new technologies that confused us. "Oliver, of what is a crayon made?" "Why don't airplanes crash?" we wanted to know. Oli bowed his head between questions—it seemed as if he were bored, or maybe as if he were thinking—and then raised it back up to give short answers, the length of which seemed to be determined by a wind-up key lost somewhere inside of him.

"Airworthiness depends in part on the distance between the leading edge of the wing and the stabilizer."

Had he worn a turban, we might have confused him with some mechanical carnival swami with a heavy head pivoting on a swivel neck.

"Crayola crayons. Introduced at the St. Louis World's Fair in 1904. Wax and pigment mostly."

Papa was fascinated with the changes he saw in Oli. He was also vexed. For the more he thought about Oli, the less the myth of Oedipus seemed to explain.

For example: Oli's lust for the woman who had raised him had seemed real—to Papa and, to be completely honest, to me as well, at least on the night that Oli produced the semen stain. Oedipus, however, had held no lust whatsoever for the woman who had raised him. None. He had lusted for and married his biological mother, and he had done that without realizing that she was his mother.

Another disparity: Oli's new, pervasive passivity suggested to Papa—and to me—that patricidal impulses boiled deep within him. Oedipus, however, had never had patricidal impulses. He had harbored no murderous impulses of any kind. Rather, he had killed a man who was attacking him, and was horrified to learn, later, that he had killed his biological father.

As Papa's fascination with Oli grew, so did his dissatisfaction with Oedipus as a general explanation of Oli's predicament. Papa began casting about for a new myth, one that would, even better than Oedipus, explain Oli to Papa and father-son tension to the world.

Alas, Papa couldn't find a suitable myth, not in Greek, Roman, Celtic, Native American, Inuit, Viking, Egyptian, Indian, Chinese, or Japanese lore. That is why, over the next two or three years, he created a myth from thin air. It was a fine myth, a pre-cultural myth, a convincing myth. Indeed, the new myth was so resonant with Papa and Oli's situation that Papa didn't even call it a myth. "This," he said, "is 'probable history.'"

Greatly simplified, the probable history that Papa spent the years 1910-1912 inventing was this:

> *Once upon a time in a small horde of early humans there was a primordial, violent father who cast his sons away from the horde as soon as they came into their manhood. By ridding the horde of his sons, the primordial father preserved for himself all of the women and most of the food.*
>
> *Challenge after challenge, the sons were unable to best their father.*
>
> *Finally, in an epic cognitive leap, the sons got the idea of collaborative fighting.*
>
> *The battle that ensued was fierce—though, outnumbered as he was, the father never really stood a chance. The sons killed him and raped all of the women—the mothers, the sisters, the cousins, and the aunties.*
>
> *Having killed their father, the men ate him at a celebration feast. While the celebration was predictably beastly, the act of dining was ceremonious, for the sons believed that by eating their father they took into themselves the meat of his strengths.*
>
> *As soon as the ceremony and celebrations concluded,*

however, the sons were simultaneously beset by a wash of guilt. This guilt—this single flood of guilt felt by all of the sons at the very same time—was literally the birth of civilization, for it signaled the recognition of two essential taboos. The first is the prohibition against parricide. The second is the prohibition against incest.

From that point on, all humans strove to control their inborn parricidal and incestuous impulses.

"And you must, too, Oliver," Papa said.

Chapter 13

On one of our last days in Bavaria that summer, Mathilde received a proposal by post from a man of her acquaintance. She accepted, also by post.

Papa was excited for her, for Robert Hollitscher was a successful businessman, and Mathilde would be well cared for. He suggested that, in celebration, we all hike. It would be a sentimental hike—perhaps our last hike ever as a family.

Dutifully, we all put on appropriate shoes and gathered outside. However, as had become usual for me in the past several weeks, lethargy and mild fear accompanied my preparations. I had a headache that I wanted to nurse. I had a book that I wanted to read. I rarely wanted to go outside, for any reason, and that day was no different.

Once we started walking vigorously, I felt a skewed sort of gravity pulling me back towards the house. Then, as is true of most people on most walks, I began to have tiny, exercised-induced explosions of intestinal gas that I tried, by squeezing, to mute. We all did.

"Is this anal eroticism, or what?" Papa muttered to Mama happily.

Yes, he said it to Mama, not Tante Minna.

Ever since discovering Oli's semen stain, Papa had been tending to Mama. For example, Papa and Mama both were extremely fond of Alpine flowers, especially of *Kohlroeserl*, a small dark-purple flower with strong perfume. When they were newly wed, they had climbed a grassy slope and spent a morning of splendor in a meadow of such flowers. Papa now brought Mama bouquets of *Kohlroeserl* whenever he could, and Mama once again began enjoying smells and sounds and sights. Not only could she walk about again, she lumbered good-naturedly out of bed most mornings, shaking off sleepiness in the early hours, humming to herself through the afternoons and evenings, and then, as day ended, turning in alongside a thoroughly roused Papa.

Tante Minna, on the other hand, seemed to turn into a cauldron of unrelieved withering. She had never in my memory been attractive—much too square-faced, and much too plump. With her billows, however, she had always seemed at least comforting, though now even the allure of her soft folds disappeared. Warmth seemed to have left her, perhaps escaping just as steam does on a cold morning when it gushes out of a bowl of hearty oatmeal, leaving what remains to turn on its own to a yellowing, charmless gel.

We nine were hiking, each of us with our thoughts, Mama and Papa and Tante Minna moving ahead of us siblings even though we had youth and agility on our side. Sophie laughed and called. I didn't bother to laugh or call back. A warming wind rushed up from the valley and the streams burst with pleasure.

As had become my habit, I filtered the day's lush beauty out of my perceptions. Preoccupied with my headache, the novel I had been reading, and intestinal gas, I managed to get no sense of birth or glory from nature that day. I sensed only dreary atmospherics. In disappointment there is no menace. I didn't actually look at the sky. I intentionally caught no sight of the horizon, for horizons had begun to scare me so.

We hiked pine-covered trails. As we moved higher, the ground became increasingly wet. I had to be careful not to slip on the needles. In places, my skin chafed from perspiration. I felt dizzy from the altitude and from want of a snack. I was thirsty but careful about using up the contents of my canteen. Eventually it ran dry. After it did, I thought that maybe thirst had turned my breath sour, so when I talked to anyone I tried to inhale.

Somewhere along the line, Oli had tromped on ahead of the rest of us siblings. He seemed to be trying to keep up with Papa. That day, I had little patience for Oli's increasing strangeness. I was glad that he was nowhere near me.

Once, when I looked up from my careful trodding, I stood for a moment to let my dizziness pass. As I pulled air rhythmically into my lungs I watched Mama, Papa, and Tante Minna round a hill way ahead of me. Then I saw Oli scamper madly to catch up.

Q: How do crazy people go on a hike?
A: They take the psychopath.

In the mountains, the subtle lack of oxygen can do things to the brain. I pulled in as much air as I could, but the air was probably too thin. Anyway, the death of brain cells is how I account for the fact that, while I rested, the mountains began to reveal their beauty. Even though the sky remained grey, I felt the gloom around me lift. Indeed, I felt a tingle—it was just the faintest shudder, really—of what I suspected was cheer.

I couldn't rest long enough to be sure of the change that was happening. Papa, Mama, Tante Minna, and Oli were now completely out of view. Martin and Mathilde had gone on ahead of me, too. I needed to catch up.

As I once again placed my feet carefully against slippery pine needles covering loose, wet stones, I could hear Sophie behind me, coming along a slightly different path from the one the rest of us had taken. She was having a hard time of it, slipping and falling and dinging her hands and knees again and again.

"Anna!" she called to me. "Wait! Hold my hand! Help me, please!"

I kept my gaze on the rock behind which Mama, Papa, Tante Minna, and Oli had disappeared. I liked the way the water on the rock sparkled whenever a moment of sunshine broke through the cloud cover.

"Yes?" I said when she called again. "All right, Sophie. I am happy. Happy to help you." Claiming an emotion sometimes makes it real. I walked to the spot where Sophie's path met mine and willingly reached a hand down towards her.

She gasped for breath and grasped for my hand. Once I had pulled her to me, she bade me wait a moment for Ernst, who was close behind and having a more horrible time even than she on the miserable path they had taken.

I held Sophie and she reached out for Ernst, giving him a steady hand while he found his footing. Then, when we three started walking together, I led.

Not more than a quarter of a mile later, we met Mathilde and Martin sitting on a boulder, taking their rest. Again, I pulled as much oxygen as I could into my lungs. Then we five continued the hike together, this time reverting to the walking order of our youth: boys led the way and girls followed. Together, we rounded the same curve that Oli, Papa, Mama, and Tante Minna had rounded. As we did we encountered the first few wisps of what would quickly prove to be dense mountain fog.

Within minutes, we couldn't see a thing. But the grey-white blindness felt more silly than dangerous. We five began calling "Hi, ho!" gaily, all to avoid losing each other. Sophie "oohed" and "ahhhhed" at things into which she stumbled. Martin made jokes, mostly at Sophie's expense and at a level of sophistication to which she was not attuned. We all laughed along with Martin—and along with Sophie, as well.

Laughter. Do you know that feeling when your emotions finally begin to run free and the muscles of your face ache with laughing and smiling, pleasure long awaited and release finally obtained? As Martin poked fun at Sophie and Sophie marveled at phenomena that did not always merit respect, my face pained me from ear to ear. We all guffawed. We all blew our noses with abandon. We passed gas freely. The fog lifted.

And as it lifted we heard Papa's cry, and we startled like a herd of dumb deer.

"Papa is hurt."

I was the one who said it. It was a statement of fact. No one else said anything.

And before anyone *did* anything, we paused—together. I want to emphasize that togetherness. We had, the five of us, just enjoyed ten minutes or so of uncommon communion. So when we heard Papa's cry—and when I numbly, dumbly uttered an explanation for it—our physical responses were unified, and they remained so for twenty seconds, maybe, or maybe only ten.

My point is that no one rushed to rescue. No one rushed to flee. During the moment in which we all paused, we each lifted our heads a tiny bit. Then, delicately, we tilted our ears towards the sound of trouble, just like deer do.

"Papa is hurt?" Mathilde said the same words as I had, but she formed them into a question.

That is when fear infected us all.

Years later evolutionary psychologists would suggest that deer at moments of confusion like this weigh two possibilities—"Fight? Or flight?"—and make hasty and necessarily self-serving choices. All animals do, even human animals.

The long and the short of it is that I made one self-serving choice that day and my sibling deer made another. No one was right and no one was wrong, or so might the evolutionary psychologists say. Out of fear, my siblings chose to run over rocks and around hills and down slippery slopes wee, wee, wee, all the way home. So, apparently, did Mama and Tante Minna.

Out of fear, I stayed to help.

"Behind every intense fear lies an intense, infantile wish," Papa always said.

I remember finding Papa at the bottom of a crevice, a bouquet of *Kohlroeserl* for Mama in his hand. But this is where my memories of the day become wobbly. This is where they skid almost entirely to a halt.

I cannot remember how I helped Papa climb out of the crevice. I can still hear his weepy gratitude when he reached safety at crevice's top. I remember his inconsolable belligerence about "that ass, Oliver."

I remember that Papa's face was aflame and that he muttered madly about the rape of mothers, sisters, cousins, and aunties. I have an idea of a not very pleasant hour spent at the top of the crevice in a meadow of Alpine flowers. I do remember thinking that it was more Mama's duty than mine to pass that sort of time with Papa. I remember that I didn't like exposing to the sun as much of my skin as I was exposing. I was cold. I wanted to go home.

I also remember a fairy tale. Papa improvised it for me as we lay among the flowers and blinked at the setting sun.

> *Once upon a time there lived a powerful king with too many children. The boys were all brave and two of the three girls were beautiful. But when Trouble struck one day as Trouble sometimes does, all of the children and their mother and frumpy aunt ran away. They left the king alone and in great peril.*
>
> *Except the youngest girl, the one who wasn't as beautiful as her sisters. She didn't flee. She helped.*
>
> *That day, the Girl Who Helped became lovelier by far than her two sisters. Before the day ended, the king gave her a luminous, golden ball. He told her to toss the ball high into the air, to hug it occasionally close to her breast, and to take care never to drop it in a lake for a frog to retrieve. If she could do that every day she would be his very favorite daughter for the rest of his life.*

"Fight or flight?" The evolutionary psychologists say that we all choose. But for some people under some circumstances, the choice is not an either-or proposition.

Chapter 14

Not surprisingly, in the weeks after we returned to Vienna, the family began to atomize. It was as though some huge force at our very center were spinning us around and flinging us each to parts unknown.

Sophie got flung away first—from me, anyway. When we were very young, Sophie's beauty had won Papa's heart. God knows it couldn't have been her personality. She was dull, even way back then. It may be unkind to say of someone with exquisite smiles and charming laughter, but it is true about her. By the sheer force of good looks, she had kept Papa's primary affection—right up to the day that I rescued him.

Then she became downright snappish with me. She could still regale Papa with her dewy eyes, but he no longer looked to her for unswerving love, and she knew it.

Indeed, because all of the family females but I had fled that day, I was now Papa's clear favorite. That is what flung Mathilde, Tante Minna, and Mama from me, as well. But I liked being Papa's favorite girl. I easily took up all sorts of helpful duties that they had left off. Papa's girl needed only to gather papers, help with the occasional translation, welcome professional dignitaries, and, most importantly, listen to him admiringly each night in his study as he worked out the twists and turns of his theories.

In the fall of 1909, Martin enrolled in a commercial college and secured an apartment of his own in a less upscale section of the city. The next to leave home was Mathilde, who married her Robert. It was a happy wedding. Mathilde wore the veiled, high-necked, white silk dress with embroidered orange blossoms that Grandmother Bernays had sewn for Mama twenty-three years before. Sophie and I wore matching yellow tea dresses. I was delighting in how feminine I looked and was enjoying my first sips ever of wine with Papa when I caught the bouquet. I caught it initially, actually, in the back of the head, though I was able to whirl around and somehow grasp the flowers with my hands before they fell all the way to the floor. People applauded and congratulated me. I smiled graciously. But, in spite of the fun, I suspected that gentle Mathilde had purposefully thrown the bouquet hard and hit me just where she'd aimed it.

Within the year, Oli rather listed away in the general direction of the Vienna Polytechnic to study civil engineering. Next, Ernst came of the age to matriculate. However, he had become increasingly anxious through his adolescent years; he was reluctant to live beyond the heavy double doors of our apartment. Understanding nameless dread perfectly well, I imagined having long talks over coffee with him about how he might best deal with all of the "what if"s that might happen were he to go out on his own. But of course he and I didn't talk, for no one but Papa was talking to me. Anyway, families have an inertia all their own. Ernst's two brothers had created an expectation that sons move on. And so he did, to study architecture in Munich.

By 1911, only Sophie and I remained home with Papa, Mama, and Tante Minna. Every single night during those years I sat with Papa for hours on end in his study, listening to him drone and wonder, recant and divine. All of my contributions to our discussions were minor, but one of my most significant roles was assigning to patients the monikers that Papa would use when writing about their cases. I feared I could never come up with one as good as Herr Lanzer's "Rat Man." So I was nicely proud when I was able to name someone "Wolf Man."

He was a Russian neurotic. And, no, he did not get hairy and violent each month at full moon. He only dreamed of wolves, and he only did that once, as a child. Still, I had fun in the inventing, and in seeing the shock of amusement in Papa's face when I suggested the name.

Every night that I sat with Papa seemed to goad Mama, Tante Minna, and Sophie. Perhaps they could hear Papa and me laughing throatily from way back in the study downstairs. Maybe the noise made them feel excluded. I really doubt, though, that they heard anything at all; the many Persian rugs in Papa's study, consulting room, and waiting room would have absorbed whatever noises we made. Regardless, every night that Papa and I met privately, Sophie sat with Mama, who was in bed again, having begun a renewed decline. Tante Minna, too, pulled her chair to Mama's bedside. The three of them sewed and tatted in a frenzied circle.

At the end of 1911, I turned sixteen years old. Around that time, I developed a new problem. Again it had to do with my masturbation fantasies. For the two years prior, Papa and I had spent as many as six hours each evening sequestered alone in his dimly lit, smoke-filled study, talking mostly about sex in its many permutations and manifestations and chuckling knowingly about the *outré* behaviors and yearnings he had discovered. Finally my emotional defenses against that much sex talk failed me. In the ensuing months, whenever I was not alone with Papa, my masturbation fantasies pursued me—and they did so with a fury so unrelenting that even I found it burdensome. The noises coming from my four-poster very late at night began also to come from my bedroom during the early evenings, at first once or twice a week but eventually almost every evening and then every morning, as well. I was embarrassed. I was exhausted. I felt like my fantasies were consuming me like a cancer, eating outwards from my heart towards my skin. I sensed that every step I took, every phrase I spoke, screeched out to my aunt, mother, sister, and father an undying itch for something that they, certainly, were in no position to scratch.

In the late winter and spring of 1912, matters between Sophie and me became especially strained. This was while I was finishing up my secondary school degree. Faced with the prospect of choosing how to spend the rest of my life, I deplored—a bit too vocally and a bit too often, perhaps—that I was facing limited options, all because Papa did not believe that women belonged in university. Sophie found my despair boorish. In whispered comments about "Princess Anna," she made that clear.

But truly: Housewifery? Teaching? Nursing? That was what my career options were if I were to be forbidden to study at university. That sort of life may have been good enough for Sophie and her sort. But I wanted to live a life of ideas. I wanted to write rich exposition alive with literary allusions and well-turned phrases. I wanted to read the classics in their original Greek and Latin and to stretch my mind in many directions. I wanted to read Galileo and to grind my own telescope lens.

Papa stood firm on his ideas about education for proper young women. And so I began losing weight. I became pale. My posture became stooped, and one night I wept at the supper table.

To his credit, Papa saw that in some measure I was behaving like a caged animal. He wasn't about to budge in his thoughts about what a young woman wants and needs. But he did kindly suggest that I forego worrying about my future at least for a while. After I graduated from secondary school I would be expected to help organize our household life, just as Sophie was doing. Those were skills I needed to acquire and practice if I was ever to put them to life-long use. But I wouldn't be expected to help as much as Sophie helped. My primary jobs for the entire year after my graduation would be to fatten up and to continue to serve as Papa's nightly sounding board.

Hallelujah, yes? But rather than thanking Papa for his understanding, out of plain old bad habit I bellyached something about Sophie, and I did it right in front of her. Without hesitation, she slapped me across the face. And without hesitation, I hit her right back.

Of course, we were both sent to our rooms—not really a solution as we still shared a bedroom.

The very next morning Papa suggested that I spend my year after graduation away from Sophie—away from home entirely if necessary, touring Europe, perhaps with Tante Minna. She and I could stay with friends of his in every major city and have twelve months of educational experience. It would "broaden me."

Ah, the Grand Tour! In the eighteenth century it had been *the* educational rite of passage for well-to-do young adults. True, we Freuds were now relatively well-to-do. But it was already the twentieth century, and the proposal seemed extraordinary! My sisters had not been allowed to travel extensively. Neither had my brothers. I was terribly taken by the opportunity it presented. But in a way, the suggestion was also worrying. For example, I didn't like the idea of Papa continuing his work without me. Would he start talking with Sophie each night in his study? I also was not sure that Tante Minna and I could provide each other with pleasant company for a year. And finally, I feared that a Grand Tour immersion in sensual delights would only foster more of the extravagant sexual fantasies that were disabling me.

I am certain Tante Minna fretted about that last question as much as I, and I am fairly sure she is the one who convinced Papa to retract the offer of the trip. A few weeks after our first conversation about the possibility of a Grand Tour, Papa had been away traveling and lecturing. Missing him intensely, I had written to him about how dull I found everything except being at his side at night alone in his study. In that letter, I offered to take him, upon his return, to an idyllic little nightspot café about which only I knew. I never imagined that signing it with an abundance of kisses and hugs (noted, as they still are in correspondence, by a string of "x"s and "o"s) would spark anyone's concern.

Papa must have forwarded the letter to Tantie, for only a few days later she visited me in my bedroom. She had the letter in hand. She was trembling head to toe. She told me that I was evidently too ill for the sort of trip Papa had proposed she and I take. Rather than tour Europe with her for a year, I was to visit a spa alone for a few weeks. There I was to think long and hard about a proper future for myself, and I was to present Tantie and Papa with a practical plan for that future immediately upon my return.

I was sent to a spa in Merano. It had more than a few guests who were, like me, emotionally exhausted.

Merano is a castle-graced spa village in the Dolomites of northern Italy. It lies in a lush valley surrounded by snowy peaks. The sky is almost always sunny—so clear and luminous that, mid-day, Merano feels like wellness itself. Indeed, Merano is famous for the quality of its light. It makes the town a haven for walkers, hikers, and bicyclists, regardless of the season.

Preoccupied with my wretchedness as I packed, I had not thought to bring my hiking boots. Neither had I brought a compass or canteen. Indeed, I had only packed a minimum of clothes and then, as an afterthought, Papa's complete set of published works, which required its own large suitcase. I'm almost ashamed to admit it, but I actually believed I would spend all of my time in the Dolomites moping indoors.

Instead, Merano beckoned! Rather than pout and study, I spent my mornings walking mile upon mile. I bought sturdy shoes and, of course, a compass and canteen. As I hiked I stood up straight, and I sang songs to match the rhythm of the canteen as it bounced against my leg. I felt the sun on my neck and shoulders, which over the past year had been unusually tense. Each mid-day, I returned to the village and dined on vegetable and fruit cocktails, bean soups, polenta, olive patés, and other foods that seemed exotic if for no other reason than that they weren't made of boiled beef. When the sun dipped behind castle walls in the late afternoons and shadows grew long, I hopped in and out of the spa's changing rooms, treatment rooms, soapy soft mineral baths, medicinal baths, steam baths, mud-baths, hot saunas, and thermal pools. In white-tiled salons, antiseptic-looking attendants massaged me, and I realized that it had been many years since I'd been lovingly held. (We Freuds were not a hugging family.) When the attendants basted my body in oils, I learned that someone else's touch can be respectful and caring, not dangerous like that of the Powerful Man in my fantasies. I felt decidedly non-sexual—indeed, it seemed to me that I was being guarded by kindly, berobed giants who agreed that I was too young for all that. I dozed and awakened, dozed and awakened, trustingly. My beating fantasies abated.

Each day in the last week of my scheduled stay in Merano, feeling almost well, I rented a bicycle. Though a wobbly rider, I propelled myself down the town's lovely streets all the way to its castle, where, at noon, I ate a picnic lunch. In the afternoons I would have a massage, after which I would bundle into a chair in the sun on the flat roof of the spa and play chess with an ancient Hungarian man who had come to Merano for a pulmonary cure.

One afternoon, I descended to my room just ahead of suppertime to find a telegram from Tante Minna telling me that Sophie had announced her engagement to Max Halberstadt, a young photographer (and the very one who later took many of the most famous pictures of Papa). A second telegram, this one from Papa, informed me that, while the family was happy to learn that my ill health and temper were becoming matters of history, it would perhaps be better if Sophie's engagement and wedding could proceed in a way that was enjoyable to Sophie. My few weeks at the spa were to be extended for the entire *four months* of wedding preparations. At the end of that time, the wedding would take place without me in attendance.

To say the least, I was distraught. For the next four months, I angrily ignored my health. I avoided the old Hungarian gentleman, the spa, and each and every nice thing about Merano, including most of the food. Instead of walking, bicycling, taking treatments, and eating delicious meals, I spent my days in my room, cultivating hunger pangs and delighting as my cheekbones and collarbone became vivid beneath my skin. Late at night before I climbed into bed I made sure to marvel at my protruding pelvis. Then, under the covers, I greedily argued with my own hands over their proximity to my nightgown's hem.

I did spend the evenings productively. I practically memorized Papa's published works.

In such a temper was born my plan for the rest of my life. I would make myself so useful to my father *and* so needful of him that I could never again be banished from his side.

Although I missed Sophie's wedding, I heard reports. One anecdote in particular struck my fancy. Apparently Papa was overcome by the sight of Sophie leaving the wedding reception with Max. She wore the veiled, high-necked, white silk dress with embroidered orange blossoms that both Mama and Mathilde had worn. Her innocence and loveliness must have brought to his mind a flood of memories and desires. In Shakespearean oratorical fashion, and perhaps at the mercy of a little too much wine, Papa bellowed out his goodbye, assuring Sophie that I, a temporarily absent Cordelia, would return quickly to Lear's side now that his two other daughters had fled in fear.

It was no doubt a strange note upon which to commence the celebratory rice throwing. Apparently, though, that is pretty much what he said.

Chapter 15

During the pre-war years in which my siblings left for lives of their own, Papa's friend Call Me Otto had family problems, too. Continuing with his promiscuity and nudism, he founded a society called The Great Unwashed, which extolled the wonders of the unbathed human body. He gave lectures throughout Europe on the spiritually and psychically liberating potential of bisexual sex performed, ideally, *en masse*.

"Lectures" is where the family problems came in. Only some people called them "lectures." Others called them "rants." Call Me Otto's father, Herr Hans Gross, was one of the latter group. Herr Gross was a world-famous criminologist and forensic pathologist with cabinets full of polished skulls and untraceable potions. In 1913, he had his libertine son arrested on a variety of indecency charges related to the lectures. Otto remained in prison until 1914, when Herr Gross had him declared legally incompetent and remanded indefinitely to a mental institution.

Sophie was by then living in Hamburg with Max. Papa, Mama, Tante Minna, and I were the only ones left at home to be presented with the news of Otto's arrest. We were, of course, outraged to hear that Otto had been deemed incompetent, for we knew that to be untrue. At the same time, we weren't so sure that a mental institution was the wrong place for him. That is because, over the previous six years, Otto had added a fondness for opiates to his list of questionable predilections.

Furthermore, he topped off the drugs each day with alcohol. As a result, while Otto almost always appeared to be having a good time, he was on an increasingly slippery slide into realms in which, had he been able to exercise full choice, he might have preferred not to travel.

This slide may have been accentuated by an underlying mental frailty that at the time was called "*dementia praecox*." The more modern term is "schizophrenia." Ironically, it is the very topic that Otto had researched when working as a psychiatrist in Munich.

Call Me Otto's father probably thought that, by institutionalizing his son, he had tidied up family matters for the better and for good. To his horror, however, the artists, spiritualists, and youth of Europe were unprepared to interpret even the most colorful of Call Me Otto's symptoms as signs of illness. The revelatory lectures, especially, they liked. The news that Herr Hans Gross had succeeded in transferring Otto to a safe hospital setting sparked an enormous "Free Otto!" fever that infected all of Europe. "Call Me Otto! Call Me Otto! Call Me Otto! Call Me Otto!" young people chanted in village squares. They waved sticks. They threatened to set fires.

One problem with the ebbs and flows of madness is that it is impossible to set one's clock by them. The revolutionaries eventually did start a few fires. They even scaled Otto's hospital walls. On the day that that they did, however, Otto was not inclined one jot towards ranting and revelation—or even towards liberty. His symptoms had gone into spontaneous remission. What's more, once he was in apparent good health, he successfully convinced his attending psychiatrists to allow him to adopt a dual role of patient and professional. When the demonstrators used a battering ram to force their way into a locked examining room, they found that they had interrupted Otto as he was giving the tried-and-true word association examination to a patient. (Her hysterical response was perhaps understandable, given the battering ram.)

"You can call me Otto," Otto said to the revolutionaries, hurrying them into an adjacent examining room and offering coffee and strong sherry to anyone with a thirst. "But you will have to wait while I finish up here. When we start, please remember that your only responsibility will be to speak the first thing that comes to your mind as soon as it comes to mind."

I like to think that within minutes of calming his patient and escorting her down the hall to her cell, Call Me Otto returned to his babbling liberators and invented group therapy and the human potential movement.

Upon my return from Merano, Papa saw that I was more thin and stooped than ever before. Intervening on my behalf with Tante Minna, he announced that I would be allowed a few weeks to settle back into family life before articulating the requisite practical thoughts about my future.

In the meanwhile, he was eager for me to begin a healthy routine. He offered, for starters, to walk with me every morning so that I could get some sunshine. He also suggested that I resume my duties as his sounding board each night in his study. During the days, I could work for him, translating some of his papers into English.

This arrangement suited me just fine. On our walks (which Papa agreed to take at a modest pace) we had wonderful talks about the rivalries within his psychoanalytic movement. I enjoyed translating Papa's papers, for it gave me an enhanced and up-to-date education in psychoanalytic matters. In order to find English equivalents for terms such as "anal-sadistic," "sublimation," "cathexis," "introjection," and "regression," I had to make sure I understood the definitions completely. Papa was gracious about answering my questions and supplying me with examples.

My English was already strong from my studies at secondary school. As I translated, my appreciation for the subtleties of Papa's newest ideas became robust. I learned in this way for far longer than the few weeks Papa had initially bargained for with Tante Minna. Indeed, this period lasted more than a year. During those months I ate heartily because again I was happy. And so it was that by 27 June, 1914, I had regained my health.

On June 28, Austria-Hungary's Archduke Franz Ferdinand, heir presumptive to the throne, was shot and killed in Sarajevo. Six million soldiers would die in the resulting war, and eighty thousand civilian Austrians would perish. My brothers would help fight the war. I would assist relief efforts. Our family and, indeed, nearly all the families of Vienna would be forever shaken.

About six weeks before the assassination, and having no idea of the momentous changes that were about to befall us, Papa asked to speak to me about my ideas regarding a profession. He made the setting for our conversation as friendly as possible. Indeed, after supper one evening, he and I remained at table, and he asked Cook to bring us coffee and then leave us alone.

In the few minutes it took Cook to make coffee, I wondered whether I was about to be sent away again. But why? Sophie was no longer living at home. I was dutifully and harmoniously helping my father. True, I had failed to do as Tante Minna had long ago demanded; I had yet to articulate a solid plan for my future.

Cook brought coffee. Papa thanked her. I tried to look calm and confident.

"You can relax, Anna," Papa winked at me, taking his first sip of coffee. "Really and truly, I mean no harm by wanting to talk."

"Of course not, Papa," I said.

"Try to think of this as an open-ended discussion of your wants and needs," he advised.

"I will, Papa."

Grinning, Papa took another sip of coffee.

"Anna, what *are* your professional wants and needs?" he asked me.

"It would be easier for me to tell you what I don't want," I answered.

"Please do."

"I don't want to be a teacher or a nurse," I replied.

"Yes, I've heard that before," he said, and then he added some sugar to his coffee. "Let's try approaching this topic from a different angle. We both know, my dear, the work of Doktor Hermine Hug-Hellmuth."

Of course we both knew her work. He was her psychoanalytic mentor, and because of that I had just translated some of her work into English for an American publication. Doktor Hug-Hellmuth was a physicist and elementary school teacher who had joined The Wednesday Psychological Society and had won recognition for her ideas about how to psychoanalyze children. Specifically, she believed that children's play reveals their innermost yearnings. This may seem obvious these days, but back then hers were the first useful suggestions ever of how to glean deep emotional information from a child too young to be introspective. Papa was so intrigued by the idea of meaning in children's play that, over the last year or so, The Wednesday Society had made analyzing children one of their primary topics of discussion. They had even begun speculating about how to gain access to children at play in school.

"I know how impressed you are with her, Papa," I ventured. "And I am impressed, too. But that doesn't mean that I need—or want—to become a teacher."

"No, it doesn't. But did you also know, Anna, that Doktor Hug-Hellmuth and I and a few others hope to create a cadre of teachers sympathetic to psychoanalytic precepts?"

I did.

"And do you know that our larger goal is to motivate basic changes in public school pedagogy?"

I did not.

"What we are learning," Papa explained, "is that Vienna's public schools are so rigid as to discourage any introspective thought in children. Children fear and hate school, and any astute observer can see those feelings expressed in their imaginative play. What we would like is for those very same schools to become environments in which children thrive emotionally, and in which they can learn not only about reading, writing, and arithmetic but also about themselves. We would like psychoanalytic precepts to inform teachers and, indeed, to become part of the language that everyone speaks. We want politicians to understand preconscious desire, for dentists to know about phobias, and for young mothers to understand that they are not to make their children fear their own sexualities. To do this, we have to start with the children. It will take at least two whole generations of work by us to change the very culture of thought in Vienna, my dear, but the benefits to everyday people of such a change should be clear to you. As should the benefits to psychoanalysis itself."

"That's an ambitious idea, Papa," I had to admit.

He didn't say anything else, and at first I didn't understand the cause of his silence. Then, when I looked at him for guidance about how we were to continue in our conversation, in his eye I saw a twinkle.

"I'm sorry, Papa. But it seems that I'm not understanding as much as you're hoping I understand."

"What would a school need in order to have a psychoanalytically-informed classroom?" he asked.

"Psychoanalytically-informed teachers, I suppose."

Then I understood what I was supposed to say, but I felt so oppressively hesitant.

"And so, Papa, you are suggesting that…"

"I am telling you that teaching may not be the loathsome way to spend a life that you believe it is."

"I see." I felt warm, but I didn't know if it was from fear or excitement. I said, "If I were to teach, if I were to become one of the first ever 'psychoanalytically-informed teachers…'" and then I felt my breath grow short. My hands had become sweaty and itchy. "If I were to teach in a way that communicated psychoanalytic concepts to children and encouraged them to think about themselves and their emotions and all of that…." My heart was pounding. I had to stop talking.

Papa let us sit in silence for a while.

"Could I still translate for you?" I finally blurted out quickly, before my nervous system could stop me. "Could we still talk every night in your study and take morning walks?"

"I don't think we'll have time for all of the walks, but we could always schedule a few," Papa answered. "And you won't have time for much translating. But, yes, I would be honored if we could continue our nightly discussions. During them, I would hope that you would inform me on an ongoing basis of your observations and intuitions about children's play."

Well, adulthood was clearly upon me, and at least I could see that it wasn't going to be as awful as I had feared. I sat and stared into my hands while Papa cleared his throat and then read a bit of the newspaper. I was still sitting quietly when he put the paper down. I had yet to move or speak. And so Papa suggested that he and I take a walk.

The night air was nice. I shook my head to ease the tension in my neck. I took his arm. And when he asked, I exhaled a few rapid bursts to still the pounding in my chest, and I agreed to take the professional teaching exam, which would be offered in a few weeks. I also agreed to accept an apprentice teaching position that he had already arranged for the coming fall at an elementary school in Vienna.

Papa was not at the breakfast table the next morning for he had an early patient scheduled. On my plate he had left a note inviting me to spend a few weeks in Italy. This was to serve as reward for my compliance and as consolation for the years of university joy I was agreeing to forego.

I smiled at the idea that I was at last to take a touring trip, and that it would not be in the company of Tante Minna. At dinner I told Papa that I gladly accepted his invitation, and that very evening we made our travel plans. We purchased tickets the following morning.

And then, almost immediately, I became ill with whooping cough, leaving Papa to use the tickets with one of his colleagues. They had a wonderful time.

On July 18, a few short weeks after the Austrian heir had been assassinated at Sarajevo, I set off on a different touring trip entirely. It was, essentially, a consolation prize for my consolation prize. Having missed out on Italy with Papa, I was to spend two weeks visiting friends and relatives of his in England.

In retrospect, I'm surprised Papa and Mama let me go. First of all, I was still coughing. More importantly, all of Europe was nervous that a war between Serbia and Austria-Hungary might ignite a continent-wide conflagration.

The morning that I left, the train station was swarming with soldiers so fresh-faced and boyish that they looked like their mothers had dressed them to play war. But my train pulled away from the station without a soldier on it. (Only later did I realize that this was because the war would start to our east, and the train I was on headed west.) Once it left Vienna it entered the brilliant beauty of the countryside. Very late in the evening we arrived at the German border. Customs agents asked to see everyone's passports, and we showed them in courteous exchanges.

A few hours after midnight, when the train crossed the Rhine into France, our experience with border agents was anything but well mannered. French agents questioned a few of us roughly. They also commanded the engineer to switch locomotives lest the train drive through France with the imposing blue and brass eagle of Germany as its emblem. During the wait for a new engine, agents peremptorily removed all posted timetables, explaining to the horrified porters that those documents specified an "Elsass-Lothringen" region rather than one called "Alsace-Lorraine," and that, in France, such a spelling would not do.

With all the delays, our train arrived late in Calais, where I was to catch the last ferry to Dover to meet a colleague of Papa's who was to be my touring chaperone. I had to rush to hail a petrol cab, and I had to use my best English to convince the driver to hurry.

Train compartments become awfully stale after twenty-eight hours of travel, but the air inside a petrol cab is even worse. I was grateful to arrive at seaside and stumble onto the ferry. I took a seat on one of the boat's outer decks. As we pulled away from France, the air was glorious—entirely clear of motor fumes and other peoples' smells, though stinking resoundingly of fish.

We had left a warm, sunny morning in Calais. Dover, on the other side of the English Channel, was chilled by fog. No doubt, after spending the ferry ride in the wind, I looked a fright. But I hadn't time to do any grooming; the whole mass of people on the boat was moving towards the gate and pulling me along. Lugging my own bag, I made my way through British customs. All the while, I hoped that the friend of Papa's I was to meet would forgive a weary traveler's appearance.

Papa's friend was entirely gracious, presenting me with flowers. He was a Welsh neurologist named Doctor Ernest Jones. For some reason that I have never been able to pin down, Papa had chosen him as my chaperone but never bothered to tell me that, in the ten years that he had been practicing medicine, Doctor Jones had thrice been accused of sexual misconduct with patients, two of whom were children.

Doctor and Mrs. Jones are visiting their Jewish friends. Their friends take them to a deli for a bowl of matzo ball soup.

"Delicious!" exclaims Doctor Jones upon tasting the soup. "And what other parts of the matzo do your people eat?"

Unfortunately, there was no Mrs. Jones.

He was thirty-five years old and a natty dresser, but not a physically impressive man. I thought he had the shape of a terrier. In the years since, I've read a description of Doctor Jones's stubby face that I like very much: "Pale but pungent—like a salad dressing."

To be fair, I admit that he was charming. When I apologized for my appearance he assured me that he preferred women whose hair stuck straight into the sky. That made me laugh, and I liked it when he manfully took my bag and hoisted it into his private car. He drove me to a lovely hotel where he had booked adjoining rooms.

Early that evening, I was able to bathe properly and dress in something fresh. Doctor Jones treated me to a dinner I shall always remember. It was fish and chips, and I had never before imagined anything as outrageous as dipping good food in cheap batter and then frying it in fat. It was wonderful.

In the morning, we had sausage and eggs at the hotel, and I was unhappy only about the absence of coffee. (I settled for gallons of tea.) Then Doctor Jones announced that it was time for us to tour boarding schools. The cathedrals would have to wait until we were in London.

That's what we did for two days—happily enough, actually. As I've said, he could be charming. He had selected two boarding schools to visit in the lovely Kent countryside. The headmistresses of both were eager to receive me and discuss matters of psychoanalysis and pedagogy. At each school, after we met with the headmistress Doctor Jones and I were assigned a student who showed us the grounds. Mostly I remember magnificent playing fields and dim hallways lit by tiny stained-glass windows. In the second school's hallway, Doctor Jones held my hand lest I stumble for lack of general illumination. He made all of the right jokes at all of the right times. Indeed, on each occasion that a solemn student guide showed us a headmistress-of-yore portrait, as soon as we were alone he made me laugh about boarding school pretensions, archaic precepts of education, and dunderheads in general. I felt relaxed with him, and sometimes merrily so. I particularly liked when he held my hand, even if it was briefly.

On the evening of our second day of school tours we drove to London, where Doctor Jones lived. He showed me to a nice bedroom in his home, ceremoniously handing me a fresh bouquet of flowers as I crossed its threshold. After a few moments of stuttering silence, he suggested that I put the flowers in the crystal vase on the night table. I did, and he excused himself to freshen up for dinner. After my bath I put on my best dress and admired myself in a full-length mirror. I looked good.

At dinner, there was a surprise. It was Doctor Jones' mistress. I must say I was temporarily speechless at the very idea that he had a mistress, as well as at the fact that she had been waiting to dine with us while I bathed and dressed. Her name was Lina. Lina was beautiful, if you could ignore the fact that her teeth were discolored and that she was a little plump. When Lina saw my consternation about her life with Doctor Jones, she explained something along the lines of, "Oh, no, I'm not really his mistress. He had a mistress and I was her maid, and she left and I took her job." Then she produced an awful, tinkling laugh.

Offering me a beer (which I refused), Lina assured me that she was very glad to meet me, and asked if I'd found the flowers and crystal vase all right.

How Papa had trusted this arrangement I'll never understand.

The next day Doctor Jones, Lina, and I toured the pseudo-gothic cathedrals Papa had specified in and near the center of London. We also saw Big Ben and walked over a bridge or two and along the riverfront. That night, Lina retired after a supper of beer. Doctor Jones and I ate leftovers from the prior evening. Then Doctor Jones invited me out to the cinema to take in a moving picture show. I was excited; I had never been to the movies.

The Perils of Pauline was a cinematic serial filmed in Fort Lee, New Jersey. It began playing in theatres in England in 1914. Week after week, episode after episode, the young Pauline evaded attempts on her life and honor. She fought buccaneers, savages, rats, weather, mountain lions, Mexicans, barracudas, and her dastardly guardian. Most familiarly, she was tied kicking and screaming to railroad tracks by one villain or another while a train rapidly approached.

The movie I saw with Doctor Jones was one of the early episodes.

He bought shelled peanuts from the vendor. He asked for one bag, which we would share.

We sat in the dark. I remember Doctor Jones arranging himself in a mannish fashion, with his legs spread apart just a bit, as we waited for the film to begin.

"The rapidly industrializing British Empire," he whispered near the end of the short subject, *News from Around the World*, "covers fully one-fifth of the world's service."

Actually, he said "surface" but I heard "service"—as though I had eavesdropped on a surge of sexual thoughts and impulses he had successfully avoided articulating.

Hoping for clarification I said, "Excuse me?"

He smiled and crunched a few peanuts, and the movie began.

What ensued was high drama, both on-screen and off. Pauline had to battle rats and gale force winds. I, in my seat, had to battle Doctor Jones, for he slung his arm around my shoulders and gave me one of those awful, neck-annoying, sideways hugs. It was entirely uncalled for, but it was hardly an assault, not yet. So I didn't shout or anything. I wanted to behave in an adult fashion, and I thought fending off an unwanted approach was the very sort of thing I could do with aplomb.

I removed his hand from my shoulder and neck and sat up straight again. I had so little idea of the extent of his intentions that I even remember laughing when "HELP! HELP!" appeared in big block letters on screen—which it did as Pauline defended herself from her guardian.

As I laughed at the movie's hijinks, Doctor Jones began tickling the back of my neck. I ignored him. I even tried to eat more peanuts; I was that intent on believing that his behavior was benign and that mine was an appropriately gauged response to his. But at one point, when I reached my hand towards the peanut bag to take some more peanuts, he caught my hand and pushed it down towards his lap.

The whole maneuver knocked me off balance, and I don't think it was just the force of his tug that did it. Equally responsible, perhaps, was that, at that moment, I realized that I had juxtaposed "service" with "surface." Quite literally, I was overcome by vertigo when I appreciated what he intended. I looked away from the screen and directly at his face. Once again he smiled and mashed peanuts with his teeth.

I'm not sure what happened next, why I felt myself go off-balance again. All I remember for sure is that my hand briefly touched what I hoped was his leg. He may have pulled on my arm again. He may have pushed on my back. I may have reached for peanuts and missed the bag entirely. Anyway, once I touched whatever it was that felt decidedly unlike anything I wanted to touch, I quickly withdrew my hand, but then he started pulling on my wrist and trying to position my hand where he wanted it. The odd thing was that, as he did, he kept chewing peanuts, and I kept chewing peanuts.

On screen, Pauline was silent, regardless of what happened to her. A lot did, but sound on film had yet to be invented.

"HELP! HELP!" The title cards in the movie did the talking for her.

I was silent, too, though I'm not sure why. I may have believed that if I called attention to myself, Doctor Ernest Jones would start to struggle in earnest (pun again intended) and overpower me. His commitment to appearing to be a typical movie audience member was what I was relying on to get me out of the mess I was in. I do remember that, at one point, Doctor Jones turned to me and grabbed at my blouse. He actually succeeded in knocking a few buttons out of their holes. It was then that I started to slap his arms and hands, not with great force—certainly not with the force that Pauline, for example, was by then using to batter her attacker—but as though I were trying to wake him out of a nightmare.

Even as I did, I kept watching that bloody movie, and so did he.

For what must have been about five minutes, he and I skirmished in our seats, sometimes a lot, sometimes a little. And although, for the most part, I kept my eyes on the screen, at one point I clearly saw Doctor Jones's own "little Britain," all "expanded and industrialized," waggle about in need of "service."

He tended to the matter himself, the music swelled, and the movie ended.

Once the emergency was over, I did not know how to begin a conversation. So I was silent on our walk that evening back to his home.

Like Papa, Doctor Jones had trained as a neurologist. He had read everything Papa had ever written about psychoanalysis. He had even translated some of it. Doctor Jones did not actually recite to me from Papa's summary of his analysis of the *feinshmeker* Ida Bauer as we walked that evening towards his home. Papa had asked Ida whether she had found the sensation of her attacker's penis against her thigh appealing. Doctor Jones said nothing of the sort, though he did ask me whether I had found our little episode of capture and near conquest to my liking.

And then he said, "Behind every strong fear is an intense, infantile wish, you know."

Jewish telegram: Begin worrying. Details to follow.

I considered the question that Doctor Jones had posed. True, my sexual fantasies had always been of rich, torturous humiliations. But I had not found our "little episode" at all to my liking. The stays and indignities that I so enjoyed in fantasy lost their appeal in close quarters.

I didn't say that to Doctor Jones, for he knew nothing of my fantasies. I have no idea what I actually said, although I am sure that when I said it Doctor Jones took the opportunity to correct my English.

He was always correcting everyone's English, even the English of the English.

I was lucky. The next day, Austria-Hungary roundly refused England's offer to mediate peace for all of Europe. This meant that I, as an Austrian and the daughter of Sigmund Freud, was a very public enemy alien. I was told to leave England, though I did have to find my own passage home, and train service across Europe had been cancelled.

Doctor Jones was a gentleman in the ensuing days as we bobbed in and out of transportation offices in our search for a safe means of travel for me. Those days were exhausting and frightening. I relied on him occasionally to make me laugh; he was good at that. He poured me tea at night even while, in my heart of hearts, I wished for coffee. Lina sometimes read me her poetry.

The bond of victim to perpetrator can be a strange one, laced with a tie no truly free person could accept. I had not, may I reiterate for the record, found my episode of capture and near conquest in the least bit appealing. However, I did upon leaving thank Doctor Jones for his concern, as well as for all the tea. Furthermore, at the very moment that I turned to board my ship to Malta, Doctor Jones kissed my hand in front of world cameras, silhouetting me in the minds of millions not as a lost and terrified adolescent, but as a proud and elegant young woman on her way back to her rightful home. For that promotion I felt beholden.

Willing victim? That dramatically overstates my fondness for Doctor Jones. I was lucky to have escaped him and terribly happy to have done so.

Chapter 16

Prior to the war, Europe had been at peace for so long that most Europeans could not remember armed conflict. We had no concept, really, of how brutally lives could be thrown away.

When war arrived, we welcomed it. The departing soldiers enjoyed the parades and rhetoric. Young women looked at mobilization as an opportunity to kiss soldiers goodbye. Everyone hoped for a chance to rise to the challenge of tragedy and to grow spiritually and morally through suffering.

Martin and Ernst joined the army as gunners within a few weeks. Oliver was initially refused the chance to enlist, though for what reason I have never quite understood.

I missed the chance to go say goodbye to Martin and Ernst, for my journey home from England was necessarily by sea. The expelled Austrian diplomat to England and I took a boat to Malta and then another boat to Gibraltar and a third boat to Genoa. In Genoa we found a safe train to Vienna. I traveled for a total of six weeks.

Oddly, once I was back in Vienna, Papa and I worried about Martin and Ernst not at all. We got weekly letters from them, and that was good enough to assure us that they would be home shortly. Musing together that extreme conditions can reveal what is most truthful about people, when Papa and I thought about Martin and Ernst it was only to wonder about what to ask them upon their returns.

Yes, as early as 1915 food shortages began, but they were hardly acute. For lack of water chestnuts and chicken one could no longer, for example, eat at one of Vienna's several Chinese restaurants.

"But we are not Chinese and so that hardly matters to us," Papa assured us all.

Throughout 1915 I worked as an apprentice teacher by day. In the late evenings I sat with Papa in his study, telling him about my work, functioning as his sounding board for his theories, and helping as I could with translations. Occasionally, on my way to and from the study, I spent a moment or two enjoying one of my favorite pastimes from my youth. I gazed at the living dioramas in Papa's Persian rugs. Crossing my eyes I saw a manticore or two. I could still see the village of one tall tower and many low, stone buildings surrounded by the sea. Shaking my head I could see that Persian women still danced together in one rug. I smiled to see what I was still sure in another were the creepily flying fruits and vegetables.

Increasingly, the fruits and vegetables interested me, for by 1916, food was difficult to find. Looking for a way to help Mother Austria in her hour of increasing need, I embroidered her flag on every one of my cotton dresses and volunteered during the evening hours with a group called Bernfeld's American Joint Distribution Committee. This was the point at which I began to perceive our war in a way that Papa did not. The "goods" that we distributed were not the chickens, water chestnuts, and the like that I expected them to be. They were instead hundreds of newly orphaned children, pierced by cold, filth, pain, and grief, and shipped to Vienna on night trains from a front hundreds of kilometers away.

Late in 1916 Oliver, who in adolescence had designed ways to tunnel out of fantastical nightmares, was allowed to assist the war effort as an engineer in charge of tunnels.

By 1917 food could scarcely be bought. Papa wrote an article for a Hungarian journal and asked to be paid directly in potatoes. Ernst, on one of his military leaves, brought home tales that Papa could not bear to hear and a sack of peas riddled with worms that Papa could not bear to eat. I opened each pea, removed each encamped worm, and cooked what was left.

Coal was scarcer than ever. Still, while most families huddled together in the evenings around a single stove, Papa wanted me to leave the stove to Mama and Tante Minna—and for the one short week of his leave to Ernst, as well. Papa and I bundled up and retired to his cold study to talk theory.

Decent cigars were impossible to find.

Papa's psychoanalytic practice was a war casualty, with all of his analysands either conscripted or too afraid and hungry for the luxury of neurosis.

Poor nutrition and constant cold helped give rise in me to what may have been tuberculosis, with which I struggled episodically for the next five years.

Nicotine withdrawal in Papa gave rise to an area in his palette tissue that was hardened and painful. This was the first sign of the cancer that would be diagnosed in five years' time and that would kill him in a little more than twenty. But back then we didn't know what it was. Papa refused to show the spot to his physician. I pleaded, but to no avail. Sucking eagerly one warmish morning on a rancid, black-market cigar, he explained, "I've never been the sort who takes to being opened up and inspected."

Life was not all war. For me there was one constant and lovely oasis in the growing gloom.

It was my position as a primary school apprentice teacher. My charges were third, fourth, and fifth grade boys and girls. The teacher handled all traditional instruction; I handled the rest. Which is to say that I began my apprenticeship by managing day-to-day emotional emergencies like friendships betrayed and mommies missed. I was also in charge of physical emergencies like belly aches, lost lunch boxes, and scraped knees. And then there was my third and favorite area of responsibility: recess.

As was typical at primary schools, boys and girls alike dressed in blue uniforms. Each day, I wore blue, too—my favorite blue skirt and jacket—because my "uniform" let me fade in among the children. But I didn't just supervise or observe the children when they were on the playground; I played with them. Indeed, from the very beginning, playing was my truly singular talent as an apprentice teacher. At it I was, perhaps, just a bit too gifted. Not much taller than the tallest of my charges and dressed in blue just like they were, I was known to scamper about the playground, bargaining about rules ("Unfair!" "You lied!" "I'll tell!"), winning turf wars, and feeling altogether like the eldest in a band of terribly hilarious siblings.

I had to rein myself in. I had to remind myself that my role in the battles swarming around me was to adjudicate, not to triumph. I had to be calm; I had to be comforting. To my satisfaction, whenever I remembered my teacherly responsibilities, my passionate little students settled down and looked at me trustingly. They actually appreciated my help. They wanted my opinion on matters of justice. They thought me as fair as I had once thought Mathilde. No doubt I also seemed as all knowing in their eyes as Oliver had been in mine.

"Can we invent the Ferris wheel again this afternoon, Miss Freud?"

"Why do things look bigger when I look through Rosa's glasses?"

"If I eat this goldfish, when I poo will it still look gold?"

During the years of my apprentice teaching, I was satisfied with my life in a way that I hadn't ever been. I would return home each evening from school, my face and hands chapped from running and shouting in the wind. Then I would immediately change out of my blue clothes and try to remember not to bring the day's events to the supper table.

"And so does apprentice teaching still agree with you, Anna?" Tante Minna or Mama would ask.

Suspecting that I might be scolded like a schoolgirl if I told them the details of my boisterous days, "Yes, it still does," was all I would answer.

Alas, the two middle-aged dears really did not need to hear that a goldfish does change color, that the voice of a single lost seven-year-old can be heard across an entire floor of the Schőnbrunn Palace, and that a ball should never be tossed in a room with a ceiling fan.

I served as an apprentice teacher for three and one-half years. As much fun as I tried to generate on the playground, as we progressed month by month through the war years, our general gaiety diminished. We had not enough coal to heat the schoolhouse, and we were all so nutritionally compromised that we weren't able to tolerate cold well. Our nerves frayed.

So it began that, after recess and when the children normally would have studied science, the teacher and I began taking them to the park, where, in the name of plant studies, we hunted things to eat—things like mushrooms but also many varieties of edible plants. During arithmetic hour, we helped them cook the foods we had foraged. There was some pedagogical validity to what we did, for to double and triple recipes one must add and multiply, and even successfully manipulate fractions. Our music classes, too, acquired a practical orientation. We sang harmonies on city streets. Indeed, we would stand below the apartments of students who were home ill. In any given week, nearly half of my poorly fed students might be temporarily felled by one or another of the respiratory infections sweeping opportunistically through the city. We serenaded those children and we even yodeled, too, for tall buildings can create a wonderful echo, and what better way to begin a geography lesson about Switzerland?

In 1918, I completed my assistant teaching obligation. As much help as I knew I might be to Papa and his colleagues as a full teacher, I was sad to see my assistant position end. It was only with reluctance that I accepted from my old secondary school a four-year teaching contract and said goodbye to my gang of "siblings."

That year the supply of cigars and psychoanalytic patients in Vienna dried up entirely. Papa's temper became very bad indeed.

We learned that Martin was missing in action. About six weeks after war's end, he came home with bullet holes to show in his cap and sleeve. But when the Armistice was signed we still wondered whether he had perished.

Bored, broke, hungry, afraid, desperate for news of Martin, in pain, and in a frenzy of nicotine withdrawal, Papa offered to take me into analysis. Bored, broke, hungry, afraid, desperate for news of Martin, and in pain from remnant tuberculosis, I acceded.

> *Two fish are in a tank.*
>
> *The first fish says to the second, "So, how do we drive this thing?"*

Part 4

Through the Danger Door

(1918-1920)

Anna and Sigmund at the Psychoanalytic Congress at The Hague, 1920.

Sophie and her husband Max Halberstadt.

Chapter 17

And so, eighteen years after I first started sitting on Papa's Persian rugs in the waiting room, and nine years after beginning nightly conversations with him in his study as his chief confidante and sounding board, I was welcomed into Papa's consulting room as an analysand.

It was 10 o'clock in the evening. The room was lit by moonlight, a single Chinese lamp, and the coal fire, just as I had seen it lit when I once looked through the keyhole at Papa and Doktor Jung. Papa walked me to the analytic couch with the same grace and routine I had witnessed him practice one day on the *feinshmeker* Ida Bauer. He followed a good distance behind me, just as I had seen him stay behind her. Although I proceeded across the floor in an extremely proper fashion, I could not help but imagine that I was sashaying, just as Ida had done. When I glanced over my shoulder at Papa, a little nervous about the strange formality with which he was accompanying me, he smiled winningly. As I prepared to lie on the couch, he extended me his hand. When I crossed my feet at the ankles and folded my hands on my chest, he covered my feet properly with the small, white, tufted rug.

An oriental music box sounded out the first few notes of a plucked-string tune when Papa sat in his chair and the thump of his descending body disturbed the music trigger. Searching out the source of the tones with my eyes, I saw a rotating Buddha shudder, seemingly in anticipation of the conversation to come. Then it settled quietly, half-hidden behind a string of colored glass beads.

I was nervous. Yes, by that time in my life I had spent thousands of evening hours in Papa's study with him. I had also read the library of Papa's publications and personal notes many times over. And while this was my first evening visit to the consulting room, it was not my first visit altogether, for I had sat on Papa's lap during one of Ida's psychoanalytic sessions. Yet as prepared as I might have considered myself, I had little idea of what was supposed to happen in the consulting room under normal analytic circumstances. I didn't know how the flow of conversation was supposed to go.

In my heart of hearts I feared that Papa would begin our session with what he had asked each of us young Freuds every night during a short period of my childhood: "And what did you do today that you would rather not tell me?"

It was some oddball idea of child rearing to which he was giving a thirty-day test, and it was certainly never brutal. Rather, it was always one of those this-is-going-to-hurt-me-more-than-it-hurts-you routines.

"And what did you do today that you would rather not tell me?" Papa would ask us as we six lined up in our nightclothes. We would make our confessions (we had to come up with something), take a slap from Papa's paddle on our flannel-covered bottoms, and trot off to bed. There was no drama about it.

Though it did hurt (a paddle always does) and it always made Ernst cry. Every night he soaked his pillow with tears. Sophie's odd laughter rang out as counterpoint. A few sighs from Mathilde. Hugs for Dolly from me. Martin punched his mattress. Oliver scribbled in his notebook. None of us ever varied in our responses to the paddle slaps, and Papa never varied in the stimulus.

"And what did you do today that you would rather not tell me?"

I remember one time on a hot spring afternoon during that child rearing experiment. None of the neighboring children would play with us because we were Jews. We siblings—all of us, from Mathilde and Martin right on down through me—hoped to fill an hour or so with a harmless game called Sardines. Most people have played it. There is some searching or "tag" at the outset, but I believe that the real point of the game is to cram together, prone like sardines, into a tiny bit of a space. The winner is the sardine who can tolerate the cramped quarters and sour body smells the longest without moving.

Papa discovered us. We were being sardines in a small crawl space underneath the cellar stairs of our apartment building. We were lying on gravel, or at least the bottom layer of us was. I was five or so years old and was so excited to be allowed to play. We were really sweaty, we were getting dirty, and the bodies around me aroused feelings I had never before felt. It was wonderfully uncomfortable and hard to breathe. I knew that finally I had found a game I could play.

I wet myself from excitement.

"AAAAA!" Ernst began to yell, for he was the sardine lying beneath me.

Papa had just set out for a thinking walk when he heard Ernst's screams.

"AAAAAAAA!"

Papa came around the back of the building to investigate just as my brothers and sisters came pouring and screaming out from under the cellar stairs. I lay there still. I had won, you see.

Papa helped me up. He picked me up, actually, for I was very small. He assumed, when the crook of his arm supported my bottom and my head rested on his shoulder, that I had wet myself in fear. He presumed that the boys had scared me and the girls hadn't tended to me properly.

So that night, when we lined up to confess our sins to the paddle, I was excused from the line. I watched each of my siblings, one by one, admit to Papa that they had been at fault. And I watched each one of them take a completely dispassionate slap from Papa's paddle, right on their night-clothed bottoms.

I hugged Dolly to comfort her, but I also giggled into her skirt.

"Now, Anna," Papa asked when the beatings were done and he could take a moment to look at me impishly. Sophie shot me the rudest of possible glances. "Tell me, do. Whatever is it that's on your mind now?"

Papa did not ask the dreaded, "And what did you do today that you would rather not tell me?" at the outset of our first psychoanalytic session.

He did, however, ask, "Whatever is it that's on your mind now?" When he asked it, I looked at the ceiling. All these years later, it still needed painting.

According to the rules of psychoanalysis, I did not need to answer with a summary, for example, of my thoughts about my life in general. Rather, I could answer the question literally. What was on my mind *now*? I mentioned the fact that the ceiling needed painting, and from there we talked about colors, and from there I mentioned the nice orange of the fire and the ochres and blues of his waiting room rugs, and from there (and this was an "aha!" moment) I remembered that I'd had a dream just the night before that featured many of the images from one of those rugs.

"There was a man who sold Persian rugs. I knew he was himself Persian because he wore a turban. He smiled a lot, and his teeth were big and white. He sat in the absolute center of a village market. Grinning, strangely dressed people poked their heads out of the windows of low, stone houses."

"Indeed, some of these are familiar images for you, Anna."

"Yes. Of course. And just like the waiting room rug that holds the village scene, the village in my dream was circular. I knew this because I momentarily viewed it from on high."

"On high?"

"That's right. I must have climbed the village's tower and looked. Though in the dream I don't remember ever being atop the tower. Still, I knew that, from on high, the village layout resembled a wheel.

The market was the wheel's hub. The spokes of the wheel were tunnels extending out towards the wheel's rim."

"You mean towards the sea that you used to imagine at the village periphery?"

"Yes!"

"Tell me about the tunnels, Anna."

"The tunnels ran through the stone houses and all the way to the ocean. Oh, my! The village had no roads!"

"No roads?"

"No! I remember wandering about the market, feeling lost and trying to find a road because Oli had always told me that roads are wonderful things to find when you're lost. But instead of finding roads I found tunnels, and I was afraid to enter them."

"Understood."

"All of the tunnels had curved ochre ceilings and cobalt blue tile floors. I remember backing away from a tunnel and practically bumping into the rug merchant."

"And?"

"It was very early morning in the market. There was a tiny man in a black shroud and a large white cap who slowly approached the village tower. He intended, I believe, to climb the tower and ask the men of the town to join him in prayer."

"So the tower in your dream, the tower that you as a child imagined in my circular rug—it was a *minaret*?"

"I suppose so, Papa. And he was a *muezzin*, logically. As the *muezzin* approached the *minaret*, the smiling rug merchant began sniffing, dog-like, at a pile of rugs. The *muezzin* saw it and visibly registered disapproval. And so the rug merchant stopped sniffing and instead began behaving like a gentleman. Very politely, he took a sip of grape juice from a translucent, tulip-shaped cup that was a lot like one of Mama's everyday china cups, but almost luminous. Then the rug merchant turned to look at me. He smiled, and even though there was nothing grotesque or animalistic any more about his appearance, his smile revealed shockingly huge, white teeth. I was taken aback at the sight. I guess his smile and his teeth are things I've mentioned already in this dream, Papa, yes? And that repetition signifies that they are important?"

"They are important."

"I also remember seeing a callused, dark spot at the center of the rug merchant's forehead. I assumed that he had gotten it from resting it on the ground as he faced Mecca to pray. He prayed five times a day. He was a faithful man, this rug merchant."

"Improbable," Papa said.

"Even though it was so early that most of the markets' merchants had yet to arrive, hanging from the stalls were strings of dried eggplant and sacks of figs, apples, and nuts. There were meats. I smelled curry and cumin and turmeric. Papa, I'm not even sure whether I know what any of those spices smell like, but in my dream I smelled them and I knew what they were. Together they created an almost irresistible bouquet. I became so hungry! But it wasn't my food, so I didn't reach for it. As I felt my hunger, the rug merchant became just a little more canine again. He sat on his haunches, licking his own teeth. He did sip his juice politely. But he also sniffed some rugs, though more discreetly than he had before."

"'Sipping his juice.' That's the second mention of that action."

"Yes," I said. "And the second mention of 'sniffing.' The more that he sniffed the pile of rugs before him, the more I began to feel hungry. I had a strong desire for…and let's see, the dawn became brighter around me."

"Hungry for what dear? Don't elide."

"Well, to be honest, I'm starting to get embarrassed, Papa. I'm happy to tell you these things if I must. But would it be all right if I spoke in metaphors?"

"You need to speak the truth plainly. Don't waste time feeling uncomfortable. People tell me these sorts of things all the time."

"All right. I will try. Well, to be honest, the hunger I was feeling was sexual. When I became sexually aroused I glanced about to see if anyone had noticed that I was blushing or that my breathing had changed. No one seemed to be watching me. But I began watching the market's other women. They all wore the *hijab*, covering them from head to foot in dark cloth. I wore my usual light blouse and dirndl. I felt very exposed. Then the touts came out and…. "

"Touts?"

"The men who entice shoppers to their masters' wares. You're not familiar with the term, 'touts'?"

"No, but that's all right. Tell me about touts."

"The touts came into the market, and even though they didn't look directly at me, I got the feeling that they were trawling for me especially. They carried jelly cookies just like those that Tante Minna makes, and they wanted me to follow them. I might have gone with them to their masters' stalls, but somehow I knew that we wouldn't really end up there. It was into the bedrooms of the houses that they would take me. We would reach those bedrooms by passing through the beautiful tunnels of ochre and cobalt blue. I wanted to follow the touts because I liked the colors of the tunnels. And I could hear the tunnels themselves thrum as though with the power of hundreds of tiny motors. That was enticing."

"And so how did all this make you feel? The touts? The colors? The thrumming?"

"Alive and happy. But I didn't think that touts were safe to follow. I was afraid of my desire to go. I hesitated and looked to the rug merchant as though for advice. As I hesitated, I watched a jowly woman wearing the *hijab* bring him a bowl of lemon water. He used it to wash his lips and fingers and feet and even his ears. She helped the rug merchant blow his nose."

"Interesting, that, about the nose."

"As the woman washed the rug merchant, the *muezzin* climbed the *minaret*'s winding ramp. He stood at the top. I envied him his view of the village and the ancient landscape around it. When the rug merchant blew his nose, the *muezzin* let out a bone-rattling cry and called all the faithful to prayer. The cry bounced off the stone walls around me. And at the tail end of the *muezzin*'s first call, the rug merchant looked at me and shook his head: 'No.'"

"'No?'"

"No about following the touts. I shouldn't follow touts."

"Is that all that happened? Is that the end of the dream?"

"No. When the rug merchant shook his head, the touts began to hiss."

"Tell me more."

"Um, I think maybe the rug merchant put his forehead to the ground and prayed."

For a moment, neither Papa nor I said anything.

"Something else happened, Anna. What was it?" Papa finally asked.

I lay there with my eyes closed, convinced that I had just told Papa the entirety of the dream. But then it seemed to me that the dream might have gone on, and the more I lay there quietly, the more I knew that to be the case.

Indeed, I remembered that, instead of leaving with the touts, I had moved towards a very old and sexless man, the proprietor of one of the market stalls. He had caught my eye by smiling reassuringly. But when I arrived, I saw that somehow the proprietor had transformed himself into the big-toothed rug merchant.

"And?" Papa demanded when he heard about that.

I didn't immediately answer.

Papa prompted, "And was the rug merchant now sexless like the old man?"

"The rug merchant did not have the old man's reassuring smile. He had a big, satisfied smirk on his face and he called for the touts' jelly cookies. He wanted grape juice, too. It and the cookies were delivered by a small boy. I drank the juice. As I did, I felt a disorienting rush of shyness, but I kept my wits enough to notice that I was drinking from the same tulip-shaped, translucent cup from which I had seen the rug merchant drink earlier."

"Tell me more about that rug merchant," Papa said, shifting in his seat.

"I stayed with him while he shamelessly courted his customers. Events always transpired to his advantage. He flattered and fawned. The customers asked questions that the rug merchant answered, but never directly. He wasn't really honest, ever."

"He wasn't really honest, ever," Papa repeated, as with appreciation for a talent like that.

"'I don't bargain!' the rug merchant would shout in a loud, happy voice. 'I am far too unreasonable for that!'"

"Now, tell me," Papa asked, and I could hear real curiosity in his voice. "What does this dream mean to you?"

In the silence that ensued, I let my mind wander. I noticed that atop the dark, inlaid woodwork above a window frame there was a row of tiny, antique figurines. Then I turned my head slightly to the left, and my gaze rested on one of Papa's bookcases. It was covered with—smothered by, almost, on all of its shelves—more of the same.

The bookcase's figurines were larger. They were from ancient Greece, Rome, India, and Africa. Papa, I knew, had collected some on travels and been given many as gifts. Most were familiar to me; he'd shown them around to family members whenever he brought one home. But for some reason, that night even the antiquities that were most familiar seemed extravagantly odd. I saw the friendly gargoyle with which I had communed during Ida Bauer's analytic session. This time he seemed stubborn and threatening—I suppose because I focused my attention on his firm, ugly snout through which rain water had once gushed. I glimpsed Pandora's Box and wondered momentarily about the ashen secrets it had gathered over the years. One fertility goddess had a belly so stretched that it might have incubated twin elephants. A hunter had an arrow with a laughably bulbous tip, of which he seemed enormously proud.

There were some half-hidden sculptures that looked downright deviant, but stacks of unbound notes partially blocked my view of them. Shifty-eyed flutists and large-breasted dancers, lounging women with chipped genitalia, people coupling, and fat men laughing, beasts and creatures and varmints—all peeked out at me from places it seemed they shouldn't have been. When the shadows cast by the firelight flickered on them, I saw them scurry about feloniously.

"It is probably significant that the rug merchant allowed no bargaining," is how I began when I tried to interpret the dream for Papa. "He was adamant in his refusal of the normal process of cordial give and take. So although I, for one, would have liked to talk to him about the price of a rug, I didn't dare try. I was afraid of what the rug merchant might do if I were to refuse his authority in any way. My fear probably arose in response to a repulsive collection of tarnished trophies that he had; it triggered in me some instinctual dread. *What are those trophies?* I couldn't help but wonder. *Are they shrunken human heads? Are they burnt genitalia? And to whom did they originally belong?*"

"Let's stop with the interpretation for a moment, Anna. Just tell me more about the trophies," Papa said. "Where did he keep them?"

"On bookshelves, on desks. Really, on almost any surface that would hold them or halfway hide them."

"Anna, it's such a remarkable thing to imagine about your rug merchant, the possession of ill-hidden shrunken heads and burnt genitalia. Why do you think you have done so?"

"The rug merchant also had vacuum-sealed safes, which I supposed were filled with rugs. I was so very curious to see the rugs in those safes. But he told me, 'No,' those doors were only opened for customers who were constitutionally up to the rigors of purchasing. I had already somehow indicated to him, probably through my shyness, that I wasn't quite ready to purchase a colorful rug, so he would not open a safe for me."

"My dearest, smallest, most loyal child, let us talk, if only for a moment, about what you might mean by the word 'safe.' Yes?"

"All right."

According to Papa, the rug merchant was he, and he had something I wanted to possess. Papa suggested that the dream's colorful rugs represented sensual pleasure, which I was not yet ready to enjoy. Furthermore, "tunnels" were vaginas; "dog-like sniffing" was sexual curiosity; "big white teeth" were the penis shaft, though by what rationale I was never quite sure. (With Papa, teeth were often penises.) The "callused spot on the center of the rug merchant's forehead" was probably not, as I thought when I first described the dream to Papa, evidence of the merchant's faithfulness to God, but instead the mark of Cain, sign of sin. And the "touts" were men beckoning me to the wonders of heterosexual life.

Yet as often as I'd easily used the word "safe" in describing my dream (three times, by my count), I had difficulty understanding that it might be significant. At that point in my life I had no conscious memory of my momentary attraction to Fraülein Sabina Spielrein. I had no awareness that I would ever love a woman romantically or sexually. Yet even a casual interpretation of my rug merchant dream shows that I somehow clearly knew (for the rug merchant pointed it out to me) that touts (men beckoning me to the wonders of heterosexual life) were not "safe" for me to follow. Neither had Doctor Jones been safe to follow, though I had never revealed to Papa any details of my encounter with him.

Rugs were held in a safe, and touts were not safe. Yet sexuality still beckoned me. For example, the "*muezzin*'s glorious cry" was probably the cry of orgasm. Both the rug merchant and I drank sweet juice from a translucent, tulip-shaped cup. Yes, that particular cup was reminiscent of Mama's everyday china. However, the imagery is also genital—female genital. Mind you, Papa never suggested that interpretation. Still, I do think that the interpretation I have just given is the correct one. The shape of the cup and the sweetness of the liquid both revealed that I, like the rug merchant, would want to partake of the fruit juice of the vagina.

"I don't bargain," spoken by the rug merchant, was vintage Papa. He set the rules, almost all of which I was someday to break. "Bargaining" also played a role in my on-going fantasy of a brave boy at the mercy of an incensed tyrant. "Tarnished trophies," "burnt genitalia," and "shrunken heads" allude to Papa's antiquities. I also interpret them as what might happen to any young woman who tried to bargain with my father.

Papa and I never discussed the "young boy" who, in my dream, brought jelly cookies and juice—which, of course, were precisely what Tante Minna had brought to me on the evening after my menarche. I suppose that the boy could have had several identities. Perhaps he was the "me" of my sexual fantasies. Perhaps he was Oliver as a boy, for surely I still felt guilty and sad about what had become of him. And surely I missed the Oliver I had once loved so dearly, the brother I'd admired and trusted. Of course, I also know that the young boy who, in my dream, brought cookies and juice might instead have been an embodiment of what was probably my central fear—that Papa, in his conversation long before with Doktor Jung, had been speaking truthfully about himself as a child rapist. The young boy, in that case, would have been Papa's victim. Papa was not safe.

Chapter 18

Papa always said that dreams are compromises between illicit desire and the censoring agents of the mind.

As are fantasies, which is no doubt why Papa wanted me to supplement our talk about my dreams with discussions of my masturbation fantasies. He was intrigued by the one from when I was very young about a nameless, passive child being beaten by a nameless, angry man. But he was far more interested in my newer fantasy, the one in which a young blond hero was entrapped and hurt by an iron-fisted Powerful Man. Papa wanted to hear this newer fantasy nearly every time we met. He had me recite the details so often that I felt like the Ancient Mariner, plucking at the garments of a wedding guest with my skinny hand and telling essentially the same tired story over and over again into the uncaring air.

Except, of course, that the garment of a wedding guest was never what my skinny hand actually plucked mid-fantasy—certainly not in childhood, certainly not in adolescence, and certainly not after our analysis each night when I was fully aroused and alone in my bedroom.

Each psychoanalytic session was essentially the same. We met at ten o'clock, which was usually after Mama and Tante Minna had gone to bed. There in Papa's moon-, lamp-, and fire-lit consulting room, we talked for an hour about dreams and beating fantasies, beating fantasies and dreams. As soon as his fancy was caught by an association I made or a nuance I reported, Papa would light a cigar and begin puffing contentedly. The air in the room would curdle. Late in each session, Papa would exhale profoundly and shift his weight in his chair. A new tension would enter the room.

"You can stop now, Anna," Papa would quickly say. "We have tunneled very deeply."

Abruptly, almost too jauntily, he would walk me to the door and shake my hand as though I were any one of his many supplicants and he needed to hurry me along.

"Goodnight, Papa. Thank you for your time," I would say.

"Goodnight, Anna."

I would be in the full flush of embarrassed excitement. After Papa closed the Danger Door against me I didn't have to waste time pinning on my hat or winking at a confused young me as Ida Bauer had done seventeen years before. Instead, walking quickly and quietly, I delivered myself from Papa's world of shape shifting and *soupçon* into our staid, twentieth century quarters. I heard two old ladies snoring. I entered my own bedroom and changed into my nightgown. Usually I sat at my desk to write a few pages of despairing poetry. It kept me for a while from masturbating, and that was important to me for, as Papa's analysand, I was under strict instructions to refrain from any sort of sexual activity. All of Papa's analysands were, lest we drain creative energy from analytic hours.

Routinely, after writing, I brushed my teeth and tried in vain to chastely sleep.

"'Colors' and 'colorful' are two concepts that you have raised, Anna. I find them both cavernous. Let us start tonight with 'colorful.' What associations can you make in relation to that word, dear?"

Remember, I had at this point no conscious idea that I would one day love a woman. I was still, I am almost ashamed to admit, completely taken by the idea of masturbating my way through a lonely life so that I could fulfill my duties as my father's favorite female.

"Well, I do remember from when I was five or six that Mama

called psychoanalysis 'pornography' and your consulting room a 'den of iniquity.'"

"Yes?" I couldn't see him, for he always sat immediately behind my head. I did, however, imagine his eyebrows leaping upwards.

"One day when I asked you what a 'den of iniquity' was, you said that it is a place where people feel free to behave more colorfully than they might otherwise."

"Yes. I remember. Go on," said Papa, lighting a cigar.

"And of course you remember a child named, in your case notes, Little Hans. He was phobic about social interactions as well as about horses. Keeping his hand on his widdler helped him feel better."

"Of course I remember Little Hans. I'm pleased and flattered that you remember him."

"When I was a young girl I heard you tell Tante Minna about Hans' strong fears. I wondered if they made his widdler turn colors. So that is another association to the word 'colorful.' Yes, Papa?"

"Yes, Anna. That is most definitely an association to the word 'colorful.'"

There followed a silence. Papa blew a nice smoke ring and played for a moment with the fringe on the shade of the Chinese lamp. Then he instructed me to continue.

"Well," I said, and then I dared: "Papa, I suppose it is possible that I, as a grown woman, feel some envy for Little Hans. You were sympathetic about his fondness for his own widdler. Yet you actively discourage me from pursuing my affection for mine."

It was unusual for me to challenge Papa in any way. But I was peeved with him, which was perfectly understandable. He expected me to dedicate my life to serving certain of his needs—to gather papers, translate, welcome guests, and listen to his thoughts—and I was eager to do so. In order to live a spinster's life, however, I needed to masturbate, and I was being told that I shouldn't.

Responding to me, Papa sounded amused.

"You want the right to keep your hands on your widdler in the same manner that Little Hans was allowed to keep his hands on his? Do you want to do that right here? In my consulting room? And do you believe yourself to have a widdler, young woman?"

"No, Papa. I don't. Goodness, you know what I mean. Let's don't be thick."

"Thick?"

"Thick, Papa. Dense. Stupid."

Papa sat for a few moments of silence while I lay just as quietly on the couch. Then, finally he said, "I didn't mean to be thick."

"I am sorry if I snapped at you, Papa. Really. Actually, I can associate in relation to 'thick' for you, if you'd like."

"I would like that very much. And the association is…."

"Orgasm. It is the feeling that I have before I arrive at orgasm. I get it when I have my fantasies and I plead and explain and beg and bargain for my life with the Powerful Man. There is tension in the air. Fear. It is thick, coagulated. And then I arrive at orgasm."

"Very good, Anna. Very, very, very good."

"But on second thought, 'thick' might just be the viscosity of my *smegma.*"

Here, I seem to have wanted to rile Papa with Yiddish while testing his tolerance for matters that were central to my femininity. Papa reminded me to speak in proper German and suggested that "vaginal discharge" was the term I wanted.

"Yes." I accepted the correction. "Vaginal discharge is thick. But I do have another association. You and I are father and daughter. We cannot ever be sensually thick. Furthermore, I cannot leak my vaginal discharge with you. How is that, Papa? Are those the kind of associations you were looking for?"

There transpired an exceptionally long bit of silence, during which I felt not the luxury of being able to talk with my analyst about anything that came to mind, but the boundaries of what I could and couldn't say to my father while pretending to a luxury I didn't have.

"Well, it seems that your hour is up, Anna," Papa eventually said, shifting his weight in his chair and shutting off the Chinese lamp that had illuminated, I then realized, only me. "We have tunneled deeply enough."

That night, for some reason, I dreamed of keening women.

There has been a death. The women wail as bells chime.

It is I who have died, smothered in one of the rug merchant's airless safes. Remembering, I feel once more the lack of oxygen throughout my body. I am a block of pain. I feel death seize me, though I cannot feel myself die.

But I am also vital and talking to the rug merchant. He laughs and explains to me that oxygen deprivation is not fatal. Rather, it is something that many people decidedly enjoy, with a little practice.

From his laughing, wide, toothy mouth his tongue unfurls a thousand-year-old rug recently snatched from the ruins of Troy. I hear the rug fall to the floor.

I don't see this, for my view of the rug merchant's white teeth holds my gaze.

The merchant calls the rug beautiful. But when I finally glance at it, it is clear to me that it is not much more than a threadbare rag. It has no splendor. There is no real color.

"You have much to learn about color and rugs, my dear," he says.

How is it, I wonder, that he does not need to close his mouth to articulate plosive and fricative consonants?

"Would you like to accompany me on a journey through the wonders of the Far East?" he continues. "I will teach you how to value carpets and colors by their smell."

"Smell?" (I am very practiced at associations, so I excitedly venture one to the rug merchant.) "Or 'Semen-al?'"

Tickled by the naughtiness of my association, I can now see in the rug brilliance and intensity, tone and tinge. I want to hear the rug merchant's answer.

"You have stopped making sense to me, Anna. And your time is up," he says, fading away to nothingness.

I dreamed, of course, in German. However, I report this dream in English, and I must admit that the German words for "smell" and "semen" do not bear the resemblance in German that they bear in English. *Der Geruchssinn* is "smell." *Die Samenflüssigkeit* is "semen." There is no alliterative logic that links to the two.

So why, I struggle right now to understand, did I just report a "smell" to "semen-al" association? Way back those many years ago, did I experience one that never existed? Or have I confabulated one in retrospect?

Perhaps the rug merchant was right. Perhaps I had stopped making sense.

Perhaps, back in 1918, I had finally lost my mind. Perhaps I was hysterical with repressed anger and desire and was, unbeknownst to me, talking in other-worldly voices while I twitched and swooned, and thought about having sex not only with Powerful Men and myself but with other hysterical women, as some hysterical women were known to do.

Aha! *Der Fischgeruch* is the German word for "fishy smell."

Perhaps that is the word I used for "smell" in my dream. *Der Geruchssinn* suggested *der Fischgeruch.*

One of the truly lovely aspects of free association is the fact that the audit trail of life can be retrospectively fudged. Streaming freely from concept to concept and from memory to new thought, one can corroborate almost any assumption one likes.

Smell, fishy smell, female fishy smell, male fishy smell, semen. Now there's an associative path. Is that the one that I took that night in my dream?

For the life of me I do not know. Memory, dreams, and a purposefully wandering mind: Together they play wonderful tricks.

Chapter 19

Hysterical or not, I walked trustingly through the Danger Door and into the consulting room the next night at ten o'clock. I lay on the couch and dutifully reported.

"I dreamed last night that I heard keening, wailing women. I followed the sound inside the ochre and cobalt passageways and found the village women gathered around a corpse. I was the corpse."

"Would these be the same ochre and cobalt tunnels from your previous dreams?"

"Yes, they would."

"So you were in the same village that you were in before?"

"Yes, I was."

"But this was the first time you entered the passageways."

"Yes."

"All right. Now go on."

And so I did. "I joined the keening women. With them I wailed and wailed to my heart's content for poor, dead Anna. My corpse lay silent, admired by all. 'She was so beautiful,' the women were saying, and so I said it, too. 'Look how lovely she looks when reclining. Her lips are even now so red and ripe. She is still beautiful and true. Our Anna.'"

I heard Papa cough and shift in his seat while he adjusted the shade of the Chinese lamp. "Please continue, but use the present tense, Anna. It will help you feel the dream more deeply."

"All right. Let me see.... The village women lift me. I am as stiff as a board. They bring me to the side of the tunnel. I hear the thrumming of the walls. Thrum thrum, thrum thrum. Thrum thrum, thrum thrum."

"What are you doing that for, Anna?"

"Doing what?"

"Saying 'thrum thrum, thrum thrum, thrum thrum, thrum thrum?' It's ruining my concentration."

"I wanted to remember how the walls sounded. They had a life or a motor inside of them. They vibrated gently and made the lightest, busiest, most thrilling noise I had ever heard. Then the women took their mouths.... "

"Present tense, please."

"Then the women take their mouths and put them up to mine, giving me the breath of life, for I have died, you see, by suffocation. I have died in one of the rug merchant's airless safes."

"Ahhhhh. You have died in the rug merchant's airless safe."

"But when the women give me the kiss of life, I hear a baby cry, and then I am not nearly as dead any more."

"The kiss of life?"

"Yes. They put their lips to mine and blow their life into me."

"It's just that at first you called it the 'breath of life.'"

"Yes. I may have."

"All right. All right. Please go on. Tell me more of your thoughts about what the women did to you. Present tense, please."

"But I am already through thinking about the women, and now I am thinking about the rug merchant. Would you like me to say what is on my mind as soon as it comes to mind?"

"But you were about to tell me all about the kiss of life," Papa seemed to protest.

"Yes. But now I am thinking about the rug merchant."

"Oh. All right. As you wish."

"In the dream I leave the women, or so I guess. You see, I don't actually remember what happened to the women. It's just that, after the kiss of life, I remember no more of them. I remember instead standing in the rug merchant's stall. We are each drinking juice from our own tulip cups. That is significant, I suppose, because in the previous night's dream he used the cup first, and then later I used the very same cup. He explains to me that, because I am dead, he doesn't want to use my cup for fear of 'catching' whatever it is that killed me. I tell the rug merchant that I have no sickness. I died in his safe. He laughs at the news. He says, 'You're not dead at all, then. Oxygen deprivation is just an acquired taste. You'll learn. You'll see.'

"Then he tries to sell me a rug. I am so happy to learn that I am alive that I am willing to buy, even without bargaining. But the rug is without the color or beauty of life so I don't want this particular one. When I tell him this he hurls the rug angrily, and he hisses at me like an ugly, scary tout. 'You have much to learn about color and rugs, my dear,' he says. Then he takes me roughly in his arms and begins to spirit me away. I am afraid. Paralyzed. I cannot breathe now through my mouth or nose. I am suffocating. I will die for real this time."

Of course in my account to Papa, I elaborated and lied. Personally, I think that honesty in psychoanalysis is over-rated. In the first place, complete honesty is all but impossible. Analysands inevitably color their disclosures with assumptions about what the analyst wants to hear. Sometimes they are aware of the assumptions they make and the editing they do, but sometimes they are not. When they are not aware of their deceit, are they being more truthful? Is ignorance any better an excuse for contrivance than egocentricity?

Furthermore, have you ever noticed yourself hold in mind two versions of an emotionally significant event—for example, one version in which you were at fault and one in which your heroism shined? One in which you were helpless in the face of dark forces and one in which you rose to the occasion, almost imperceptibly but perhaps just enough?

When, in disclosure, you offer one version as opposed to its counterpart, is that lying? And if so, is the lie necessarily in the telling?

Or is the lie in the event itself? Who is to say that reality is unambiguous? Maybe all events transpire in two ways or more. Maybe all time is a-synchronous. Maybe the universe generates confusion by creating indefinable incidents, and we just compound the perplexity with our crude, linear reporting styles.

This is silly talk, of course. Still, these are the kind of matters about which we wondered in 1918, my first year of analysis. It was the era of Einstein and his relativistic notions of space and time. Nietzsche had declared that "to tell the truth is simply to lie according to a fixed convention." In parlor talk, everyone but mothers and aunties wondered if right and wrong were necessarily good and bad, or instead, variable and relative. When I lied in analysis, as I frequently did with Papa, it was easy for me to believe that the lies were only an inevitable manifestation of my very slippery facts.

Papa, I knew, was not above the occasional lie. I watched him publicly proclaim himself an ever-rational scientist. Sunday afternoons, however, he enlisted me in telepathy experiments. Sundays with Papa were the only times I was allowed to touch a deck of cards.

I also heard him argue with Mama and forbid the God of the Jews a seat at our table. At the same time I knew him to be morbidly afraid of the spirits that might animate telephones.

In 1918, like virtually everyone I knew, I forgave myself my occasional lies by speculating about mankind's incomplete understanding of simultaneous occurrences in time and space. I am older now and done with thoughts like that. We lie not because facts lie but because we hold in mind our intended places in hearts and history.

As Nietzsche said when he had gotten over his own youth, "We have art lest we perish from the truth."

"Anna, I have a list of words that you have used in describing to me what I would like to call your Ochre and Cobalt Dreams. Let's go through those words one by one. I will say a word. Then I would like you to say a word. Please voice your association no matter how illogical or meaningless it might seem. Later we will talk about what your associations reveal about your inner self and possibly about your experiences and desires as an infant. Ready?"

I was. From "thrumming tunnels" I associated right away to vaginas ready for thrills and desire, and I was able to do so without embarrassment. From "smothered in one of the rug merchant's airless safes" I associated to my tuberculosis, but since then I have arrived at another association. Suffocation for me was symbolic of my withering from the lack of freedom to be my real self in Papa's consulting room—or, indeed, in any compartment of my life that was open to him. "Drinking juice from my own tulip-shaped cup?" At the time of my session with Papa I could make no association to that at all. Neither Papa nor I realized that I was inching closer towards a realization of my desire to love a woman.

Now I see that the rug merchant encouraged me to accept a life deprived of oxygen. *It is something that many people decidedly enjoy, with a little practice*, he had said. *Nota bene*: When the rug merchant tried to sell me his approved brand of sexuality—a rug in which I could perceive no color regardless of his claims on its behalf—I refused. When I refused, he hissed like a tout.

And that is when I got excited. But of course I did! What would be the punishment administered by a rug merchant whose real human incarnation had once wondered aloud whether he is a child rapist? A rage-infested beating, perhaps! I never imagined actual rape, but in my dream I certainly felt excited at the possibility of that beating. Indeed, it was only at the thought of such a beating that I could begin to see color in the bland rug.

Actually, it may have been my bold request for a "fishy smell tour of the world" together with the possibility of a beating that awakened me to the rug's color. Mind you, with regard to the beating, I am not sure that I actually wanted to be abused by my own father. I believe instead that I was happy to have the dream take notice of my fantasies and of the complex young woman they showed me to be. I loved my beating fantasies, loved them truly and dearly. For it was only in fantasy that I was ever allowed to be strong and brave. I required a cloak of creativity to see myself in a way that was separate from Papa's limiting definitions of what was womanly or appropriate for me. It was only by imagining myself a boy that I could also imagine myself to be autonomous, self-determined, and actively engaged with the threatening world around me. And that was truly exciting.

But for the remainder of that session, as Papa led me through a chain of associations originating from within my dream, I felt uncomfortable. Perhaps my discomfort was due to a wobble that had crept into Papa's voice, or to the tiny, nervous coughs that he had begun to produce every few moments. I lay with my arms crossed over my chest, as though trying to protect myself from exposure. With Papa's prodding, from the "white" of the rug merchant's teeth, I associated to "too big" (from afar, white things appear larger than dark things) and from there to the "gaping mouth" that had held infinite appeal. From "gaping mouth" I moved on to "horse" (horses have big mouths, too) and then to "penis" (for horses have big penises).

It was at "penis" that Papa interrupted me to suggest the following interpretation of my associative chain:

In my ice-capped virginity (which Papa said was symbolized in my dream by the frosty translucence of the coffee cup) I desired him, Papa, the rug merchant, the horse-penised father in possession of sexual secrets that he kept in his "safe," which was a symbol for his under drawers. Instead of dying, what I did in my dream was have an orgasm. I did it when I thought I had burrowed into said "safe."

"So you understand and are not upset?"

"Of course so, and of course not," I replied, my arms still folded.

Chapter 20

In any psychoanalysis, the analysand eventually learns that objecting to an analyst's interpretations is counterproductive, for analysts understand objections as covert affirmations.

"Having diagnosed a case," Papa once wrote, "we may then boldly demand confirmation of our suspicions from the patient. We must not be led astray by initial denials. If we keep firmly to what we have inferred, we shall in the end conquer every resistance by emphasizing the unshakeable nature of our convictions."

In other words, with Papa, gentle, courteous questioning was hardly ever the order of the day.

"Heads I win, tails you lose," as the joke goes.

"Now for the connection between your dreams and your beating fantasies," Papa began our session the next night. "Your earliest fantasies I have now heard aplenty. 'A child is being beaten.' Which child? It doesn't matter. All we really know is that it is never you. Who is doing the beating? Again, it doesn't matter. All we know is that it is always a man.

"While your earliest fantasies were repetitive and fairly devoid of nuance, your current fantasies are rich in overtones and significance. Your protagonist, interestingly, is always a boy, *and* it is you. Your antagonist is always a powerful and evil man who clearly enjoys delivering the blows.

"I would like to suggest to you that in your childhood fantasy—let's call it the 'Phase One Fantasy'—you were a mere onlooker while I was the prominent figure. I was the beater, and the child whom I beat was one or another of your siblings. This early fantasy was a perfectly normal one. Its emotional impact was 'I am watching my Papa beat everyone but me. Papa doesn't beat me. Papa loves me best.' Often you masturbated in your happiness after that dream. It's possible that sometimes you didn't. No matter. All was good for you.

"Your current fantasy, the one in which a powerful man beats a beautiful and brave boy who also happens to be you, let us call the 'Phase Two Fantasy.' For personal reasons, perhaps, I find the fantasy discourteous. For, again, the person doing the beating is I. Now, however, I am finding pleasure in inflicting pain, and this I don't understand.

"So, I have a question that I would like you to answer. How did your fantasy life evolve from Phase One to Phase Two? How did you proceed from your once-harmless Oedipal preoccupation to your current problematic focus?"

I lay there trying to understand and then conjure answers to Papa's questions. As I did, I thought I heard a stray note or two from the music box, but when I looked at the Buddha atop it, he was stoic and smiling, with no sign of recent motion. An image of my mother and aunt, snoring obliviously and chastely in their adjacent beds, ran through my head. Then I thought of all the empty beds in the apartment—Mathilde's, Martin's, Oli's, Ernst's, and Sophie's. The boys' beds were as severe as army cots, and the girls' as frilly as doll furniture. Sophie's long-abandoned stuffed animals were no doubt reflected dumbly in her gilded mirror. My bed was waiting for me. I should have been in it.

My eyes rested for a moment on Pandora's Box, now relegated to a shelf also inhabited by figurines. Though Papa no longer used it as an ashtray, I imagined a burning ember still in it, and one or two of humankind's pressurized vanities escaping on a wisp of old combustion.

"Anna, again: How did your fantasies evolve from Phase One, in which I was the expected and worthy object of your gaze, to Phase Two, in which I am a purveyor of sadistic pleasure, in a frenzy over a boy whom I do not recognize but who turns out to be my daughter? Do you have an answer to my question, Anna?"

"No, Papa."

"Well, I believe that I do."

Papa then suggested to me a rather curious answer to the question he had posed. He said that my Phase One and Phase Two Fantasies were actually Phases One and *Three*. According to Papa, the space between them was occupied by an intermediate, *Real* Phase Two Fantasy. In the Real Phase Two Fantasy the person doing the beating derived no undue pleasure from administering punishment. The person receiving the beating was I. I was a girl and I wanted and welcomed pain.

"Indeed. The Real Phase Two Fantasy was born of the guilt that you felt as a result of Phase One, when you happily watched me dispassionately beat one or another of your siblings. After Phase One, you needed to punish yourself for the pleasure you had felt. You created a masochistic Real Phase Two Fantasy that was the twin of the Phase One Fantasy except for the fact that you had become the victim and were grateful for that. You do not remember this particular fantasy because it threatened to please you forever, and thus to enslave you.

"But never mind. Your amnesia about that Real Phase Two Fantasy is evidence that it accomplished for you a necessary step in personal growth. You began to move beyond your feelings of competitiveness with your siblings. And, my dear, these days you continue to grow emotionally. Granted, sometimes your progress has been shaky, as is made evident by the fact that in your current fantasy you are a boy and you bargain and plead for relief from punishment and pain. So today, right now, I want you to understand irrevocably that you must set aside your Phase Three Fantasy. Move on to a Phase Three-A Fantasy, one in which you are a woman and you enjoy whatever pain you receive. But keep in mind that any continued fascination in your sexual fantasy life with me as a pain giver should be terminated."

"I..."

"I know. Hearing that is difficult for you. Let me assure you, then, that even though you can no longer focus your sexual attention on me, you can, and indeed should, cultivate your womanly enjoyment of pain. Such an enjoyment will always serve you well—as long as some other man feeds your womanly needs."

"I...Papa, are you are suggesting that I create a Phase Three-A Fantasy in which I am beaten by a lover?"

"By a husband."

"And would it also benefit me to create a *reality* in which I am beaten by a husband?"

"Let us say 'captively protected.'"

"But why on the earth would being a captive of someone be good for me?"

"It might not be good for you in fact, but it would be good for you to want. As a woman you must condition yourself to accept situations such as first intercourse and childbirth that are exceedingly uncomfortable, but that, in the end, serve you well. A readiness to experience pain and even life-threatening danger affords an advantage to any woman who wants to live life to its fullest. I see the fact of your newly discovered and intensely feminine Real Phase Two Fantasy as a harbinger of happy, procreative days to come. I am correct in my key assumption about the Real Phase Two Fantasy, yes, Anna? Of it you have no memory?"

"None whatsoever, Papa."

"Excellent! Excellent! It is possible that there is more than repression at play here. In the normal course of life we forget much of what we know. And you may never have had this fantasy at all. No matter. Even if you didn't personally have this fantasy, you would still have it in your history, for it is undoubtedly the experience of a queenly lineage before you, all rumbling with their sisters as you rumbled with yours in an attempt to possess the horse-penised father's big love."

We had just arrived at a landmark moment in my analysis. Papa had always assumed that I accepted the proposition of inherited general tendencies. To some extent I did. Yes, I knew that Papa's ideas about the lust of sons for mothers and of daughters for fathers derived, at least in part, from Papa's experience with Oli. Still, for the most part I was willing to believe that Oli, like all of us, had fallen prey in some measure to overwhelming instinctual urges.

Now, however, Papa was asking me to accept, almost without blinking, the idea that virtually anything he wanted to say about me was irrefutable fact. I bridled at the very thought of allowing Papa to compose my past for his own purposes as whimsically as someone might compose a tune on a piano. At the same time, I knew that to resist Papa was risky. The antique figurines spilling from bookshelves, tabletops, and even inkpots were vivid reminders of the headless busts and burnt genitalia of the rug merchant. I truly feared the potential consequences of trying to get Papa to bargain.

Mind you, I am not the first analysand to whom Papa made outlandish suggestions followed up by an explanation that personal history and mathematically probable ancestral experience are infinitely swappable. Indeed, by the time of my analysis, the interchangeability of personal experience and archeological hokum was central to his theories. More to the point, Papa actually welcomed those occasions on which an analysand could not remember any given "memory" as ratification of the genius of his work.

Taking such liberties with truth had started in the years immediately leading up to the First World War, when Papa had treated the patient I had nicknamed "Wolf Man." Wolf Man's actual name was Sergei Pankeieff. He was a wealthy, handsome Russian aristocrat who was disabled by gonorrhea, which he had acquired at age seventeen from an obese and unwilling chambermaid. He traveled by coach with the aid of a personal physician and a valet who helped carry him, feed him, arrange things for him, and perform the bizarre rituals that an obsessive fear of animals compelled him to have performed.

One of Herr Pankeieff's presenting symptoms when he entered analysis was a continuing lust for women with large behinds, whom he hoped to take with force, *a tergo*, accompanied by the scintillating music of their screams. Together, Papa and Herr Pankeieff discerned what they believed to be one of the contributors to his unruly cravings. It was an early childhood of precocious sexual stimulation. Herr Pankeieff had specific memories of an older sister enticing him into erotic play. A nanny had warned him that such play would give him a penile wound. In terror, Herr Pankeieff had retreated with his prematurely awakened sexual feelings into sadistic masturbation fantasies and into the real-life torture of butterflies.

Working with Papa to divine other roots of his preoccupations and problems, Herr Pankeieff recalled a dream. When he was four he had dreamed one night that his bedroom window had opened on its own to reveal six or seven wolves silently sitting on branches of a big tree.

"In great anxiety, evidently of being eaten by the wolves, I screamed and woke up," Herr Pankeieff explained, according to Papa's notes.

Within six months of having that early dream, Herr Pankeieff had developed the animal phobia that would, for years, compel him towards irrational acts and rituals. Meanwhile, young as he was, he grappled with attacks of ferocious urges to rape amply bottomed women.

Associating from the symbols of his wolf dream, Herr Pankeieff produced for Papa some memories that had lain unexplored for nineteen years of his twenty-three. He remembered illustrations from fairy tales, horrible drawings that his preposterously sexualized sister had shown him with cruel pleasure. He remembered frightening, morality-shorn stories, tales like *Little Red Riding Hood* and other fables in which terrifying wolves did awful things to little girls, little boys, grandmothers, and grandfathers, and flocks of humbled sheep.

Papa noticed a pattern. Wolves. Violence. Victims. For all dreams and memories reported by Herr Pankeieff, Papa interpreted the fearsomeness of wolves as evidence of Herr Pankeieff's primitive fear of his own father. From this observation, Papa surmised that Herr Pankeieff held within him a deep, homosexual longing for his father. "Behind every strong fear is an intense, infantile wish," Papa always said.

When Herr Pankeieff related to Papa his dream of the silent wolves in the tree, he remarked at length about the stillness of the wolves. Papa at that time was particularly fond of a new rule of thumb:

When the dreamer is unable to tolerate a representation of what he fears most, he sometimes transposes what he fears into its more acceptable opposite.

The stillness of the wolves, for which Papa could find no interesting explanation, might be more productively examined if one saw it as its opposite, savagery. Where Herr Pankeieff related a tranquil scene, Papa imagined an agitated one in which Herr Pankeieff's father forcibly impaled his wife on his member.

If you read Papa's notes, you will see that in relating the Herr Pankeieff case, at this point he paused.

"I fear," he wrote, "that this is where my reader's trust will abandon me."

Papa was right about that. For this is where his interpretation of Herr Pankeieff's dream took fabulous flight. Herr Pankeieff and Papa's mutual rummaging for memories had produced not a single scene of any kind of parental sex, whether rough or tranquil. Still, Papa concluded solely from the silence of the wolves and the size of the womens' bottoms that Herr Pankeieff so ominously desired that, at age one-and-a-half, Herr Pankeieff had witnessed his parents have violent sex. He had watched his father rape his mother not once but three times, and at least one of these times *a tergo*. (It was a position that would have allowed Herr Pankeieff to get a good glimpse of both parents' genitals and of the extremities of his mother's amplitude.) Furthermore, Papa declared that the thrice-witnessed scene charred into Herr Pankeieff's mind images that, although they were never actually remembered, were also not forgotten.

I am not one to quarrel with the idea that traumatic memories can be buried. The "never remembered but never forgotten" part of Papa's summary of this case is specifically *not* the part with which I quarrel. It is the fact that, in the absence of memories to help him create a logical story *with* and *for* his analysand, Papa confabulated scenes, convinced his analysand of their truth, and recorded them for posterity as truth. He re-wrote someone else's psychic history.

Mind you, even Papa was not inclined to believe his interpretation in its entirety. It filled in too many leaky crevices by jumping to too many specific conclusions. Furthermore, the question of whether and how much to believe—of both his interpretations and of Herr Pankeieff's memories—Papa found "[N]ot really very important.... [S]cenes of observing parental intercourse, of being seduced in childhood, and of being threatened with castration, are undoubtedly inherited property, but they can just as well be an acquisition through personal experience."

A dangerous notion, but not as dangerous as what was about to come.

"It would also not surprise me, Anna, that, signaling as your newly discovered Real Phase Two Fantasy did an acceptance of your receptive female sexuality, that particular fantasy was accompanied by yet another fantasy—a fantasy of special reward. You took comfort and pleasure in imagining that after I beat you.... Ah, but let us stop for a moment. I want us to appreciate the full meaning together. Present tense. I am through beating you. I have beaten you oh-so-mercilessly but somehow gently enough. I cool you. I comfort and cool you with a strategically applied moist cloth. I weep to you. I rage to you with my face aflame, and you accept all of the power and thrust and attendant magnitude of emotion that is so apparent in me. And because of your gentle acceptance of my failings, I show you special kindness and admiration. I weep even more freely in your presence, perhaps, than I otherwise would. I show my jugular to you—quickly. As I do, I make my breathing stop. You are so kind as to not move or laugh or even touch. And then I give you a gift, perhaps. I give you a special pet name, something from Shakespeare or from the Greeks. "Cordelia," yes? I also give you something golden. Orbed, even. I favor you above all others with a golden orb, a ball that you can hold to your breast and toss, and that you promise to play with forever. Did you ever have such a fantasy, Anna?"

Well, how did he know? And whose fantasy had I inherited, anyway?

Chapter 21

In early 1920, I left analysis with Papa. My refusal to continue has been compared by some to the *feinshmeker*'s refusal. Let me be clear. My reasons for leaving were not the same as those of the wide-winking Ida Bauer. Ida left analysis willingly and determinedly. As bizarre as the particulars of my analysis had become, I left analysis reluctantly, the foot-dragging born from my realization that I had gained insight, wisdom, and even entertainment from my sessions with my father.

Indeed, I had found not only my own psychoanalysis, but also the psychoanalyses of many people in and beyond my social sphere, absolutely fascinating. Princesses and queens, movie directors and debutantes, scientists and literary giants, our family's accountant and my personal physician: I had heard from Papa about them all, and I knew them, really knew them, inside and out. So it was not general dissatisfaction with psychoanalysis that drove me from Papa's couch. Nor was it specific dissatisfaction with my analysis and its increasingly hairy overtones. It was the discovery that Papa played as fast and loose with my secrets as he did with everyone else's.

Given his unabashed history of casual betrayal, the question of why I supposed that Papa would keep the contents of my beating fantasies confidential remains open. Regardless, that is precisely the assumption that I made, perhaps because the very consulting room with its antiquities and its rituals of reclining and rising, shaking hands hello and goodbye, donning the foot rug and doffing it made much of what we did feel sacred. More likely, I suppose, my assumption of confidentiality was an artifact of analytic transference. No doubt drawn to Papa erotically throughout the period of my analysis, I somehow confused our analytic life with marital life. There we were, alone, together, six nights a week. Papa was mine, I was his, and pillow talk is private.

So you can imagine my shock when I appeared with Papa at a psychoanalytic congress at The Hague. I sat, as I usually did in those days, in the chair reserved for wives at the side of the podium. I must explain that I felt a touch more vulnerable than usual to begin with that day; at Papa's suggestion (and for the first time ever) I wore a modern-style dress that reached only four inches below my knees. Furthermore, I did not wear my usual buttoned boots and thick, dark stockings, but something called a "dress shoe," along with stockings that were almost entirely transparent. Once I was seated, Papa began to read from his newest work. The title itself should have been a giveaway: "A Child is Being Beaten."

He had told me he would be discussing ideas about masochism that he had developed in our sessions, but he had never really told me exactly what he was writing and what he would be reading. I sat in that very public chair beside the podium as Papa read and then spoke extemporaneously and took questions. Mine was not the only set of beating fantasies presented in the paper but mine was the lion's share of the clinical material. At least Papa declined to mention my name. He made it clear to his listeners that he did not hold out great hopes for the young woman primarily depicted in his paper. Her probability of ever achieving sexual normalcy was low.

An hour, maybe more, passed in this way.

A doctor tells a man in bed that he is dying. "Is there anyone you want to see?"

Patient, feebly: "Yes."

Doctor: "Tell me. Anyone."

Patient: "Another doctor."

"Anna! Anna! Yoo-hoo!"

I had not seen Doktor Call Me Otto Gross in eleven or twelve years. I had heard that in 1914, after the Free Otto! revolutionaries liberated him from the mental hospital, he had joined the Austro-Hungarian army as a physician. While in the army he had enjoyed a bottomless supply of morphine and had not by any means let the war stop his socio-sexual revolution. He required that all of the medics reporting to him have sexual relations with his lover, whose name was Mieze, at least once a day, as long as Mieze was willing. Most, I am told, were more than happy to comply with the rule, as was Mieze.

Otto called out his "Yoo-hoo!" directly after Papa's question and answer session concluded. I don't suppose that anyone else at the congress that day even recognized Otto. If they had, I'm not sure they would have acknowledged him. His reputation had declined precipitously. His fame was now mostly as a Dionysian enemy of patriarchy. In Papa's psychoanalytical kingdom, that new stance bought him no favors.

Outcast, broke, downright silly at times, and periodically so afraid of his father's henchmen that he would starve himself rather than sit at a respectable table and eat a good meal, he looked fowl and wonky. His eyes were bulging. His teeth were decaying.

"How have you been, Doktor Gross? You look wonderful," I lied, taking the hand that he offered.

"No I don't, dear, I look awful. I smell, too, worse than usual. But you know? In its own outré way, being psychotic is the most glamorous thing a person can do."

He took my hand with much the same tenderness that he had once shown when taking the hand of Papa's analysand Herr Lanzer. Then he began to walk away with me, heading for the door and pulling me helplessly along behind him like a toy train.

"Call me Otto, please, Anna," he called backwards over his shoulder. "We simply must talk. Care to buy me coffee and a snack?"

Papa was surrounded by well-wishers and members of the press. I had only to tell him a quick, "I'll meet you later at the hotel," and Otto and I were off walking the streets, looking for a coffeehouse where we could sit and visit.

Many people have an idealized picture of true friendship. They say things like, "He knows me so well. I don't even have to explain to him what I'm thinking," and, to some extent, those words reflect reality. But when I was a child and adolescent, Otto had not known me very well. And after the evening of Herr Lanzer's visit to the Wednesday Psychological Society, he and I had slipped out of each other's sight. Still, "knows just what I'm thinking" does describe what transpired between us on the day that Papa debuted "A Child is Being Beaten." Watching me watch Papa on the podium, Call Me Otto had guessed that I was the fly *du jour* under Papa's glass, and that I was deeply ashamed about the disclosure and about my lustful inner self.

We sat at a table. Otto munched and sipped and gently held and squeezed my hand. I stared down at the table and slowly but surely tears began to fall, not in torrents but one every so often and then another. Like any good friend Otto said nothing, just continued the squeeze. I don't know how long we sat that way.

"What is the matter, Princess? Tell me, how I can be of service?" Otto asked froggily.

"I beg your pardon?" I said.

"I am not sure how I can help, Anna, but I know that I would like to."

He munched and sipped some more. He asked me about my childhood. I told him much of what I already mentioned at the start of my account here—about getting lost in the woods when I was little and being retrieved by Mama just as the weather was getting cold and the woods were turning dark, about my early fascination with the people in my father's waiting room, about the mushroom hunts of my childhood, about Mama and her sadness, about Oliver and his.

Very gradually and gently—we must have sat at the table for well over three hours—Otto began to suggest alternative interpretations of the beating fantasies about which I felt such deep shame.

"A child raised in a house with a joyless mother can herself feel joyless and dead. From the perspective of a child who feels dead, even the excitement of humiliation may be of potential appeal." That was one interpretation, and it sounded good.

"In a family that witnessed the demise of your brother, Oliver—a family whose children were fed early on luscious days of mushroom hunting and jelly cookies but who eventually existed on a starvation diet devoid of song and spirituality and Hebrew and Yiddish—pleasure can seem like a precious commodity. 'Whatever pleasure I take will be missed by you, my sibling.' In a family like this, developmentally normal sexual pleasures are snatched privately, greedily, guiltily. When guilt is folded into whatever fantasy elicits the pleasure, punishment may occupy a place of prominence in the plot." That was another way that Otto tried to get me to see things. It, too, seemed a perfectly sensible one.

"A reasonable interpretation, Anna, of your father's analysis of you and his focus on your solitary carnal pleasures is that it was itself a sexual beating of sorts. It was a drama in which your father was wonderfully free to flirt with what we *goyem* call venial transgressions, but at the same time was restrained from coming close to what even he knew would be mortal sin."

I cried silently some more. "Thank you, Otto. But really, I would be most grateful if you could just tell me how to stop being a pervert."

Leaning forward with happy assurance, Otto whispered confidently, "Ah, but as you've probably guessed by now, my definition of perversity is different from your father's. By my definition, my dear, you are no pervert—though I couldn't say the same thing about Sigmund Freud."

I don't know what came over me at this point. Maybe it was the proximity of his filthy hair, which seemed as likely as not to have been infested by bugs. In any event, I felt newly, vaguely, repulsed by Otto. As a daughter, I also felt defensive on Papa's behalf.

There must have been a slight challenge in my voice when I asked my kind friend, "Well, pray tell me then. What is perversity, Otto?"

Otto checked over his shoulder (for his father's henchmen?) and confided, "Perversity is whatever arouses curiosity but discourages understanding."

"My father is not a pervert!" I countered loudly. Too quickly, too melodramatically.

People were looking, which Otto didn't like. Grabbing for his assorted smelly things, he stood up to leave the coffeehouse.

"Otto, stop it," I urged in a stage whisper. "Sit down!"

By this point he was almost at the door. I followed, hot on his trail. "Otto! I think I am entitled to an apology. So is my father."

Otto was apparently nonplussed by the idea. I took the opportunity provided by his bafflement to return to the table and leave money for the food and service. Otto followed me.

"Why ever would your father be entitled to an apology?" Otto asked, palming the tip.

"You exasperate me to no end! Otto, you of all people have no right to pronounce about perversity!" At this Otto looked offended, so I added, "Well, of course, really, I mean, what right has anyone to pronounce about perversity? The very idea of anyone imposing egocentric values on the habits and preferences of another person is potty!"

And then Otto was all smiles. "My point exactly, Anna," he said. Impulsively, and in parting, he gave me a huge hug, leaving on the front of my dress a vague hint of his grimy form. "Love to all!" he called out.

He attempted to exit through the swinging kitchen door. A moment later, a waiter shoved him right back into the dining room. The diners who saw his re-entry laughed. A few pointed. He accepted the unwelcome attention nobly.

"Whatever happens, Anna, and much will," he said a moment later as, making his way to the front of the coffeehouse, he stopped at an unbussed table to stuff scraps of food into his pockets, "I want you to abide by a promise you are about to make to me."

"What is that promise, Otto?" I asked, suddenly worried about him in his poverty and illness, and wanting very much to open my purse, heart, and home to him.

"That you will not let them do to you what they've done to me. Say it."

Now it was my turn to be nonplussed. He apparently didn't want the kind of help I'd been eager to pledge. Yet I could not imagine myself ever becoming a penniless, marginally oriented, winsomely gracious vagrant. So why must I repeat such a promise? Still, I obliged him.

"I will not let them do to me what they have done to you."

Satisfied by my obedience, sated with coffee and empty calories, and dribbling vanilla cream from a sleeve, Otto rushed out of the café and disappeared into the crowd on the street.

When I told Papa I would no longer meet with him nightly, he cried.

I remember sitting up on the couch for the last time when I heard the weeping begin. I was tempted to hold him in my arms and retract everything I had just said. Regardless, with due deliberation and a great deal of *savoir-faire*, I removed the small rug from my feet and legs.

He remained in his chair as I walked to the door and opened it. "We have tunneled very deeply," was what he blubbered from across the room.

As I closed the door behind me I heard Papa blow his nose.

Danger. Danger. How is it that we can be so thoroughly taken with someone? How is it that we are both transformed and confident while love proceeds apace and both sniveling and ugly when love leaves?

I was deeply afraid. Where would I go when I walked out of the waiting room door? What on earth would I do?

What would Papa do?

I thought back to the years in which I had sat so happily on the Persian rugs in Papa's waiting room, guarding his consulting room door. I remembered the frog prince from my re-written fairy tale. He did not have love but he did have the courage and dignity it took to raise his little rump and hop into the water all by himself. He swam down the creek to the river and down the river to the sea and what the salty sea eventually did to his green skin no one but him ever knew.

But you know? Maybe the river and the sea were better off for his lonely visit. Maybe the frog prince was better off, too.

Maybe Papa and I would be all right.

That night I had a dream.

> *"'A history forged of disaster' is how we refer to our land," the rug merchant warns me. We wander together through lava-encrusted landscapes, stepping over as we do the disembodied heads of Roman statues toppled only the day before by a seismic jolt. "From the beginning of time our land has sometimes come completely alive with seismic shaking. The sea turns a familiar red. Schools of wiggly fish leap into the air. And as jaggedly as a ship sailing into a difficult wind, the earth cracks open and welcomes into its caverns entire villages of fleeing children."*
>
> *The rug merchant and I climb high on a lamppost to drink our grape juice from tulip-shaped cups. As the cup comes to my lips, I hear the muezzin call. I survey from our privileged perch a scene of blackened bodies under carts, and swollen heads behind lampposts.*
>
> *The rug merchant climbs down, faces Mecca, and touches his forehead to the ground. He is the only thing on the vast landscape that is alive.*
>
> *But then I hear a mother weep.*
>
> *"Weeping Mother, please, tell me where you are! Tell me how I may help!" I call from on high.*
>
> *She walks out from behind a statue of the moon goddess. She answers me in a language for which I do not have words. Still, I know that the day before, her daughter ran with*

friends away from the village and through cobalt and ochre tunnels during the chaos and the trembling. I somehow know that the mother has wept all night for her daughter. Now that the day is new, she has started a search—not for her daughter but for a trace of her daughter. She hopes to find, perhaps, a piece of her daughter's white veil, a relic of her chastity to have and to hold.

"Help me! Help me!" is what I know she cries.

I look to the rug merchant for permission to go. He pauses in his prayer just long enough to whisper, "No. No. Please don't go."

When I climb down to join the weeping mother, we hope to follow the children's footprints at the outskirts of town. There is no joy in our steps for we know that the best we can find is a talisman for the mother in her loss. As we come close to the seashore, though, the futility of even our despairing venture becomes clear.

We commence keening. We see that the blinding dust clouds that rose from the collapsing village the day before and swept grandly towards the shore erased the children's footsteps from the sand, and with them, the last earthly traces of innocence and glee.

The mother turns to me. My ears are so filled with the sound of my own terror that I cannot hear the words she slowly utters. I can see her mouth move, though, and I can read her lips.

"They are dead," her lips say in her language, "but thank Allah they are safe."

Somehow, from somewhere, I hear laughter.

Chapter 22

People who share their lives with analysands sometimes prefer the pre-analysis neurotic to the post-analysis one. Pre-analysis neurotics are good losers. They are selfless, inhibited, and undemanding; they make especially good wives and daughters.

Post-analysis neurotics, on the other hand, lose their endearing self-effacement. They feel and act from self-love and self-respect, not from passive fear. The desire and relief that the post-analysis neurotic's newfound strength arouses in family members and friends is often matched by envy, which is ugly.

When I left analysis, Papa was saddened. He was also desirous of me, or so I thought. Perhaps it's just that transference clouded my view of him. He was envious; of that I am sure. It was ugly.

In 1920, the year in which I discontinued analysis with Papa, Sophie died. It happened in late January, only days after my analysis ended.

I had just returned to our family apartment after a day of teaching. Papa's envious eyes were on me as I reached for the ringing phone.

She had died of influenza, was all that her husband Max could communicate across the crackling long-distance lines.

The epidemic of Spanish Influenza had started in 1918, and it ended the war. When men on the battlefield die before bullets even reach them, it is time for everyone to go home. Except that they shouldn't go home.

Returning soldiers brought Spanish Influenza with them. The worst epidemic since the Bubonic Plague, during the winters of 1918 and 1919 it killed twenty to forty million people in Europe, or roughly five to ten percent of the population. Then it abruptly tapered—lingering, though, just enough to kill a few people the winter after.

Sophie and Max had been living in Hamburg. Telephones lines were terribly fallible in the first years after the war, so it is as likely as not that a call for help from Max would not have gotten through. But he hadn't even had time to make such a call.

Usually influenza kills by filling the lungs with fluid. It is a process that takes a few days at least, maybe a week. Spanish Influenza was different, though. Some say that it infected the brain sooner than it infected the lungs. Asymptomatic until almost the end, an apparently healthy person could die with only a few hours' warning.

Sophie was pregnant with her third child at the time.

My first thought at word of Sophie's death was not of her or the why's and how's of her death. It was not of her husband shouting his grief from Hamburg to Vienna. It was not of her two little boys and their anguish, or of my parents and theirs. It was not of a public health menace or of the need for better contagion control. My first thought was of me. Sophie had mostly hated me. I had responded in kind. How, though, would I carry on for a lifetime without her?

Some mothers teach their babies about family by intoning for them the names of all family members in a kind of lullaby. My mother did that for me. "Papa, Mama, Tante Minna, Mathilde, Oli, Martin, Ernst, Sophie, Anna. One, two, three, four, five, six, seven, eight, nine." Not surprisingly, I was a precocious counter. I could count on to nine before I had learned to stop at, say, two, three, or six.

I do not mean to skip lightly over my sister's death. From the moment I heard, life seemed to have a hole in it. But it was a numerical sort of missing that I felt for Sophie. It was not sorrow.

"I do not know," Papa wrote to a friend in late February, "whether cheerfulness will ever call on us again. My poor wife has been hit too hard."

We treated Mama with special kindness when Sophie died. We had long been used to her battles with resignation and sadness. With Oli mostly lost to her and Sophie dead, it seemed only natural that Mama would become more resigned and sad than ever and would need the gifts of our presence and love.

I remember distinctly, though, when the first turn for the worse came. It was only two days into the whole affair—the day of Sophie's cremation, which we missed because a train strike prohibited us from traveling to Hamburg. Mama moaned that bands of metal circling her skull were pinching her beyond her tolerance. During the rest of the week the sound of her voice inspired in all of us a feeling of dread.

Then a severe attack of grippe incapacitated her for several weeks, leaving her physically depleted, as well.

One afternoon, sensing that a calamity was about to happen, I knocked on Mama's bedroom door. Hearing no response, I opened it without permission. I discovered Mama in the midst of a curious act. In a surprisingly flimsy nightgown, she was separating her voluminous cache of engagement correspondence with Papa into "his" and "hers" piles, and tossing all of the "hers" letters in great, glorious arcs into the fireplace. I called to Tante Minna for help. She and I tried to dissuade Mama. Up until then, we hadn't even known that the letters had survived the period of her engagement. We wanted her to save them for posterity.

Mama explained that the time had come to quit the business of womanhood.

She was able to answer whatever questions Tante Minna asked her, and that fact diminished my apprehension. With her artfully tossed letters to Papa creating a roaring fire, she took to her bed, where I was pleased to see her remain warmly, safely, and indeed even a bit contentedly, until late April.

Alas. How can a woman who is not herself kill herself?

Our apartment one floor up from ground level at Bergasse 19 was Mama's place. It was a world of draperies and cautious choices. Papa was an intellectual bull charging through the china shop of staid thought, but nowhere in our apartment's orderly plenitude was there a piece of art or furniture that could not be called Perfectly Hapsburgian. Bizarre figurines were reserved for Papa's suite of rooms. The family apartment had the trappings of pre-War Viennese domesticity. The things that Mama had chosen in the good old days were genteel and plush, and appreciating them did not require deep thought.

However, the life of prescribed ideas and rectitude was precisely what Mama tried to flee one morning when the maid carried the milk towards the building from the curb only to be greeted by Mama's body rushing past her face.

Mama had on the same nightgown she had worn when she burned her letters to Papa. She told me later that she wore that flimsy gown as a badge of honor, perfect for the moment she would hurl herself head first out the window and onto the stones below. Unaccountably, though, she actually exited the window feet first, and just after she did she changed her mind entirely about how she wanted the rest of her morning to go.

She was able to cling to the windowsill for a few minutes, but she did so with her characteristic silence. With no cry for help there was no rescue. When she finally let go of the sill, she managed to twist her body enough so that, upon hitting the ground one very tall story below, she missed the stone walkway and struck a small patch of garden. She remained upright. She was proud of that, she told me later. Because her heels dug deeply into the soft dirt and her knees locked in place, Mama's posture remained completely matronly and correct, though later the maid remembered seeing Mama's nightgown fluttering in the breeze, covering her modesty only about as well as a spider's web might have.

Mama crushed her heel bones as well as most of the small bones in the arches of her feet. Her feet would heal but she would never again easily bend those knees. She gave her spinal cord a shock from which it, too, never quite recovered.

Still, it was only the starchly-aproned maid who lost consciousness. Of that Mama was forever proud.

The next year I spent my workdays teaching penmanship, English, French, arithmetic, and hygiene to secondary school students. Then, every day from late afternoon on, I baled chicken soup to Mama. Sitting exhausted in the chair by her bed, I served with the soup crackers and conversation.

"Tell me anything you would like to tell me," I would prompt. "Say the first thing that comes to your mind as soon as it comes to mind."

"Like what, dear?" Mama would ask me cheerfully.

"For example, how do you feel today? What did you dream last night?"

Apparently, during much of her thirty-four years of marriage, no one had ever asked Mama a personal question. I may have been talking like a psychoanalyst, but I was also speaking the language of friendly intimacy. Mama behaved as though she had never heard it before.

She did answer my questions. And she had plenty to say, though she occasionally asked me if I was sure I wasn't bored with all my listening. I know that I made a difference. I saw it in her face right away. Indeed, the maid told me that the very sound of my footsteps seemed to inspire in Mama a state of anticipatory wonder.

Martin, Oli, and Ernst, all now married and living as far from Vienna as they could manage, sent cards daily. Mathilde visited every afternoon while I taught. She plumped Mama's pillows and helped her bathe. Tante Minna was really too old for that kind of labor. She was fifty-five, and Mama was fifty-nine.

Each afternoon, my sixty-four year-old Papa retired to his study only moments after I entered the apartment. The one time I dared to knock on his door and ask if he needed anything, "…anything at all, even if it is just to sit and talk for a moment?" he sat behind his big desk and issued a rather strange statement, as if he had long prepared for such a moment.

"I am not necessarily the sole author of your little melodrama, Anna, though I can see that you regard me as its primary villain. Unfortunately, it is never the aim of an analysis like yours to create conviction. Our discussions were only intended to bring the repressed complexes into consciousness, to set the conflict going in the field of conscious mental activity, and to facilitate the emergence of fresh material from the unconscious. I think you will agree with me that is precisely what we did."

He did not look me in the eye as he spoke.

I was unable really to follow the logic of Papa's statement. I was not sure how what he said had anything to do with my question of whether he needed anything, anything at all, even just to talk. I said so.

"I see," said Papa. "Then I will continue to mourn the loss of my dearest daughter, Sophie, and to find consolation solely in my work."

Which he did for four long years.

Papa mourned Sophie's death intensely, shutting me out emotionally during all four of those years. I am at a loss to identify for certain which of these two events—Sophie's death or my abandonment of his couch—contributed more to his grief. But my refusal of further analysis—and his feelings about that refusal—did seem to color much of what he taught and wrote.

Papa's work during those years was an expansion of his early theory on penis envy.

He had first mentioned the theory in 1905, in *Three Essays on the Theory of Sexuality*. In introducing the concept, he had not sounded terribly pejorative. He had said that little boys assume that everyone has a penis. When presented with evidence to the contrary, they deny the absence that they behold. Little girls, on the other hand, immediately recognize that a boy's genital is bigger than theirs, and they want one more like the one a boy has. Penis envy as described in 1905 was much like the envy that any child with a small scooter might have for another child with a large tricycle. Size matters.

During the years immediately after Sophie's death, Papa elaborated on his early penis envy formulation. He proposed that the moment at which a girl first discovers her lack of a penis is a moment of calamitous shock. No later normal developmental event produces such ineradicable psychic change, for from that instant on, the girl will want a penis. Soon enough, of course, she will realize that she can never grow one. Hoping, then, for second best, she will begin to desire her father's.

Of course, according to Papa, humans inherit from the seminal human horde the knowledge that incest is taboo. For this reason, any girl's desire for her father's penis will be wrapped in shame and eventually sublimated to become a desire for a child, which is a worthy penis substitute. To fulfill her obsession to have children throughout her childbearing years, she will need to secure and retain a man.

One may reasonably wonder where either Sophie or I fit into this labyrinth and how I may have come to imagine that the loss of me from his psychoanalytic couch might have outweighed in Papa's heart the death of his "dearest daughter, Sophie." The clues lie in what Papa said about how penis envy causes moral unreliability in girls.

It all has to do with the castration complex. Papa suggested that, descended as we all are from a horde governed by a beastly father, any little boy inevitably worries that punishment from his father may go dangerously beyond a slap on the bottom. Specifically, a boy fears that his father will actually chop off his son's penis in anger. Fear of castration, then, is what helps a boy form moral virtue. A penis is so precious and the fear of its loss so complete that, once a boy acquires moral virtue, he does not easily forget or misplace it.

A girl, however, never has a real penis to lose, and therefore has no good incentive to develop moral virtue. Whatever virtuous behavior she manages to exhibit derives from her incessant crusade to catch and keep the man who can provide her with cute and cuddly penis substitutes. A woman lies, cheats, steals, and pretends to be good, all in her quest to be loved, invaded, and impregnated. She is essentially and forever untrustworthy.

"But can't you see, Anna?" Call Me Otto asked me excitedly. "Can't you see that your father had to rationalize your abandonment of his psychoanalytic couch? Can't you see that he saw your rejection of him as a sexual rejection and a terrifying indication that you and possibly all women prefer your men younger and more virile than he was? My God, if he was sixty-four years old he was probably losing some of his sexual powers. Talk about a castration complex! And can't you see that the great Herr Professor Sigmund Freud blamed you for the fact that we really do seem to be governed by the taboo against incest? Even though he respected you for adhering as closely as you could to both the letter and spirit of that law, your absence from his couch was a terrible, narcissistic blow. Does it not make ready sense to you that he soothed the wound you caused by assigning to all women the moral virulence that he self-defensively assigned to you?"

Good questions, all. However, it was not really Otto who asked them of me. Otto died just a few days after he watched me sit through my father's public presentation of my beating fantasies, and after he talked with me compassionately while I cried.

Forgive me if I introduce the idea of Otto's demise a bit too casually—and this after sounding so detached about Sophie's death. Let me honor Otto by saying that his passing was a loss that, to this day, I have not comfortably absorbed. Otto was found dead in an abandoned warehouse of causes that the coroner could only tag "entirely mysterious." Coming as his end did just days after he had tried to help me appreciate some of the perfectly permissible in what many might call deviant about me, the mystery surrounding his last moments drove a cold stake of fear into my heart. I had always suspected that moneyed members of the European middle class were not prepared to tolerate flagrant and popular bohemians like Otto, or even chipper little masturbators like me.

And, indeed, I have always suspected Otto's father and his henchmen as the culprits in Otto's mysterious demise. Who else but a world-class criminologist and forensic pathologist would have been in a position to so thoroughly baffle Vienna's coroner? Who else would have had the motivation, except for the man whose son had consistently and inventively diminished the stature of a treasured family name?

I was not alone in my suspicion. As Papa said on the night he saw notice of Otto's death printed in the newspaper alongside a tally of international soccer scores, "That's King Laius one, Oedipus nothing."

Papa believed that, as children grow, they internalize the perspectives and wisdom of their parents. I know that I did. Still, I seem to have internalized Otto's, as well. Otto's final gift to me was a set of moral biases that I would carry forward through adulthood despite the fact that his corporal self was unavailable to guide me through the remaining crises of my life.

So the questions about my father's unconscious motivations in elaborating his theories about penis envy and the castration complex were, in fact, questions that I asked myself in the privacy of my room. I believe that, in 1920, Papa felt that he had lost two of his daughters forever. He blamed me for my departure and maybe for Sophie's, as well.

Papa called the psychological mechanism in which we assign to someone else ideas and feelings that we believe would be unacceptable in ourselves "projection." I think that Papa was right about projection. I think he felt guilty about having once withdrawn his love from selfish Sophie and given it instead to me. Holding "Sophie" and "blame" so proximate in his heart, he blamed himself as he mourned her death. In psychological self-defense, he projected the blame onto me.

That's all right. The tendency to project is nearly unstoppable. I project onto dear, departed Otto all of the time. To this day I count on Otto to raise whatever kind of personal Cain I need.

Part 5

Beating Fantasies and Daydreams

(1920-1925)

Chapter 23

It was in the four years after Sophie's death, those years in which Papa was most creatively expressive about his disappointment with me, that I became an analyst. Here is the story of that.

Siegfried Bernfeld was the young man who, in 1914, had founded Bernfeld's Joint American Distribution Committee—the organization with which I had volunteered during the war. By 1922, Siegfried was a bit of a celebrity among young Jewish intellectuals in Vienna. Photographs made him look woebegone, but I can guarantee that there was nothing hesitant or dismal about him. He was animated and droll and, when he spoke publicly, a crowd pleaser. He was also a secular Zionist and socialist and a leader of Vienna's post-war Youth Movement.

Siegfried was interested in psychoanalysis. Beginning in about 1920, he occasionally attended meetings of the Wednesday Psychological Society. Papa, deep in mourning for both Sophie and me, was gladdened by Siegfried's interest, for he saw Siegfried's engagement with the Society as a chance to bring psychoanalysis out of private consulting rooms and into social welfare institutions.

By 1922, I had developed a sort of silent crush on Siegfried. I was smitten with the carefree elegance of his manner, with his endurance, and with the apparent depth and breadth of his heart. Four years after war's end, Siegfried was still tirelessly distributing and re-distributing displaced children. Most of them he hoped to one day redistribute to Palestine, where they could live free of anti-Semitism.

In the meanwhile, Siegfried had founded the Kinderheim Baumgarten, a home in Vienna for 300 Polish war orphans. Some were handicapped; all were traumatized. He could call every one of them by name and make each one laugh.

Still unnerved by my war-time experience of unloading freshly orphaned children like produce from trucks, I volunteered at the Kinderheim Baumgarten, leading after-school play groups. Truthfully, the fact that I secretly fancied Siegfried was not part of my motivation in volunteering, for I could not have pursued a man in any meaningful way. I remained too shaken by the exposure I'd felt when, all dressed up and on display, I'd heard Papa read "A Child is Being Beaten." I even recall feeling particularly upset one afternoon when I realized that Siegfried was watching me with the children. Indeed, he watched for a few afternoons in a row, and his notice was so disconcerting that I considered resigning my volunteer position.

Of little children, of course, I was not shy. I still had the old flair for running and shouting with the best of them, and that's what I did during those several afternoons that I knew I was being observed. By plunging myself into hilarity and solidarity with my "siblings," I was able to shut out almost completely my awareness of Siegfried's observing eyes. At the very end of the last afternoon that Siegfried watched me, as I was saying goodbye to my gang and blowing my own chapped nose, he asked to walk me home. I was relieved when a handsome young woman appeared almost out of nowhere to join us. She was his girlfriend. Without her confident presence I doubt that I could have withstood the intensity of his.

As we walked, Siegfried told me how impressed he was with my manner with children, and he asked that I play privately, daily, with three of the most clearly troubled orphans.

He also asked that I psychoanalyze them.

My throat seized up at the very thought, but my vocal chords worked better than I feared they would. I was able to express to him my willingness to spend special time with any child of his choosing. But I begged off analyzing them, explaining that I had no psychoanalytic training. Though I didn't tell him this, I was unable to imagine that psychoanalysis of the sort that I had endured would be helpful to any child.

So, six days a week during the evenings, I met with each of the three children individually for an hour. We played. When we played, we of course talked, and when we talked I couldn't help but ask open-ended questions and see deeper meaning in the little things a child said and did. Which is to say that, each and every one of those evenings, I found myself sliding down a slippery slope towards analyzing children. The progression from private play to psychoanalysis is one that I suspect Siegfried knew would happen.

Whenever I wondered at the legitimacy of my work with these children, I assured myself that no one who practiced psychoanalysis at the time had formal training. One simply read psychoanalytic literature, which I had done since puberty. One attended meetings of the Wednesday Psychological Society, which I had also done, albeit spottily, since puberty. And finally, one was analyzed by Sigmund Freud—and that I had certainly done. Then one started analyzing others.

For a brief while during 1922, I also undertook what was known in those days as a "training analysis" with Papa. It was not really an analysis at all, but a series of scheduled question-and-answer sessions between Papa and me. For the most part, I asked him about psychoanalytic theory; he answered me graciously but guardedly. Also, when I became stumped by aspects of a specific case I was handling, I sometimes asked Papa for his professional opinion.

Today the term "supervision sessions" might be used rather than "training analysis." Anyway, this series of sessions increased my confidence in my knowledge. It also afforded Papa and me a way to pretend that matters between us were easy. As a result of these training analysis sessions, I felt sure enough about my psychoanalytic abilities to expand my patient load. I even began analyzing a few children of the analysts in the Wednesday Psychological Society. That income along with some translation work I took on allowed me to resign my teaching post at the secondary school for bored and boring girls.

By 1922, the Wednesday Psychological Society had evolved beyond the backwater organization it once had been. Its name had been changed to "The Wednesday Night Meeting of the Vienna Psychoanalytical Society, a branch of the International Psychoanalytic Association." The IPA had members throughout Europe, America, and Asia. They met at periodic congresses that were generally held in Eastern Europe and that drew impressive press attention. While the guiding light of the IPA was always Papa, it did have presidents who directed the organization. In 1922, the president was none other than Doctor Ernest Jones—still (thank goodness) residing in England.

Even though the IPA was international, Vienna remained the center of the psychoanalytic movement. Indeed, the best minds in psychology, medicine, and even literature and art made a point of regularly traveling all the way to Vienna to attend and present at Wednesday night meetings. Regular attendees included Sandor Ferenczi (who believed that hysterical women reporting sexual abuse in their pasts were telling the truth), Otto Rank (applying psychoanalytic theory to the study of legend, myth, creativity, and art), Helene Deutsch (theorizing about female sexuality), Karl Abraham (collaborating with Papa on the study of melancholia), Sabina Spielrein (Fraülein Spielrein had long before disentangled herself from Doktor Jung, gone to medical school, and become a psychiatrist known for her interest in masochism and the death instinct), Hugo Heller (Papa's publisher), and Lou Andreas-Salomé (a poet and novelist who had been the consort of Nietzsche, Rilke, Turgenieff, Tolstoy, Strindberg, and Rodin). This is just a sampling. Virtually everyone associated with Vienna's meetings was a luminary of some sort.

One consequence of the increasing caliber of the discussions and discussants was that attendance at Wednesday meetings was no longer open to just anyone. One applied for provisional admission to the Vienna Psychoanalytical Society of the IPA, and one was elected to membership on the basis of recommendations as well as on the merit of an original paper.

I had never been a fixture at Society meetings, but I had certainly been an occasional presence, pouring cognac and hanging coats whenever Papa had a large crowd. Now that I was psychoanalyzing children, however, I dearly wanted to regularly attend. Yet I knew that if I did, I could no longer get away with behaving like a servant. I would need to formally apply for membership, and to present a case study of my own.

This presented me with a dilemma. Only two years before, I had been wounded by Papa's public disclosure of my secrets. I knew that I could not begin my career as an analyst by similarly betraying the trust of the children I helped. Whose case study, then, would I present?

My qualifying paper was called "Beating Fantasies and Daydreams." It was an analysis of my own beating fantasies, though I certainly didn't present it as such. Rather, I described a "little girl"—and it was years before anyone dared speak aloud the thought that surely crossed everyone's mind that night. The patient to whom I ascribed the beating fantasies and daydreams was suspiciously similar to the primary little girl described by Papa in "A Child is Being Beaten." Surely we were talking about the same child, for the ages and clinical descriptions and even the masochistic fantasies of the two patients were the same. Yet we could not have analyzed the same child, for when Papa presented his paper I had yet to begin analyzing children. The most likely explanation for the similarities was the real one; my paper was a presentation of my self-analysis, and Papa's paper was a presentation of his psychoanalysis of me.

Analysis, Papa had often lectured, is a fundamentally erotic relationship laden with transference and countertransference. For this reason, analysts must never psychoanalyze a family member.

Presentations of papers at Wednesday meetings were generally followed by spirited discussions of the paper's contents. I received only a few polite questions. All questions were vague and just a hair off-topic. No one asked the obvious, "Just who is the little girl about whom both you and your father have written?" I can only imagine that the august members of the Vienna Psychoanalytical Society feared the shattering real-world repercussions of what my answer to such a question might be.

Perhaps to err is human; perhaps it is just a Freud family trait. I failed to anticipate that the idea of Papa psychoanalyzing me would spark gossip among his colleagues.

Papa made mistakes, too, but not always. For example, he seems to have been right in 1920 when, in presenting "A Child is Being Beaten," he said that my probability for ever achieving sexual normalcy was low. But of course that depends on how one defines "normal."

And as right as he may have been on that one point, he erred regarding another matter related to me.

Papa believed that fathers are to blame when daughters fail to fulfill their heterosexual promise and instead form passionate relationships with other women. According to Papa, a blame-worthy father allows something to go awry during his daughter's Oedipal phase of development. To be specific, the temperature of his love for her during that critical period runs either too hot or too cold; as a result, she does not feel "safe" (a significant word in my dreams) forming a healthy, lusty bond with him. This means that she cannot later transfer her father-directed desire onto a man she might reasonably marry. Wallowing throughout her Oedipal years in childish, mother-directed love, she later mates with women.

To a small extent that baroque theory matched my reality. Arguably, my father's love for me had once run too hot. But I know that a far stronger force overrode the influence of that paltry one in pushing me into homosexuality.

That stronger force was Eva Rosenfeld. My attraction to my first inamorata had absolutely nothing to do with my father and nearly everything to do with my sister.

Chapter 24

Eva was my Sophie substitute, and a new, improved version, to boot. Like Sophie, Eva was gorgeous. She was *zaftig* and raven-haired, just as Sophie had been. Eva was also giggly as Sophie had been, but she was delightfully less so. She knew when to stop laughing. And Eva was smart, where Sophie had not been just naturally stupid; she had cultivated it.

"Growing is for vegetables" was a motto Sophie embroidered as a teenager onto a pillowslip that she used on her bed. She never quite explained what she meant by "growth," but I have to imagine that she had both "increased intellectual understanding" and "expansion of useful self-knowledge" in mind. For while I read and studied and looked inward, Sophie primped and preened and gazed into her gilded mirror. I never once saw pretty Sophie and a good book or challenging conversation so much as glance at each other from across a room.

Eva, on the other hand, read and talked. She looked inward, as did I, but she also ran forward in life, full speed ahead. Married to her wealthy cousin Valti, who had since given himself over to bitter jokes and self-pitying shrugs, Eva remained happy and resplendent. She was proud of her house, her intellect, her few extra kilos of flesh, her garden, and her mothering.

Especially her mothering. Eva had been a mother ever since she was a child.

Eva's family had lived in Berlin. The grown men were theatrical impresarios, and life with them was as lively as any vaudeville routine they produced. Eva's father and his brothers weren't well educated and they weren't particularly well informed. They were, however, happy. Drunkenly and cacophonously they argued with each other every Sunday at a big, extended-family dinner. They bumped heads about art, philosophy, and politics, and at least twice they quarreled so boisterously that the police had to be called.

But one Sunday her father died at the dinner table. He went mid-sentence, right in front of everybody. With his death, his wife withdrew into a lifetime of mourning, his brothers drifted off into new business ventures, and his three teenage sons became irretrievable drunks. From before her menarche Eva tried to keep the family together, but by the time she was sixteen she had given up on all of them. She began living as a full-time volunteer at Zellerhaus, a depressingly seedy orphanage for young girls.

Eva fully intended to devote her entire life to mothering uprooted girls. But upon becoming a woman, she fell in love with Valti. Together they moved to Vienna. He worked as a lawyer and they started a family of their own. They had a daughter and, too briefly, two little boys who died within a day of each other in Vienna's 1918 dysentery epidemic.

At which point Eva, in her despair, reinvented Zellerhaus on a much smaller scale and without the squalor. She opened the two tragically emptied bedrooms in her rambling, comfortably furnished home to girls in need. Each girl was a war orphan, brought to Eva by her friend Siegfried Bernfeld.

It was through Siegfried that I met Eva. One of my analysands was a girl named Minna. She was a boy-crazy liar and thief. Six hours of analysis from me a week was never going to be enough to give her the re-start in life that she needed. She needed more than clinical care. She needed a home.

In their most strictly Freudian interpretations, transference and countertransference in psychoanalysis are about sex. But when the analyst is an unmarried woman and the analysand is an orphan, transference and countertransference are surely also about mothering—the need to get it as well as the need to give it. I had already become Little Minna's surrogate mother, and I took those duties to heart. I worried about her. I sent her strudel on the days that I couldn't be with her. I nagged. I wanted her to become a doctor. I would gladly have provided Little Minna with the full-time mothering she needed, if circumstances had allowed.

But they did not. Mama was in frail health and needed peace and quiet at home. Tante Minna, in her old age, was easily frazzled.

Siegfried, therefore, arranged to "redistribute" Little Minna.

I accompanied Siegfried on the morning that he brought Little Minna to Eva. My intention was to make the transition easier for her. I had never met Eva, but considering all of the opulent possessions Eva no doubt had in her exquisite home (there actually were no opulent possessions and the home was far from precious), I wanted to do her the courtesy of warning her about Little Minna's thieving and dishonesty. Psychoanalysis had not yet remedied those problems.

More importantly, I hoped to secure from Eva permission to continue analyzing Little Minna.

I expected Eva to refuse this permission. I expected her to perceive a continuing emotional tie between Little Minna and me as ruinous to a potential emotional tie between Little Minna and her. In which eventuality, I would have to dutifully sever my relationship with my new-found dear heart, and hope that she would accept the loss of me as just one more grimy lump in an already boulder-strewn life.

I expected to write despairing poetry that night and for many nights to come.

I did not have to. Eva explained that afternoon, as she prepared supper in a large, yellow-tiled kitchen with her daughter Mädi and four foster daughters, that families are like balloons. They can stretch more impressively than one might ever imagine. They can also deflate without being destroyed, and that is especially important for everyone in a foster family to remember.

That afternoon I was struck by the unforced originality of the metaphor Eva had used. I wondered if it was typical of Eva's way of thinking. I could tell already that, in spite of her husband's money, Eva was inventive and found joy in being of service. I found joy in being of service, too, but Eva seemed to live with a lightness of being that I had yet to own. Impressed, I knew I wanted to learn from her. If I had been asked on that first afternoon to describe exactly the sort of relationship I wanted with Eva, I might have answered, "I want to *be* Eva."

I knew I couldn't be Eva. So I told her that I wanted to help her help Little Minna and all of her daughters. Was there a way I could be of service?

This was four years after war's end. Vienna was still mostly impoverished; few households had servants. Valti's income was large enough that Eva probably could have hired a maid, a gardener, and a cook. She realized, however, that the era of class divisions had probably passed forever. She certainly did not want to make her daughters used to archaic luxury. So, she told me that, yes, she did need an extra pair of adult hands around. When she welcomed my offer of help, she pulled me into her large, friendly body and gave me a hug.

So it was that the morning that Siegfried and I brought Little Minna to Eva, both Little Minna and I acquired a new family. Just as Eva became my substitute Sophie, I became her substitute Valti, for her husband was tired of marriage and was overly invested in his work. He was also a passionate patron of the arts. He had better things to do than come home, and I was more than happy to fill his shoes.

Because I was no longer teaching, I could arrange to analyze and play with my Kinderheim Baumgarten children during school hours. This meant that I could spend nearly every evening helping Eva indulge the girls with stabilizing childhood rituals. I fetched them from school late each afternoon and rode the streetcar to Eva's with them. Eva would have a wonderful dinner waiting for us, and, if the season were right, much of it would have been made with ingredients from her garden. The girls and I were expected to set the table, and we always made a point of making it look nice. After dinner, we formed a production line and washed and dried dishes. Then Eva and I helped the girls with their homework. Once all of a day's labors were done, we all ate cookies at the kitchen table and chatted in a style that Eva insisted be positive and mutually supportive. Then the girls washed up and changed into their nightgowns, finally joining Eva and me in the parlor for fairy tales. We all took turns reading the tales aloud, and I was proud to discover that I could tolerate even the scariest of stories.

All of the girls called Eva "Mama Eva." Even I did when I was with them. I was "Annafreud"—all one word. It's how I sign my name to this day.

Papa noticed that I was spending nearly all of my free time with Eva. And when Valti came home late from the opera or a gallery opening, he could see traces of the many ways Eva and I were creating a loving home for Mädi and the foster daughters.

Papa and Valti thought that Eva and I should be stopped.

"Stopped from doing what?" Eva wondered aloud one night as I put on my coat and kissed everyone goodnight.

We guessed that they didn't object to the haven we were giving the orphaned girls, or to the affection that we showered on Eva and Valti's own Mädi. It must have been something else they didn't like. We asked them what it was, though of course they wouldn't name it.

Certainly Eva and I couldn't name it, for in those months Eva's and my love was enlivening to everyone who cared to be touched by it. But it was also entirely chaste. We could have been wearing white veils the whole time for all the sin we mustered together. Like good sisters, I did not touch Eva sexually, and she did not touch me.

It must have been our happiness that peeved Papa and Valti. Having found such voluminous joy in each other, we ceased to be as prisoner-like as women sometimes are. We forgot to make the expressive groans and patient sighs of suffering that grease the wheels of family and community, and we taught our girls not to make such sounds either.

Chapter 25

Psychoanalysts think of fantasy as a force that organizes both internal and external experience.

They're right.

Several months after I met Eva, the year turned to 1925, which is about when I developed a non-sexual fantasy that I called the Phase Four Fantasy. In that fantasy Papa was not a Powerful Man. He was a shorter, frailer man who also happened to be forever incensed about one matter or another. He yelled at me at the top of his lungs for having humiliated him in front of his friends and colleagues. He blasted his ire with the same barbaric abandon that Eva's father and uncles had used on each other at Sunday dinners. The police were called. I yelled back at Papa, and the police were impressed by my spunk. Peace was somehow duly imposed on the two of us. Papa exuded meekness even though he didn't like being meek. In this fantasy, before our relationship had a chance to deteriorate again, Papa died mid-sentence one night at table.

All these years later I can see that I was still angry with Papa for having psychoanalyzed me, and that I was feeling guilty about having presented to his Vienna Psychoanalytical Society my "Beating Fantasies and Daydreams" paper in counterpoint to his "A Child is Being Beaten."

I couldn't, however, bring myself to express my anger and guilt. It wasn't that I was afraid of regressing to the intemperate version of myself that I had been in the months after my graduation from secondary school. It was more like I had developed something akin to Rat Man's omnipotent thoughts. I tamped down my negative feelings so that they wouldn't injure Papa. Hurting him was an intolerable thought, for of late he had seemed delicate. He truly appeared to be shrinking.

What I didn't know was that, almost two years prior, Papa had discovered a lump in his jaw similar to the one he had found during his wartime nicotine privations. He was anxious about what the lump portended. He knew that he was losing vigor, but he believed that, if he were to reveal the lump to his physician, he might be ordered to forego cigars. So Papa kept his lump a secret.

Eventually, the growth became too large to be ignored. At Papa's request, Eva and I took him to see Doktor Felix Deutsch. (He was the husband of Vienna Psychoanalytical Society member Helene Deutsch.)

"Be prepared," Papa told the doctor, "to see something that you don't like." Then, looking directly at Eva, he opened his mouth.

At first glance, the doctor knew that he was looking at cancer.

Doktor Deutsch was a compassionate man. Considering Papa's age and the losses our family had experienced in the not so distant past, Doktor Deutsch decided to be less than forthright with Papa, and with Eva and me, as well. He encouraged Papa to have the lump excised, but he said nothing of cancer.

Papa was relieved. Thinking that removal of a benign lump would be relatively minor surgery, he entrusted himself to the care of a rhinologist friend. Apparently, however, this rhinologist was no more competent surgically than the rhinologist Doktor Wilhelm Fliess had been in 1895 when he botched the operation on Emma Eckstein's nose. Papa bled heavily during the operation; the rhinologist stanched the bleed, bandaged Papa, and arranged a cot for him on the ward. Then, believing that all was well, the rhinologist went home.

Only an hour or so later, blood started to gush. No one was in attendance. The bell to summon help had no clangor. Papa's hospital mate, a friendly, mentally retarded dwarf, heaved himself up from his own recovery bed to run down the corridor screaming for help.

The dwarf saved Papa's life. Mama, Tante Minna, Eva, and I were summoned by a bevy of apologetic nurses. By the time we arrived at the hospital, all had been brought under control. Not only was Papa alive, he was sitting up and smiling.

Because technically no visitors were allowed on the ward during lunchtime, we were sent away. We came back after an hour only to find that, in our absence, Papa had bled disastrously again. Again no medical professional had been nearby. Still the bell had no clangor. The whole sequence of events played itself out again.

Except that this time Papa was not expected to survive. Once the bleeding was stopped I asked Eva to take Tante Minna and Mama home in a cab. The dwarf and I sat at Papa's bedside through the night, hand in hand. We drank black coffee to keep a steady vigil.

Papa did survive, but for months afterwards he needed tending. His bandage needed changing. His wound needed monitoring. His mouth needed draining. He needed someone to give him pain medication. He needed someone to talk to him about his fears and to reassure him.

"How are you feeling, my Papa? Is there anything that you need? Please. Tell me whatever you want as soon you want it." I said it all day long every day to poor, broken Papa.

The caretaking tasks were far too involved for Mama, whose own knees and spine were still not functioning properly and who had never learned to ask a verifiably intimate question. Tante Minna's lungs and heart had become weak as she aged. She couldn't have born the strain of constant watchfulness and worry.

That is when I became Papa's nursemaid around the clock, tending to him in ways that exceeded the care and feeding of his mouth and face. Papa was frail. He could not stand. He needed bedpans. He needed wiping, and he needed the cloths used to wipe him to be fresh and warm and for the wiper to be silent and respectful. He could not sleep in his bed alone, for he was afraid. He needed my altruistic surrender. Yes, in his bed.

Performing fundamental bodily tasks for another is an act of delicacy, intimacy, and love. It is no surprise that it brought Papa and me together, healing the hurts of several years.

When Papa was strong enough to walk we planned a celebratory trip to Rome for the autumn. The lump had been benign, or so we thought. It was gone. Hurrah.

Papa spent the summer eating and drinking and gathering the strength to travel. However, in spite of all of my patience and Papa's obedience, by the end of the summer Papa had more lumps to show Doktor Deutsch. Doktor Deutsch said that Papa required a second, even more radical excision, and possibly a refashioning of the entire jaw.

It was at this point that I began to suspect that Doktor Deutsch was protecting us all from an ill-favored truth. I decided to ferret out the true diagnosis by subterfuge.

I told him of our plans for a trip to Rome, and he encouraged me—"By all means!"—to take Papa before the operation.

"Suppose that we have an especially good time in Rome. Might we stay a while longer?"

"Absolutely not," was the doctor's quick reply. "Give your father the vacation of a lifetime this year in Rome. But above all, promise me you won't stay longer than expected."

The day that we returned from Rome I told Papa the truth.

In October Papa had not one operation but two. They left him unable to speak or eat. In late October he set his affairs in order.

In November he had a minor operation on his testicles to restore his fading sexual potency.

By December my fantasies had evolved to a Phase Five version. The characters were again the Powerful Man and the boy with blond curls, whose responsibility was to care for willows waving significantly in brooks. As usual, out of lack of attention to important details, the boy had somehow fouled the brook. He had enraged the Powerful Man. He had engendered an apparently irreconcilable antagonism.

As usual, in fantasy, I experienced the full excitement of the youth's fear and valor. No longer, however, did the scene proceed from transgression directly through wretchedness and then to orgasm. Rather, in my Phase Five fantasy, at the very moment that the Powerful Man could have chosen to become angry and beat the boy, he spouted pity and compassion. Bliss and harmony oozed from him like syrup. It stuck to everything. It gushed from the boy with blond curls, too.

Adrift in my fantasy each night, I didn't even need to masturbate to achieve a state of complete physical and emotional peace.

I wanted to tell Papa about this development in my fantasy life but I couldn't easily, for most of our time together was focused on meeting his dire needs. True, we talked about less pressured matters than medicines and prosthetics at breakfast, dinner, and supper, but at those times Mama and Tante Minna joined us.

I suppose that I could have asked to speak to Papa alone. Yet I believed that if I were to tell Papa casually about the changes in my fantasy life, I might re-awaken old wounds that my physical devotion to him had only recently begun to heal. For one thing, I would have to reveal that I had disobeyed him; I had failed to drop him from my fantasy life entirely, as instructed. Furthermore, any confiding about the forgiveness and compassion that now flowed reciprocally in fantasy might have constituted a too explicit acknowledgment that lingering conflicts needed to be resolved because his death had been foretold.

Still, I had concerns about the symbols in my fantasy. For example, what were the willows that the boy with blond curls had for so long protected? Were they tacit agreements between the Powerful Man and him, agreements that allowed the Powerful Man to be the only one who held the prerogative to choose between punishment and forgiveness? Would my disclosure of the change in status—the fact that I, the boy with blond curls, now apparently also held the power to forgive—be the sort of transgression that might pollute the very brook of tender understanding that at last ran between Papa and me? In other words, would an announcement that harmony now ruled mean that, forever after, only disharmony could?

I spent a few months caught up in such questions by day and sleeping deeply, heavily, dreamily beside my father at night after pleasuring myself solely with the ebullience of my thoughts. Each night I grew happier. By day I grew sadder.

And so one morning my Papa said to me, in a voice weakened by age and with words mangled by his own fermenting mouth, "Come out! Come out! It's safe to come out!"

I recognized it as his mushroom hunting call from years and years before. When Papa whooped it out this time, he and I were sitting in the parlor waiting for breakfast to be announced. We were each gathering our strength, having just exhausted ourselves with a twenty-minute struggle to get his slippery prosthetic in for the day. Both of us had our feet up on ottomans. I was leaning my head back in my armchair, looking upwards, numbly. I was especially sleepy that morning, for I'd spent most of the previous night with Eva. (More about that soon.) Papa, evidently, had been looking straight at me and had chosen that moment to let me know that he knew I was hiding a secret or two that I'd actually rather tell.

After his hunting call, there followed a pause of perhaps three seconds. I looked at him questioningly, my eyes not quite acknowledging what I'd heard and not quite indicating a need for an explanation.

The kind amusement I saw in his smile seemed part of his reply.

And then, with a slurp, he asked, "Shall we?"

Chapter 26

How did I so completely misread Papa's intentions? I knew that "Shall we?" was an invitation to formally re-enter analysis. But why did I assume that "Come out, come out, it's safe to come out?" was an explicit acknowledgment that my concerns were his concerns, as well as a promise that the matters I might have wanted to discuss were matters that he would take on compassionately? Why ever did I think another analysis with him would be less perilous than the first?

"Come out, come out, it's safe to come out" is hardly an unambiguous guarantee.

I have no single explanation to offer, only an array of possible ones.

One hearkens back to an idea that I learned from Siegfried Bernfeld. War orphans frequently expose themselves to unnecessary peril even after they have been redistributed to safe settings. Siegfried suggested that, by actively seeking out and then escaping danger again and again, orphans assure themselves that happy endings can conclude stories whose horror still rings. Perhaps that's what I thought I could get by re-engaging analytically with Papa—a happy clinical experience that would quiet the echoes of a once-sordid tale.

Another possible explanation for my lack of caution: Papa was sick and needed me. The balance of power seemed finally to have shifted in my favor. I imagined that, whatever Papa's faults or intentions, I could keep myself safe.

A third: I had found my initial psychoanalysis intriguing.

Narcissistic curiosity had been aroused by lying supine for an hour each evening, enjoying the undivided attention of my favorite parent, and searching for unconscious logic in what at first seemed to be only randomly chosen thoughts. I fancied that I had displayed mental processes that were uncannily clever. I wanted to show them off again.

Papa had made egregious errors with me; of that I was sure. For my part, I carried a lot of shame about what I had concealed from him and why. Still, at that age—about thirty (it seems both old enough and far too young, yes?)—I couldn't quite name either his mistakes or mine.

I do believe that I re-entered analysis with Papa in the hopes that he had learned the error of his ways. A selfless father and great theorist and practitioner, he would at last conduct my analysis impeccably. Together we would masterfully arrive at an understanding of the mistakes that he undoubtedly had made as analyst and father, and of the mistakes that I surely had made as analyst and and child. We would together write a better ending to our mutual horror story. Such an epic display of psychological competency would provide us a reprieve we could cherish for the rest of our lives.

All that, and I hoped that analysis would help me understand the perplexing change that my relationship with Eva Rosenfeld had just taken.

It had been one of those glorious Saturdays. Siegfried took the children on an outing, as he usually did, leaving Eva and me to relax in her house and lovely yard. Tante Minna and Mama were caring for Papa that day. They always tried to spell me once a week. Eva and I sat in the garden and lazed in its hammock, watching the sky for much of the day. We marveled at the atmospheric changes we witnessed. Clouds and sun competed fiercely for possession of the vast, blue expanse. Sometimes we shouted out encouragement to the sun or clouds. Why not? No one was listening. When the stars came out we were inspired to get up on our stockinged feet and dance wildly together under their resplendence.

HYSTERICAL

It was Eva's idea to play Statues that night. It's a game from almost everyone's childhood. The "It" person grabs the hand of the "Other" and whirls her around and around, very suddenly letting go. Torn away by centrifugal force, Other stumbles about.

Then It yells, "Freeze!" And, at that moment, Other becomes a statue until a touch from It releases her.

Eva was It; I was Other. She whirled me and twirled me until I begged to be set free. She let go. I flew, and then she yelled, "Freeze."

I found a very sensible posture in which to become statuesque. It was so comfortable a posture that I was sure I could maintain it indefinitely if Eva got lazy about delivering her touch of release. She had certainly been lazy about it once or twice before when we'd played. This time, too, Eva left me frozen for far longer than I expected. It was an excruciatingly long time, but she finally did touch me.

When Eva at last graced me with her hand in the starlight, it was my breast that she touched.

She looked not at me but up at the night sky.

To this day I don't know why I touched her. Considering the indefinitely maintainable posture I had chosen, I suppose I might have stood still all night, or at least until she touched me in some less personal place.

Instead, I melted free. My melting was almost instantaneous; that's the way Statues usually goes.

When I touched Eva's breast, she, too, melted. We lay back down in the garden. An hour or so later that is where we remained. Like two little earthquakes we had finally, fatally disturbed sensible ground.

As we drifted off to sleep in the warm night air I could almost see the heads of broken Romanesque statues littering the landscape around us. I had an image of myself surveying the scene from atop a lamppost perch. There were bloated heads and blackened bodies everywhere.

Let them rot, I thought to myself. It was a history forged of disaster. But then, from somewhere I couldn't place, I heard keening. I was sure that I recognized the sound.

Ah! It is the mother of the little lost girl! Did her poor, dead, daughter rush again from a dusty town and die again in the greedy caverns of the earth? Did Eva and I make the earthquake that killed her?

Terror and guilt drenched me from within. What an awful thing to do to a child! But then laughter—my own dream laughter—followed. No, it was the girl's. No, it was mine.

"I have been swept forever from the reach of my family," I hear. "The crying that fills the night is that of my Mama in mourning. But Mama is always in mourning; there is nothing I can do for her. Thank Allah for warm bodies and the greedy-mouthed earth that opens and closes. Thank Allah that I am safe."

It is the little girl calling out those words.

No, it is I.

That night I laughed myself the rest of the way to sleep.

Chapter 27

A man goes to meet a new neighbor.

"What brings you to our town?" the man asks.

The new neighbor replies, "My job. I'm a professor of deductive reasoning at the university."

The man says, "What exactly is deductive reasoning?"

The new neighbor explains. "I'll give you an example. You have a tea kettle, so I deduce you like to drink tea."

"Right."

"And from that I can deduce that you like to share tea."

"Correct."

"From that I can deduce that you have a wife."

"Why, yes!"

"And from that I can deduce you are a heterosexual."

And the neighbor says, "Okay, I see."

They finish talking and the neighbor goes and talks to another neighbor.

"I was just talking to the new neighbor," he announces.

"Yes?"

"Yes, he's a professor of deductive reasoning."

"Hey! What's that?"

"I'll give you an example: Do you have a tea kettle?"

"No."

"Homo!"

I sneaked into bed beside Papa the next morning before the sun rose. The next day at dawn, I sneaked into Papa's bed again.

At breakfast both days, I ignored Papa's significant glances. For some reason, he dared not ask why I had taken to coming to bed so late. It never even crossed my mind to tell.

Monday night, about a day-and-a-half after he invited me and I accepted, my new analysis began.

At first glance it seemed that nothing in Papa's consulting room had changed in the nearly five years since I'd left analysis—not the placement of his chair at his desk, nor the angle at which the moonlight struck the couch, nor the strangeness of the décor and lighting.

Of course, some things had changed. There was a framed photo of the electroplated, star-dusted elderly woman who had been a patient of my father's when I was very young. The frame's glass had a big, slobbery, female lip print on it, as though the woman, despite her age, had tarted herself up and kissed it just before giving it to Papa. Leaning against the picture frame was a short paragraph of newsprint. It was her obituary.

There were a few postcards and letters that I hadn't seen before. They'd been sent by tragedians and opera stars and politicians and philosophers, all thanking Papa for the insights that he had given them into the human condition. There was a letter from Samuel Goldwyn, Sr. of Hollywood, California. In it, Mr. Goldwyn asked Papa to come and work for him as a script consultant on the topic of love.

And there were new antiquities. Papa gave me a proper tour. He brought elephants and horses and rotund fertility figures out of the shadows for my inspection. There were frogs and princes and dancing maids, most of which I had never seen. There was a Venus with a broken spear.

And so "Venus with a broken spear" is what I said when Papa asked me to say the first thing that came to my mind as soon as it came to mind. I had just walked Papa to his chair and then skittered across the room to the couch, hopped on it, and covered my legs.

"Well, we're off to a running start then, aren't we!" said Papa with a little surprise in his voice. "Associate in relation to 'Venus with a broken spear,' please."

Like an eager student, I quickly delivered the sort of association for which I supposed he searched.

"Venus's spear is broken, which is to say that she mourns the penis she never had."

"She mourns her missing penis. Very interesting, Anna. Can you please elaborate on that idea?"

"Well, of course she never had a penis. Perhaps she had a penis substitute."

"Which would have been…?"

"That would have been a child. Venus had a child but the child has died. Perhaps the child was never even born. Perhaps Venus's child was never even conceived."

"Which would bring us to your status as a spinster. But does the association that you have just made seem of immediate concern to you? Is this something on which you would like us to waste time? I respect it as an association but I am mildly drawn to another possibility. I wonder if that is because you, too, are drawn to another association, something new that is very much on your mind but about which you are reluctant to speak."

What? When I had associated to "Venus with a broken spear" I hadn't been thinking about my interactions of the previous two nights with Eva. But Papa had evidently noticed me climb into bed with him later than he thought acceptable. It seemed that now he wanted to talk about that.

"You want me to explore whether Venus had an actual penis and the penis got broken just like her spear got broken?" is what I responded.

I had asked the question with playful pleasure. I wasn't ready to talk about Eva. Withholding information, I imagined Papa and me in our own metaphorical game of Statues. In our version of the game, I was

It and he was Other. By offering up "Venus with a broken spear," I had twirled and whirled him. In asking me to associate, he had grabbed a familiar and almost indefinitely maintainable stance. Now, in suggesting a specific direction for my associations, he had stuck himself in that stance—and in fear and ignorance. He would remain frozen there until I chose to release him.

Papa somehow seemed to appreciate the power that I held. He didn't push for answers and he didn't condemn me for the levity of the one that, moments before, I had given.

"No, no. Not at all," Papa said. "I want you to talk about whatever you would like."

"Let's see, then."

And then I took a while. I really slowed down in an effort to decide what it was that I might want to understand during this conversation with Papa, not what it was that the overly bright parrot in me thought she should squawk.

I remembered that my overarching goal in re-entering analysis was to talk about the new quality of Papa's and my relationship. But I also wasn't ready to discuss that yet.

What to say? I thought about my situation as the youngest in a family of genius and eccentricity. I thought about my lonely years of self-comfort, and of my identification with the good-hearted hero of my fantasies. I thought about the time I had already spent on Papa's couch, time during which I had worked to defeat the ardency with which I reached for myself. I thought about Papa's analysand, Emma Eckstein who, in the year of my birth, had lost her nose over the very practice that I was still tirelessly trying to surmount. I thought of the new way that I had discovered just two nights before to find comfort and rapture, all without touching myself.

"Venus is a woman," I said. "She has a clitoris. She enjoys touching her clitoris just as many young men enjoy touching their penises. The sole function of her clitoris is to bring her pleasure and comfort. She has been told, though, that her clitoris can no longer serve that function for her when she is alone. She is forbidden to touch it, so, in a metaphorical sense, I suppose that it could be considered useless if not broken. That makes her feel frustrated."

I stopped talking for a moment. He said nothing.

"How is what I said, Papa? Shall I go on? I have more to say if you want to hear it."

Evidently, Papa did not.

"No. No. No," he mumbled. Then he spoke more clearly. "This is not about masturbation, and it is not about any form of clitoral pleasure." I heard him move his chair and lean his head close behind mine. "You are past worrying about clitoral pleasure, are you not, dear Anna?"

"Well, it is true that I didn't masturbate either of the last two nights."

"Good enough for now. Let's agree that the association you just produced was an unconscious cover-up, a ruse to hide from me the real truth that you want to tell and that I want to hear."

Now I was confused. Cover up for what? Was Papa actually asking me to talk about Eva? Between non-phallic sex with her and the concept of a broken spear I could draw a clear connection. But if he was referring to Eva, did he actually want me to tell him about the previous two nights?

"Anna, let's get specific. Why is Venus's spear broken? Please. I insist that you tell me everything."

"Well, all right," I said, a little hesitantly. I opened my mouth, took a deep breath, and spit out about half a syllable when he prompted again: "Why is Venus's spear broken, Anna? Why?"

So I took another deep breath. But then I realized that I didn't know how to begin, not really. I didn't know how to talk about the things that I had done with Eva, not within the context of an answer to a question about a broken spear. I was incapable, I now see, of thinking about Eva's and my love as a manifestation of either phallus or damage.

"Just say what comes to your mind as soon as it comes to your mind," Papa interjected.

"Yes. I am trying. But what you just said confused me. Can I begin afresh?"

"Just begin, please, where you were—with 'Venus is a woman. She has a clitoris. She once enjoyed touching her clitoris just as many young men enjoy touching their penises. The sole function of her clitoris was to bring her pleasure and comfort. Her clitoris no longer serves that function for her, and never will again.'"

"Papa, there is something that I might like to try thinking about and perhaps even talking about. But I really don't know how to, given the conversation that we're having. Can I begin afresh? Can I talk about what comes to my mind as soon as it comes to mind?"

"I am going to ask you to trust me, Anna. In the course of analysis many analysands resist my line of inquiry, and in this respect, you apparently are no different from them. But I am onto something here, and if we go about things your way we may never arrive where we need to arrive. Venus no longer touches her clitoris. Like the very, very, very good girl that she is, she doesn't touch it anymore because she has grown past all of that. She knows now that to allow anyone, including herself, to give her sexual satisfaction by this immature route would be to remove herself from the chain of humanity in which the primary object of sex is the survival of the species."

"Oh."

"Go on, Anna."

"I am not quite sure how to go on with what you have begun. I think that I may be just about ready to talk to you about a matter that admittedly has nothing at all to do with survival of the species. Of that I am fairly sure."

"I see."

"I am not sure that you do, Papa."

"Anna, be a good girl and do what I ask. The chain of thought through which you would like to travel is dangerous. The chain of thought through which I am trying to lead you is for your own good. It is time for you to come to the understanding that Venus's clitoris will someday soon pulsate with pleasure, but neither as a result of her touch nor the direct touch of anyone else. Rather it will throb because Venus has learned to ignore the demands of her clitoris and instead to quietly, graciously, and eagerly accept the urgent and only-at-first pain-inducing thrusts of penetration."

Q: What was the first thing that Adam said to Eve?
A: "Better stand back. I'm not sure how big this thing gets."

"Go on, Papa."

"She will also feel pleasure at having received that which speeds incipient life on its way up her vaginal channel and towards the safe home of her uterus. For Venus to continue even to think about the needs of her own pitiful spear would be to refuse herself her rightful and necessary position as a link in that purposeful, vibrant, and sometimes radiantly sacrificial chain of life. It would also be to deny herself the intense pleasure of a vaginal-centric orgasm, knowable only by women who comply deeply and willingly with the dicta of biology and destiny. And finally, for Venus to remain focused on her spear, broken or otherwise, would be to place herself as a boat without rudder on the sea of life. Women have no internal navigational instruments with which to judge right from wrong. Afloat without guidance or support on an unpredictable and crashing sea, her spear would soon be broken anyway. Pity the Venus without a man to make moral determinations for her and to thrust them with stony vigor into her again and again."

A little girl tells her mother that she has learned where babies come from.

Her mother says, "Yes?"

The little girl explains, "The mommy and daddy take off their clothes. The daddy's widdler stands way up high, and the mommy kneels on the floor and puts the widdler in her mouth. Then the daddy's widdler sort of pops and makes

> *sticky juice into the mommy's mouth. The mommy swallows the sticky juice, and that's where babies come from."*
>
> *The mother looks lovingly at her daughter and whispers, "Oh, honey, that's not where babies come from. That's where jewelry comes from."*

"Well, I wouldn't want any of that happening to me, would I?" I said.

"No. You would not want to navigate the sea of life unguided and alone. Anna, trust me. It is time for you to move forward in your developmental process. It is time to marry. I would like to make for you a small introduction."

Papa paused a moment to gather either his thoughts or his courage.

"It is to your cousin, Edward Bernays," he continued. "You surely don't remember him, for my sister and her husband emigrated with him years and years ago. Anyway, Edward lives in New York City. There, he has been accepted by Gentiles into their society and has become both a Protestant and a very wealthy man. He is the preeminent practitioner of a new American art form called Public Relations. It seems that your cousin is so brilliant at this art form that he has convinced all of the architects serving the middle class and wealthy to design new living rooms that include enormous display cases for books. And all because he is under contract to a major book publisher! He seems a genius, that Eddie—a real genius, not one like me who spins theories out into the culture of the Western world only to have the vast majority of people who matter titter about them over sherry in the parlor but never read the original text. Eddie Bernays gets things done! Why, if he wanted to, Eddie Bernays could bring psychoanalytic theory and thinking into the average home at last! A cultural revolution is what I'm talking about, Anna! Eddie would do it, don't you think? For you? He is in Vienna visiting this week."

The entire room became quiet. I doubt that even my breathing made noise.

"Well, we have tunneled very deeply tonight," Papa confidently whispered after a good block of silence had transpired.

Then, because in our psychoanalytic routine Papa had always followed remarks about our success at deep-tunnel-making by rising and walking to the door, and I had always arisen and walked with him, I tried to sit up and leave.

I could not. While my arms and head and torso were as free as ever, I found that the moonlight coming through the window held my legs in place under the foot rug. It was as though the light itself were a giant biologist's prong that pinned me, the lowly insect, quiescent for analysis, direction, and dissection.

"Papa! I can't move! My legs are frozen!"

"Your first hysterical paralysis. Well, it's about time, my girl. Congratulations! We are apparently dredging up issues that will be illuminating to discuss. I say! I'll just leave you for tonight, shall I?" Papa's eyes, which had looked tired only a moment before, twinkled. His voice was now positively chipper. He covered me with a full-body blanket. He shut off the light. And he toddled out of the room, careful not to fall.

I suppose that it took me about five minutes to stop gasping, panting, and screaming. It took me about two more minutes to realize that I had an unforeseen problem.

"Who is going to help me winkle?" I called out.

No reply came, for the bedrooms in which we Freuds slept were many doors, walls, stairs, and hallways away from the consulting room in which I reclined.

I would have to make do. It would be a night of discomfort. I began a few more minutes of gasping and panting. Eventually, though, I saw that fear would do me no good. I resolved to try to tolerate the pain in my bladder—nay, to enjoy it. For, you see, during the long minutes of analytic silence, I had begun to wonder whether my destiny as a woman really did dictate that I ignore the demands of my clitoris and even enjoy receiving pain. This presented the former teacher in me with an interesting problem: If I needed to enjoy pain, how would I learn to do so?

Practice makes perfect, we educators always say.

Quieted, and with new purpose, I resolved to attempt sleep. Left to my own devices in my father's consulting room, where kings and princes had writhed and snarled in psychic agony and been tenderly ministered to by the very doctor who had just left me to sort things out on my own, I gave sleep a go.

As I nodded off, I had a few last, fleeting images of the sort that one gets when one leaves the plane of everyday activity for that of slumber. A tremendous, slate-grey microscope. Colossal knobs mechanistically turning. They govern the mirrors and the glass under which I lie. Godlessly, monotonously, they whirl back and forth trying to bring me, a small insect, into focus.

They utterly fail in their attempt.

Chapter 28

I awoke early the next morning, but not as early as Papa. Birds were singing their dawn chorus when Papa entered the consulting room dressed for the day. He was pushing and leaning on Cook's wheeled cart, which held a tray of coffee and biscuits.

"One can have remarkable power even without physical strength, don't you think, Anna?" he asked me cheerfully.

He got no dutiful "Yes, Papa" from me that morning.

I told him I needed to winkle.

"Yes, I can help you with that right now. I am sorry I didn't remember last night that you would need some arrangement. It actually occurred to me as I got into bed, but at that point I hardly wanted to disturb whatever emotional abreaction your hysterical paralysis had set in motion."

"Abreaction" was a term that Papa had coined for the psychic healing that comes from allowing a flood of once-repressed feelings to flow.

Papa parked the wheeled cart and began limping about like a painfully frail waiter on fire. "I can serve you whatever it is that you need this morning. Biscuits, jam, coffee."

"Yes, Papa. But first, please..."

"Yes?"

"Papa, I really need to..."

"Yes?"

"...winkle."

"Ah, yes." Papa handed me a chamber pot and hobbled out of the room. With much heaving of my torso I was able to release my skirt from my hips and settle myself down. I completed my necessary task.

After a gentle rap on the door Papa came back into the consulting room.

"All done?"

"Papa," I said calmly and clearly. "You shouldn't walk about so much. You will fall. I need to see a doctor. I need to be in hospital. I cannot move my legs; they have no feeling whatsoever. This is an emergency."

"Nonsense, my dear. There is nothing at all wrong with your eggs. Legs! Freudian slip. Hah!" he said merrily. "But, Anna, just to reassure you. Here. Regard this pen that I now hold about one foot before your nose. Follow my pen as I move it slowly up, down, and to the right and left. Yes? Ahhhh. Very good. You see? No jitter. No trouble. Biscuit?"

"But I have no sensation."

"One can have remarkable sense even without sensation, don't you think, Anna? Coffee?"

"Yes, please. No sugar."

"They are uterine pains," he announced to me as he handed me my coffee. "They are pains writ on your psyche by the dead children woven into your womb."

"What are?"

"The pains that you are feeling."

"Papa," I said, feeling quite concerned. "I have no pains in my uterus. No pains and no dead children. I have no pains in my eggs."

"Legs! Slip!" Papa called out.

"I have no sensation whatsoever from my waist down."

"'The children are safe, though.' Isn't that what you concluded, even though the children were dead? Paradoxical, of course, but you might have been right. We'll find out. A whole dusty town of girls and boys. All safe. All dead. All woven into your womb."

Cold fear is what I remember of the moment when I realized that

Papa had stepped over the line demarcating propriety from impropriety, sanity from insanity, and perhaps even the natural world from the supernatural. He who was a doctor was behaving childishly about a potentially grave medical matter. He who was erudite was resorting to sing-songy conversational tones. He who claimed to scientifically approach the meaning of dreams was razzing me about a dream of mine—a dream that I had never confided to him.

My dream of children fleeing a tumbling village and being safe by virtue of having already been killed dated from a night five years before, hours after I had left his analytic care. Because analysis had ended, I had felt no inclination to tell the dream to him. Indeed, I had never felt any urgency to tell anyone about that dream, and so I hadn't. I knew that I hadn't.

How in the world had he learned about that dream?

Where before I had been annoyed and exasperated with Papa, now I was afraid both for him and of him. If Papa were hysterical, or worse yet, crazy, I probably needed to get help. Now. I needed to stand up and quickly leave the room.

I tried. My legs, however, still would not work. Again and again and yet again I gave my legs mental "One-two-three-go!" commands, hoping they would swing off the couch and take me straight towards the door. But they lay placidly. They simply would not work.

"As if they ever did," Papa said.

"As if what ever did what?"

"As if your eggs ever did work."

Slip! I thought about calling out, but if I had I might have shrieked it endlessly, madly. It might have been the end for me of composure as I knew it. So instead I resumed my "One-two-three-go!" commands. One-two-three-go! One-two-three-GO! This time I even articulated them, softly, but, of course, to no avail.

"We have so much to talk about," Papa said, contentedly. "There are all of the matters that you neglected to tell me in your last analysis or that you distorted. Shall we begin with the earthquake dream and the vanished daughter? Or shall we begin instead with Doctor Jones? You do remember Doctor Jones, don't you, Anna?"

I had also never told him about my episode of capture and near conquest with Doctor Jones.

Papa had been conducting telepathy experiments with me as his partner. Had he and I become truly telepathic?

Papa had been my analyst and in that analysis I had realized some of the dangers of transference and countertransference. Could experiences and secrets be transferred and countertransferred just as commonly in analysis as erotic longing?

I believed my friend Call Me Otto Gross to have been murdered by his father, Hans, a forensic criminologist with access to untraceable potions. Papa knew Herr Gross professionally. Had he obtained from him a truth serum? Had I, without my knowledge, been chemically induced to spill some of the very beans I had spent so many years counting?

There were too many frightening implications at hand. Not wanting to rile myself further and thereby render all of my faculties as useless as my legs had become, I decided to proceed with Papa as civilly as I could. I did my best to conversationally engage Papa as though he were behaving normally. I took comfort during the attempt in the realization that, for the first time ever, my psychoanalytic session would be conducted in a consulting room bathed in the full light of day. No half-shadow tricks would be available to Papa if he tried to toy with me.

As sensibly as I could, I chose from the platter of questions that Papa had presented me a topic for us to discuss: Five years before, I had not communicated to him the dream of the earthquake, the fleeing, and the girl who was safer and perhaps even happier dead than she had been alive. How had he known?

"Strictly speaking, Papa, I was under no obligation to communicate that dream to you. I had it the night after terminating analysis, not the night before."

"Associate, please, Anna, in relation to, 'a history forged of disaster.' In your dream, did the rug merchant not use that phrase as you and he toured 'your land'—a land ruined by earthquake?"

"'A history forged of disaster.' That would, I suppose, be our family."

"Indeed. Associate, please, Anna, in relation to (and then he checked some notes he had made) 'Our land has come alive with shaking.' Ha! While you are at it, associate also, please, to, 'The sea turns a familiar red. Schools of wiggly fish leap into the air.' I love that last one."

I closed my eyes and obediently said, "'Land comes alive with shaking.' That would be sexual intercourse, or maybe deep, family tremors. 'The sea turns a familiar red.' That would be menstrual blood or perhaps the blood of childbirth. 'Schools of wiggly fish.' Those are probably penises."

"Exactly. By the way, it's all right to slow down, Anna. Spitting out the words and punching every syllable is hardly required. Try, in general, being a little less urgent about all of this if that is at all possible for a sensibly shod young woman like you. What we are doing this morning is an easy-paced introspection, a gentle foraging for mushrooms, not a battle for a hilltop or a rumble over dead mammoth meat. Now: 'Welcome into its caverns.' My notes tell me that you dreamed of the earth doing that to children. Think softly and peacefully about that image, Anna, and tell me what it means to you."

I thought as softly and peacefully as a young woman can who is a daytime prisoner of her mad father. Which is to say that I settled on associations that followed what I calculated to be his line of thought.

"I believe that it has to do with suffocation."

"No, it doesn't. Nothing in your dreams has to do with suffocation, not even when you suffocate in your dreams. Those dreams are about orgasm."

"Then perhaps…"

"No. Think softly and peacefully for a while. Then speak."

After a few appropriately soft and peaceful moments I ventured, "I think that the image of children running has to do with children."

"Of course it does, Anna."

"I think that it has to do with children running."

"Of course it does, Anna. Where do children come from?"

I somehow knew that "cabbage patches" was not the answer that he wanted.

"Mothers and fathers."

"Can you be a little more specific this time? We are done with the general foraging. From whom do they emerge?"

"Mothers."

"Not bad. Do you remember, Anna, that all fears are repressed wishes?"

"I do."

"And do you remember that, during my work with Wolf Man, I said that sometimes an experience that is fearfully repressed manifests itself as its opposite in dreams?"

"I do."

"So while in real life fears can be wishes, in dreams the experiences that we fear the most can be most pleasant? We agree?"

"Yes. We agree."

"How do you feel about the children who rush blindly into the earth's caverns?"

"I don't know. Sad I suppose."

"No you don't. You thought they were dead, yet you thanked Allah they were safe. And you dreamed they were laughing. Remember?"

"Ah, yes. I feel thankful. Intensely happy."

"Precisely. You feel thankful and intensely happy that the children are rushing into you, the earth. And might I suggest to you that this image is an inverted wish? You would also feel thankful if the children were rushing out of you—that is, out of the cavern of your greedy vagina and into life. But this is something that you fear."

"Yes, Papa. I think I see the logic that you are building."

"Good. Now it is time for us to talk about Doctor Jones."

"Why?"

"'Alive with shaking,' Anna. It is the image of sexual intercourse from your dream, the one that we have just discussed. I would like to discuss the image specifically in relation to Doctor Jones's penis, the wiggly fish that I believe you almost caught during your brief visit to England at the very beginning of the war. Think about Doctor Jones, dear Anna. And when you do, please associate in relation to 'alive with shaking.'"

Well, I had to. I had to tell him what had happened so long ago and far away, even though I had escaped unharmed, and even though I had resolved that episode in a way that I found tolerable. I had arrived home safely. I was still a virgin when I did so. I had retained Doctor Jones's esteem and that was important to me since, in my family, obtaining and retaining the esteem of well-connected, Christian men was a laudable goal. Furthermore, Doctor Jones was a friend of my father's, and that, in and of itself, had value in my eyes. And in photographs that ran in newspapers around the world I had been portrayed as a proper lady getting a buff on the hand from a very proper gentleman.

I did not want to tell Papa what had transpired with Doctor Jones. I did not, I did not, I did not. For, in spite of all the victory and resolution that I had salvaged from those miserable five days, I imagined that, in my father's eyes, my behavior would not have seemed up to snuff.

My paralysis threw the family into a logistical crisis. I needed caretaking, which meant lifting and bathing. Furthermore, someone needed to take over the caretaking role that I had long played for my father.

In those days, caretaking was almost always assigned to a family member. Professionals were not likely to be invited into a place so close to the family core. With both my mother and Tante Minna too old for heavy labor, what we needed, it seemed to all of us, was a man young enough to lift me and a woman young enough to bathe me. Either the man or the woman could tend to my father's jaw. We needed a couple that could live with us.

Enter my brother, Oliver, who was then (as he often was) between jobs. He was accompanied by his amiable wife, Henny, and their eighteen-month-old daughter named (confusingly enough for me) Eva.

Paralysis was not the only affliction pinning me to the consulting room couch. As analysis continued and my love for and trust in my father met nightly with the eager thrusts of his thorny questions, my entire self seemed to relinquish its vigor. Muscles throughout my arms and neck progressively weakened. I coughed in a demoralized but appealing way. Night by night in analysis, my body rendered my mind (or was it my mind that rendered my body?) increasingly accepting of the (only at first pain-inducing) thrusts of penetration.

Politely but insistently, Papa asked questions like, "'Stubby and terrier-like' indeed! Associate in relation to that, please." And, "The rapidly industrializing British empire? But that's so classic! Do tell! Go on!" And, "Well, my dear. Did you find your episode of capture and near conquest appealing? How else to account for your work with war orphans?"

"I don't see the connection at all, Papa."

"Why, in deep mourning for the seed that you swallowed, you were mothering children whose actual mothers, by dying, had refused them."

"Swallowed? But I…" And then, for a moment, I wasn't so sure. Confusing tableaux from what might have been a second unfortunate encounter with Doctor Jones began to flood my brain.

"Papa!" I shouted. "For God's sake, STOP!"

Papa laughed. "All right. You can calm down. But that reminds me. Have you heard the joke about where jewelry comes from?"

This is how we continued for the next few days. He wore me out. Eventually I began answering all of his questions without a struggle, and as I did I accepted the bloody sundering of psychic muscle that ensued. I reclined submissively.

I had become a real woman.

Within another week and with luck, I calculated, a real woman could become too thoroughly transpierced and emptied even to talk.

I agreed to meet with my cousin, Edward Bernays. Henny dolled me up, giving me a fresh dress and combing my hair nicely. Oli lifted me from the couch in the consulting room onto a ladder-backed chair that had been brought from the family apartment for the occasion. Papa and Eddie talked for a while in the waiting room just beyond my sight and hearing. It sounded to me as though Papa were offering a dowry, which may seem shocking to people today and was certainly out of date then, but only by a generation or so.

Eddie was a nice enough looking man and certainly a sympathetic and pleasant one. He spoke excellent German. After he took my hand and shook it in the American style, he grabbed a footstool and sat on it so that his face was a little lower even than mine, though my own face seemed to me to creep perpetually towards his as gravity allowed me to slip towards the floor.

He had a wonderful sense of humor; I have to say that about Eddie. Every once in a while he would spring to his feet, grab me by the arm opposite the one that had just dipped as low as the floor, and shout, "Let's give her the old heave-ho!" Then he would pull me back into a proper sitting position. We both did a lot of laughing.

Truly, I liked Eddie. I liked him a great, great deal, and I think that he liked me. We could have had a lovely marriage if it were to be based on mutual respect and loud guffaws. Who knows? Maybe Papa was right about Eddie. Maybe he was an artistic genius of a sort.

Alas, Eddie didn't want me. He was honest enough to tell me straight out that he thought we could always be "the best of buddies," but that marriage, as he understood it, wasn't based on admiration and warm feelings.

Good old Eddie. Those PR people really see to the heart of things, don't they?

Chapter 29

It wasn't long before I deduced how Papa had learned of my never-disclosed dream and about the episode with Doctor Jones. He had read my diary, clear and simple.

It wasn't even a real diary. Over the years of my childhood and adolescence I had written poetry and stories. I'd also written personal notes—letters to myself, really—and I kept all such writing in a set of five thick folders. I had brought them into the bedroom that Papa and I shared. This was so that, if I awoke at night and wanted to write or to quietly contemplate the evolution of matters that confused me, I could do so while Papa slept.

I had never imagined the danger in such a practice. Papa was infirm. He rarely walked anywhere without my help. I always made it to the bedroom alongside him.

When he left me in his consulting room the night of the onset of my hysterical paralysis, however, he apparently enjoyed a surprising rush of agility. He made his own way to the bedroom, where he benefited from a hale night of rifling and rummaging.

Alas, dreams of earthquakes and rug merchants and encounters with a stubby-shaped terrier with a face like salad dressing were not the only topics about which I had written notes to myself. I had also written a few lines about lovemaking with Eva. I had done so on both occasions, as soon as I returned home. Which means that Papa had confirmed any suspicions about Eva via the unambiguous evidence I had left.

I'm sure it was already obvious to my whole family that Eva and I were in love. As analysis continued and my infirmities proliferated, she visited daily, bringing me candied hearts and flowers—anything she could think of to cheer me up. She fretted and worried. It made me sad to see her wring her hands in tiny tweaks. The day that I met with Eddie Bernays in the consulting room, Eva sat in the garden with Henny and Oli, both of them holding onto her and assuring her that everything would turn out all right. And it did. Eddie went away.

I told Mama, Tante Minna, and Henny first about Eva. I waited one evening until Oli, who had just delivered me to a chair at the kitchen table, left the room to go off and look after Papa. It was not so very late—eight o'clock, I suppose. Tante Minna poured tea and we women sat and talked. My hand shook when I tried to raise my glass. I was making good progress towards my hysterical goal of complete incapacitation; I was already too damaged to lift a few sips of lightly flavored water to my trembling mouth.

I spilled quite a splash of piping hot stuff on my thigh. Then I began to weep, first from shock and pain, and then because I apparently had the permission of the women of my family to continue.

No one, of course, even thought to point out that my leg had registered pain when even I thought it could not. They all rushed at me with a flurry of feminine "Don't you think?"s and "What if you?"s and "When that happened to me I…"s that also produced an ice bag and a hankie. When I quieted down, Tante Minna scooted her chair closer to mine and suggested that I had just done an awful lot of weeping for a big girl like me.

"What, darling, is the matter?" she asked.

"Minna, dear," Henny chimed in, "when you ask 'what is the matter' do you mean 'what is the matter aside from the fact that her fine, strong legs are mysteriously paralyzed and that, weak as a kitten, she has to spend an hour every night pummeled by her father's endless questions about private matters?'"

"Precisely. What's the matter, dear? How can we help?"

That old urge to rescue. Tante Minna still had it. I knew I was still a sucker for it.

I looked around the table at the three women who, I was beginning to realize, might be on my side in an epic battle I had yet to understand. They sat under the glow of a vapor lamp, the color temperature of which made their lips and cheeks and tips of noses look faintly blue and their foreheads' worry lines hyper-grooved.

My nervous system, like my muscles, had begun to deteriorate, making my vision that night not as good as it normally was. The heads and shoulders of my mother, aunt, and sister-in-law were clear in my gaze. However, within inches of their heads, the room fell into a blur; the colors and shapes of the kitchen cabinetry were a mass of clumsy, dark color chunks. Beholding the three of them staring at me with great concern from within a unified glow of light, I thought of a haloed coven of fretting angels rising from the mist of household hell.

Do they meet here nightly? I wondered. When? After Papa and I have gone to bed? Do they speak their real thoughts? Do they join hands and bow their heads in a ritual of quiet, competent pother? Do they ever, perchance, giggle? Why do all three of them seem so solicitous? Am I not safely under my father's medical and psychoanalytic care?

"Anna, what is troubling you so, dear? We love you, but we cannot help you if you won't let us," Tante Minna said.

I looked at the three of them. Henny had just set her freshly washed hair in bobby pins. Tante Minna wore her pink and green flannel robe and was eating a pastry. Mama had slathered her face with night cream. Well, they didn't look judgmental. Taking a deep breath, I decided to reveal the cause of my suffering.

"Tante Minna. Mama. Henny," I said. "Everything I've been going through is my fault. I have brought sickness on myself and shame on you, as well." All of them raised their eyebrows. "You see, I am not the kind of woman you think I am."

"No?" they asked in unison.

"No. You see, I—well, I do not feel about men in the way that you do. What I mean to say is—I love a woman. Specifically, what I mean to say is that I have loved Eva. Sexually. And now my body is punishing me." When I saw all six eyes well up with moisture I began to weep. "Forgive me. I am sorry to disappoint you."

Again a flurry of hankies and ice and "Don't you think?"s and "What if you?"s and "When that happened to me I"s.

I was struck—indescribably struck, I might add—by the fact that one of those angels had just said, "When that happened to me I…."

It was Mama who had said it, Mama with whom I had sat nightly the year after Sophie died, ladling chicken soup and listening to her lifetime full of stories. In that year I thought that I had learned everything there was to know about her, and indeed all of the Bernays family and all of the Freuds. We were Ashkenazim—*shtetl* Jews. Still, the Bernays family was a rabbinical lineage, more highly situated socially than the Freuds, who were without pretenses or refinement and had a few notable scandals in their past, most recently a world-wide counterfeiting operation involving Papa's two eldest brothers and perhaps his father, too.

"When that happened to me I," Mama started again, but Henny asked her to wait while she tended to a whistling pot.

While Henny futzed in the kitchen, my thoughts raced like a hound chasing rabbits. Mama may have been willing to marry "down" and enter the Freud family. But could she ever have forgone her essential passivity and reached out to a woman? No! Goodness, no!

But "When that happened to me I…." was what she had said.

Childhood rape! The hound had a prize rabbit in his jaws, and I had achieved a flawless psychoanalytic understanding of that dear, old woman. Mama had been raped as a little girl, and I knew it as surely as I'd ever known anything. She had always been emotionally incompetent. Perhaps, for the last sixty or so years, she had actually been hysterical!

"How awful for you!" I cried out to her in amazement and sympathy. As I cried out I meant to surround her in a comforting embrace, but, of course, I hadn't the strength to move my arms all the way up and towards her.

"Yes, it was," Mama said, taking one of my flailing hands. "Truly. When that happened to me, I—well, we were both so afraid, so afraid. In the end my lover refused to leave her husband. She and he moved away in shame, leaving me in deep mourning and at the center of quite a public scandal. Then I met your father. It took him over nine hundred love letters and quite a lot of cocaine, but he finally convinced me of my true destiny as a woman."

"She was your *lover*?" I asked.

"Yes. I was eighteen, and she was twenty and the love of my life. It is true, though, that I have loved your father since. He is an interesting talker."

"A persuasive one, too," Tante Minna added, after which Henny muttered "Hmmm."

"Mama, why didn't you tell me this? In all of those evenings that you poured out your heart and history to me, why did you never mention this one incredibly central, unbelievably non-peripheral fact?"

"Because you never poured out your heart and history to me, dear. Beloved Anna, these things aren't freely talked about, even in our modern times. Listen. Do me a favor. I have wasted my life; don't waste yours. Go on and love your Eva. Love her with all your heart and soul. Kiss her for me, as hard and deeply as you like, and with that kiss let your own froggish skin melt away. Whatever you do, though, don't let anyone try to turn you into the sort of woman you are not. I let people do that to me, and look where it got me. Give up your instincts and your right to self-determination, and you give up your vigor and will to live. Even your children see little in you to love. Anna Freud, I have never given you one ounce of worthy counsel in my life but I intend to do it now: Promise me that you will not let them do to you what they've done to me."

Promise me that you will not let them....

Thinking about my mother's words, I realized that Otto Gross had said precisely the same thing. It was the very last thing he ever said to me.

"Been *schtupping* the *maidlach*, have you, Anna?" That was the very first thing that Oli said to me when I told him about Eva.

He was sitting on the living room floor. I was in a chair across the room. Oli was thirty-four-years-old, and his once tow-colored hair was already grey.

Though a change had come over Oli since his return to the Freud home. Now my father's full-time caretaker rather than crazed teenage assailant, he was doing whatever the opposite of aging is. He was "youthening," becoming playful. He was even regaining his childish lisp, which he, like all of us, had worked so hard to lose.

He had also started to laugh regularly and to make jokes. Although the humor often sounded bitter, it never ultimately settled that way.

Oli was sitting on the floor with his daughter. Little Eva played with crayons. "Wax and pigment, mostly," I remembered Oli dryly explaining about Crayola crayons years before, after his breakdown. As Oli and Little Eva sat, she drew. Scribbled, really, for that's all an eighteen-month-old child can manage artistically. While she scribbled, she extorted drawings from her father.

"Draw airplane, please."

And Oli drew an airplane next to her scribble.

"Draw airplane, please."

And Oli drew another airplane next to another scribble. This one he gave a smiling face.

"Draw airplane, please."

Oli drew another airplane next to a third scribble. This one he gave wing flaps and landing gear.

"Draw airplane, please."

It went on for quite a while. By the time the evening ended, Little Eva had drawn a fleet of scribbles and Oli had drawn a fleet of airplanes, each more elaborate than the one before. None were capable of fighting. All were built for short, buoyantly doodled hops of escape. Or so I imagined.

"What are you drawing?" I asked Oli.

"Airplane."

"I know 'airplane.' But can you tell me about the airplanes that you are drawing?"

"Let me guess, Anna. You want me to tell you the first thing that comes to my mind as soon as it comes to mind?" That sounded like a challenge to me.

"I don't suppose that I do. But helplessly confined as I am to this chair across the room, I am not at a good angle to see the airplanes that you have drawn. Can you tell me about them? Show them to me, perhaps?"

Oli brought me sheets and sheets of paper. At that point I was not a very experienced psychoanalyst. I am now. To this day I have the airplane drawings. Regardless and still, I cannot for the life of me see anything special in what Oli drew. They were just a large stack of smiley-faced, winged and wheeled, completely charming "draw airplane"s.

"Nice, Oli. Really nice," I said.

"That's 'Oliver' to you, Anna," Oli shot back, though with a smile.

What was going on? What message was I to read in any of grey-haired Oli's childish and challenging behaviors? In his brittle beaming?

"Perhaps now you would like to tell me what's on your mind as soon as it comes to mind," I ventured.

"Not until you promise me that you will stop telling him (gesturing towards Papa's suite of professional rooms) what's on yours."

That was a statement to which I could not yet offer a response. So I kept the conversational focus on my brother.

"Oliver, can you tell me why airplanes don't crash?"

The question may have seemed a *non sequitur*. But, after all, in the very way that Checkovian characters talk about tea when what they are really communicating is sorrow over the catastrophic loss of everything they have held dear, the conversation that Oli and I were having about airplanes and airplane drawings was really about something else. Admittedly, I wasn't quite sure what it was about; I certainly couldn't address the topic directly. That hardly mattered, for I was at least as interested in observing the manner in which Oli would answer as I was in learning the content of what his answer might be.

As an endlessly curious child Oliver would have delivered a long and impassioned lecture, complete with pictures, loopy guesses, and inspired pratfalls. As an adolescent, after his breakdown, Oliver's answer to that very question had been, "Airworthiness depends in part on the distance between the leading edge of the wing and the stabilizer." It was a remarkably accurate answer for such a young thinker, but it was delivered with all of the emotion of a mechanical genie whose head bounced on a metal neck.

"Homosexuality may be a family trait, don't you think?" was Oli's surprise response.

"Now there's a *non sequitur*," I blurted out. I had not told him anything about what I had just learned about Mama. "Who in our family, aside from me, is a homosexual?"

"Papa."

"Oli! On what evidence do you call Papa a homosexual?"

"Actually, given the chance to be more precise, 'polymorphously perverse' is how I would describe him. I have no hard evidence. But I have read his published notes on the Rat Man case. I know that in it he confessed to an intense, erotic longing for Rat Man and then blamed Rat Man for the whole mess. In other contexts he has confessed that eros infects all of his analytic relationships, with men as well as with women. That is significant, don't you think?"

"Perhaps not. Perhaps he is just stating a fact universal to analytic situations."

"Perhaps. But have you ever heard another analyst make such a sweeping personal admission?"

"It is a fine trait of Papa's that he can hold himself up to public scrutiny."

"But if he is wrong, and if these are not universal tendencies that he is pronouncing, but only idiosyncratic ones that he is promoting, then what he has burdened us all with is psychoanalysis by delusion."

I closed my eyes and took an uncomfortable breath.

"Anna, I say. On top of the problem with your legs, you're looking a bit more autumnal and death-haunted than is probably good for you. Are you sure that you are taking care of yourself?"

"Yes, quite sure," I said, popping my eyes open with as much verve as I could display. "If I am looking momentarily ill to you, it is possible that the matters Papa and I are discussing in my psychoanalysis have become temporarily externalized. I will look better once we can get them resolved. You can count on that."

"I don't suppose you would care to tell me what those matters are."

"Oh, you know…."

"No. Truly. I have no idea."

"Of course you do. You have been psychoanalyzed. You and your analyst talked about what a young man needs to discover and accept about his real self. Papa and I talk about what a young woman needs to discover and accept."

"And that is…?"

"If you must know, the pleasure that I can gain by sacrificing myself in the sexual act. The gratifying death shudder that will absorb me once I know that, in spite of my iron will, the enemy is inside me at last. All that."

"Ah. All that."

"Yes, well."

"We all have a preposterous curiosity about the perfectly private things other people do in bed, don't you think?"

"Not at all," I said firmly. "Not at all."

"Well, then, I guess it's getting late. Look, Little Eva has fallen asleep on the rug. I will say, goodnight."

"Goodnight, Oli."

"Goodnight, Anna."

"Oh, Oli!" I called out softly just as he was about to carry his slumbering baby from the room. I would have waved the pictures of airplanes he had just drawn, but I hadn't the strength. I could only indicate the pictures with my eyes. "I asked but you never directly answered. Can you tell me why airplanes don't crash?"

"They crash all the time," he spoke in a low tone. "They're surprisingly non-airworthy. I do have an idea for mechanisms that could be contained in indestructible boxes, and that could record the pilots' voices and maybe even mechanical details communicated by the engine itself. They wouldn't stop an airplane from crashing. But, after a crash, the indestructible boxes could be found, the recordings retrieved, and information gleaned about what went wrong."

"Fascinating, Oli! What a marvelous idea!"

"Thank you. I am delighted that you like it."

"I think the idea smashing!"

Shifting Little Eva so that he might more comfortably hold her he said, "Smash-resistant is actually what I have in mind. But if I could just for a moment, Anna.... You know, Anna, I'm more than a bit worried about you."

"I will be fine, Oli, as soon as I get a few analytic matters resolved."

"Yes," he started, but then Little Eva snorted and stirred, probably because Oli and I were talking too loudly. Oli lowered his voice again, and he rocked back and forth on his feet in the way that parents for tens of thousands of years have rocked while holding sleeping children.

"What I want to say, Anna, is that I would like you to think about those smash-resistant boxes. Do me a favor, will you? For any airplane that Papa asks you to get on, I want you to make sure that the entire plane is made out of that same substance. Promise me?"

"I..."

"Don't answer yet. I can see that you're not ready. But think about it. Goodnight, Anna."

"Goodnight, Oli."

Chapter 30

"We all have a preposterous curiosity about the perfectly private things other people do in bed, don't you think?" I asked Papa later that night at the beginning of our ten o'clock analytic hour.

"Well, aren't we frisky tonight?" Papa answered. "You're looking well. There is color in your cheeks. Your pulse is…let me see…. Your pulse is strong. Have you been eating, my girl? Getting up and about even?"

"I have not been getting up and about. But, yes, in fact I've just finished a snack. And now I am feeling quite well, thank you."

"Let us begin, then. I believe we are now through with our discussion of Doctor Jones, unless there is something we have missed that you would like to bring to consciousness."

"No. Nothing. Thank you just the same."

"Then please close your eyes and say the first thing that comes to your mind as soon as it comes to mind."

I kept my eyes open. Quite calmly I said, "We all have a preposterous curiosity about the perfectly private things other people do in bed."

"Yes, you have said that. There is a gold mine full of associations to be retrieved from that statement, I'm sure. Yet I don't know quite where to begin exploring such a far-reaching proclamation. Do you have anything less precipitous with which you would like to begin?"

"It is just a statement of fact, and it has been on my mind."

"On your mind? Since when?"

"For about an hour. Oli said it. I thought that it was actually quite catchy."

"Oli? Since when do we absorb our wisdom from The Newly Sibilant Sayings of Oliver Freud?"

"I thought it was catchy. That's all."

"Catchy."

"Yes."

I couldn't see Papa. From the sounds that I heard I did suspect, however, that he had gotten up from his chair and was moving about unsteadily out of my view.

"Venus with a broken spear. Do you remember her, Anna?"

"Of course. We spoke about her at length just a week or so ago."

"Yes. Very good."

"How is dear Venus, Papa? Is she well?" I teased. "Please convey to her my condolences about her terrible loss."

And then there was an appalling silence in which Papa responded not at all to my little joke. As the seconds ticked by, I realized that he had accepted what I'd said not as a lighthearted comment (which was how I believed I had intended it) but as an insult—or, worse yet, a provocation. I lay there aghast at my apparent instinct for self-destruction. The last thing in the world I actually needed that very night was an analytic session even more unpredictable than this entire set had so far proven to be.

I heard Papa wind up the Buddha music box and put it back on the shelf where it would make its tinny song.

But the Buddha remained silent.

"Drat," I heard, and then I heard him shake the Buddha and then give it a smack. "There's no telling what's going on inside that thing."

Papa began again to roam stiffly. I thought I heard him leave the small area illuminated by the Chinese lamp and move into the room's moon- and fire-lit shadows.

"Anna," he finally said. "Do you know the Tibetan term *mandala?*"

"I believe I do," I said. "They are intricate, circular designs that represent the full expression of Buddha's perfectly enlightened mind, are they not? Is that why you were playing with the Buddha music box, Papa? I've read the term *mandala*, but I don't think I've ever seen one."

"Ah, but you have," Papa said. "Right here, in the center of the room."

Though I couldn't see Papa directly from where I lay, I saw his shadow gesture outwards, and so I directed my gaze at the large, circular rug occupying the major portion of the nicely polished floor. Less than five feet away from me, it was not only in the center of the room, it was the centerpiece of the room, the visual anchor for all of Papa's magnificent furnishings and embellishments. I say "anchor" because it was not dramatically engaging in the way that many of the room's *objets d'art* were. Rather, it seemed strong, solid, and quiet. A series of deep colors and interdependent designs radiated outward from its magenta core all the way to the rug's braided edge.

"Persian provenance, Tibetan influence," he explained. "But pedigree is not what is important here. Please, Anna, look at the rug. And when you do, I want you to concentrate on…."

"Perfect enlightenment?" I interjected, optimistically.

"No, Anna," he said. "On Eddie Bernays."

"Papa, no. Really? But…"

"Yes?" Papa said, and I could hear impatience in his voice.

"It's just that I'm disappointed, Papa. I had hoped…"

"Of course you've had hopes, Anna. Actually, I'm glad to hear you acknowledge them. Now, please, look at the *mandala* and at the circles growing ever wider and think of Eddie. Eddie. Eddie." He was slowly and mesmerically repeating the name, and at the same time, pressing intermittently on my forehead in a way that he had learned in Paris from the great Docteur Charcot.

Now I was embarrassed for both of us. Here Papa had started droning on like some sort of mountebank mystic, and I was supposed to be thinking about Eddie, a very likeable man but hardly the human manifestation, to my eye, of Buddha's perfection.

"Papa, I just can't do this," I finally said after a few more "Eddie"s.

"Just too disappointed?" Papa asked.

"For heaven's sake, Papa. What are you getting at?"

"I asked you to think of the *mandala*, Anna. Let's look at it. The reddish core at rug's center—that is you. You have a burning procreative instinct. It's your biological imperative, your birthright, your menstrual blood, your driving force. The ever-widening circles are your sexual and psychical maturation. As you pass through developmental stages, the circles get bigger, more lush, more weighty. They have brought you from your pre-Oedipal stage through your Oedipal complex and on to first crush. They may have gotten you as far as serious infatuation. They can bring you even further, Anna, to love, to commitment, and to motherhood, if only you will let them. I want you to live all of the circles of your life, Anna, and you should want that, too.

"I think you're stretching a metaphor, Papa."

"Anna, let's talk about Eddie."

"Why Eddie?"

"If not Eddie, someone like him. Whom do you desire, my dear?"

"Oh, my!" I said. And then, "Papa…."

For here was my chance. I felt strengthened by the way the rest of my family had received my disclosure about Eva. Papa was only just beginning to steer our current conversation with truly misguided force. If I was ever going to stop him from systematically confusing us both, the time would be now.

"Papa," I began again. "If I could be happy without being married, would you be happy for me?"

He didn't say anything right away. I distinctly remember hearing him light a cigar and exhale slowly. I smelled the acrid smoke. I heard him arrange and re-arrange figurines on his shelf—the flutists and dancers, people coupling, fat men laughing, men with large phalluses, and women with full *derrieres*.

Then I heard a few sounds that told me he had found Pandora's Box and removed the lid. After only as much time as it would have taken him to peek cursorily inside, he knocked a few burning ashes in, put the lid back in its place, and slid the box back onto the shelf.

I was surprised to feel a pang of sorrow for the box, clearly tiresome to Papa now that it was no longer the everyday catcher of his spark. True, it was nothing special to look at in comparison to the more frolicsome members of its shelf community; it had entirely regular angles, predictable blue tiles, and it was shut up tight, revealing no trace, ever, of fires within.

"Ah, me," Papa sighed. Then there was a long silence. But then, "Anna, I give up," he said, more decisively that I had expected. "I have tried. But I see now that I have failed." And here Papa hobbled quietly to his desk and dropped himself into his chair, reeking, I must say, of age.

"You have tried what, Papa?" I asked.

"We have talked about almost all that you once kept hidden. I have worked the crannies and crevices of your dreams. I have steadfastly tried to steer you towards your best destiny. I have drummed into you the value of a womanly life."

"Yes, we have. You have," I said. And for a wonderful moment as I contemplated his admission of failure I felt my spirit lift with so much joy that I feared my body might float off the couch.

"I have constructed an analysis of your dreams and actions that, without fail, ignored the thrumming, the earth tones, and the abundant vaginal imagery. We have discussed your episodes with Doctor Jones at length. Oops! 'Length.' Slip!"

"Slip," I agreed.

Then Papa said, "I am sorry, Anna. Sorry and, I guess, more than a bit sad, actually. I hope you don't mind. We have spent these days talking about Doctor Jones, Venus, and almost anything we could except for the matter at hand—or I should say the woman at hand. Eva. I have lost the battle. You want to disclose a change in your relationship with her to me, do you not? This will be difficult news for me to hear, I hope you realize."

"Yes, Papa," I said, trying to sit up but only getting as far as lifting my torso just a bit. "I want to disclose to you the new nature of my relationship with Eva."

"All right then," he said, and he rose from his chair and ceremoniously stood at soldierly attention in order, I supposed, to take hard news in the most time-honored way he knew.

If I could have rolled my eyes politely, I would have.

Instead, "Why, Papa?" I asked. "Why is this so difficult for you? Why 'difficult' for the man who has boldly explored the terrain of human sexuality and its endless permutations, as well as its indelible mark on the psyche?"

His chin wobbled for a moment before he spoke.

"You have asked me an enormously private question, and before I answer it I need your assurance that you are as able as you ever were to keep a secret." He was still standing like a soldier.

"I am, Papa."

"Very well." He relaxed a little. He noticed a piece of lint on his clothes and brushed it off. This odd, impromptu grooming behavior communicated a *gravitas* that made me wary.

"Anna," he began, "you see before you a man of waning physical power. The surgery that I had on my testicles when I was sick with cancer has made no difference in my ability to perform. For about a year now I have been without my spear."

"I am so sorry to hear that, Papa. I didn't know." I wasn't quite sure what the etiquette was for speaking with one's father about his virility, so I tried to match his tone, which was sober and solemn. "For a man of your vigor such a loss must be heartbreaking."

"I am a living, breathing, castration complex. No more, no less."

"My condolences, to be sure."

"Thank you. The real matter that more rightly concerns you, though, is the lens of distortion that my castration complex may have placed upon my ability to absorb your news about your…shall we call it 'spinsterhood?'"

"We could probably just go ahead and call it 'homosexuality.'"

"Let's not. Not yet."

"All right."

He rose out of his chair, but this time, thank goodness, he did not set about re-arranging his tiresome treasures. Instead, he crossed the *mandala* rug to a bookshelf, and he took from the shelf what looked like a diary. Shuffling with it back to his desk, he began making lengthy notes. He would write, stop, think, scratch his beard, and then write, stop, think, and scratch some more. If the choice of activity was meant to make me feel excluded and superfluous, it worked—so much so that when he spoke to me at long last, I was grateful and unguarded.

"Have you told your mother about Eva?" he asked me.

"Yes."

"Have you told Minna?"

"Yes, and I've told Henny and Oliver, as well."

"May I ask what their reactions were?"

"They were all very reasonable and supportive."

"And that warmed your heart, yes?"

"It did."

He stopped asking questions and gazed for a while out the window at nothing in particular. Perhaps he was lost in thought, envying the people on the street, the normal folk who lived unexamined lives. I can remember thinking right around then that it would be lovely to live that way.

"Well, you won't get reason and support from me," he finally announced. "I'm sorry, Anna. You see, I really have failed you here. Try as I might, the lens through which I perceive your news is one of sorrow and repugnance."

He put down his pen and looked out the window some more.

I had no trouble believing that he was sad, and terribly so, for his voice had cracked when he spoke.

"Is that something you would like to talk about?" I asked him, trying to keep us engaged with each other in some productive way.

"Not really."

"Well, I would," I countered. "I think we need to work this out a bit more."

"If you insist," he said. There was something in his voice that reminded me of a child saying "but you're not going to like this." He rose from his desk chair and took his place in his analyst's chair directly behind my head. Rather than asking me a question, he began to talk about himself.

"I will begin by being frank and confessional. It is difficult for me, a man of great appetite, to imagine my daughter in salacious heat at a time when the loss of my own torridity weighs heavily on my heart."

Then, after a pause—a very long one, at that—Papa asked, "Are you not afraid of me right now, Anna?"

When I wrote about the Wolf Man case, I wrote that, at one point, Papa's recounting of the case took "fabulous flight." I mention that now in order to signal that what follows in my recounting of the session that day may also be fabulous, though I have intentionally distorted nothing. Still, my ability to perceive events clearly as they happened may have been compromised by confusion. They may be compromised to this day by guilt.

"Are you not afraid of me right now, Anna?" he had said.

Now, that was really a *non sequitur*. I had told Papa about Eva. He had correctly anticipated what I would say, had dodged it for as long as he could, and in the end had acknowledged the news. All had not gone smoothly, but it had gone about as well as I could have expected. He had not died on the spot, for example, of shock and grief. He had not even gotten angry, or at least not angry enough to shout. He had not really blamed. Goodness, he hadn't even tried very hard to dissuade me! And he had actually spoken honestly about his feelings of inadequacy.

But then he had asked, out of nowhere it seemed, “Are you not afraid of me right now?”

“Afraid? Why, Papa? Why on earth would I be afraid of you?”

“I am afraid. I am so afraid of me.”

I knew right away that something extraordinary was happening with Papa because the locution he had used, “I am so afraid of me,” was unsophisticated—not at all like him. Also, the very topic of our conversation seemed to have changed without warning. I needed to understand what was upsetting him.

“Papa, please,” I said. “Come from your chair and let me see you more easily. Of what are you afraid?”

He stood up and came around to face me. As he placed himself near the analytic couch for inspection, his head wagged high over mine. I looked into his eyes and saw that he was almost weeping!

“Papa, why?”

“I am afraid that as a homosexual, you will entice young children,” he said, and his eyes raced around the room as he did. “I am afraid that you, like others before you, will become a child rapist.”

“Papa, don’t be ridiculous!” I said. “Homosexuals don’t necessarily rape children!”

His eyes stopped their wild evasion and settled directly on me when he said, “Libido is a force to be harnessed, and Anna, you haven’t been harnessing yours.”

I was more perplexed than defensive when I said, “Actually, Papa, I have. It is only very recently that I’ve stopped.”

He looked at me even more meaningfully, as though I were supposed to know what he would say next. But I didn’t, and he remained silent.

“Oh, hell’s bells, Papa! Does my relationship with Eva really make you think I would harm a child? Why ever would you imagine such a thing?”

“Imagine? Do you think I imagine? Let me be clear, Anna Freud. I, like you, have occasional attractions. And I may have harmed a child.”

I took a very deep breath, and then another and yet another. Yes, I had heard him talk about this years before with Doktor Jung. Still, I was too astonished to speak.

I spent a few moments feigning clumsily at plumping my pillows while I gathered my thoughts. For his part, Papa shuffled across to the bookshelf to place his diary back where it belonged. Having done so, he looked at me sheepishly. As I avoided his eyes by focusing on the pillows I was arranging, he began to roam nervously about. For the most part, he walked the perimeter of the *mandala* rug, as though he were examining its edges.

Toddling as he was, he seemed simple and naive—characteristics that I knew how to deal with, for by that time I had been either teaching or analyzing children for eleven years. The very idea that an "innocent" like him could do actual evil was beyond my ability to absorb that evening. Indeed, I began to refuse that notion almost as soon as I heard him express it. I began speaking to Papa in the conversational tones that I usually reserved for teenagers. Vocally, I offered safety and care.

"I'm going to ask you some questions about what you just said, Papa. But before I do that, I want to reassure you that I, personally, have never hurt a child. What Eva and I do with each other in no way has anything to do with children. We have loved each other for a long time. Our sex is not casual or meaningless. It isn't necessarily mannerly, but I'm beginning to understand that sex generally isn't. Furthermore, there are no children physically present when Eva and I are sexual with each other. Child molesters? Hardly. It is just Eva and me, Papa, with each other."

"It's just Eva and Anna," Papa repeated as his walk around the rug brought him in and out of shadow.

"Yes, Papa. I do fear that you are inflating your concerns about us. But now I need to hear about you. You said that you might have hurt a child. Tell me more."

He looked up for a moment, meeting my eye. "Of course you could be right," he said.

"About Eva and me. Yes, I am right. Papa, I need you to talk to me about that child now."

"Talk?" And right then and there I saw a very large tear spring into his eye. It was accompanied by a slight squeaking sound from high in his throat.

Oh my! I thought. I am about to say, "Tell me what comes to your mind as soon as it comes to mind." And just as Mama did when I said that, he is going to respond as though I am the first person in his life ever to ask him a personal question.

I did it. I said, "Tell me what comes to your mind as soon as it comes to mind. I would be happy to help you sort out your thoughts and feelings."

He squeaked again, and I must report that hearing my father do that was most disarming. He stood on the edge of the *mandala*, protected (I truly hoped) by its power from the evil spirits that seemed to have overrun his room and maybe even his mind. He just stood there, making tiny, high noises and holding Venus. Soon enough he was weeping copiously, though without any more sounds.

"Pauline."

"Pauline? Who is Pauline? You don't mean *The Perils of Pauline,* do you, Papa?

"No. No, I mean the real Pauline. She was a little girl. She was my cousin."

"What about Pauline?"

"I took her."

I did not immediately realize what my father was talking about. Was I emotionally protecting myself by shutting down my intellect?

"You took her. You took her where?"

"I took her flower."

"You took Pauline's flower? Did she have a pretty one?"

"Her brother held her down. I approached from above. I took her flower."

Implosion. Exhaustion. Horror. My mind was again fully awake.

The interdependent circles near which Papa stood seemed suddenly to scream out a logic of which I had long been vaguely aware but had never allowed to reach consciousness. I realized precisely what Papa was talking about, and I feared I would be sick.

It was right about then that the worst thing of all happened. Papa began to move with surprising speed down on top of me. His whole self descended. I could smell the tobacco of his breath. Our eyes briefly met in the split second before his face smacked into mine. I could feel his heat on my chest and his breath in my ear. He grunted. And then from somewhere (a draft from the window? a gale from my memory?) I felt cold air on my skin—more skin than I would ever willingly expose to the sun, I remember thinking in that instant.

"HELP! HELP!" I yelled, and as I yelled I saw those words in my mind's eye, as though they were the block-lettered, silent screams of the heroine in *The Perils of Pauline*.

When Oli rushed into the room, he found me perched high up on the back of the couch. Papa was on the floor, and he must have looked to be in far greater distress than I. For one thing, he was sobbing and holding his groin.

"Papa! Papa! Are you all right?" Oli asked.

"She kicked me, Oli! She kicked me!"

Papa held his testicles as he cried all night long in a corner of the parlor. Oli, Henny, Mama, and Tante Minna sat together in the center of the room, huddled near the coal-burning stove. I sat in the opposite corner. By the time dawn neared, Papa's eyes and face were leathery with sweat and bloating. He looked positively reptilian.

"I didn't leap on you—I fell on you!" he called at one point from his corner. "I'm an old man and I'm not very good at walking."

"I'm a young woman, and I'm not so good at it either," I countered, "thanks to you."

Oli tiredly trod back and forth between the two of us every once in a while, delivering hot coffee. "I would like to point out that apparently you both can manage your limbs more readily than you've been letting on."

"Ask him about his little cousin Pauline, Oli. Go on. Ask him!" I shouted.

"The confidences of the consulting room are not to be betrayed!" Papa thundered as he stood up to his full height. He moved towards me, his face set in angry stone. He got almost all the way to me and then he fell, keeling straight over.

This time when I screamed, it was in fear for him, not of him.

"Papa! Are you all right, Papa? Oh, Oli! Help him! Help us!" I had tried to catch Papa in my arms but had only succeeded in giving his face a nasty scratch and then dropping him to the floor, where he rolled about, crying.

"Are you all right, old man?" Oli asked. He pulled Papa into a sitting position.

"I've just fallen again, blast it," Papa blubbered. "That's the second time tonight."

Hearing him sniffle, Tante Minna came over and dutifully held a hankie for Papa while he blew his nose. After that little exchange, he looked at me with fierce eyes. "And neither time did I do it purposefully!"

Well, now I felt like I needed a hankie. For with the second fall he had some evidence for a claim of innocence. I was not about to give up my side of the consulting room story entirely. But I was feeling newly confused and chagrined. Had I grossly misinterpreted what had happened a few hours before between Papa and me? Did I not have the full breadth of the high road supporting me?

"Who is Pauline?" Henny called out.

"She was my cousin—my niece, actually, though we were about the same age." Papa answered quickly, almost as though he were afraid that I would give my version of the Pauline story before he could give his. "I have a memory. It is a disturbing one. I was a very young boy. I remember Pauline's brother, John, holding her down in the grass. She was lying on her back and she was terrified. John held her by the arms so that I could approach from above. My memory beyond that point is not clear, though I know that she held to her breast—her fully clothed breast, I might add—a bouquet of *Kohlroeserl*. I do not—I repeat do not—know for sure what I did to Pauline. How much, really, could I have done, considering that this is a very early memory for me, one that preceded puberty by a handful of years? I only know that to this day I am filled with revulsion and remorse. I know that the refrain in my brain is, 'I took her flower. I took her flower.' I know that Pauline always seemed sad afterwards—though it was a sadness that, in all fairness to me, I may have projected onto her. Little boys can have vivid imaginations. I took her flower. What sort of flower I took I do not know. Was it from the bouquet? Was it the entire bouquet? Was it actually her virginity? I don't believe that it was. But being the honorable gentleman that I am, that is what I must take full blame for, whether or not it is the truth."

I looked over at the other women in the room. Mama, Tante Minna, and Henny, who had welcomed my own (I thought shameful) disclosure so warmly, did not rush at Papa with the ice bags and hankies and "Don't you think?"s, "What if you?"s and "When that happened to me, I"s that I had found so dear. They looked at Papa. They looked at each other. They looked at Oli. They looked at me. And they said nothing.

We all said nothing.

I, for one, was struck by how closely life resembled film. The visual clues were all so pat. Only a few hours before the consulting room had seemed awash in the sort of cinematic hints that spell "horror story." It had been night. Exotic, evil creatures had been watching me mutely, having paused in their barbarous cavorting in a sin-charred room. Sirens had screamed anonymously on the streets outside.

But the images my mind produced when Papa talked about Pauline created a different sort of horror scene. *Lust Spills in the Gorge* might be that movie's name. And here would be the scene: The girl was wearing a blouse and dirndl; the sun was in the sky; the girl blinked to fight off the glare of the sun; her assailant carried *Kohlroeserl.*

No. Wait. In Papa's story it was Pauline who carried the *Kohlroeserl.*

It was in *my* story of the day of our family's disastrous Alpine hike that someone—Papa!—carried *Kohlroeserl.* In the aftermath of listening to Papa describe his possible rape of Pauline, I found myself in a blur of details that—let me say it right here—led me to re-experience sensations from that day sixteen years before.

Oli had pushed Papa into a mountain crevice, and my siblings and I had heard the sound of his cry.

> *Papa is hurt. Everyone is running. I am helping Papa climb out of the crevice. His face is aflame with emotion. He is angry, weepy, needy. I hold him close to me. He holds me. He mutters about the rape of mothers, sisters, cousins, and aunties. We spend an hour or so in a meadow. It is Mama's duty, not mine, to be in that meadow with him. The cold air is on more of my skin than I normally reveal. I want to go home.*

What was I remembering? What had I forgotten?

As Oli brought Papa a clean handkerchief for the badly bleeding scratch on his face, the impact of what seemed to be retrieved memory fragments began to seep in. Had I been assaulted a few hours earlier in the consulting room? Already it was impossible to know for sure. Had I been assaulted sixteen years earlier on the mountain? It was theoretically possible. After all, Papa had just wept to us all that he may have hurt a child. Indeed, I once overheard him confide to Doktor Jung that he was a child rapist.

The only way to find out was to ask Papa.

And so, "Papa," I started, gently enough. Mama, Tante Minna, and Henny were still huddled near the parlor's stove. They had listened raptly, albeit from a fairly long distance, to Papa's story about Pauline.

When I started to speak to him, they scooted their chairs closer to us. Oli, too, came closer.

"Papa, I want to ask you something. I can see that you are troubled by your memory of Pauline. That is an event about which I can offer no real insight. Either it happened or it didn't, and I do not know how you will ever discern the truth, given that Pauline is probably now dead."

"That's right," he said. "And I know that John is dead, too."

How does one say to one's father, "But while we're on the matter of child rape…?" One just says it.

"But while we're on the matter of child rape, I thought that I might ask you about something that happened sixteen years ago."

"Yes?"

"Did you rape me the day that we hiked in the Alps and Oli tried to murder you?"

"I did not try to murder him!" Oli shouted.

Chapter 31

Sometimes facts can behave like trick billiard balls, crashing deafeningly into one another, scattering spectacularly, careening recklessly off what is known and unknown, and then coming to rest in suspiciously tidy patterns.

Dabbing carefully at the deep gash I had made on his face, Papa resignedly said he "had no memory" of raping me sixteen years before. I said that I believed him, though I also made clear to him that his story about Pauline was ample demonstration that memory can self-defensively enshroud whatever the mind might prefer to keep secret.

Oli was upset that I had mentioned so casually the defining traumatic moment of his life. With my utmost composure I listened to him explain that he had only "inadvertently fallen" on Papa, never even for a second intending to push him. Papa allowed that he believed Oli, given the fact that, within the last several hours, he had twice "inadvertently fallen" on me.

Oli and Papa mutually requested that they accept each other regardless of whatever mistakes they had made. Acceptance and forgiveness were duly granted.

Forgiveness—whether deserved or not—can, by displacing guilt, create a vacuum that giddiness, the helium of human emotion, quickly fills.

Helium expands infinitely, as do all gasses.

Touched by the sheer gassiness of the moment, Mama and Papa

mutually requested and granted both acceptance and forgiveness, as did Papa and Tante Minna.

Mama and Tante Minna also mutually requested and granted acceptance and forgiveness, Mama laughing all the while. “Thirty years she’s been *schtupping* with my Sigi off and on. Now she asks me?”

By then it was morning. Henny and Oli brought the baby into the room when she awoke. She was a scrumptious reminder of happy possibility, and we were all grateful for a chance to help her welcome the day.

I then rather timidly asked Papa if he could hold acceptance and forgiveness in his heart for me regarding all that I had told him about myself the night before.

“No. I can’t say that I can, Anna. I can’t say that I can.”

He wasn’t visibly angry or disgusted when he said it. He was only firm and sorrowful. Still, quicker than you can say “hysterical transferential identification,” I was once again the young boy of my masturbation fantasies. Once again I was on a platform in the sun. Once again I was being publicly beaten by an enraged, iron fisted man. This time, however, the scenario was a bit different. This time the boy with blond curls got mad.

“You are impossible!” I screamed. “And this is so unfair! This is the way my awful life goes, over and over and over again! You accept and forgive Oli, he accepts and forgives you. You accept and forgive Mama, she accepts and forgives you. You accept and forgive Tante Minna and she does the same for you. Mama accepts and forgives Tante Minna, who accepts and forgives her. There was so much acceptance and forgiveness in this room a few minutes ago, it felt like Yom Kippur! But what about me? When is anyone going to get around to accepting and forgiving me?”

“I do!” “I do!” “I do!” Mama, Tante Minna, and Henny each cheered. They came rushing at me, babbling about “Don’t you think?” and “What if you?” and “When that happened to me I….”

“Silence, everyone, please!” Papa shouted. “This is between Anna and me. It is important.”

He offered me his arm. And in the light of a new day I walked with him all the way to his suite of professional rooms, through the waiting room, and into his consulting room.

Walked with him. *Nota bene.*

Need I even say that the rest of them shuffled behind us, entered the suite of professional rooms, and gathered to eavesdrop at the Danger Door? Papa heard the whispering and jostling for position and bade me walk him back to the door, where he gave three sharp raps that sent them all scurrying.

I then returned Papa to his chair. Once I was sure that he had firm hold of it, I turned towards the couch. I proceeded steadily enough. Then I heard a quick few steps and found Papa at my side, guiding me the rest of the way, afraid that I would fall. I arrived safely at the couch, thanked him, and then walked him back to his chair.

Once he was settled in the seat I said, "If we're not careful we'll be walking each other conscientiously for the rest of the day."

That is why my final analysis took place with me standing at Papa's side, leaning on him for support whenever I needed to.

"Let me begin by suggesting to you that you are wrong about your feelings, Anna. You are neither a homosexual nor in love. Instead, you are merely feeling ambivalent about men—probably about Eddie Bernays himself. He was, after all, a bit too smooth a talker."

"Papa, you are wrong in your interpretation of what I've told you about Eva and me."

"No, no. I insist. Ambivalent you are. Ambivalently but firmly heterosexual."

"I am a homosexual."

"Anna Freud! Are you questioning my authority?" He actually roared it—like the Hapsburg Empire father that he was, a man used to firmly ruling the entirety of his family. He even looked imperial when he roared, to the extent that any wobbly man with a crumbling jaw can.

"Anatomy is destiny!" is what I think he tried to bellow next, but

I'm unsure, for mid shout he coughed up mucous and then had to lurch towards a spittoon. "If I am sure of anything," he said, spitting, "it is whence real sexual satisfaction for women derives!"

"Whence, then?"

"Inside the vagina—not outside, on the clitoris."

"Do tell," I said.

"I am not deaf to the superior tone that your voice has taken. I will pay that tone no heed. I have only your best interests in mind, my dear, in telling you what I know about female satisfaction. I have more experience in this matter than you. You will just have to trust me."

"Ah, but while I do still love you, Papa, I don't quite trust you as blindly as I once did. I must admit, though, that as a reasonably competent psychoanalyst I am open to the possibility that you are right. I am not convinced, mind you, but I will consider your argument, for you have been my primary teacher and you are a brilliant man."

"Thank you, Anna, for your open-mindedness."

"You are welcome. But I must tell you that even if you are correct in your idea that real sexual satisfaction must come from inside the vagina, I do not intend to change my decision about sexual preference one jot. The vagina can be filled with just about anything. And if other responsive areas of the body can be brought into play and stimulation, so much the better."

Most probably, a man who is already sitting in his chair cannot fall into his chair. Still, that is the memory I have of that moment.

Papa fell backwards, grasping at his heart and his jaw. "It's all my fault!" he sputtered by way of explanation to no one in particular. "I was much too driven by my own libido. I never provided her with a figure upon whom to safely Oedipally attach. And once I, the father, had ruined her developing psyche, I, the analyst, failed to cure her. I left her in the muck and mire of penis envy, and she will swim there for life!"

I was mildly amused imagining an unseen confessor in the room. But I was also unmoved. If I have ever in my eighty-seven years spoken with the quiet dignity of a proud homosexual, I did it then, at age thirty.

"Nonsense, Papa," I said. "Penis envy explains my homosexuality no more than dildo envy explains Tante Minna's lack of it. Now let us sit here for the remainder of the hour and keep our thoughts to ourselves." I walked quite well and independently over to the couch, where I sat down.

At the end of the hour, Papa said, "Our time is up. We have tunneled very deeply." We each rose from our sitting positions with no aid whatsoever and walked separately to the door.

"Papa," I said when he put his hand on the doorknob. "I will not be coming to analysis again."

What was I to think, how was I supposed to respond, when he protested, "I am an old man, and you do not think it worth your while to love me!"?

First of all, precisely that sentence was language that I knew he had already used on Hilda Doolittle, an American writer, when she left analysis. Second, I was not amused. He was being manipulative.

Though I did feel sorry for him. He was right. He looked ancient.

So I stayed calm.

"There is an old rabbinical saying, Papa. 'If I myself am not for me, then who will be for me? And if not now, when?'"

He didn't even bother gasping and fuming at my having brought rabbis into the conversation. He smiled. "Well, I don't know what I object to more, the pious overtones or the stiff-armed goodbye." And, with that, Papa gave me a most pristine kiss right on the top of my head.

He watched as I crossed the waiting room and entered the hall. Before I could make it into our family's apartment, however, I heard him pursue me.

"Anna, I wonder if I might ask a favor."

"Of course," I said.

"Would you consider attending the upcoming conference of the

International Psychoanalytic Association for me? I fear that I am too old and sick to travel."

"Of course, Papa."

"Thank you, Anna."

"You are welcome. It is no problem at all."

"Ven a gonif kisht darf men zich di tzein ibertseilen," my grandmothers might have known to warn me. When a thief kisses you, you had better count your teeth.

Just a few short weeks after my final analysis, I traveled for Papa to the conference at Bad Homburg. I wore my pearls and sensible shoes. I strode strongly to the podium, being the "reasonably competent" psychoanalyst that I was. I opened the sealed envelope containing a freshly written paper.

Its title was "Some Psychical Consequences of the Anatomical Distinction between the Sexes." It was the formal setting forth of the ideas about penis envy that Papa had been developing ever since Sophie's death. Little girls, he said, "notice the penis of a brother or playmate, strikingly visible and of large proportions, at once recognize it as the superior counterpart of their own small and inconspicuous organ, and from that time forward fall a victim to envy for the penis." Then the paper explained that penis envy underlies the fierce emotional attachment typical of fathers and daughters.

Maybe I entered some peculiar, stress-induced trance as my eyes moved across the pages; I don't know. At any rate, I read the paper aloud and at the very same time was somehow able to read between the lines. It was a curious sensation, and apparently, also a transient skill, for I've never been able to repeat that particular feat.

Am I angry that he has tricked me into reading aloud a text subtly insulting to me and to my lover? I wondered this to myself at paragraph breaks.

Am I embarrassed to be the daughter compliantly narrating matters so revealing of my father and his foibles?

How do I really feel about him, this man who has written with such misguided force and fear? How do I feel about any of this or all of this?

I was the center of public attention, and so I didn't stop to ponder my questions. I just kept calling out the words, and I suspect, blushing at least once or twice.

And then I got to some particularly graphic sentences about clitoral masturbation and phallic pulsing. Mentally, I had to make them fade from the page even as I spoke them. But having done that, having made the most lurid parts of his paper literally disappear, I came to a realization:

The treatise itself was fiddle-faddle. But beneath the nonsense were relatively unadulterated expressions of emotion about fathers and daughters.

Papa said that family affection is anchored in the instinctual life of humans. Which it is, undeniably. He also said that family affection is insurmountable. As driven as we all are by the quest for genital stimulation, we are driven far more by the unnamable desire to create and preserve people to love.

What he'd written was actually quite touching. For, in truth, it was a declaration of the higher-purpose indelibility of the ties between daughters and fathers. It was also a declaration of his love for me.

Part 6

Wish Fulfillment

(1925-1938)

Anna with Bob, Tinkey, and Mabbie Burlingham.

Anna and Sigmund on the train in Paris, after escaping from Austria.

Anna and Princess Marie Bonaparte in Paris.

Chapter 32

A priest and a rabbi took tea together for many years. One evening the priest asked the rabbi, "Tell me, friend, for I've wondered. Have you ever tasted ham?"

The rabbi smiled. "There was a time when I was very young and curious when I tasted ham. Now you tell me something, friend. Have you ever been with a woman?"

The priest smiled. "When I was very young, yes, I was with a woman."

The rabbi said, "It's better than ham, isn't it?"

Eva did not turn out to be the love of my life. Dorothy Burlingham did.

Eva, you see, became an analytic client of my father. He bade her lie on the ornately draped couch in his den of iniquity. He turned upon her all of his charm. And he successfully convinced her that she was unswervingly heterosexual and should be loyal to her gloomy husband.

That is why Eva and I became "good friends." Though it was a complicated relationship, indeed. Quickly Eva became as dismal as her husband. They had another child. I resolved to move on and find another love.

Which I did one night not terribly long afterwards, although it would be more honest to say that love found me.

Our family was dining at home. A series of loud, frightening knocks threatened to rupture our apartment's thick, oak door.

Cook answered, and into the foyer rushed a small, elegantly dressed, dramatically gaunt woman with four young children. I had followed Cook into the foyer, so I saw Dorothy's whole entrance. Right away and even before she spoke, I knew that the intruder before me was both wealthy and American for she wore a long string of tiny, precious stones and had one of those "bob" hair styles. Even so, she dropped to her knees and began kissing the floor. "*M'aidez, m'aidez*" she muttered with each buss. It embarrassed her children.

"What's all that ruckus about?" Mama called out, and then she, Papa, and Tante Minna abandoned their dinners and appeared in the foyer to see.

Papa was never one to tolerate groveling. He insisted that Dorothy stop kissing his parquet and stand up properly. Once she was erect, Papa gave her one of his trademark handshakes. He also nodded courteously at the children, who nodded back at him. The two little girls even curtseyed. All four children were redheaded and freckled. The oldest two wore adorable, metallic orthodontic braces of a kind yet to be seen in Vienna.

I was intrigued by what I took to be the rampant exotica of the strange new creatures. In their comportment and accoutrements, Dorothy and her children were actually typical of upper crust Americans from that country's eastern seaboard. Dorothy Tiffany Burlingham was from New York City as well as Cold Spring Harbor, New York. Her husband, Robert, of New York City and Westchester society, was a convivial young physician who unfortunately suffered from what, by the 1980s, we have come to call manic-depressive disorder. It episodically rendered him angry and abusive. During one of his institutionalizations, Dorothy had gathered up her children and fled his reach, leaving America entirely for refuge at the home of a sympathetic family in Geneva. For about four years, she had been with that family off and on, using their home as a base while wandering expensively about Europe in a Model T car to sites that she hoped her children would find educational. The wandering was a strategy; she believed it would render her difficult for Robert to locate. By the time she and her children had arrived in Vienna, however, Robert had found her and begun legal proceedings to bring the children back to America.

Dorothy was skeletal from exhaustion and fear. She did not speak German well and was visibly embarrassed about having disturbed our supper.

Mama knew how to handle the situation. She invited everyone in and asked Cook to commence dessert—and, of course, to set extra places. The language of the evening, Mama announced, would be English.

Which we Freuds all spoke well. We spoke it better, in fact, than Dorothy's children did.

Dorothy's eldest boy, a feisty youngster approaching puberty, had a loud and almost unintelligible American twang. Though he deigned to sit with us at table, he refused Cook's dessert, declaring Austrian cakes "too brown" and us all "too old and boring to eat with."

I didn't need to be a psychoanalyst to correctly guess that this child, Robert Jr., was an *enfant terrible*. I also guessed that his awfulness was at least partly to blame for his mother's distress.

At table, Dorothy asked Papa for psychoanalytic help. He explained to her that his schedule was full; he would refer her to a trusted colleague. When Dorothy asked me for psychoanalysis for her children, I assured her that I had the time to work with the eldest right away and would fit in the others as needs developed and she saw fit.

Considering the behavior of Robert Jr., I guessed that all four siblings would be a goldmine of information about deviations from normal developmental paths.

I didn't learn much about the children that first night. My impressions were limited to "adorable" (for Mikey, a blushing four-and-a-half year-old), "opaque" (for Tinky, a six-and-a-half-year-old with the posture of a convict), "admirable" (for Mabbie, an eight-year-old who hung on Dorothy's every word), and "boorish" for eleven-year-old Robert Jr., or "Bob."

I did eventually take them all into analysis, beginning with Bob and then working age-wise down the line. Eros did not infect my psychoanalysis with any of them. Parental love did, however, and that surprised me, given how extraordinarily unlovable Bob, especially, was. Of course, it was psychoanalytic countertransference that gave birth to my parental love. In these four cases, the force behind it was terribly powerful. Dorothy had become too frail to extend her love steadily. The children needed someone like me to stabilize them.

One might, I suppose, assume that my love for Dorothy began as an extension of my countertransferential love for her brood. Indeed, I freely admit that may be true. Though I do think that I would have fallen for Dorothy regardless. Yes, she was almost impenetrably private. Yes, she chuckled but never really laughed. She was infirm and weepy and temporarily not up to the task of making simple decisions. But she needed me, and I liked being needed. Furthermore, her lineage was easily as colorful as mine. Where else was I going to find that in a woman?

Dorothy's grandfather had been Charles Lewis Tiffany, an immigrant to America from Ireland and a jewelry designer of unparalleled success. As rich as he was, he was also frugal. For economy's sake, C. L. (as he was called) walked the nearly sixty blocks from his upper-east-side home to his jewelry and diamond store on Union Square in New York City each day. He did so even during the blizzard of 1888, which grounded 200 ships and killed 500 people.

Dorothy's father was Louis Comfort Tiffany, the famously difficult and free-spending designer of stained-glass windows and lamps. Her mother Louise (yes, it was a "Lou and Lou" marriage) had been a suffragist before marrying. As gracious and loving as her husband was extravagant, Mama Lou had always felt uncomfortable in the Tiffany's ostentatious mansion on East Seventy-Second Street. Three seasons a year, she and the children lived simply at The Briars, a modest country estate in Cold Spring Harbor.

Mama Lou died of bowel cancer when Dorothy was only twelve.

When she took ill, Dorothy's Aunt Bessie came to help out, for Louis had no talent at being gentle. Neither, it turned out, did Aunt Bessie. She insisted on bringing Mama Lou from The Briars to the hated New York City mansion. She moved the children onto an upper floor of the mansion, leaving Mama Lou on a lower floor so that her moaning wouldn't disturb anyone. Each day when Dorothy asked if she could please, please see her mother, Aunt Bessie said, "Tomorrow." After several months of this, Aunt Bessie and Louis together announced one morning that Mama Lou had died during the night.

Almost immediately after Mama Lou's death, Louis had The Briars torn down, the property expanded, and Laurelton Hall built. A San Simeon of sorts, it was about the size of an ocean liner, a monstrosity of museum-quality rooms. The estate included a full-sized, replica Moroccan village in which Dorothy and her siblings were instructed to play. It came complete with costumed peasants as well as real goats, cows, chickens, doves, pheasants, and Clydesdale horses. There were fountains (one interior and nine exterior), a clock tower (clocks were everywhere; Louis insisted on punctuality), and a smoking room that had a throne for Louis that was very much like the couch in my father's consulting room. Dorothy especially liked to tell me about a mural-sized painting called "The Opium Fiend's Dream" that hung behind her father's throne. It featured images from the life cycle of a Chinese prostitute and, better still, it included a manticore. Laurelton Hall itself even had a *minaret*, and from its top Louis regularly screamed.

In the years after her mother's death, Dorothy found just about everything in life too strenuous. She left boarding school before graduating and returned to New York City on the pretext of wanting to care for her father as he aged. The result was nothing short of disaster, for Louis didn't need caretaking, and he loved Dorothy only as a bit of stage dressing for his pretentious life. He threw huge, costumed affairs, for example, for which he expected Dorothy to serve as a decoration. Once he dressed as the Kubla Khan and had Dorothy and her friends dress as slaves and fan him and the guests with ostrich feathers. Another time Dorothy was an attendant to the King and Queen of the Nile, the Queen being Louis's new and (according to Dorothy) slutty girlfriend.

A few years into this arrangement, Dorothy met Robert Burlingham, the man she would marry. He seemed a perfect match. He was amused by her father, although not hostile to him. He was a medical resident. He had graduated from Harvard in the Class of 1910, along with T. S. Eliot. He was even of Mayflower stock. Best, his physical appeal was so quiet and intense that he set Dorothy to quivering.

Dorothy first learned of Robert's manic depression only six weeks before he and she were to marry, when Robert rapidly cycled from his normal romantic gentility to feeling unsure about himself to feeling unsure about Dorothy to becoming verbally abusive of Dorothy and to terrifying her with threats of violence. A few weeks in hospital seemed to set things right; Robert emerged picturesquely apologetic and the wedding plans proceeded. Just two months after the wedding, Dorothy was merrily pregnant. Eight months later, Robert had another episode. About the time he emerged from hospital, Baby Bob was born.

That was 1914. Robert had suffered a few more episodes by 1917, when Mabbie was born. Twenty-one months of menace and reconciliations later came Tinky. Two harrowing years after Tinky, a pregnant Dorothy escaped with her children to Geneva and gave birth to Mikey.

And a little more than four years after Mikey's birth, Dorothy and the children arrived in our foyer.

There was no immediate attraction between Dorothy and me. Indeed, Dorothy was by nature heterosexual. Any handsome man's proximity was to her like a potent perfume. Robert's presence (he did eventually visit and try to reconcile) was altogether destabilizing. So the attraction between Dorothy and me was not fundamentally physical. Rather, it was a choice we made. It happened by way of her children, and that is its own story.

I began with Bob, analyzing him once a day. He was an awful brat, but his selfishness and impetuousness were equaled by his charm. Indeed,

I learned from his mother that, on the voyage from America, he had charmed the ship's cellist out of his spare cello, then fallen in love with the instrument and refused to give the cello back when the ship docked in Geneva. And by "falling in love" I mean just what one would expect. He'd never heard cello music before; once he did he was physically and emotionally changed by it (obsessional thoughts, unabated desire, and disrupted sleep).

Of course, Dorothy made Bob return the cello to its owner, but when she did she promised to buy him a new cello and a whole fleet of smaller instruments. She spoiled him. Children don't become impossible louts by accident. It's interesting, though; with each instrument Bob's mother gave him, he fell in love in rapid succession. I suspected that this pattern of intense infatuation with one object of desire after another was one he would later take up in relation to women, and I was right.

I also suspected that Bob might take up the serial acquisition pattern in relation to men. In the classic style of some pre-teens who have decided that their brand of sexual desire is off-target and must be sublimated, he was obsessed with death. He talked about it, read about it, came to supper once dressed as a veiled widow, and, indeed, killed several small animals. He claimed the deaths were accidents, but I suspected torture.

My first task in creating an analytic alliance with Bob was the same as it is for any patient; I set out to initiate transference and countertransference. But Bob disliked women of his mother's generation almost by creed, and I disliked Bob, so this was not going to be easy, I knew. I began our relationship by befriending him in a way that both of us found disorienting. Here he was, an American boy of enormous good looks, musical talent, and athletic ability, but he had no peer group because he wasn't enrolled in school. He couldn't enroll; he did not speak German. I became his sidekick.

He was only at first uneasy at having me in my proper skirt and nicely done hair accompany him on larks and pranks. I say "only at first" because I came to enjoy our adventures as much as he, and quite soon he saw the advantage in that. We built soapbox cars and raced them down hills. We hung ropes from trees and swung like monkeys. He and I climbed a trellis together so that I could give him a last boost into an upper-story window of a library, which enabled him to sneak an overdue book back into the stacks and then claim he'd returned it long before. That particular caper was my idea entirely. In all of this I only scraped my knee once and twisted one wrist badly. The other children looked on jealously; I promised them all they would have their turns with me later.

Dorothy looked on jealously, too. I promised her nothing.

On a more mundane note, I also typed Bob's letters to his father in America. I returned things he had stolen from his siblings, sneaked him money he wanted for candy that his mother didn't want him to have, and plea bargained with Dorothy on his behalf when she found out he'd been eating sugar again. In short, I facilitated Bob's most harmlessly impish self and protected him from the consequences of his darker impulses. Furthermore, I enjoyed every moment of both tasks. In return, Bob transferred onto me some of the Oedipal lust that rightly belonged to his mother.

Then, one by one, I added Dorothy's other children to my roster of neurotics. One by one, I garnered their dependence.

Mabbie was the Burlingham child whose character most corresponded with mine. She lived to please her favorite parent, which in her case was her mother, and she became strangely desperate whenever she suspected that Dorothy was experiencing discomfort of any kind. Mabbie also had an unusual approach to language. It was as though she were overly adept at speech. Even at age eight, she had an enormous four-language vocabulary of nouns, adjectives, adverbs, verbs, and prepositions. She had so many borderless words that she found it difficult to keep the languages distinct in her head. When speaking excitedly, she would construct her sentences from whatever words were rolling around in her mouth. Even when speaking calmly, she couldn't get things entirely straight. I considered her inability to keep languages distinct in her mind and her inability to see her mother's needs as separate from hers to be manifestations of the same problem. She had an interior self that she was unable to anchor.

Where Mabbie was overly concerned about her mother's comfort, Tinky seemed concerned about no one but herself. I am not sure, however, that I always understood her correctly. She was reluctant to disclose in analysis. And, as I've said, she had an odd posture with hunched shoulders and a defiant glare. Tinky also had a disconcerting habit of aggressively staring at other people, and I could never quite decipher whether she was envying or pitying the people she watched. Like Dorothy, Tinky was rail thin. Furthermore, she was allergic. Many foods gave her terrible rashes, as did certain pollens. She claimed to be allergic to baths, as well, or at least to soap.

There was not much deviant about Mikey, the youngest of Dorothy's children. Only four-and-a-half years old the evening his family arrived in our apartment, he was hypersensitive to his mother's attenuated state and to her social insecurities. That's what I tried to help him with in analysis. On the whole, though, I found Mikey's happy manner unfailingly ambrosial. Apparently, he knew that about me, for periodically while he played he would look up and catch me watching him. He would smile at me as though to acknowledge applause.

I didn't have to be nearly as inventive to gain the affection of Mabbie, Tinky, and Mikey as I had been with Bob. I just needed to be present, friendly, and not in tears. This sort of behavior made time spent with me infinitely preferable to time spent with their mother.

To no one's surprise, Dorothy became anxious about my relationships with all of her children. This is actually to be expected between any child's analyst and the analysand's mother. A general, broad, leonine circling between Dorothy and me ensued. Warily, she growled. She worried that her children were talking about her failures. She didn't want my judgments. She had done, she let me know in no uncertain terms, as well as she could by her children under circumstances that would have daunted any woman.

If I may be reductionistic, I would say that it was all the ringing around each other that brought us together. Dorothy desired in me what she had once desired in her husband. She wanted me to prevail in a contest of wills. She wanted to be held captive by someone both able and lusty who would emotionally disrobe her. This time, though, she wanted things to proceed more gently.

I was hardly in the mood to hold her captive. That sort of thing is not my cup of coffee. However, by creating a dependence on me in each of her children, I suppose I had done precisely that. And by asking pointed questions, I accomplished the second, "stripping bare" deed that she wanted done.

"Can you name for me what is making you avoid my gaze?" I asked one day as we conferred about her family.

When she didn't answer I said, "If you can't talk about how you feel, may I make some educated guesses?"

Then, when I saw beads of perspiration gather on her brow, I said, "I can help you feel more comfortable if I take your shawl and hang it for you. Would you like me to? Then we can talk about the anger that is making you warm."

Somehow things became animated—"peppery," I might actually say. My memory is that it was the removal of the shawl that set us both off. I truly didn't know that any of this was about to happen. But as she warily withdrew her shawl from her delicate shoulders I felt as though I were being dared to be bold. So I touched her neck when I took the shawl in my hand.

"What would you like me to do next?" I heard myself ask.

The windows were open. The sky was bright blue and the few clouds white and puffy. We heard the children play a fantasy game in the yard below, with Bob as a pirate and the girls helping a blindfolded Mikey safely walk Bob's plank. We locked the door and had our privacy.

Within a few minutes the opera was over. Dorothy's hand lay

warmly on my bare belly. I saw the edge of the discarded shawl stir in the breeze. Charmed by the harmony of hues—the ebony shawl lay on the pink, ecru, and peacock blue of the pillow onto which I had tossed it—I wanted to write a poem about color or perhaps sing a song about the wonders of draped outerwear.

I kissed Dorothy's eyes and discovered a few tears.

I accepted them as bereavement at her long-awaited letting go of Robert, not as shame or reluctance about her irremediable harvest of me.

Chapter 33

The house that Dorothy and her family first rented in Vienna was a suburban mansion that belonged to a Hungarian prince. It sounds impressive, but it was really just a drafty edifice with too much lawn and too many rooms.

Though, soon enough, we needed the extra space. Dorothy's friends from Geneva, Arthur and Ruth Sweetser and their two children, came to live with Dorothy and her children.

Dorothy and I agreed not to enroll her children in either public or private schools, for even if they could rapidly improve their German, the four of them had little experience with schooling to begin with, much less with schools as rigid and unforgiving as the schools in Austria. Instead, Dorothy and a host of tutors educated them. I visited the mansion every day and met with each child for an hour individually. A second host of tutors educated the Sweetser children, whom I also analyzed. My psychoanalytic practice was at last more than full, with most of my patients residing at the same address.

I even negotiated a cordial peace between Dorothy and her husband. He was in good mental health when he visited, and so he was appallingly attractive to her. I worried that her strong heterosexual tendencies would re-ignite. She worried as well, and so she and I agreed that whenever he visited Vienna I would determine the frequency and location of their interactions, and I would chaperone them.

But in those first wonderful months after meeting Dorothy, Robert was still thousands of kilometers away. Even so, we did not have the lazy weeks of rapture and mutual revelation that typify the beginning of many love affairs. Dorothy and I were rarely free of children, tutors, and duties. Mostly in my late afternoon reports to her about her children's progress, as we sat with our feet up on ottomans and coffee cups in hand, I revealed choice tidbits of my own life story. She fed me morsels of hers. And so it came to pass that we believed our compatibility would last for a very long time.

But then late November came.

In Vienna, the end of November marks the beginning of a frenzy in Christians for Christmas. Dorothy was Christian. Most of Vienna was, as well. And, of course, the whole idea of Christmas is intensely religious. Vienna accomplishes a world-class sacred celebration every year, epitomized by the spectacular midnight mass at St. Stephen's Cathedral on Christmas Eve—a mass that spills out onto the cobblestone streets while bells ring deliriously in joy.

But really, Christmas in Vienna is not only about God, because the Christians of Vienna are easily as romantic as they are religious. For them, the holiday is partly a celebration of horse-drawn carriages, of being swaddled in furs, of listening to the high voices of the Vienna Boys Choir, of dropping *kronen* into pots held by cheerful old men in *loden* who toot on little brass horns, and of skating on frozen ponds. Religion shares the stage with lights, cheer, family, winter fun, and giving. For those reasons, even I had often enjoyed the season.

But the Burlinghams were Americans. So for them Christmas was not about the seasonal niceties I had come to favor. It wasn't even about God, for they weren't religious. For them, Christmas was about gifts and overeating.

Beginning in late November, Dorothy and I began spending money in the style of her father, frenetically acquiring presents that we wrapped and squirreled away in a closet to await Christmas Eve. For their part, the children penned long letters asking *Christkindl* for items they had seen in a magazine or store window or perhaps had even sought out and priced in one of Vienna's special Christmas markets. While Dorothy stayed home baking (with the intention of filling the house with the aromas of cloves and cinnamon), I trudged through drizzle and fog to shop. The days became steadily shorter, the children more demanding, and Dorothy and I more worn out.

Do you know the joke about the Pope, the Dalai Lama, and the Rabbi?

> *A new flood is foretold and nothing can be done to prevent it; in three days the waters will wipe out the world.*
>
> *The Dalai Lama pleads with everyone to become a Buddhist; that way, they will at least find nirvana.*
>
> *The Pope has a similar message: "It is not too late to accept Jesus," he says.*
>
> *The Rabbi says, "We have three days to learn how to live under water."*

Flooded by the intensity of the children's desires for gifts and food, I thought I might try to interest them in a more Viennese approach to the season. To this end, I suggested that, in the style of our Christian neighbors, we incorporate Advent into our holiday plans, for Advent traditions teach children patience. And so, one evening after supper, Dorothy and I announced together that we would all fast until Christmas Eve.

"By which I mean we will forego meat, desserts, and between-meal snacking," she explained.

I had just served everyone an after-supper cookie with a scoop of ice cream. Mikey looked as though he thought I might take his plate away. Tinky looked as though she might steal it from him.

"Mother, you've finally gone mad," Bob taunted Dorothy.

Mabbie, of course, defended Dorothy, because that's what she always did: "I think it's all right to be more European about this. Other people keep their cookies in tins until Christmas Eve. We could do that."

"In the meanwhile, we also could decorate the tree with some of our cookies," Dorothy added, to build enthusiasm. "Anna and I can cut a tree tomorrow."

"Wrong," said Bob. "I don't know how this bit of tradition escaped you, but in Vienna the tree doesn't get cut and decorated until Christmas Eve."

"Well, we'll make other kinds of decorations then," Mabbie countered as Tinky actually slipped the last few bites of Mabbie's cookie into her own mouth. "That's what we'll do while we..."

"Starve!" Bob added nastily, spitting crumbs because he spoke, as usual, with his mouth full.

We did, as it turned out, make decorations. I set out art supplies I had bought just for the occasion. I explained that the children could make lace, dip candles, or hand-wrap wreaths: their choice.

"*None* of this is our choice," Bob snarled.

Mikey and Mabbie happily opted for candle dipping. Bob said he was going to find the mistletoe I'd bought and hang it by its neck until it begged to be taken down. Tinky was grim, saying and doing nothing.

Of all the children that holiday season, I worried the most about Tinky. Just that week, she had begun a habit of scowling quietly at Dorothy, me, and her siblings for long periods. Sometimes she took notes. She had also recently begun a new private pastime she called Scaling. She would enter a room in which family members were doing one thing or another, watch for a while, and then begin to climb about the room quietly, over and around people so that she could perch in odd locations and observe the goings on further from there.

I wasn't sure that Tinky's purpose in Scaling was only to see or listen better. I thought she also was trying to unnerve us. That evening, after about five minutes of watching the candle dipping, she began Scaling. Almost as soon as she settled herself on top of a sideboard and peered brazenly over Mikey's shoulder, she cried out, "Boo!" Mikey startled and burnt himself on the wax. His scream then startled her, and she made the sideboard wobble. The wobble knocked over a vase, which landed on the floor with a crash.

"You did it on purpose!" Mikey accused her, flabbergasted.

"What are you, some kind of raven?" Mabbie demanded of Tinky, annoyed.

Tinky calmly climbed down from the sideboard and left the room, her skinny shoulders hunched in a bird-like way.

She headed for the kitchen and started Scaling again.

Bob found me in the kitchen doorway, silently observing Tinky. As complicated as the evening and situation were, I was silly enough to anticipate some friendly (if snide) commiseration from him, considering what good chums we had become over the past several months. I was disappointed.

"Don't you think the idea of us celebrating Christmas as a family is a bit offensive," he asked, wrinkling his nose for emphasis, "considering that neither of you two 'parents' has a penis?"

There may be much that is romantic about snowflakes and good cheer, but there is also something lonely about it all. After Bob's remark, I watched Tinky climb the kitchen cabinet that held the everyday stemware. She was nimble as a goat—more so, in fact. She reminded me of Tinker Bell, fluttering from toehold to toehold. As I watched, I saw Tinky's tiny nightgowned body framed by the kitchen window. Through the window I could see frost-covered tree limbs sparkling. Farther down the street were snow-speckled automobiles, children caroling, and blanket-covered tourists in a horse-drawn carriage.

Neither Tinky nor I said a word as she made it past the cabinet and across the sink and stove.

I heard a noise coming from Dorothy's bedroom. Tinky, too, heard it. She paused before mounting the icebox. I left the kitchen to investigate the noise.

The bedroom door was locked, but it was clear to me that Dorothy was weeping behind it. I went into the parlor to ask the children what the problem had been. Bob said it was his grand hanging of the mistletoe that had set her off.

"She and my *father* used to kiss and tickle under it," he explained smugly.

Dorothy's enchanted Christmases with the once-perfect Robert: She'd warned me about the sorrow of those memories earlier that evening. She also had told me that she still had hopes for some day being in a relationship in which it was acceptable to express physical affection in front of her own children.

In the week leading up to Christmas Eve of 1925, seventeen people in Vienna committed suicide.

The next day, Bob took a holiday from being rude. And on Christmas Eve, all of the children were better behaved than I had anticipated. They appreciated their gifts. Bob pronounced the tree—decorated with ornaments that we as a family had made and with candles that we as a family had molded—well worth the wait. Christmas Day visiting my parents and Tante Minna was occasionally awkward. But we all got through it. We had brought Bob's cello with us. After dinner, Bob got everyone laughing with stories about his and my hijinks. Mikey, who had somehow never heard about most of these adventures, clapped his hands and howled at the comedy. He sat on Tante Minna's lap, and that made her very happy, indeed. Mabbie wrapped herself around Dorothy's shoulders while Bob talked, and then she even draped herself around Mama for a while. When Bob's tales ran dry, he played a little concert for everyone. Meanwhile, Tinky slipped off to the foyer and started Scaling. Papa followed her in to watch and smoke a cigar.

By April of 1926, I was completely sharing parental responsibility with Dorothy. I stayed each night until we'd put all four children to bed, and I arrived each morning in time to wake them. I left only for a few hours each day to meet my non-Burlingham, non-Sweetser patients, which I did in a small office in Papa's suite of professional rooms.

Eventually, Dorothy began studying psychoanalysis in the hopes of one day practicing at my side. She was even my pupil. She began her studies by attending my four-lecture series on child analysis, which I gave on Monday nights at the Training Institute that had just been founded by the Vienna Psychoanalytical Society.

As Mama had pointed out to me the evening of my great disclosure, matters of sexual preference were not easily discussed, not even in those more modern times. Dorothy and I decided, therefore, that I would not take up residence in her home. Neither would we mention the depth of our feeling to anyone—certainly not to Papa (for fear that he would meddle), but not even to Mama or Dorothy's psychoanalyst. People could believe what they wanted.

It wasn't only that matters of sexual preference were not easily discussed. It was also that the word "queer" had come into use, and it was freighted with contempt. "Spoiled," "ruined," "alien"—all are synonyms for "queer." With Papa's pronouncements about homosexuality and perversity, he had fostered a honeycomb of prejudices that Dorothy and I knew would not serve the reputations of two child psychoanalysts well. Neither would they serve Dorothy if Robert were ever to carry through on his threats to sue her for custody in American court.

Eventually Dorothy began studying analysis three nights a week, reading all of the psychoanalytic literature (and there was quite a lot), and attending the Society's regular Wednesday night meetings, as well. She also started a training analysis with Papa and began seeing patients of her own, under his supervision. And, of course, she mothered her four children. In an attempt to eliminate her commute from the suburbs and thereby simplify her life, she commissioned the architect Felix Augenfeld to renovate an apartment upstairs from the apartment in which I lived with Mama, Papa, and Tante Minna at Bergasse 19. When the apartment was ready, I moved most of my things from

Papa's and my bedroom into her new bedroom. And when I did, no one—not even Papa—so much as commented.

Papa never again mentioned the word "homosexuality" in reference to me. In conversation and correspondence, he referred to both Dorothy and me as " virgins," and to me as a virgin of the "vestal" kind. At the same time, he never again spoke of my supposed ambivalence towards men, nor of any possibility that I might one day marry.

Chapter 34

In 1927, Dorothy and I opened a small school for Viennese children who were in psychoanalysis. To be honest, there weren't a lot of Viennese children in psychoanalysis aside from our children, the Sweetser's children, and Eva's children. But Dorothy and I each had small clienteles, and none of the children we analyzed were doing well in school.

Part of the problem, we knew, was culture shock. Our patients' homes and analytic environments were inquisitive and supportive. Their schools, on the other hand, were punitive and restrictive. All Austrian schools were. Navigating those two worlds successfully was difficult; learning suffered.

When we built The Matchbox School, we built it with Dorothy's money in Eva's back yard. Immediately, Tinky, Mabbie, and Mikey acquired a large peer group, and Bob got new girlfriends.

The Matchbox School was profoundly different from Austrian public schools. For one thing, the teachers played with the children during recess. Another difference: art, music, and athletics were braided throughout the academic curriculum, so that a musical exercise or competitive physical activity might be used, for example, to teach a mathematical concept. There were no tests. There were no lists of facts to memorize. Teachers created guided experiences, often in the natural world, and in that way taught students valuable skills and concepts while helping them become creative problem-solvers. Through

The Matchbox School we were part of an entire movement of progressive educators like John Dewey and Rudolph Steiner. Such schools are more common today, but back then Dorothy and I were proud of our little experiment.

But four short years after we founded The Matchbook School, we began to perceive its significant disadvantages. Bob had just turned seventeen. His approaching departure for university was making everyone edgy. Bob had made great progress. No longer a charming, selfish terror, he was a true romantic—so sensitized to music and thrilled by nature that a chord from a violin or a song from a robin could set him to trembling. And coughing, actually. He had developed asthma. But he also had become eager to talk about his deepest feelings and most daring ideas. The new Bob wasn't going to easily sally forth in the rough-and-tumble world of university, and we all knew it. In awe, really, of the enormity of the social problem we had created for him and for the others, we began to consider closing The Matchbox School.

In the end, our hand was forced. With inadequate notice, two of our three teachers announced that they were moving on in their careers. And so the bubble of protective enchantment that we had built for the children was, at last, burst.

Alas, public school turned out to be more polarizing than we had imagined. Street violence against Jews had begun in Vienna, and even the halls of elementary schools weren't safe. And Nazi teachers did not go out of their ways to be kind to socially tormented children being raised by two women, one of whom was Jewish and both of whom were psychoanalysts.

That year—it was 1931—Doktor Carl Jung wrote Papa a letter. Plagued by reoccurring nightmares and waking hallucinations of a Europe so flooded with blood that only the Swiss Alps were left in greenery, he wrote, "Bring everyone to Switzerland, Sigmund, I beg of you. You will be safe here."

In 1931, the Creditstalt, the main bank of Austria, crashed.

Politicians argued in favor of Christian values and for the removal through legal and economic means of "the harmful influence of the Jews on our public, cultural, and economic life."

Throughout these years, and in spite of the troubles the children had in public school, we Burlinghams and Freuds thought ourselves fortunate. Our Austrian government was controlled by anti-Semites, yet they seemed to be more reasonable than the anti-Semites in Germany.

In 1933, spouting rhetoric about the profligacy of ignoramuses and the possibility of more moneyed times, Adolf Hitler was elected Chancellor of Germany. Almost immediately he suspended civil rights. His Nazi party burnt the Berlin Parliament. They opened the first concentration camps, imprisoning many of the 10,000 people arrested during and immediately after the Parliament's conflagration. All Nazi enemies were subject to confinement in those camps. High on the list of "enemies" were Jews and homosexuals.

Dorothy and I were glad we had remained discreet.

Because Dorothy was an American and a Christian, she had nothing to fear from Adolf Hitler. We Freuds, too, thought we were safe. We were Austrians, not Germans. There were far too many Jews in Austria for us to believe that any one family was threatened by Hitler in Germany. We counted on history to grab the occasional German Jew but to pass us by, doing no more damage, perhaps, than rattling a window or two.

But we underestimated the degree to which Austria depended culturally and financially on Germany, as well as the speed with which a nation can fall.

In May of 1933, Aryan culture became official German policy. Non-Aryan books were burnt in Berlin, Papa's among them. "Against soul-disintegrating exaggeration of the instinctual life, for the nobility of the human soul, I commit to the flames the writings of Sigmund Freud!" a soldier shouted as marching bands played patriotic music. Then he threw Papa's books on the pyre. We heard the radio broadcast.

By October of 1933, German Jews were excluded by decree from all culture and arts.

Meanwhile, the Great Depression in America was contributing to economic upheaval throughout Europe. By 1933, one-third of Vienna's adult men were unemployed. Unable to tolerate such economic inefficiency so close to Germany's borders, Hitler threatened to annex Austria.

All around us, friends began to flee to whatever countries would have them. It was not easy to gain entry papers to other countries, however. Not America nor France nor Sweden nor England nor Belgium nor Switzerland could afford being overrun by refugees.

Oliver, Henny, and Little Eva were lucky enough to gain entry to France. Ernst and his wife were accepted into England.

In 1935, Germany began drafting young men into the armed forces, and an international hue and cry arose. The Treaty of Versailles that had ended the first World War forbade Germany from maintaining an army larger than 100,000 men. Fortunately, it also barred Germany from manufacturing armored cars, tanks, submarines, airplanes, and poison gas; only a small number of specified factories could make weapons or munitions. And so Germany had to delay activating its machinery of slaughter, if just for a bit. We had a lull of almost three years.

This time we Burlinghams and Freuds fancied that history had passed us by altogether. Perhaps it had knocked once or twice on our door, but we had been wise enough to make sure that we were not at home when it did. Dorothy and I opened The Edith Jackson Nursery, a day care center for toddlers of impoverished mothers. The Nursery presented us with an unparalleled opportunity to study the development and psychology of one- and two-year-olds, and it made an enormous difference in the lives of the families who made use of our free services. But the nursery was short-lived, coming to a chaotic end in 1938.

For in 1938, Hitler made clear to Austria that he considered it to be a part of "Greater Germany." Abruptly and without a struggle, the Chancellor of Austria resigned. In his radio address he urged his countrymen to avoid bloodshed by complying with the German forces when—not if—they invaded. "God save Austria," he concluded. (*Gott schutzë Ostterich.)*

No chance that God was listening. The next day was *Anschluss*; Germany annexed Austria. The fact that Germany and Austria were now one and the same meant that, with no process at all, the entire set of Germany's anti-Semitic laws became our governing law.

All that day and the next Papa, Mama, Tante Minna, Dorothy, and I listened to the radio. Despite the counsel of our Chancellor, some brave Austrians resisted the German troops. Yet every time resistance turned into collapse we heard the sound of overwhelming rejoicing—and then news of violence against Jews. There was indiscriminate, casual brutality. There was efficient, systematic brutality, too. Soldiers helped louts force Jewish families to scrub streets on their hands and knees. Catholic prelates celebrated *Anschluss* from pulpits. Heads were clubbed. Swastikas were everywhere. The Ringstrasse trembled with the thunder of storm troopers' boots.

Civilization in Vienna was dead. On the day after *Anschluss* the Vienna Psychoanalytical Society disbanded. Everyone was to flee and reconvene, if they could, wherever it was that Papa settled.

It may seem with my quick description that events happened at the speed with which wind whips around mountains and tall buildings. But seven years had elapsed since we'd closed The Matchbox School. By *Anschluss*, Bob and Tinky were both students at colleges in America. But Bob was visiting us in Vienna on that very day, as was his father, Robert.

Mabbie, too, was no longer living with Dorothy and me. She had a fiancé, a young Jewish architect named Simon Schmiderer with whom she'd set up house—though, while Robert was in town, she had us ruffle her bedclothes each morning. That way, during her father's daily visits to Dorothy and Mikey, it looked like Mabbie was living the life of a respectable if untidy ingénue.

Mikey was still an adolescent. During Robert's visit the morning after *Anschluss*, Dorothy asked Robert to escort him to America immediately, which he did.

Bob would stay a few days and help Dorothy pack. Then he would accompany her to Switzerland, whence she would proceed to England. She wanted to keep her Tiffany inheritance safe and use it to help others flee.

Despite everyone's pleadings, Mabbie refused to be separated from her Simon, even for a moment. As an American, she could have left Austria easily and legally, yet she chose to do things in a way that would ensure Simon's safety, as well. Together Simon and Mabbie slipped over the border into Switzerland on the pretense of his being the beleaguered employee of "an American, a Mrs. Dorothy Burlingham" who had hired him to show her atrociously spoiled daughter potential investment properties in Switzerland. To the border guard, Mabbie feigned a complete ignorance of German. She also put on haughty airs. The ruse worked; in German, the guard wished Simon luck dealing with Mabbie, and let them pass.

Mama asked Cook to make Dorothy and Bob a lovely beef supper the evening that they were set to leave for Switzerland. They would be riding on a night train. On their way, they would stop at the sanatorium to gather up Tante Minna who, suffering from pleurisy and having no possessions that the Nazis might want, had received an exit visa.

After our meal, I kissed Bob goodbye and struggled for my composure as he and Mama walked into the hallway. Papa, I assumed, would join them. Soon we would all be going to the train station; this was the only time that Dorothy and I would have a chance to say a private goodbye.

I suppose that, considering our many years of successful discretion, she and I might have been a bit subtler. We weren't at all. We grabbed each other and hugged and cried, not knowing if I would ever receive an exit visa. If I did not, I might die at Hitler's orders. And all of the time that we hugged we writhed, one body against the other, expressing a longing about which, in all of our years together, we had hesitated even to hint at, to anyone.

When at last we broke free of our embrace, I turned to help Dorothy with her bags. Then, heads raised with determination and hankies at noses, we expected to join Bob and the others in the hall. Instead we encountered Papa. He was blocking the door.

I glanced over my shoulder at Dorothy, and in that glance noticed that, during Dorothy's and my embrace, every drape in the room had been silently drawn.

"Have you homosexuals no shame?" he snarled. "What will the neighbors think?"

Indeed, it took the non-theatrical equivalent of *deus ex machina* to extricate my family and me from Vienna.

Specifically, it took Princess Marie Bonaparte, a member of vertiginously high international society and an analysand of Papa's. Princess Marie was real royalty twice over; the great-grand niece of Emperor Napoleon I, she had married Prince George of Greece. She is her own colorful story.

It is no betrayal of Princess Marie's secrets for me to say that her marriage to Prince George was unhappy. Everyone knew that, for she wondered aloud at society parties whether he was homosexual. She seemed to have been somewhat of a homosexual herself. She was in Vienna visiting her lover. And if I perceived matters correctly, the lover was Ida Bauer, the very *feinshmeker* whom Papa had analyzed thirty-seven years previously. (Ida was probably the first case of homosexuality that Papa had diagnostically missed. She had told Papa at the outset of her analysis that she regularly shared a bed with her assailant's wife, but Papa hadn't appreciated what that implied.)

Whether Princess Marie was heterosexual, bisexual, or homosexual is probably inconsequential. It is certain, though, that she was not a perfect match with Papa's definition of "woman." In spite of her beauty and flirtatious manner and her long history of heterosexual affairs, Papa referred to her as "more than half masculine." She had a mind that would not stop asking questions, getting answers, and taking charge.

The Princess had entered analysis with Papa for her inability to have orgasms during missionary position intercourse. She could have orgasms with direct stimulation to her clitoris, but she was concerned that her inability to achieve one by penetration alone meant that she was technically frigid. Papa explained to her that, indeed, she was; real female sexual pleasure is concentrated in the vagina. But the princess was "more than half masculine," indeed. She was skeptical. She asked questions. And when the answers Papa gave didn't satisfy her, she set out to gather evidence.

In the course of gathering evidence, she spent a year measuring the distance between the vagina and clitoris of over two hundred women, and she "interviewed" (her word, not mine) all of them. The interviews convinced her that, if Papa's theory was right, the problem for her and her 200-plus women was that their clitorises and vaginas were set too far apart.

Princess Marie couldn't do anything for the ill-built multitudes, but she did talk to a gynecological surgeon. She had her own clitoris surgically repositioned, hoping to sensitize her vagina by lending it some of her clitoral nerve endings.

The surgeon had no trouble removing the clitoris but a good deal of trouble reattaching it meaningfully. So many of the nerves in her genital area had been snipped that she could not, after her wounds healed, feel much of anything. But even half deadened, her clitoris continued to give her more pleasure than her vagina.

So she had her clitoris repositioned again, this time placing it even closer to the vagina. By then the clitoris was almost dead. Still, it ruled.

It was actually Ida Bauer's Vienna apartment that became the launching pad for Princess Marie's rescue effort.

Ida and the princess invited Doctor Ernest Jones, who was again enjoying tenure as president of the International Psychoanalytic Association, to join them at Ida's. Part of Dr. Jones's role as president of the IPA was to expedite the emigration of Jewish psychoanalysts from Germany and German-occupied territories.

Papa was embarrassed to see Ida again. He would have liked his jaw and face to look less scarred.

Ida was still a fancy dresser and a bit of a clown, and now she was a flirt, as well. She did Papa the favor of looking him in the eye and giving him a gorgeous smile just before she smooched his mauled cheek. Then she turned and smooched me, and when she winked, we both broke into grins that threatened to run away with us.

For his part, Doctor Jones kissed my hand primly. It was twenty-four years since I had slipped from his grasp. Now I was famous—in Vienna, anyway—as a lecturer on child psychoanalysis. He had his reputation as a neurologist and the foremost psychoanalyst in England. I inquired after his health. He inquired after mine.

Princess Marie led the meeting.

The plan, she explained, was for Doctor Jones to work through diplomatic channels to gain written assurance from England that they would accept as permanent immigrants everyone in the Freud family as well as attendant doctors and household help. At the same time, Ida would see what could be done locally to expedite emigration papers. She would probably accomplish little, for she was a Jew. Still, she would try to provide logistical support for Doctor Jones and the Princess, who would immediately commence bribing every Austrian and German official who mattered.

The very next day the Gestapo arrived at our door and took me away.

The Nazis had come once before. It had been the S.S. that time. They came unannounced and searched the apartment. I wasn't at home then. All the while that the S.S were there, Mama pretended that the soldiers were just impolite visitors. She reminded them to wipe their feet at the door. She offered them use of her umbrella stand. She scolded them when they mussed the sheets in her linen closet. Papa sat and smoked. Together the two of them pulled off their "I'm too old to know what's going on, so you can't scare me" gambit and kept their own fears at bay. By the end of the day, Papa and Mama were proud of their emotional resourcefulness, but they were also poorer, for the S.S. had taken the six thousand shillings Papa was keeping in our safe for eventual use in England. They had also taken all passports.

The passport confiscation was very bad news. We couldn't arrive in England without them. Even with visages as famous as Papa's and mine were, we would not be allowed in the country without incontrovertible proof of our identity. So we actually had two barriers to our escape—no permission to leave Austria and no possible way to enter England.

Actually we had three barriers. Papa refused to leave Vienna without his collection of antiquities. We had turned it over to the authorities so that they could evaluate its monetary worth, after which the Princess could pay on our behalf an emigration tax on the pieces' value. (We couldn't pay the tax. No Jew could pay such a tax, as all Jewish bank accounts had been confiscated.)

Until those antiquities were returned, Papa would not be budged.

The day that the Gestapo took me, the Princess bravely demanded to be arrested alongside me. They took me alone. Ida walked the floor all day alongside Papa, who cried and tottered, and, indeed, prayed until evening. Doctor Jones called the British ambassador. The Princess rushed off looking for someone to bribe.

They arrested me at about noon. I sat for hours in a corridor with many others—so many others that I realized they could never question us all in one day. My biggest fear was that our captors would realize they had a crowding problem on their hands. With too many of us to interrogate, the "excess" might be herded off to somewhere unknown, perhaps as soon as that evening. Who knew what might happen then? I managed to insinuate myself into the queue in a room where only a small number of people were waiting to be questioned.

When the Gestapo talked to me it was the International Psychoanalytic Association they wanted information about, for they were tracking a group of Jewish terrorists and were suspicious of any predominately Jewish organization. Once I explained the IPA's educational and research objectives I was sent home. Though I was warned by one soldier that they were only waiting to kill the likes of me later.

On April 1, the first trainload of Vienna Jews left for Dachau.

When we heard, I suggested to everyone in my family that we take Veronal and kill ourselves while we had the chance. Papa quietly ignored me. The rest followed his lead.

Shortly afterwards, the Princess's efforts paid off; we got our passports back, although now they were German passports, not Austrian, and they were stamped with swastikas. Still, they would get us into England if England would have us.

Doctor Jones finally wrested assurances from England that we were all welcome there. My brother Martin and my sister Mathilde and her husband left immediately, Martin departing just in the nick of time. He ran the publishing house of the International Psychoanalytic Association. The Nazis were on their way to his apartment at the very moment that he crossed into France.

Papa, Mama, and I still awaited the return of Papa's antiquities. On May 14 they arrived, clumsily crated but unharmed, with an emigration tax notification attached. We began packing our things in earnest. Princess Marie paid the tax.

It took the Princess until June to obtain in return for the tax payment the official tax receipt and the accompanying *Unbedenklichkeitserklärung*—declaration of no impediment. Without the *Unbedenklichkeitserklärung*, we could not leave.

It was delivered to our apartment on June 2 by the Gestapo. The officer demanded that, in order to receive the *Unbedenklichkeitserklärung*, Papa sign a document stating that he and his entire family had been treated fairly and that he had been allowed to work in freedom. A legend has circulated in the years since that Papa pulled out a pen, signed at the bottom, and with an understandably impish flourish, added, "I can recommend the Gestapo to anyone!"

He didn't. He was somber when he signed.

The Princess and I ran immediately from the apartment to secure reservations on the next train out. We packed the dog and grabbed the household help. We needed to bring a doctor, but Doktor Max Schur, Papa's personal physician, needed an appendectomy. So we brought in his stead a pediatrician whom we knew wanted to flee. (Doktor Schur did get permission to emigrate; he met us in England within a few weeks.)

We could not obtain exit visas for Papa's four elderly sisters, so Princess Marie arranged for their apartments to be stocked with money, medicine, coal, and food. We left them for what we imagined would be a long but not entirely uncomfortable few years.

Then, on June 3—after three months of intense wrangling by Princess Marie and Doctor Jones, unrelieved pressure from the international community, and unswerving emotional and logistical support from Ida Bauer—we boarded the train west.

After years of fear, danger becomes not so much an enemy but a novel companion with which one travels. You give it the slip whenever you can. If you are inclined towards humor, as Papa was, you try to laugh at its expense.

A Jew, a homosexual, and a gypsy walk into a Nazi bar.
The bartender sees them and says, "What, is this a joke?"

Vintage Papa.

At 2:45 in the morning on June 5, our train crossed the Rhine from Germany into France. Papa, our maid Paula Fichtl, and I were the only members of our entourage awake to celebrate the crossing.

"Now we are free," said Papa quietly as he looked through the train window towards where the sun would, in a few hours, rise over his lost homeland. *"Jetzt sind wir frei."*

I, too, gazed back towards Austria and all that we had left behind.

Of course, it had been naïve of us to assume that, given money, medicine, food, and coal, my father's sisters would fare the maelstrom passably well. We had left them with precisely those possessions that German army officers covet. Needless to say, my aunts were soon relieved of their provisions and apartments. Dolfi Freud died of starvation in Theresienstadt. Mitzi Freud, Rosa Freud Graf, and Pauli Freud Winterlinz were murdered at Auschwitz.

Part 7

England

(1938-1982)

Sigmund and Martha, Maresfield Gardens, London.

Chapter 35

When we arrived in Dover on the night ferry we were reunited with Mathilde, Martin, Ernst, and Dorothy. A crowd of admirers had gathered. They waved and threw flowers. A news photographer asked Papa to stand inside the ferry building where the light was good and to remove his hat; the idea was to create a photo that would show that Papa's brain, for all its capacity, rendered his head no larger than that of a mere mortal.

Ernst drove us past Buckingham Palace on the way to 39 Elsworthy Road, on Primrose Hill near Regent's Park in London, where he had rented a house.

Papa was able to walk by himself into the house. He requested immediately, however, that he be carried upstairs to see Tante Minna, who was seriously ill with her pleurisy. No one was allowed in the room so I cannot report how the reunion transpired.

Three months later, on September 3, after a remission of thirteen years, Papa's cancer returned. At first it was just a suspicious spot on his cheek. Doktor Schur arranged for Papa to receive diathermy. It was an early form of radiation that is still used therapeutically, but no longer as a cancer treatment. Indeed, the spot dissolved, though another quickly replaced it.

Doktor Schur then arranged for surgeons to split the cheek open and give Papa the most radical operation in eighteen years. They promised him he would fully recover within six weeks.

He never quite did.

On September 16, Mama and our maid, Paula, moved from Ernst's rented house into a lovely house in the Hampstead section of London. It was at 20 Maresfield Gardens. They moved in order to prepare it for the rest of the family. After Paula had scrubbed and Mama had decorated for eleven days, Papa, Tante Minna, and I joined them there. Our new home was roomy—far larger than our Vienna apartment. There was a garden. There were shrubs and birds. Mama loved the house. In tribute to its splendor and airiness she called it our "white bread castle."

Dorothy rented a house just down the street at 2 Maresfield Gardens, and she was joined there by Mabbie and Simon. She was also joined by Bob, who over the previous several months had given up his pattern of serial infatuation with beautiful women. He had actually married one of them—a charming Norwegian girl named Mossik Sørensen, whom he had long known as a friend of Mabbie and Tinky's.

Papa was very frail. He could not easily talk. Still, he enjoyed having us all around him. And he was such a celebrity! He had visits from H.G. Wells and Salvador Dali. The International Psychoanalytic Association reconvened, and they did so in our parlor, drinking cognac and smoking cigars just like in the good old days.

Papa received a huge welcome from the two major English medical journals, and this made him very proud. *Lancet* wrote, "His teachings have in their time aroused controversy more acute and antagonism more bitter than any since the days of Darwin. Now, in his old age, there are few psychologists of any school who do not admit their debt to him. Some of the conceptions he formulated clearly for the first time have crept into current philosophy against the stream of willful incredulity which he himself recognized as man's natural reaction to unbearable truth." The *British Medical Journal* wrote, "The medical profession of Great Britain will feel proud that their country has offered an asylum to Professor Freud and that he has chosen it as his new home."

I took up my duties as Papa's chief nurse and confidante. He needed so much tending that I did not work in any other way. Papa recovered enough by the end of the year to resume his psychoanalytic work. He conducted four analyses daily.

Even though Papa felt stronger, he approached the end. We all knew it. He urged any friend who intended to visit at some future date to do so soon. Princess Marie kept in constant touch.

The writer Virginia Woolf and her publisher husband, Leonard, came for coffee one day at five, though they drank tea. Papa formally presented Mrs. Woolf with a flower, and Mr. Woolf noted later that he had done so with the smoldering grace of a half-extinct volcano.

Papa's last book was *Moses and Monotheism*. Largely a cultural-historical speculation on violence and religion, it was the means through which Papa attempted to make sense of what had happened to the world around him. He had finished writing in July. The American publishing house of Alfred A. Knopf wanted English language rights. By November, Papa's only hope was that he could live to see it published.

In February, a new cancerous growth was discovered.

Late in April, Doktor Schur traveled for eight weeks to America to settle his wife and two small children and to apply for citizenship papers and a license to practice medicine. In his absence, Papa took a general turn for the worse. By the time Doktor Schur returned, Papa was as afraid of living as he was of dying.

Papa called Doktor Schur to his side. "Promise me, Schur: When the time comes, you won't let them torment me unnecessarily. You will talk to Anna, and she will tell you to let me go."

Even though at one point in that single conversation Papa showed his first slight signs ever of mental confusion, Doktor Schur understood Papa's new cognitive problems to arise from pain and exhaustion, and the plea to come from a man of abundant mental faculties. He promised not to fail Papa in the end.

In May of 1939, *Moses and Monotheism* was published in America.

In July, Papa dismissed his four psychoanalytic patients. He refused all drugs other than aspirin. In August, Papa's cancer ulcerated and began to stink—so badly that his beloved dog would not even go near his room. Papa got very weak. He lay in his bed at the window all day and watched the garden.

Dorothy left for America to help Mabbie, who was due to have a baby.

On September 1, Oli and Henny's daughter, Little Eva, by then fifteen years old, visited from France.

In early September, an air raid warning sounded. It was a false alarm, but we moved Papa away from the window to a room at the center of the house.

There in that room blessed neither by visual pleasure nor breeze, the cancer ate its way through Papa's cheek. Papa could find no words up to the task of describing the pain.

Doctor Jones came and said his formal goodbyes to Papa.

On September 21, Papa suggested to Doktor Schur that it was time for Doktor Schur and me to have that "little talk about letting go."

I did not give my consent lightly, nor did I give my consent alone.

I gathered Mathilde, Martin, and Ernst. We telephoned Oliver and told him about the decision that we all needed to make. He said that he would come right away. However, he also said that he had lived under a cloud of patricidal suspicion for too much of his life. He could not take a position on what to do about Papa. We had his emotional support navigating the difficult choices ahead of us. We could not, however, have his participation.

Mathilde, Martin, Ernst, and I retired to the garden. There was due deliberation but there were no dissenters. We gave orders to Doktor Schur.

We really had no opportunity to say goodbye. Having spoken to Doktor Schur, Papa quickly entered a realm of pain and confusion. He no longer responded to words, only to gentle touches.

Mama and Tante Minna remained in the kitchen, crying into cups of coffee. Mathilde, Martin, Ernst, and I entered Papa's room. Martin peacefully laid a hand on Papa's brow. Ernst rested his hand on one of Papa's knees. Mathilde and I each took one of his hands. I remember squeezing the hand I held ever so gently and whispering, "We have tunneled very deeply, Papa, you and I."

Doktor Schur injected Papa with 1.5 times the normal dose of morphine.

Papa slept. We waited by his bedside. Doktor Schur repeated the dose when Papa became restless. Still, Mathilde, Martin, Ernst, and I waited. We waited all through the night.

Oliver arrived the next morning and, that day, Doktor Schur repeated the dose again. Papa slipped into a coma.

Late that evening, Martin, Oliver, Ernst, and Mathilde left Papa's bedroom to get some rest.

I slipped into bed beside Papa for the very last time.

On September 23 at three o'clock in the morning, Papa's heart succumbed to the onslaught of morphine.

There was quite a lot of sorrow—too much, I would say, from Oliver and me. Oli was a perfect mess. His lisp positively flamed. Henny and Little Eva worried that he would harm himself, although he didn't.

I, who had tended terrified orphans and needy toddlers and thought myself so wise about sorrow and mourning as to be immune, was lost in anguish. Because the war had accelerated and the seas were dangerous, for almost a year Dorothy could not come home to comfort me.

Mama, who in some ways knew me best, feared that I would be lost forever.

But amidst the sorrow there was also celebration. Gathering in the white bread castle over a nice dinner just three days after Papa's death, Mathilde, Martin, Oliver, Ernst, and I ceremonially took into our bodies the flesh and knowledge of our father.

No, we didn't eat him.

It was all Mama's idea. Once, almost four decades before, despite her fainting and guided by my trail of stones, it was Mama who had found a lost and terrified little me. Mama was the only one who could see how to save me once again.

"Take his strength and wisdom into yourself, Anna," she said. "Nobody will think any worse of you."

Oli opened a bottle of wine. He was trembling so much that he had trouble with the corkscrew.

I sprinkled ashes into my wine. Like the primal father of the bestial horde, Papa had been a man of considerable insight, sometimes in spite of himself. I drank in Papa's strength and wisdom. We all did. And for forty-three years now we have protected his legacy and institutionalized his wisdom.

I, especially.

Chapter 36

Dorothy returned from America in 1940. Immediately after, we began setting up temporary shelters for families whose homes had been bombed out. In 1941, with help from the British War Relief Society and the American Foster Parents' Plan for War Children, we established a residential nursery for war orphans. Eventually it occupied three houses on our suburban street. From then until well beyond the end of the war in Europe, we took care of 191 newborns, toddlers, and children. Some of them were literally orphans. Most, though, were sent to us by mothers who were nurses, firefighters, or workers for civil defense. They needed to tend to London and to the soldiers and civilians in the rubble pile that London was becoming. Our great humanitarian contribution was that we restored the children to physical and emotional health as best we could.

Our great theoretical contribution was that we saw that they needed much more than a bomb shelter, good health care, and clean institutional living. They needed to form attachments with adults who were willing to love them continuously. Like Dorothy and me, most of our staff were refugees from Eastern Europe. Loving those children, we risked our lives. We were shot at and strafed. We held newborns and teenagers while they screamed in terror because windows were exploding and autos combusting. We celebrated first birthdays and eleventh birthdays and first steps and first puppy loves. Meals were not always served on time, but we did all eat something every single day, and before we ate we washed our hands.

Dorothy and I continued the war nursery after war's end, receiving children who had survived Theresienstadt. After every one of those children got redistributed to families who pledged to love them forever, our work there was done.

Dorothy never achieved the repute that I did as a child psychoanalyst, although she did perform with admirable competence. She always sat in the "wife's chair" when I lectured. She was my partner in all things, great and small. I was hers, as well. We raised our four children psychoanalytically. They were mothered by psychoanalysts, analyzed by their mothers, and educated in a psychoanalytically oriented school. And when their mothers worked with other people's motherless children, they were proud of us.

Dorothy and I lived together until she died quietly in 1979.

I do not consider the deep details of Bob's, Mabbie's, Tinky's, and Mikey's emotional lives mine to disclose here. More than anyone, I know that they might find revelations to which they had not specifically agreed painful. Though I can say that Dorothy and I didn't do as good a job with our four as we did with other people's children, and I can say that because it is a matter of public record.

Bob began drinking in college, and as that picked up speed, his fanciful, romantic demeanor dissolved and his snot-nosed behavior resurfaced. As unappealing as that comportment is in a child, it is less so in an adult. For the rest of Bob's adult life, he drank and smoked angrily despite physicians' warnings about what smoke and drink could do to his asthma. Mossik left him, and a second marriage lasted only a brief while. Bob threatened suicide often, and exasperatingly followed the threats with tearful letters of apology to Dorothy and me. When he finally died in his mid-fifties it was of an asthma-induced heart attack.

I had thought Mabbie had paired so nicely with her Simon. Although it's true that they stayed together for the rest of their lives, their marriage didn't wear well. They lived mostly in America. Simon had professional troubles that depressed him. Mabbie, whenever she was apart from Dorothy, was emotionally fragile.

It's silly to talk about precipitating events to a suicide; that is just an exercise in blame. But although she had talked a good deal about wanting to die just before she did die, Mabbie had seemed to both Dorothy and me to carry realistic ideas about her future close to her heart. Then she encountered a work of art that may have set her off. *L'Inconnue de la Seine* was a death mask lifted from the face of a woman who had drowned herself in the 1920s and whose body had washed up on the banks of that famous river. For some reason her face was rapturous in death, and Mabbie was delighted by the idea of finding heavenly peace. While visiting from America in 1974, she took an overdose of sleeping pills, and she died two weeks later.

Tinky and Mikey remain pretty much all right. Tinky still scales life's difficulties, room by metaphorical room. At sixty-one, Mikey is the sunny boy he always was.

Still, one has to wonder about the emotional price paid by the analysand when the analyst is one—or both—of the child's parents.

Two fish are swimming in a pond. The first fish says to the second fish, "Hey, look! A worm!" He lunges towards it.

The second fish jumps in the way. "Stop! That worm is impaled on a hook that is connected to a thin, strong, almost invisible string. At the top of the string there is a pole. Holding the pole is a man in a boat. If you bite the worm, the hook will stick in your mouth. The man will tug you out by the string. He will pull you into the boat, open you up with a knife, scoop out your entrails, and feed you to his family."

The two fish swim away.

Later that evening the first fish swims back. "What could go wrong?" he thinks. "I've looked and I've looked and I've looked and I've looked. For the life of me, I don't see any line or hook."

He bites. He feels a pinch. He feels a pull. He finds himself at the top of the water. There is a man with a pole. The man is in a boat. Attached to his belt is a knife.

No, it's not funny. It's not a joke. I of all people should have known better than to psychoanalyze Dorothy's and my children.

It's an awful personal legacy that I have left. *So what did I do that was right?*

I do sometimes ask myself that question.

For starters, I was one of several women who were early practitioners of child analysis. I distinguished myself from my peers by distinguishing child analysis from adult analysis.

Which is to say that some of the early practitioners of child analysis—most notably a rather famous one named Melanie Klein—proclaimed themselves "real" Freudians and conducted the analysis of children as harshly as they conducted the analysis of adults. They derived what they called "deep interpretations" of the feelings and thoughts that the young children in their care vocalized, and then they conveyed those interpretations directly to the child.

"You had a scary ghost in your dream, sweetie? Why, that's your mother's nipple! It looms before you, inviting and repelling at the same time."

Needless to say, if and when I found deep interpretations when working with children, I did not convey those interpretations to the children.

Instead, I wrote them on index cards. Dorothy and I developed a diagnostic profiling system that used index cards. In our nursery for war orphans, we taught an entire staff of teachers and nurses how to fill out index cards.

It doesn't seem like a lot.

It was in our homes for children that we discovered that, allowed to choose by themselves from an attractively served array of healthy foods, even toddlers devise for themselves a well-rounded diet. It's an insight that's been passed on by pediatricians to worried mothers for years.

A gulf always exists between high aims and accomplishments. I meant to further my father's claims and stick closely to his guidelines. I meant to be a real Freudian, a better one certainly than Melanie Klein. I intended to be completely scientific and neutral in my psychoanalytic sessions with children, and to write on children's index cards notes about primitive impulses, penis envy, and maybe even nipple lust. But my patients were war orphans, blast it! They couldn't have managed if I had behaved in a strange, clinical way.

So instead of writing drivel on index cards, I wrote down what the children ate and how they seemed to be feeling. I fed and hugged and nurtured hungry, scared, sick children, and kept detailed accounts of the progress they made towards being able to talk, laugh, and trust again. If their mothers were dead or were bound to be absent for long periods of time, I gave them teachers and nurses who were more than willing to serve as stable, surrogate mother figures. Dorothy and our staff and I may have looked schoolmarmish. However, we and we alone understood that the symptoms of despair that we see in children do not always have to do with infantile sexuality or other primitive impulses. Children need families, and when neither the mother nor father can provide one, they need someone else to hold them for long periods of time and to cherish them.

The point just seems good common sense now, but it wasn't nearly as obvious then.

We made that point. We saved those children. We mattered.

> *A worried little boy was seeing Anna Freud, the famous child psychoanalyst. "I can't stop thinking about my mother," he said. "As soon as I go to sleep, I start dreaming, and everyone in my dream turns into my mother. I wake up in such a state, all I can do is go downstairs and eat a piece of toast."*

Anna Freud replies: "What, just one piece of toast, for a big boy like you?"

Tante Minna never recovered from the pleurisy that had her confined to the bedroom the day that Mama, Papa, and I arrived in England and Papa had to be carried upstairs to say hello. She outlived Papa, though. She died in 1941.

Right after Tantie died, Dorothy moved out of her house at 2 Maresfield Gardens and into the house at 20 Maresfield Gardens with Mama and me. It's where I still live.

Mama was a joy to behold as she approached very old age. A closeted bisexual for sixty-five years, she threw off the constraints of public decorum entirely. No, she did not take a lover. She took to walking precariously down the yellow lines of busy streets. It was nice, she explained, to see what the drivers would do. She poked fun at Dorothy and me for our horrified reactions and for chasing her wildly down the high street of town.

Finally, in the summer of 1951, Mama was too crazy to be allowed to walk alone at all. She was ninety. By autumn her body was failing as quickly as her mind and she was unable to leave her bed. Mentally she had returned to the winter of 1920, which was the winter that Sophie died and that Mama burnt her half of the engagement correspondence and then lay in bed working up the courage to hurl herself from her bedroom window.

Dorothy and I loved to sit with Mama, even though as we did we saw infirmity sap the last of her sparkle. As we watched Mama, she watched the fire. She had the bedroom that I use now. She thrilled when we threw onto the fire tiny chips of wood or pieces of paper. "Toss it high! Make it roar!" she would thunder. Mama died on the second of November. As she left us she bellowed out, "Sophie!"

Except for the times when work took me around the world, for the thirty-nine years between our arrival in England and the day that Mathilde died, she and I saw each other every morning and evening for coffee. That degree of closeness with Mathilde was a happy development for me. I got nearly four decades of daily-double love from her. By the way, soon after her husband died in 1956, Mathilde became friendly with a widow named Tini. Mathilde referred to Tini as her "very first very best friend." They were not sexual with each other, just widows who were truly companionable. They were together until Mathilde's death in 1977, after which Tini became so distraught that Dorothy and I took her in for a while.

Martin and Ernst lived in nearby London. Martin was a lawyer. He was widely gossiped about as a case of "arrested development"—which, in Freudian terms, means that he forever hovered in the phase of life before the castration complex would have imbued him with moral sense. These days we just call people like him "promiscuous." His wives and women were beautiful, as were his children. When he died in 1967 he was still at it with every woman who would give him a chance.

Ernst died in April of 1970. Even as an adult, Ernst was despairing, fearful, and self-protective to a fault. He also became perfectionistic, as many anxious people do. Still and all, Ernst was capable of surprising loyalty and family love. He spent most of his professional life as an architect. In his later years, he gave as much care to the posthumous translation and publication of Papa's work as I did. Everything about Papa's legacy needed to be just so for Ernst to be satisfied.

Henny and Oli never joined the rest of the family in England. In 1940, as the Germans occupied France, they made their ways to America, where Oli worked for some years as a civil engineer for the Budd Corporation in Philadelphia. When he retired, they lived on a pension in the Berkshire Mountains of Massachusetts. Oliver died in 1969. After the funeral I put Henny in a nursing home, where she died two years later.

Sadly, Oli and Henny's Little Eva did not survive the years of World War II. The circumstances surrounding her death were something that Oli and Henny refused to discuss. There is some talk that she died of a brain tumor. Others have said that she died of blood poisoning brought on by an amateurish abortion. She was eighteen.

Fraülein Sabina Spielrein, Doktor Carl Jung's beautiful young Russian patient who became a psychiatrist and psychoanalyst, did not survive the war years either. She had married, borne two daughters, and divorced. After representing Papa's psychoanalytic movement in cities throughout Europe, and after psychoanalyzing the likes of the Swiss developmental psychologist Jean Piaget, she had returned to live in the Russian city of her birth. In August of 1942, Doktor Spielrein and her young adult daughters were herded along with the entire Jewish population of Rostov-on-Don onto the synagogue steps, where they were shot.

Before his death in 1961 by natural causes, Doktor Carl Jung had begun to claim that he was the Sun God. At the time the British Intelligence Services were actively investigating him for indications of former Nazi collaboration.

Eva Rosenfeld died in England in 1977.

Siegfried Bernfeld emigrated to San Francisco, where he died in 1953.

After helping us flee Vienna, Ida Bauer escaped to America. She committed suicide in New York in 1945.

Princess Marie, our family's savior, is probably most famous for what my father once asked her in exasperation: "What does a woman want?" She lived a long and joyful life, much of it in Saint-Tropez. She died in 1962 at the age of eighty.

During my forty-four years in England I encountered Doctor Jones quite a lot. He had been very helpful in our family's attempt to flee the Nazis. For his emergency act of kindness, I remained grateful. In recognition of the service that he gave my father and our family, I gave Doctor Jones privileged access to many family papers. Indeed, I helped him research *The Life and Work of Sigmund Freud*, Papa's only authorized biography. It became a best-seller. It omits most of the details of

Freud family life. No, I didn't share the complete skinny with Doctor Jones. I had shared plenty with that dog already. Doctor Jones died a wealthy and famous enough man in London in 1958.

Paula Fichtl, Dorothy's and my maid for fifty-seven years now, says that she continues to consider it her pleasure and honor to bring me my coffee and meals, clean my bedroom, and plump my pillows. Paula, I consider it my pleasure to have known you and to have received your care. I leave this manuscript to you. Please keep my secrets safe until I am gone, and then release them.

—Annafreud

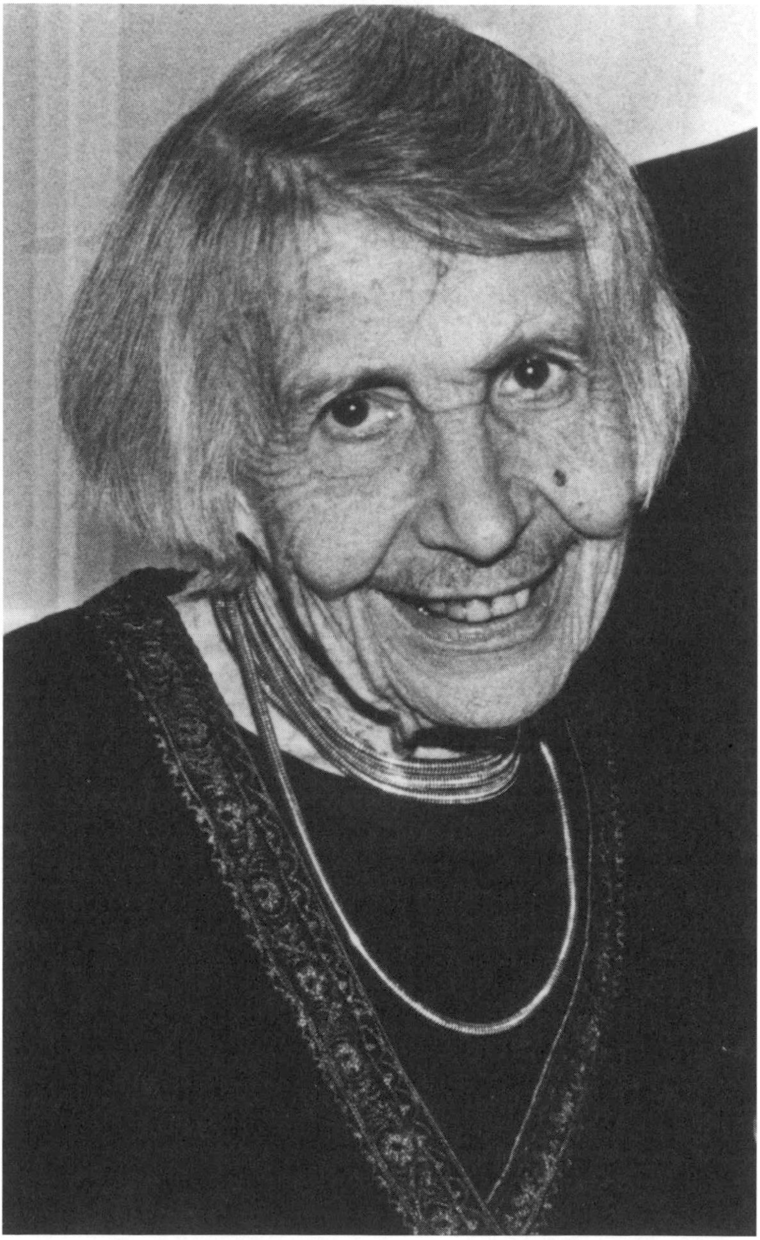

Bibliography

Appignanesi, Lisa and John Forrester, *Freud's Women* (New York: Other Press, 2001).

Bakan, David, *Sigmund Freud and the Jewish Mystical Tradition* (Boston: Beacon Press, 1975).

Bertin, Celia, *Marie Bonaparte: A Life* (New York: Harcourt Brace Jovanovich, 1982).

Cole, Robert, *Anna Freud: The Dream of Psychoanalysis* (New York: Da Capo Press, 1993).

Crews, Frederick, (ed.), *Memory Wars: Freud's Legacy in Dispute* (New York: The New York Review of Books Press, 1997).

____, *Unauthorized Freud: Doubters Confront a Legend* (New York: Viking Press, 1998)

Davis, Whitney, *Drawing the Dream of Wolves: Homosexuality, Interpretation, and Freud's "Wolf Man"*(Bloomington: Indiana University Press, 1995).

Doolittle, Hilda, *Tribute to Freud: Writing on the Wall* (New York: New Directions Publishing, 1984).

Dyer, Raymond, *The Work of Anna Freud* (Northvale, NJ/London: Jason Aronson, 1983).

Forrester, John, *Dispatches from the Freud Wars: Psychoanalysis and Its Passions* (Cambridge: Harvard University Press, 1997).

Freud, Anna, *Lectures for Child Analysts and Teachers 1922-1935* (Madison, CT: International Universities Press, 1974).

___, *The Ego and the Mechanisms of Defense1936* (Madison, CT: International Universities Press, 1967).

___, *Psychoanalytic Psychology of Normal Development* (Madison, CT: International Universities Press, 1981).

Freud, Martin, *Glory Reflected: Sigmund Freud—Man and Father* (Melbourne: Angus & Robertson, 1957).

Freud, Sigmund, *The Diary of Sigmund Freud 1929-1939: A Record of the Final Decade* (London: Hogarth Press, 1992).

___, *The Standard Edition of the Complete Psychological Works of Sigmund Freud.* Ed. And Trans. James Strachey *et al* (London: Hogarth Press, 1953-1974).

Gay, Peter, A *Godless Jew: Freud, Atheism, and the Making of Psychoanalysis (New Haven: Yale University Press, 1987).*

___, *Freud: A Life for Our Time (New York: W. W. Norton, 1990)*

Gilman, Sander L., *The Case of Sigmund Freud: Medicine and Identity at the Fin de Siecle* (Baltimore: Johns Hopkins University Press, 1993).

Heller, Peter, *A Child Analysis with Anna Freud* (Madison, CT: International Universities Press, 1990).

Jones, Ernest, *The Life and Work of Sigmund Freud, Vol. I, The Formative Years and The Great Discoveries (1856-1900).* (New York: Basic Books, 1953)

___, *The Life and Work of Sigmund Freud, Vol. II, Years of Maturity (1901-1919)* (New York: Basic Books, 1956).

___, *The Life and Work of Sigmund Freud, Vol. III, The Last Phase (1919-1939)* (New York: Basic Books, 1957).

Kerr, John, *A Most Dangerous Method: The Story of Jung, Freud, and Sabina Spielrein* (New York: Knopf, 1993).

Masson, Jeffrey Moussaieff, *Against Therapy* (New York: Atheneum, 1988).

___, *The Assault on Truth: Freud's Suppression of the Seduction Theory* (New York: Farrar, Straus and Giroux, 1985).

___, *(trans. and ed.), The Complete Letters of Sigmund Freud to Wilhelm Fliess, 1887-1904* (Cambridge, MA: Harvard University Press, 1985).

___, *Final Analysis: The Making and Unmaking of a Psychoanalyst* (New York: Ballantine, 2003).

Newton, Peter, *Freud: From Youthful Dream to Midlife Crisis*, (New York: Guilford Press, 1995).

Noll, Richard, *The Aryan Christ: The Secret Life of Carl Jung* (New York: Random House, 1997).

Person, Ethel Spector (ed.,) *On Freud's "A Child is Being Beaten"* (New Haven: Yale University Press, 1997).

Roazen, Paul, *How Freud Worked: First-Hand Accounts of Patients*, (Northvale, NJ/London: Jason Aronson, 1995).

___, *Meeting Freud's Family* (Amherst, MA: Univ. of Massachusetts Press, 1993).

Rosenzweig, Saul, *Freud, Jung, and Hall the Kingmaker* (St. Louis: Rana House, 1992).

Sayers, Janet, *Mothers of Psychoanalysis: Helene Deutsch, Karen Horney, Anna Freud, Melanie Klein* (New York: W. W. Norton, 1991).

Young-Bruehl, Elisabeth, *Mind and the Body Politic* (New York: Routledge,1989).

___, *Anna Freud: A Biography* (New York: Summit, 1988.)

Acknowledgments

I extend my thanks to two women who, in my writing life, are giants. Ruth Greenstein of Greenline Publishing Consultants lent her editing skills, commitment, broad appreciation of history and literature, and knowledge of Yiddish to this endeavor. Mary Bisbee-Beek brought patience, friendship, publishing advice, and a mass of publicity contacts and ideas. The influence on me of Ruth and Mary has been immeasurable.

Thank you also to the friends and family who read drafts. This book was nine years in the research and writing, leaving too many people to name. But each one helped me understand the novel in a way I hadn't before. My friends Cor Trowbridge and Sally Mattson, my husband Bob Schwartz, and my mother's husband Sid Spies do merit special mention. They did double and triple duty in this regard. Thank you, thank you, thank you, thank you.

About the Author

photo © Deborah Lazar

REBECCA COFFEY is an award-winning print journalist, documentary filmmaker, and radio commentator. Coffey contributes regularly to *Scientific American* and *Discover* magazines. She blogs about sexuality, relationships, crime and punishment, social media, and psychology for *Psychology Today*, and is a broadcasting contributor to Vermont Public Radio's drive-time commentary series. Her most recent major work of journalism is the March 2012 eBook *MURDERS MOST FOUL: And the School Shooters in Our Midst* (Vook), which landed her appearances on Fox News, CBS Radio and NPR, among others. Her narrative nonfiction book *UNSPEAKABLE TRUTHS AND HAPPY ENDINGS: Human Cruelty and the New Trauma Therapy* (Sidran Press) was widely praised, and was named an Outstanding Academic Title by the American Library Association's *Choice* magazine. Her television documentaries about health and mental health have been broadcast nationally.

Coffey is also a humorist. Her *NIETZSCHE'S ANGEL FOOD CAKE:*

And Other "Recipes" for the Intellectually Famished was published by Beck and Branch in 2013. Her humor has appeared in *McSweeney's Internet Tendency*, *The Rumpus*, and a large handful of literary magazines and e-zines.

SELECTED TITLES FROM SHE WRITES PRESS

She Writes Press is an independent publishing company founded to serve women writers everywhere. Visit us at www.shewritespress.com.

The Rooms Are Filled by Jessica Null Vealitzek
$16.95, 978-1-938314-58-2
The coming-of-age story of two outcasts—a nine-year-old boy who just lost his father, and a closeted young woman—brought together by circumstance.

The Belief in Angels by J. Dylan Yates
$16.95, 978-1-938314-64-3
From the Majdonek death camp to a volatile hippie household on the East Coast, this narrative of tragedy, survival, and hope spans more than fifty years, from the 1920s to the 1970s.

Bittersweet Manor by Tory McCagg
$16.95, 978-1-938314-56-8
A chronicle of three generations of love, manipulation, entitlement, and disappointed expectations in an upper-middle class New England family.

The Geometry of Love by Jessica Levine
$16.95, 978-1-938314-62-9
Torn between her need for stability and her desire for independence, an aspiring poets grapples with questions of artistic inspiration, erotic love, and infidelity.

Clear Lake by Nan Fink Gefen
$16.95, 978-1-938314-40-7
When psychotherapist Rebecca Lev's father dies under suspicious circumstances, she becomes obsessed with discovering what happened to him.

Cleans Up Nicely by Linda Dahl
$16.95, 978-1-938314-38-4
The story of one gifted young woman's path from self-destruction to self-knowledge, set in mid-1970s Manhattan.